GOLD DIGGERS

Also by Tasmina Perry

Daddy's Girls

TASMINA PERRY

Gold Diggers

HarperCollins*Publishers*

HarperCollins*Publishers*
77–85 Fulham Palace Road,
Hammersmith, London W6 8JB

www.harpercollins.co.uk

Published by HarperCollins*Publishers* 2007
1

A catalogue record for this book
is available from the British Library

978 0 00 722888 1 (hbk)
978 0 00 725217 6 (tpbk)

Set in Sabon by Palimpsest Book Production Ltd,
Grangemouth, Stirlingshire

Printed and bound in Great Britain by
Clays Ltd, St Ives plc

Mixed Sources
Product group from well-managed
forests and other controlled sources
www.fsc.org Cert no. TT-COC-2139
© 1996 Forest Stewardship Council
FSC

Acknowledgements

All my thanks to my husband John for making me laugh, making me finish and whose suggestions and editing make my work so much better.

To my mum and dad for surrounding me with books from an early age and always encouraging me to be creative. To my brothers and sister for their support and my son Fin for making me smile when a deadline is looming.

I couldn't ask for better publishers than Harper Collins. A huge thank you to my wonderful editor Wayne Brookes, as good a dinner companion as he is a publisher. To Amanda Ridout for her enormous support and infectious enthusiasm. To the fantastic sales, marketing and press teams and art wizard Lee Motley – I appreciate all your work so much.

Continuing thanks to my agent Sheila Crowley and Judy-Meg Kennedy, Linda Shaughnessy, Teresa Nichols and Valentina Zanca at AP Watt (sorry for being so disorganised.)

Thanks to all my friends who told me things I needed to know: Tamasin, Sam, Louise, Niki, Heids, Scott, Will, Jenny – I owe you all cocktails.

Last but by no means least, to all the wives and girlfriends of rich men who told me their secrets – thank you for the stories. Fact is sometimes more incredulous than fiction.

To my parents

PROLOGUE

The 175-foot superyacht *Zeus* bobbed silently in Turkbuku Bay, the recently anointed St Tropez of Turkey's Turquoise Coast. The night sky seamlessly blended into the oily-black waters of the Aegean Sea, wrapping the spectacular yacht in a cloak of darkness. A ghostly hush had fallen on the decks. Everyone on board had gone to beach clubs after dinner several hours ago, with only the crew playing cards below decks and enjoying an evening off from their demanding guests. All the guests except one. Sebastian Edward Cavendish, Old Etonian, minor aristocrat and owner of Cavendish Gallery, the most prestigious photographic gallery in London, sat in the *Zeus*'s smartest stateroom feeling as if his whole life was unravelling. Not even the luxury of the cabin, with its walnut-panelled walls and huge picture window looking out onto the inky sea could diminish his sense of being trapped. Sebastian had returned from The Supper Club, the Bodrum Peninsula's hottest nightspot, an hour earlier, drunk and angry. Unable to relax due to his escalating problems back home, his anxieties had bubbled over at the club and he'd had a furious argument with his wife, accusing her of flirting with their host. Tongue loosened by ouzo and goaded by his wife, he had blurted out that he'd slept with his new gallery assistant, a dazzling blonde recruited straight out of the Courtauld Institute. His wife had erupted like Mount St Helens, getting it into her stupid pampered head that it was some kind of ongoing affair and had threatened him with divorce. He had pleaded with her to come back to the yacht to discuss things away from the DJ and the cocktails and eavesdropping jet set, but she had turned on her spike heels and disappeared. Frustrated, seething, he had stormed back to the boat.

Now, staring out of the window of the cabin, he was feeling terrible, the alcohol buzzing round his bloodstream. He looked at his watch. Three a.m. and she still hadn't returned to the yacht.

That bitch, he thought.

Sebastian stripped off his clothes, throwing them onto a leather club chair and chopped out a line of coke on the dressing table in the hope that it would make him feel better. As soon as the white powder hit the back of his throat he knew he had made a mistake. He felt even worse.

Pulling on a white towelling bathrobe, Sebastian padded out on deck to get a hit of cold, salty night sea air. He leant against the waist-high rail at the aft of the yacht and rubbed his eyes. The lights of Turkbuku twinkled in the distance like tiny flickering candles. Beyond that his eyes strained to make out the heavily wooded Turkish hillside, the tall spike of a mosque's minaret. He wondered if this would be his last holiday on the big yacht with the glamorous friends. He snorted scornfully. They were friends now, but would they still want to know him when he was bankrupt? Like hell – and he was living on borrowed time. Despite the high-profile launch parties and exhibitions of some of the world's finest fashion photographers, the Cavendish Gallery was failing, his gambling debts were mounting, and a particularly nasty North London family were chasing him for money he'd foolishly borrowed. He stood to lose everything. He had already put the Holland Park house, that stucco-fronted jewel, in his wife's name where it would be out of reach, although after tonight he was beginning to doubt that was such a good idea. Christ, he hoped she had cooled down. Sebastian hated confrontation; that was the root of his trouble. In business, in life, in love.

He pushed himself upright and picked up a glass from the table beside him, pouring in a splash of ouzo. It was time to sort his life out, he thought, throwing the drink back. The yacht was due to sail to Istanbul in the morning, he reflected. They could get off at the port and enjoy a couple of days together strolling around the exotic bazaars, walking along the Bosphorus, and try and recapture that exquisite feeling of falling madly, addictively in love.

He listened for the hum of the tender again, but the yacht was silent, the only sound the black waves lapping against the hull; a hollow, hypnotic sound, matching his sense of hopelessness.

Suddenly he turned, convinced he had heard something – a soft flurry of footsteps on the deck, perhaps? No, just the same gentle slap of water against the boat. He was becoming paranoid. Even in London he was beginning to feel watched wherever he went. Defiantly he tossed his crystal tumbler overboard and leant right over the railings to hear the satisfying plop as the glass fell into the sea. He didn't notice that his solid silver Asprey cigar cutter had slipped out of his pocket and landed on the deck with a quiet thud. He never would.

Early next morning, a Turkish fisherman, sailing in the bay on his small wooden *gulet*, discovered a white naked body, quite dead, floating in the water, and contacted the local police immediately. About the same time, the guests of *Zeus*, stirring from their party-sleep, were quizzing the captain about the whereabouts of one of their number. Sebastian Cavendish had rightly prophesied that it would be his last holiday on board the magnificent yacht. A Turkish inquest pronounced the incident death by accidental drowning. His wife, Karin, inherited the Holland Park mansion, a spectacular photographic collection and £5 million in life insurance.

1

Six months later
'Doesn't she look fabulous?'
'And after everything she's been through. Still a bit pale, though, don't you think?'
'No wonder. Apparently she stayed in Kensington for Christmas.'
'London? I thought I saw her in St Barts?'
'On a yacht? No way, not after the accident. I heard she never wants to set foot on a yacht ever again.'

Sipping from her flute of pink champagne, Karin Cavendish tried to ignore the whispers coming from every corner of Donna and Daniel Delemere's Eton Square ballroom. A woman of impeccable manners, she was mortified that her presence at the christening had completely upstaged her new goddaughter's big day. Her leave of absence from the social scene after the death of her husband Sebastian had only heightened Karin's considerable allure, and in the last six months she had become the subject of gossip and fascinated speculation.

Still, nothing could detract from a party like this, thought Karin. It really was impressive. The one hundred guests who had attended St Peter's Church an hour earlier for Evie's baptism were now circulating around one of the most beautiful ballrooms in London. Forget power christening, thought Karin, popping a caviar blini on her tongue: this was more like a royal wedding. Waiters milled around with trays of bubbling Krug and delicate canapés. Filipino housekeepers were discreetly plumping up silk cushions and taking coats to the cloakroom. The net worth of the guests in this room alone must be over £10 billion, she calculated, looking at Ariel Levy, Martin Birtwell, and Evie's grandfather, Lord Alexander Delemere. She had not seen such a fine gathering of billionaires since her own wedding to Sebastian six years earlier, at the Cavendish family seat of Hopton Castle. She thought for a moment how Sebastian would have loved it. He had been so handsome and well connected, she sighed.

Back-lit by a long, gilt-framed window, Karin's elegant figure was attracting discreet admiring glances from the men in the room and she tried not to smile. It had been a difficult six months, during which time Karin had thrown herself into her work and seen only the closest of friends, but now she was back on the circuit, it seemed that her new status of widow was not without its advantages. It gave her a whiff of tragedy, a veneer of respect. It removed the suggestion of predatory desires that so often accompanied a glamorous divorcee or single woman. Suddenly she was available, romantic and loaded. Not a bad place to be, thought Karin, taking in the super-rich lifestyle in front of her. Not bad at all.

'We can't tell you how honoured we are that you agreed to be Evie's godmother,' said Donna Delemere, approaching Karin, clutching her three-month old daughter Evie.

Karin leant forward and gingerly pulled back the voluminous folds of the Brittany lace gown covering the child with an elegantly manicured finger.

'Oh, I wouldn't have missed it for the world. Lovely ceremony. And how is my goddaughter?'

'A darling,' smiled Donna with pride. 'Don't you think she's just so pretty? I want to put her in for modelling. I'm thinking Baby Dior; none of those vulgar nappy ads you see on TV. But I don't think Daniel likes the idea. Says it's too gosh.'

'Gauche?' asked Karin with a small smile.

'That's the one,' she said flushing prettily. 'Maybe he's right. Anyway, let's mingle.'

Karin followed Donna through the crowds, nodding at acquaintances, accepting compliments and flattering looks. While many of the rumours about Karin Cavendish were fanciful or downright scandalous, one thing they all agreed on was that Karin looked fabulous. At thirty-one, in a cherry-red jersey dress which seemed to slide off her slim curves, it would be easy to mistake her for a model. Her long tanned legs, full-lipped pout, and the glossy brown hair which bounced onto her shoulders, all gave her the striking appeal of a sultry yet aloof French actress. And currently there was extra sparkle in Karin's wolf-green eyes. She had just sold her five-storey home in Holland Park for £12 million to a prominent Iranian businessman, downsized to a de-luxe Georgian townhouse in Kensington, and ploughed the profit into her company, Karenza, the sexiest, chicest swimwear company after Erès. Yes, there were prettier girls, there were richer girls but, looking around the party, where London's entire beau monde were sipping Krug, she knew that nobody was quite the dynamic package she was.

Donna led her to a corner of the room where society giants Christina Levy and Diana Birtwell were huddled.

'And is this the gorgeous godmother?' laughed Christina, a stunning redhead wearing Lanvin, five hundred thousand pounds' worth of emeralds and a cloud of bespoke scent. 'Kay's just the perfect choice for godmother, darling,' she smirked to Donna. 'She has a fabulous archive of Chanel, for which Evie will one day be very grateful. Although I hope you're not seriously looking to her for Evie's spiritual guidance.'

The wife of Ariel Levy, the biggest British retail tycoon since Philip Green, Christina had only just managed to squeeze the christening in between a post-Christmas stint at Amansala's Bikini Boot Camp in Tulum and the haute-couture collections in Paris. Sitting next to Christina was Diana Birtwell, a decorous Paltrow blonde and wife of Martin Birtwell, the Internet gambling king. Together they were Karin's closest female friends. The three woman had shared a house in Chelsea almost a decade earlier, when Christina, a former Californian beauty queen, had come over to London to score a record deal. She had run into Karin and Diana at Hobo's nightclub, where the two school friends spent night after night drinking cocktails and chasing floppy-haired banking heirs. Hitting it off, the three of them had rented 23b College Mews, a tiny pink terrace in Chelsea, and had painted the international social scene red, white and blue, jetting around the globe at the expense of rich men. *The three Mustique-ateers* smiled Karin, that's what they'd called themselves. They had promised lifetime loyalty to each other and swore they'd never be without De Beers diamonds.

Donna passed Evie to her Australian nanny and sat opposite Diana and Christina on a huge leather ottoman.

'Who is that with Rula?' asked Karin, discreetly pointing to a tall, slim porcelain-skinned woman with long, buttery-blonde hair. A reigning Miss Adriatic Coast, she was standing with her arm wrapped proprietorially around a stout man in his sixties, with a bald head and a white tuft of hair on the point of his chin. Rula's four-inch Louboutin heels meant there was almost a foot height difference between the two of them.

'That's Conrad Pushkin,' whispered Christina. 'The novelist. Apparently they've got engaged but haven't announced it yet. Not until she's handed over the pageant crown.'

'A novelist?' said Diana with surprise. 'What's she thinking?' Rula was one of their more beautiful acquaintances, which was a significant achievement considering their social group consisted of some of London's most groomed and striking women. Rula was wearing a sable mink poncho and cream leather trousers that made her legs look endless. In the women's opinion, Rula could have had anyone.

'He has a *Nobel prize*, honey,' said Christina, wide-eyed. 'I have to hand it to her – it's pure genius!'

'What's genius?' asked Donna, taking a sip of champagne. She had stopped breast-feeding especially for the party.

'Deferred gratification, darling,' said Christina, as if it was obvious. Seeing Donna's blank look, she patiently explained. 'Rula's decided not to go for the really big catch,' replied Christina thoughtfully. 'Not immediately, anyway. Conrad's not good-looking, but he's not exactly rich either, so all the decent men, and I'm talking top fifty on the *Sunday Times* Rich List here, they'll see this gorgeous woman marrying an egghead and think, "Ah! Rula isn't interested in money! She married him for love, the lucky dog." So when she's done with him, mark my words, that honey is going to be in hot demand. The world thinks she's a beautiful woman not interested in money, but the kicker is that her ex-husband was a world-class brain. Rich men are desperate to feel clever. Marry Rula and they can bask in Conrad's glory.'

Donna whistled, in awe of Christina's wisdom.

'Do you spend hours thinking about this stuff?' asked Karin, taking a Parma-ham wrapped fig from a platter.

'Darling, we *all* spend hours thinking about this stuff,' smiled Christina with a wink.

'Anyway, on to more serious matters . . . who did the catering, Donna honey?' Christina continued. 'I'm looking for someone to do Joshua's birthday. We're looking for something tasteful but simple.'

'Like recreating Narnia?' said Karin, recalling the last birthday party Christina had arranged for her nine-year-old stepson, Ariel's child by his first wife. Their whole Mayfair mansion had been transformed into a C S Lewis novel complete with real snow, actors dressed as fauns and shoulder-high piles of Turkish delight.

'We want Joshua to have the best of everything,' said Christina knowingly.

'Actually, it's the chefs from the farm who have put this together,' said Donna. 'Everything being served here today you can buy in the farm shop.'

Donna had recently opened a spa and organic farm store on the Delemere family estate, a bucolic 2000-acre parcel of land in Oxfordshire. You couldn't seem to move these days for socialites setting up children's clothes shops or designing handbags, thought Karin wryly. Of course, she wouldn't class herself with the bored lunching classes and their expensive hobbies. Karenza swimwear was becoming big business: turnover of £20 million a year, two more shop launches planned for the autumn and ideas for a lingerie line rolling out next year. Seb's death had made her a rich woman, but within the next five years she was determined that the money she now had in her Coutt's bank account would seem like pocket money.

'You really should be thinking about promoting yourself as the Eco-Brit Martha Stewart,' said Karin, looking at her slim, eager friend. 'I know the farm shop is doing well, but you should start expanding the franchise as soon as possible. The possibilities of lifestyle brand extensions from Delemere are endless.'

'Do you always have to talk business?' grumbled Diana, draining her flute of champagne.

Karin smiled thinly. She felt sorry for women like Diana who had nothing to do except shop. After drifting into fashion PR, Diana had been working on a promotion for a Savile Row tailor. Dropping into the showroom one day, she had met Martin Birtwell, rising Internet gambling tycoon, coming out of the changing room. Diana was seduced by Martin's drive and by his convertible Sports car; Martin was dazzled by the fashionable society world that Diana moved in. They instantly became one of London's most attractive couples. But the second Diana had married him, in July the previous summer, she had given up work. She now filled her days with blow-dry appointments and baby showers. Karin pursed her lips just thinking about it. How silly, she thought. Karin wanted a man to enhance her position, not to depend on him for it. She looked around the room, sizing up all the fabulously wealthy men in front of her. It won't be long, she thought. It won't be long.

On the other side of the room, Molly Sinclair wasn't sure what was making her feel more sick, the calorific cupcake she had just eaten, or sheer naked envy. Molly had just been treated to a tour of the house, which had brought home to her the extent of Donna Delemere's good fortune. Evie's nursery was bigger than Molly's entire apartment, taking up a whole floor of the Georgian pile, complete with a nanny annexe and a Mark Wilkinson cot in the shape of Cinderella's carriage. White French armoires were stuffed with Bonpoint clothes, while a huge photograph of Mummy and Daddy's wedding hung over the fireplace like a gloating reminder of everything Molly didn't have.

It didn't seem two minutes ago since Donna Jones, as she was known back when Molly had first met her, was a bottle-blonde tramp looking for city boys at Legends nightclub. *Now look at her*, she thought bitterly, taking a long swig of vodka. Donna had swapped her Dolce & Gabbana hot pants for Brora cashmere twin-sets the minute she had met Daniel Delemere, an art historian with a huge family fortune, at the Cartier polo three years earlier. But that had been just the start of her incredible transformation into society wife. Her hair was now a soft nutmeg brown, her wardrobe an elegant mixture of Marni and Jil Sander and, bearing the Delemere name, Donna now sat on the most important charity committees and holidayed for the entire summer in the best villas around the Med. Nobody seemed to mention that she had once been a mobile beautician from Hull.

Of course, Donna had only done what girls with humble back-grounds and explosive good looks had been doing for decades. What really needled Molly was that it hadn't been *her*. It was an eternal mystery to Molly why she hadn't managed to elevate herself into this strata of society. Acquiring a husband with an impressive surname and a gull's-egg sized rock on her finger was something she had expected ever since her modelling career had taken off like a bottle-rocket in the 1980s. She had been voted one of the world's most beautiful women *four times*, for Christ's sake! Not quite in the Christy Turlington league, but Molly had certainly been on the next rung down in the supermodel pecking order. And Molly had weathered well. Even at forty-three, Molly could have passed for someone ten years younger, and the smouldering sex appeal that had made her famous had not been dimmed. Her hair was long and thick with glossy tawny highlights. Her cheekbones were high and noble and her tanned skin, regularly treated with cell-regeneration shots, from a distance looked fresh and young. Today she was wearing a winter-white cashmere sweater and cream trousers, and she looked as if she had stepped off a plane from St Barts that very morning, not out of her home in the slightly more 'bohemian' end of Notting Hill.

But no, the good marriage hadn't happened. Bad luck, bad judgement, bad drugs – who knew? The bottom line was that her mid-forties were around the corner and Molly was still single. Even worse was that she was slowly being shut out from the most exclusive society events. Those girlfriends she had spent night after night with at L'Equipe Anglaise, Tramp and Annabel's in the 1980s and 1990s had all disappeared to grand Scottish country estates, to Manhattan's Upper East Side, or to mansion houses on Palm Beach. Every now and then she would receive a invitation to an event like today's christening, but she was never invited to spend a week at the villas, or to intimate dinners with the prize husbands. It was obvious why. She was a single, beautiful woman and therefore a threat, plus Molly was part of their past, a past she knew they did not want to be reminded of.

She picked on a crab claw before throwing it into a plant pot behind her. She took a deep breath, assuring herself that the situation was purely temporary. She was Molly Sinclair, the super-model. She had lived longer on her wits than any of these nobodies. She stalked off to the bathroom to take a line of cocaine. She'd show them. All of them.

Karin popped open her compact and checked her reflection. She had to be looking her best for a charm offensive. As godmother, Karin's attendance at Evie's christening had, of course, been *de rigueur*, but it was also an ideal opportunity to drum up business for the charity benefit gala dinner she had planned for the following month. With so many society players in the room in such a buoyant, benevolent mood, it would have been foolish to let the opportunity pass to sell tickets for her 'Stop Global Warming' benefit gala. Like many of the women in the room, Karin had dipped her toe in charity work before, but after Sebastian's death she had needed a more substantial project to sink her teeth into, and an exclusive high-profile dinner for eight hundred was just the solution.

'How are the auction prizes coming along?' asked Christina, who had already donated a week on the Levys' yacht the *Big Blue* as a lot.

'Fine,' replied Karin. 'Except I had to fire the events assistant yesterday. You don't know anyone suitable, do you? I need someone young, keen, presentable – someone with a brain.'

Christina shook her head blankly.

'I can ask Martin if you like,' said Diana. 'I think his company use some agency.'

'I'd be grateful,' said Karin, in her usual cool, efficient manner. 'They don't have to be experienced, just keen. I'll be handling the important matters like guest lists and table plans.'

'Ahh, I see,' smiled Diana, playing with a pebble-sized solitaire diamond dangling around her neck. 'Now you're single . . .'

'Don't be ridiculous,' said Karin, waving a hand dismissively. 'I'm only interested in raising as much money as possible. Do you know what's happening to the icecaps?'

'Of course I do,' said Diana. 'The snow was awful in Megève this year.'

'Hey, why don't we ask Molly Sinclair?' said Donna, nodding towards the tall woman across the room. 'She's a consultant at Feldman Jones PR and Events. She must know someone suitable.'

'If we must,' said Karin coolly. Karin barely knew Molly, but knew of her; an eighties almost-supermodel, a coked-up has-been, still on the circuit peddling her overt sexuality, trying to bag whatever half-rich man would have her.

Donna waved her friend over.

'Everyone here knows Molly, don't they?' said Donna, getting weak smiles from all three women. 'Do you know of any good PAs or events assistants, Molly?'

'What's it for?' purred Molly in her smouldering smoker's voice.

'Karin's Stop Global Warming benefit. She's trying to do it without a committee,' said Christina sternly.

Karin smiled thinly. A committee was the last thing she needed. She was happy to let a handful of select, connected friends sell tickets on the fund's behalf, but the controlling streak in Karin would not allow any meddling in her vision. She wanted the glory to be all hers.

'Will you be coming, Molly?' asked Diana, absently wondering how Molly managed to look so good. If she'd had a lift, it was amazing.

'Tables are very expensive,' said Karin quickly. 'One thousand pounds a plate and selling out quickly.'

Molly shook her head, hair swooshing from side to side across her shoulders. 'Can't make the actual dinner, unfortunately. I have friends coming from the States that night,' she said, accepting another glass of champagne from a waiter.

Inwardly, Molly was wincing at the ticket price. A thousand pounds! It was outrageous! Her coke allowance for a month. Six months' gym membership. A good dress. She knew the event was a worthwhile investment, but she just didn't have that much money sloshing around.

'Speaking of friends, I tell you who you should invite,' smiled Christina, taking a delicate sip of a white Russian. 'Adam Gold.'

'Who's he?' asked Karin.

'Karin, darling, you're slacking,' smiled Christina through glossy lips. 'New York real-estate and investment guy. He's behind some of those fabulous new condo developments in Manhattan, Miami and Dallas. He's also very sexy and very wealthy. Just made the *Forbes* list this year.'

Molly's ears pricked up. *Forbes* list! That meant net worth a billion dollars *minimum*.

Karin gave Christina her best uninterested ice-queen expression. 'Billionaire or not, he's unlikely to come from New York for a party, even this one.'

'Oh no, haven't you heard?' said Diana, widening her baby-blue eyes. 'He's just moved to London. Martin says he's rolling out his property developing all over Europe, Moscow and Dubai and the Far East.'

'We could do with a shot of new blood,' said Christina, smiling. 'Not that I want to touch, of course,' she added, stealing a glance at her husband, who was smoking a Cohiba on the terrace, 'but I *do* like to look.'

15

'Darling, get him invited,' smiled Christina, touching Karin's knee meaningfully. 'The tickets will fly out the door once word gets out that he's coming.'

'Well, I am in London that evening,' said Molly slowly. 'Perhaps I could pop by afterwards . . . ?'

Karin and Molly's eyes locked and they recognized in the other something they had encountered many times before. Rivalry.

'I hate to disappoint you, sweetheart,' said Karin coolly, 'but there won't be any after-dinner tickets for the benefit night. It's just not that kind of event.'

Molly smiled. It was her sweetest, most earnest smile, a smile that had lit up a dozen magazine covers and persuaded many people, people much richer and more powerful than Karin, to do her bidding. Yes, thought Molly, Adam Gold sounded like just the sort of man to get her right back where she belonged, and she wasn't going to let an uptight, jealous little control freak like Karin Cavendish stop her from getting him. And her smile grew just a little wider.

2

Cornwall in January is beautiful. Not the hazy beauty of midsummer, when the sea shines turquoise and the sun blurs distant hillsides into deep green smudges, but a bleak, eerie beauty so strong, crisp and immediate that it turns your cheeks pink and sends a shiver through your bones. Erin Devereux pulled her scarf a little higher around her chin, too wound up to appreciate the chilly splendour around her. *My life is going nowhere*, she thought grimly, thrusting her hands deeper into her pockets and marching on along the cliff top. Usually, whenever she felt uninspired, there was nothing like the granite rocks, crashing surf and the whiff of smugglers to get her creative juices flowing. But nowadays, more often than not, she found herself wondering what she was doing in the prime of her life – well, at twenty-four – living in a tiny village at the end of the earth, trying to write a book about . . . well, nothing very much at the moment. Erin felt so hemmed in by all this open space, she couldn't get off the first page. She kicked at a pebble in frustration, missing by inches and stubbing her toe on a tree root. She howled in pain and irritation. Just then, as if someone had turned on a tap, it began to rain hard. *Story of my life*, thought Erin, and began to run for home.

'These boots are going straight in the bin,' declared Erin, pushing open the back door of Hawthorn Cottage and feeling the blast of warm, sweet air on her face. She flopped down on the nearest chair, pulled off her sheepskin boots and threw them in the corner.

'Got writer's block again?' said the elderly woman standing in

17

front of a scarlet Aga. Jilly Thomas, Erin's grandmother, was as small as a mouse, with a shock of wiry grey hair and a proud, handsome face. There was a line of flour across her lined cheek and she was wearing a navy apron smeared with something white.

'Yep, writer's block, writer's clog, writer's jam, the lot,' said Erin, pressing her cold toes against a lukewarm radiator.

'Well, don't you worry, lovey,' said Jilly, 'I've cooked you a nice chicken pie and some mash, too – just the ticket to warm you up.'

Erin smiled at her grandmother. No wonder she had put on seven pounds since she'd been back in Cornwall. But her tall frame could take a little extra weight, hidden most of the time in jeans and a thick sweater. Erin glanced in the mirror above the fireplace and saw a ruddy, pretty farm girl. Her lips were full and naturally pink and long russet curls fell down her back. She'd always envied redheads who had startling green eyes – the classic Irish colouring that gave them bold, cat-like strikingness, but Erin's eyes were cognac brown and it softened the look. Although right now her cheeks had been stung pink by the sea air and ribbons of wind-lashed hair were still stuck to her face. The glamorous authoress, she thought. Erin wrapped her cold fingers around a steaming mug that Jilly had placed before her.

'The problem is that there's nothing to write about round here,' she complained.

'You make it sound like it's Cornwall's fault,' said Jilly with a hint of a smile.

'Well – it is!' said Erin. 'I'm not doing anything. I'm not experiencing anything. What am I supposed to write about? Seagulls?'

Erin saw a look of sadness pass over Jilly's face and felt an immediate stab of guilt. She hadn't meant to sound so critical of the warm, welcoming village she had called home for the last twenty years, nor did she want Jilly to feel in any way inadequate. She owed her grandmother everything. Erin's father Phillip had committed suicide when she was five, and her mother Hillary had disappeared twelve months later. Erin had immediately moved in with Jilly Thomas, her maternal grandmother and had been brought up as her own daughter. And she had had an idyllic childhood in Port Merryn, running along the beaches, playing in the narrow, twisty streets. It had been like one long summer holiday; even the winters were cosy and warm in Jilly's kitchen. But, like much of Cornwall, Port Merryn was a dying community. The Atlantic was all but fished out, removing the village's traditional income, so the quaint stone fishermen's cottages circling the harbour were being snapped up by rich Londoners as holiday homes. With property prices soaring and no prospect of work, the families had moved to the cities, leaving only a retired community and a handful of locals running tourist-trap cafés and fudge shops. It had been five years since you had been able to buy a pint of milk in Port Merryn, and in the dead of winter the village was like a ghost town.

'I'm sorry, gran, I didn't mean to make it sound like I wanted to leave . . .'

'Now, now, lovey,' said Jilly, wiping her hands on her apron and reaching over to touch Erin's hand. 'You're only saying the truth. I know you love the village, but it's no place for a young girl, not when you've seen what's on the other side of the hill.'

Erin nodded with melancholy. It had seemed like a good idea to move back to Port Merryn after she had graduated from university six months ago. She could save on rent, and move to the city when she'd made a proper start on her writing career. At least, that had been the plan, but it hadn't quite worked out that way. Raised on a diet of Daphne Du Maurier and John Fowles – Jilly had always made sure the house was full of books to enrich and inspire her granddaughter's mind – Erin's one ambition had been to write the Great British Novel, and had spent every spare moment of her time at uni crafting her debut book. By the end of the last term it had been ready: 120,000 words, double spaced and printed on one-sided white paper. She sent it to a dozen agencies and waited. She had almost given up hope when she had been summoned by Ed Davies, senior partner in Davies & Sisman Literary Agency, to his office in London. Almost numb with excitement, Erin had spent three days deciding what to wear in order to give the right balance of 'literary genius' and 'commercial winner' and had spent the whole journey there planning her Man Booker Prize acceptance speech. She had thus been badly deflated when Ed Davies had sat her down in his Holborn office and spent twenty minutes telling her why he thought her novel sucked. However, he had seen enough promise, he said, that he was prepared to represent her.

'I'm taking a chance on you,' the agent had told her, 'and this book certainly isn't going to be your debut novel. But if you can come up with the right premise and execute it as well as I think you can, then I want to be the one negotiating your first deal.'

Erin looked across at her battered old laptop sitting at the desk by the window, almost buried under a mound of papers and notebooks. The screen blinked at her, an open document white and empty. The novel, her great escape route from the village, just wouldn't come, however hard she tried.

'Someone called for you while you were out,' said Jilly, waving an oven glove towards the phone. She was removing a thick crusted pie from the oven, which she placed on the gingham tablecloth.

'Who was it?' asked Erin, picking up a Post-it note scrawled with illegible writing. 'Richard?' Her relationship with her boyfriend at university was still limping along, even though Erin was now back in Cornwall and Richard was based in London.

'No, lovey,' smiled Jilly sympathetically. 'Katherine someone from an agency, I think?'

Erin felt a rush of excitement. 'The Deskhop Agency?'

'That's the one,' nodded Jilly. 'Who are they, then?'

'It's a secretarial agency in London,' said Erin slowly.

'Secretarial work?' said Jilly, raising one eyebrow. 'What about the book?'

'Gran . . .' she replied, hoping not to sound too exasperated, 'the Deskhop Agency acts for all sorts of media and publishing companies. I thought I might be able to get in through the back door. But don't worry, it probably won't come to anything.'

Her grandmother smiled kindly and put her oven gloves down. 'Erin, don't you dare go worrying about me. You have a talent, and a talent should take you places, not leave you stranded in a cold little backwater with a pensioner and her stodgy cooking.'

'But I love the village and I love your cooking!' protested Erin.

'I know you do, love,' said Jilly, running her hand up and down Erin's arm, 'but you're climbing the walls. It's about time you got out and had some fun while you're young.'

'I don't have enough money to move to London.'

'You know you do,' said Jilly.

'But I can't use that . . .'

Erin thought about the nest egg sitting in the bank. Her father had died almost bankrupt, but over the years he had squirrelled away money for his daughter, which had added up to a tidy sum. Erin had never touched it, keeping it for 'something important'.

'Maybe it's time to use it, lovey. Your mum would have wanted you to.'

Erin looked at her grandmother's deep blue eyes and knew she loved her more than ever. But she also knew she was right.

'Well, I'll think about it,' said Erin, wondering how much of Jilly's rice pudding she would have to eat before she could slip off and make the phone call.

'Ah, Erin Devereux. Good of you to call back. I tried your mobile but I'm not sure it's working.' Catherine Weiner's voice was brash and over-friendly. It had been so long since Erin had been up to London for her agency interview, but she remembered how scarily efficient the woman was.

'Then I tried this number on your CV. Didn't recognize the dialling code. Where are you? Surrey?'

'Er, Cornwall,' said Erin, putting on her best telephone manner.

'Cornwall,' replied Catherine, surprised. 'You've not moved down there, have you?'

'Just staying with friends while my new London flat completes,' Erin quickly lied. 'Solicitor tells me it'll be Friday. Then I'm on the first train back to London.'

'Well, that's good news,' said Catherine, briskly. 'Because Cornwall is hardly commutable and I think I've got a job for you.'

Erin's interest was piqued. 'Oh yes?'

'I see from the notes I took at your interview that you were looking for secretarial cover at a publishing company. Well, this is not that, but it should be lively work for a girl your age.'

'So what is it?'

'Events management. It's a three-week job. The client, a very glamorous lady-about-town needs help staging a benefit dinner. Sending out tickets, lots of admin, lots of running around. She wanted someone bright, organized, presentable. Doesn't need particularly sharp typing skills, which is why I thought of you. Starts ASAP, mind you. She wants to interview tomorrow. Lots of my girls are committed to long-term contracts, but I thought you might be free . . .'

Charming, thought Erin.

'So I have to come up to London for an interview?' said Erin, thinking about the cost of a train ticket.

'Erin,' said Catherine, her voice sharp and reprimanding. 'This is what's known as a very sexy gig. Now, are you in or out?'

Erin looked out of the window at the grey emptiness There was no denying it was beautiful here; it even smelt wonderful, with the tang of the sea air mingling with the scent of the wild flowers on the cliffs and the oily trawlers in the harbour. She knew that when she was her grandmother's age there would be no better place in the world in which to live, but, right now, aged twenty-four, life seemed to be on pause. Cornwall was so cut-off, so disconnected from the rest of the world, she had to get to London to wake herself up. To connect with society. To connect with people.

'Count me in. I'll be on the first train tomorrow.'

3

'Last shot and then that's it for the day,' shouted Sally Stevenson, art director of *Your Wedding* magazine, adjusting the tiara on Summer Sinclair's head and smoothing down the undulating layers of the Vera Wang gown. Summer groaned with relief. She could see it was already pitch-black outside the French windows of the location house, and she was dying to get home and soak her feet. All day she had wriggled in and out of white meringues and slinky ivory columns, her hair had been pinned up and blow-dried down and she had run through every expression from poetic wistfulness to carefree laughter. In short, she'd spent the day being trussed up like a toilet doily and she was exhausted. Still, at least some of today had been fun, thought Summer, glancing at Charlie McDonald, the male model who had been playing the dashing groom to her blushing bride. Charlie had made her giggle all day long, doing impressions of Stefan the surly Swedish photographer, and chasing the three tiny bridesmaids around the studio creating pandemonium. He was good looking, too, in a preppy, Ralph Lauren kind of way, she thought. *Although not my type at all*, she corrected herself quickly. Summer tended to go for older men – rich, older men – something her mother had drilled into her since she was a girl.

'*He might be handsome,*' she could hear her mum saying, '*but can a handsome man get you a private jet?*' No, Charlie was no more than her age, and the last time she had been out with a twenty-four-year-old she had been sixteen – and, even then, he'd been a banking heir.

'Right now, I want something sexy, something romantic,' said

23

Stefan sternly. 'Charlie, can you move to the side of the staircase?' he directed. 'And slip your arm around Summer's waist.'

Charlie moved in close. *Bloody hell, he was handsome.* Narrow green eyes framed by sooty lashes, clear, lightly tanned skin, a mop of dark blond hair. Without the square jaw he would have been pretty, but the angles of his face toughened him up like a fifties film star. 'Now, I want you to kiss her gently on the lips.'

Awkwardly, Summer turned her head, feeling her heart beat faster as his lips brushed hers. Charlie was so good looking it was hard to be completely professional, to dissociate desire like you were turning off a tap. It had been over a year since she'd had any sort of intimate contact: despite her looks, Summer rarely dated.

'Come on, Summer. You're supposed to have just married this guy!' shouted Sally. 'Don't look at him as if you're scared stiff.'

Summer forced a smile and moved closer to Charlie as Sally and her assistant began throwing silver and white balloons into the shot.

'Come on, pretend that you love me,' Charlie whispered with a soft smile. 'Then we can all go home.'

The highly strung photographer threw his hands up in the air in frustration. 'These British!' he moaned. 'They are so uptight!'

Sally Stevenson rushed in, clapping her hands. 'Okay, thank you everyone, that was great,' she said, lifting her hands above her head for the traditional end-of-shoot applause.

'So, who wants to come for a drink?' she asked, looking hopefully at Charlie, who she had booked specially because she fancied him.

'Don't mind if I do . . .' he said, not taking his eyes off Summer as he spoke.

Summer went into the bathroom to take the thick foundation off her face. She scrambled out of the creamy meringue. Bloody wedding shoots, she thought, staring into the mirror. Then again, she wasn't exactly Kate Moss, was she?

Come on, Summer, get real and stop grumbling, she chided herself. A fashion shoot for *Your Wedding* wasn't the edgy, ground-breaking high-fashion editorial she had dreamt of doing when she had first started modelling; but at least it was work, something she hadn't had a great deal of since Christmas. At twenty-four, Summer knew that her modelling shelf-life was running out.

Charlie McDonald was waiting for her in the marbled hall, swatting at the balloons as the bridesmaids were bundled into thick duffle coats by their beaming parents.

'Are you coming for that drink?' asked Charlie, throwing his bag over his shoulder.

'Only if you're buying,' said Summer playfully.

'So, how come I haven't seen you in castings before?' asked Charlie as they walked towards the door.

'I've been out of the country for the last few years.'

'Oh yeah? New York?'

'Japan,' said Summer, a little embarrassed. She knew Tokyo was considered rather down-market as far as modelling was concerned. The very top girls went to New York where they could make millions of dollars, while the tall, skinny girls went to Paris where they would make couture dresses look even more exclusive and luxurious. Toyko barely even made it onto the fashion map, but the commercial Japanese market had loved Summer's glorious girl-next-door perfection, with her flawless, peachy complexion, rosy lips and watery, lavender-blue eyes that shined with such innocence that no one noticed that they were there to sell you overpriced cosmetics. She had been one of the top girls at her Tokyo agency, a big star in her tiny neon universe. It was four years of hard work, but it had boosted her confidence, given her plenty and, most importantly, it meant her mother's seal of approval.

'Wow, Tokyo? That's fantastic!' said Charlie, without any hint of snobbery. 'I thought about going out there myself to make a bit of money. Apparently they don't mind short-arses over there.'

Summer laughed. Charlie probably just scraped six foot, but she could sympathize. The lack of work in London for girls her height – five feet seven – was one of the reasons why she went to Japan in the first place.

'You should go,' said Summer, 'it's an amazing place. A little strange and fantastically polite, but amazing all the same.'

Charlie shrugged. 'I have a band. The only reason I model is to pay for guitar strings.'

'Ah-ha!' said Summer triumphantly, 'I knew it! So you're the next Noel Gallagher.' She had always been jealous of male models. While they rarely got the big bucks that the top female models could command, most men she met on the circuit were using modelling as a stopgap or a passport to other things: students working off a bank loan, wannabe TV presenters getting visibility or actors making a quick buck.

'Yeah, just like Noel Gallagher,' smiled Charlie, 'but with better teeth.'

They walked out onto the streets of Belgravia. With the tall white Georgian houses stretching up around them, her hair still in a bouffant, carriage streetlamps glowing like dandelion clocks, she felt like a heroine in a Jane Austen novel. Sally, Stefan and some of the crew were still huddled in the doorway of the house, sheltering from the spitting rain and debating where to go to drink.

'What about the Blue Bar for a cocktail?'

'I'm not paying a tenner for a drink,' grumbled Charlie. 'Aren't there any pubs around here?'

'Well, what about the Grenadier?' said Sally looking directly at Charlie. 'I saw Madonna in there once.'

'No one famous is going to be out tonight,' said Jenny the make-up artist, lighting a cigarette and taking a long drag. 'It's that big party in South London tonight, isn't it?'

Summer felt a sudden sense of panic. 'Oh shit!' she said, and started looking up and down the street for a taxi.

'What's up?' asked Charlie.

'I promised my mum I'd go out with her,' groaned Summer.

'Hot date at the bingo?'

Summer laughed at the image. 'My mum is probably more rock 'n' roll than anyone you've ever met in the music industry.'

'Excellent! Get her down to the Grenadier!' said Charlie.

Summer doubted her mum had been to anywhere as down-market as a pub since the 1970s.

'What are we waiting for over there?' said Sally Stevenson irritably, unhappy that Summer was monopolizing Charlie.

A black cab pulled up to the kerb, and Summer quickly spoke to the driver. 'I'd better go,' said Summer apologetically, clunking the door open.

Charlie rifled around in his bag and pulled out a CD. 'My band,' he said, handing it to her with an endearingly nervous expression, like a twelve-year old schoolboy who'd just plucked up the courage to ask a girl out for the first time. 'Give it a listen. If you like it, we're playing at the Monarch a week on Thursday. You should come down and hear us.'

She felt a little spike of affection as he pulled a copy of *NME* out of his bag and held it over his hair as the rain got harder.

'And if I hate it?' she asked.

'Come down anyway.'

As the cab began to turn back up the street, Summer pulled down the window to tell Charlie she would try to make it. As she passed the group, she could see Sally Stevenson sidle up to Charlie and say, 'Funny fish, that one, isn't she?'

She couldn't hear Charlie's reply.

4

Karin strode into the Great Hall of Strawberry Hill House to give it one final check before heading back to London to get a blow-dry. It was certainly a magnificent room and Karin had very, very high standards. The marble pillars had been wrapped in gold-tipped ivy matching the mansion's incredible gilded ceilings. The ballroom was studded with bay trees sprayed white, and a long catwalk extended through the sea of tables – Karin had insisted that the vital ingredient of the night's entertainment would be a showcase of the Karin Cavendish cruise collection. There were ice sculptures, huge vases of Calla lilies and a small stage festooned with waves of ivory voile on which Havana's finest jazz band were due to play. She stood back and smiled. She knew she had got it just right.

Karin had spent three months deciding on this venue for the global warming benefit dinner because it had to be perfect. Central London was out; the venues which could accommodate big numbers for dinner and dancing were so over used and frankly, a little déclassé. No, Karin knew that if the Stop Global Warming benefit was going to make a splash, it would have to be somewhere elegant and original, and in Strawberry Hill House, a stunning Gothic mansion fifteen miles outside London, she knew she had found the place. Even being so bloody far from Chelsea had its benefits; at least thirty guests were arriving by helicopter, adding a further dash of exclusivity to the evening. The irony of using helicopters in place of cars or taxis to arrive an event aimed at highlighting the perils of global warming was not lost on Karin, but then her heart was in the party, and certainly not the cause. Global warming!

Why on earth would she want to trade her BMW X5 for one of those ridiculous hybrid cars that looked as if they were used to transport OAPs? The way Karin looked at it, if she was raising a few million for the penguins and the polar bears, then they could turn a blind eye to a few teensy helicopters.

'Hey, look lively, here comes the dragon,' whispered one of the hand-picked models-cum-waiters who started polishing the crystal goblets frantically as Karin approached. Erin stifled a giggle before putting her head down to examine the table plan.

'I said Verbena roses, not Iceberg roses,' snapped Karin at Jamie Marshall. Jamie was one of the country's premier florists, and was currently working like a camp demon on islands of roses for the table centrepieces.

'But Karin, darling,' he whined. 'They are both white roses, who will notice the diff—'

'Change them,' said Karin emphatically, and moved on before he had time to object.

'You!' Karin had turned her attention to a waiter who was putting the menus on the crisp white tablecloths. 'Get me some blueberries to nibble on. Organic . . . And you! Haven't you been home to change?'

Erin winced, feeling for the poor waiter about to get a tongue-lashing.

'Erin! I'm talking to you!' Karin snapped.

'Me? I . . . I thought . . .' said Erin, flustered. 'But I *have* changed.' She looked down at her outfit, embarrassed. It was a knee-length black shift dress with a little diamanté buckle she had bought at the Next January sale to wear to Richard's Law School Ball. It made her feel pretty, slim and demure.

She caught Karin rolling her eyes. Five minutes ago she had felt a little like Audrey Hepburn; now she felt hopelessly inadequate.

'Oh well. At least it's black,' sighed Karin.

Since Erin's first call from the Deskhop Agency, three weeks had passed in a blur. Erin had been surprised to have been offered the job on the spot by Karin Cavendish, especially as she had been so nervous in the interview after recognizing Karin from the society pages of the *Mail*. Karin had wanted her to start immediately, so Erin had been forced to make the awkward call to Richard asking if she could stay at his flat for a couple of

weeks while she sorted herself out and decided whether her
future was in London or Cornwall. From her first day at Karin
Cavendish, it had been a trial by fire for Erin. Eighteen-hour
days were commonplace and the attention to detail Karin
demanded was phenomenal. Thankfully, Erin was not organising the Stop Global Warming event by herself. Karin had
recruited a production company to sort out everything from
furniture to lighting and a PR company whose responsibility
seemed to be keeping the press away from the event rather than
persuading them to cover it. Even so, the volume of work
required to coordinate everything made Erin's head ache. It didn't
help that Karin was such a demanding taskmaster. Every bit as
particular and exacting as she was glamorous, Karin was the
ultimate perfectionist, insisting on signing off every last detail
personally. She had spent days hand-picking the best-looking
waiters from catering agencies all over London, and would spend
hours agonizing over whether to have Tattinger or Perrier Jouet
champagne at the reception. As far as Erin had been concerned,
champagne was champagne before Karin had explained the
difference. Just being in Karin's company made Erin feel more
chic and worldly.

'I'm going to Charles Worthington in ten minutes,' said Karin.
'So we need to run through everything now.' She held up a finger,
then touched her earpiece. 'Hi, darling. No, can't talk now. See
you tonight, yes? Ciao!'

She sat down at Erin's table and fingered the cream floral centrepiece critically. 'You understand that I won't be anywhere near the
door tonight?' she asked Erin. 'So I'm leaving that to you.'

It was the thing Erin was most excited about. She was to be in
charge of the guest list and would be checking people in as they
came through the velvet rope. There were plenty of celebrities on
the VIP list: Robbie Williams, Yasmin Le Bon, even Hector Fox,
one of Britain's hottest new actors; Erin had recently seen him as
a troubled hit man in an ITV drama and he had made her feel
weak at the knees.

'You have got to be *beyond* strict,' continued Karin, snapping
her fingers to summon a waiter and barking the word, 'water.'

'Remember, no ticket, no entry. And cross-reference with the
guest list, I don't want anyone slipping through. I'm diverting all
calls to you from now; they'll all be blaggers trying to get a last-

minute ticket for after dinner; you'll get loads of press too. Tell them this is a bloody charity night and let them buy a ten-thousand-pound table if they want to come. Anyway, *Tatler* has the exclusive.'

Karin ran through her list of strict rules and regulations. She wanted a car to be outside for her from 10.30 p.m. and to wait indefinitely until she was ready to go. Under no circumstances was either Erin or any of the PR girls allowed to smoke or drink.

'Not even water, Erin,' said Karin firmly. 'People think it's vodka tonic and it looks really, really unprofessional.'

Erin nodded solemnly at each instruction and, when Karin finally stalked off, she took a deep breath, part of her wanting to run all the way back to Cornwall, but another part of her more thrilled and excited than she had ever been in her life.

Summer's taxi arrived outside her basement flat in a slightly scruffy house in W10, a shade after 8 p.m. She had promised the taxi driver a ten-pound tip if he could get her home in fifteen minutes and he had screeched into Basset Road with seconds to spare.

'Here you go, love,' he beamed, shoving the notes into his breast pocket. 'Hope he's worth it.'

As the cab pulled away, Summer turned and looked up at the tall thin terrace and sighed. It was home, she supposed, although living with her mother at twenty-four wasn't exactly her ideal life plan. Molly had bought the building for a song fifteen years earlier when a boyfriend had convinced her that Ladbroke Grove would one day be the new Chelsea. Not that Molly had waited around for that to happen. Living for most of the nineties in various apartments paid for by lovers, by the time Molly moved back into the property after the demise of yet another relationship, Ladbroke Grove had gentrified sufficiently to be acceptably bohemian. Summer had moved into the basement flat directly under Molly's house after her return from Japan. Theoretically that made her independent of Molly's interference, but it seemed nobody had bothered to tell her mother. It was like being twelve years old again, only this time, she was expected to accompany her mother to parties instead of wait at home with the babysitter.

Summer closed the front door, then used another key to let herself into Molly's apartment. Molly was sitting in the lounge in her bra and knickers, her hair set in a mountain of curlers, feet propped up on a desk as she painted her toenails scarlet. Summer thought she looked like an Ellen Von Unwerth photograph.

'You're about an hour late,' said Molly tartly, putting the bottle of polish down on the table.

Summer noticed that the laptop Molly had open on the desk beside her was blinking on the eBay home page. It was her mother's latest source of income, converting gifts from boyfriends into cash – a Hermès scarf here, a Tiffany cocktail ring there; in the last twelve months she had made at least £50,000, tax free.

'What are you selling this time?' asked Summer, trying to deflect her mother's annoyance.

'Suleiman gave me a Kelly bag,' sighed Molly.

'And you're getting rid of it?' asked Summer, surprised. She herself had always coveted the legendary Hermès bag, but had never been in the position to part with £3000.

'You have a Kelly when you're over fifty, a Birkin when you're under fifty,' said Molly patiently, looking at Summer as if she had suggested that the sky was green. 'So, what kept you? I thought the shoot finished at six.'

Summer slipped off her coat and flopped onto the plump cream sofa. 'It ran on a bit. The crew wanted to go for a drink. I got away as early as I could.'

'You went for a drink when you could have been home getting ready to go out with me?' snapped Molly. 'I hope you weren't wasting your time with any bloody photographers. Did he tell you he can get you in *Vogue*? Believe me, the only thing you get from a fashion photographer is an STD.'

'I didn't even go for the drink,' said Summer tetchily. 'Anyway, it's only eight o'clock and we don't have to be at the party till ten.'

'Which would be fine if it wasn't in Surrey. Honestly Summer, you drift back from Japan, I let you live downstairs paying *half* the rent I could be charging somebody else, and this is what I get: selfishness and inconsideration. Oh well,' she huffed, 'you might as well be useful and tell me which dress you prefer.'

Summer followed her mother upstairs into the bedroom feeling wretched. Molly knew exactly the right buttons to press to make her feel guilty and ungrateful. Not for the first time since she got back from Japan, Summer wondered why her mother actually wanted her in such close proximity, considering she spent so much time making her feel like an inconvenience. But then it was a familiar feeling; Summer had always felt as if she had personally held Molly back, both in her modelling career and her love life. Even though a string of cheap Swedish au pairs had been a fixture in the Sinclair household, it couldn't have been easy for Molly to jet off on a modelling job to Manhattan or Marrakech with Summer weighing her down like a ball and chain. Worse than that, Summer felt she had scuppered Molly's chances of finding love. Despite being one of the most fabulous women in the world, Molly had never married and it was obvious why – what man wanted a screaming brat in tow? So Summer had learnt not to complain when she constantly changed schools as Molly drifted from lover to lover, had never complained when Molly left her alone all night to romance the latest rich target, hoping that one of these 'uncles' would become a permanent fixture and rescue them from the nomadic lifestyle. If she was lonely and frightened, Summer would never show it, because she knew that her mother was trying to find a man to marry, to provide a better, safer, more stable existence for them both and she didn't want to blow it.

'Now, I do hope you're going to be more sociable tonight,' said Molly as they walked into Molly's bedroom, which had dresses of every colour and size strewn over the floor, bed and chairs. 'You can be so sullen when you want to be, and there're going to be some very promising men at this benefit.'

'Well, as long as you don't abandon me with some fat seventy-year-old with wandering hands like you usually do,' said Summer, moving a £2000 Dior gown from the corner of the bed so she could sit down.

'Oh, don't bring that up again,' said Molly. 'Sir Lawrence just happens to be a very tactile man. Anyway, you can hardly blame him, when you're always playing this moody "hard to get" game with everyone I introduce you to. It's almost as if you've got something against rich men.'

Well, maybe I have, thought Summer.

Two months after Summer's fifteenth birthday, Molly came home terribly excited. She announced that she had met a man called Graham Daniels, an electronics tycoon who apparently 'ticked all the right boxes'. Within a week, Molly and Summer had moved into 'Tyndale', Graham's huge house in Ascot. Summer liked Graham. Unlike many of Molly's other boyfriends, he didn't treat her like an irritation. In fact he treated her as an adult, even letting her sit behind the wheel of his red Ferrari Testarossa and kangaroo-hop up and down the gravel drive in front of the house. Summer enrolled in the local private girls school, where she made lots of new friends, and was given her own pink bedroom with an *en-suite* bathroom and a balcony that overlooked acres of wooded grounds. Summer loved her pink bedroom until one night when Graham came to say goodnight. Summer could still hear the click of the door opening and see the white of Graham's teeth smiling in the shadows. On that first night, Summer had felt fear as his hands moved under her nightgown. On the second night she had felt a terrible sense of shame for the unfamiliar but pleasurable feelings her young body had experienced. On the third night, Graham Daniels forgot to lock the door. He froze like a rabbit when the door creaked open and Molly's silhouette loomed in the doorway. Summer had pulled her candy-striped duvet tightly around her body, waiting for the screams and anger to erupt. But none had come.

'Get out,' Molly had said quietly, as Graham scampered across the floor on all fours, then fixed her daughter with an icy stare. 'Get dressed,' she said, bundling Summer's belongings into a rucksack. Molly did not stop to collect her own things or even to change out of the floor-length silk negligee before she grabbed her car keys and dragged Summer from the house, bare feet crunching across the gravel.

The next day, Summer enrolled back into her old comprehensive school in Ladbroke Grove. They never saw Graham Daniels or his magnificent Ascot mansion again.

'So, which do you think?' asked Molly, jolting Summer out of her thoughts by waving two silk Cavalli dresses in front of her face. Summer pointed to the scarlet red halterneck with the dangerously low back.

'It matches your toes.'

'Good. That's what I thought. I want everybody to see me coming tonight,' she winked. 'Did you want to borrow the other one?' she continued, holding out the older, plainer black gown.

'No. It's okay. I'm just going to pop downstairs and have a quick shower.'

Molly nodded towards Summer's hand. 'What's that?' she asked.

Summer was holding a CD box she had just pulled out of her bag.

'This? Oh, one of the guys on the shoot gave it to me. It's his band.'

'Pass it here. I might as well entertain myself while you're getting ready.'

'Great,' smiled Summer, pleased at Molly's interest. 'Charlie wants to know what I think of it.'

'What? Charlie?' said Molly distractedly as she fished around in her handbag and producing a wrap of cocaine. She put the CD case on the bed and tipped the cocaine onto it. 'Did you want some?'

Summer felt a plunging sense of disappointment. She didn't approve of her mother's lifestyle, but Molly was her mother. Molly had made sacrifices and it was Summer's duty to accept the choices she made. She'd never had the power to do anything else.

5

Sitting in the back of a midnight-blue Bentley, Karin tried not to smile as she felt the driver's eyes on her in the rear-view mirror. She didn't need the admiring glances of a chauffeur to know that she was looking sensational. Her glossy raven hair fell loosely onto her bronzed shoulders and her strapless jade organza gown floated around her body like a cloud. She had sourced the outfit at the LA vintage couture store, Lily et Cie; having tried on the best that Bond Street had to offer, she decided that she could simply not take the chance of another guest turning up in the same dress. Including flights, a three-day stay at the Beverly Hills hotel and the actual cost of the dress . . . well, it had cost her a fortune but, as her father had always told her, you have to speculate to accumulate. Daddy was always right, thought Karin.

'We're here, miss,' said the driver, taking the opportunity to give Karin another long look. 'Do you want to go to the front or in the back way?'

'The front, of course,' she replied aloofly.

She was not going to miss this for the world. The driveway of Strawberry Hill House was lit by a string of torches in a glorious ribbon of fire, while its spotlit Gothic frontage was pure Brothers Grimm fairy tale. She picked up the well-thumbed guest list and the paper crackled like crisp pound notes. There were well over 800 on the list, with 2000 more begging for tickets. Not even the £1000-a-plate price tag seemed to have presented any sort of obstacle. There was so much money in London right now, thought Karin, a thin smile growing on her highly glossed lips – bankers, Russians, footballers, actors, and powerful old-money families –

and they were all on the list. The car crunched up to the house, the light from the windows illuminating Karin's guest list just as her manicured fingertip rested on one final name – Adam Gold. Smiling, she pulled a fox fur around her tanned shoulders and stepped out of the car to the pop of paparazzi flashbulbs. It was going to be a good night, she could feel it. Her father would have been proud.

Karin's father, Terence, was a good-looking East End boy with the gift of the gab who, during the jazz boom that hit Soho in the 1950s, had discovered a love of fashion. As the big bands and zoot suits gave way to bebop and modernists in the early 1960s, Karin's father had spotted a trend and had made a killing supplying the young designers of Carnaby Street with fabric imported from Morocco and the Far East. His enemies called him ruthless and whispered of cut-throat business methods. His friends, who numbered many, called him a charming success story; the embodiment of Harold Wilson's new Britain: dynamic, classless and very well dressed. When the heat of Swinging London finally cooled and SW3 was no longer the epicentre of the western world, Terence married Stephanie Garnett, a stunning Pan Am air hostess as socially ambitious as he was and moved to a mock-Tudor mansion in the Surrey countryside. By the time their first and only child Karin was born, Terence was a millionaire several times over, but he had moved among enough lords and earls to know that it would take more than a pile in the bank to remove the stain of his lowly background. So, from the age of three, Karin was packed off to ballet class, French tuition and the Pony Club – anything that might help her fit into the world of the upper classes. At thirteen, she was dispatched to Briarton, a liberal, cosmopolitan institution with a student register made up of rock-star offspring and pretty daughters of super-rich Greeks.

'But I want to go to Downe House, Daddy,' the young Karin had complained as she packed her shiny new monogrammed trunk ready for school. 'That's where Abby and Emma from Pony Club are going.'

But Terence didn't want Karin mixing with daughters of stockbrokers and solicitors; he wanted her to befriend Euro-royalty and billionheirs. 'You go to Briarton, my darling,' he had said, 'and you make friends with the richest, most connected girls that you can, and you keep them for life.'

'How do I do that?' Karin had asked, never wanting to disappoint her father.

'Don't you worry, baby, you are beautiful like your mother and strong like your father,' Terence had told her, stroking her hair. 'You will be popular. Trust me.'

It was Karin's five-year stay at Briarton, tucked away in the Berkshire countryside, which was to shape her desires and ambitions for life. Karin was a bright girl and, by thirteen, already a beauty, with long chestnut hair, greeny-grey eyes and, thanks to her parents, a highly sophisticated dress-sense that got her noticed. While some of her classmates had closets full of couture, Karin experimented with cast-offs from her mother – Halston, Bob Mackie and Ossie Clark, mixed together with bargain finds from Chelsea Girl. A strikingly beautiful and offbeat character around the corridors of Briarton, her father was correct; she became popular with the richest girls in a very rich school. Rarely did a half-term break pass without a trip to one of her friend's homes overseas. By the age of sixteen she had skied in Gstaad, sun bathed in Palm Beach and shopped in Hong Kong. She became an expert in excuses as to why her roster of glamorous friends should not be invited to her parents' large home in Surrey which, in contrast to Fernanda Moritez's cattle ranch in Brazil, Juliette Dupois's chalet in St Moritz, and Athena Niarchios's villa in Greece, seemed rather small and unremarkable indeed.

When she left Briarton at eighteen, Karin had a handful of GCSEs, a couple of middle-grade A levels and the steely glint of ambition in her eyes. Her school friends had given her a taste of a rich, jet-set lifestyle that she was unwilling to give up, so she sold her eighteenth birthday present, a cherry-red Alpha Romeo Spider, to fund a gap year of travel, during which she mined her school contacts ruthlessly. She spent winter in the attic of a beautiful townhouse on Paris's Ile St-Louis, which belonged to the aunt of a French friend, Natalie. Aunt Cecile had divorced well and had impeccable manners, wore couture and had impressed upon Karin the importance of grooming and social ammunition.

'*Cherie*, you are so beautiful,' Aunt Cecile had told her, 'but you must take care of yourself.' She had then shown Karin her exquisite collection of jewellery, spread out on her Louis XV bed. 'Remember this: men like to fix things. So when a man sees a pretty thing, they want to make it even prettier. You be as pretty as these jewels, *cherie*, and men will never stop giving them to you.'

So Karin was initiated into the habit of weekly facials at Carita, polished nails, waxing, and daily exercises to keep the neck firm and youthful. At chic Left Bank cocktail parties, she acquired the art of polite conversation and etiquette that would stay with her for life. She learnt to play bridge and baccarat and appreciate classical music and jazz.

The following summer, Karin moved to New York after her father, pulling strings in the industry, landed her an internship at Donna Karan. Her weekends were spent in The Hamptons, where she was surprised to find that friends' 'cottages', in English-sounding places like Southampton, were actually vast coastal mansions straight out of *The Great Gatsby*, with shingle drives and white verandas that looked straight out onto the ocean.

She rarely saw her parents but they didn't mind. They fully approved of Karin's 'grand tour' and were glad their daughter was capitalizing on Terry's success. In Karin's absence, however, Terry's fortunes were fading. He had sunk his money into a new venture manufacturing cheap jeans for the high street just as the designer denim market was exploding. Terry's instincts had been correct, but the punters wanted branded jeans, not cheap imitations, and he had been forced to close his factories. Karin was oblivious to this until the day her mother called her in Palm Beach to say that her father had wrapped his Rolls Royce around a lamppost.

She had returned to Surrey immediately, but was an hour too late. She attended the funeral wearing Dior, sandwiched between her aunties and uncles in their East End market suits, and vowed that her destiny would be much bigger and better than this.

'Darling! This place is just *A-mazing*,' said Christina, kissing Karin on the cheek. 'Ariel wants to know if it's for sale.'

'Actually, my wife is the one with the English country house obsession,' corrected the chubby middle-aged man at Christina's side.

'Ariel, sweetie,' said Karin, air-kissing him. 'You already have an amazing English country house.' The Levys had recently purchased a vast shooting estate in Yorkshire.

'It's too far and too draughty,' said Christina, prompting her husband to turn purple. 'But this is perfect. I could be in Harvey Nicks in thirty minutes *and* it's got one of those Rapunzel towers. I wonder if there are bears in the grounds?'

'Karin, can't you do something about this bloody table plan?' interrupted Martin Birtwell, Diana's husband. Karin forced a smile. Of all her friends' husbands, Martin was Karin's least favourite. He was a loud, pompous, new-money bully: the complete opposite of elegant, refined Diana. When they had first married, their circle had considered it to be a good match. Diana was from a upper-crust family that had buckets of class but no money, while Martin had hustled his way onto the Rich List from an inner-city start. But Martin's increasingly obvious drinking and Diana's growing timidity made Karin suspect that, if not violent, Martin was certainly difficult to live with behind closed doors.

He sidled up to Karin and slid his hand around her waist. 'Sort it out, sweetheart,' he said, patting her on her bottom. 'Pop us on the top table with you, eh? Our table is full of Diana's New Age freaks from her colonics clinic. What if they want to examine our shit after the meal?'

'I asked Martin to invite some of his friends, but I don't think he was listening to me, as usual,' said Diana.

Martin flashed her a threatening look and Karin was disturbed to see Diana flinch. It was such a shame she had picked so badly, she thought, because she looked so gorgeous in that white Grecian gown with an ivory mink stole across her shoulders.

'But good luck with your table,' whispered Diana with a knowing smile. 'I've seen him, and he's a dish.'

Karin smiled. 'Talking of which, I really must fly.'

As the guests began to settle down into their seats, Karin moved regally through the sea of bodies, greeting as many people as she could, finally sitting down at a table at the end of the catwalk. She picked up a place setting between her manicured fingertip and turned to the gentleman on her left.

'I believe I am next to you,' she smiled.

Adam Gold turned and took Karin's hand.

What a fox! she thought, slightly surprised. Short salt-and-pepper hair, a handsome, lightly tanned face with a firm jaw and a wide smiling mouth. His round, intelligent eyes were dark, like liquid chocolate, framed with thick black lashes.

How the hell has Adam Gold not been snapped up before now?

'Great party,' he smiled, eyes darting up and down her long jade gown.

'Thank you,' she said. 'Of course, you do know it's all for you, don't you?' She instantly regreted her flirtation.

When Karin had telephoned Adam's office to invite him personally to the party, she had only been able to get as far as his assistant. She had decided then and there that if Adam Gold did deign to attend, she was not going to treat him like anything special. Seeing how sexy he was, feeling his eyes undress her, she knew that was the correct approach. Men like Adam Gold would have had women flirting, simpering, flaunting themselves all their lives. It wouldn't do any harm to make him work a bit.

Adam was laughing. 'Well, thank you,' he grinned. 'But I'm sure you say that to all your guests.'

Karin smiled coolly. 'Only the ones with the big chequebooks and a love of the environment.'

Adam laughed again. 'Well, it's good to know you're not after me for my sparkling personality,' he said. 'Still, thanks for asking me. It's been pretty crazy since I moved. There hasn't been much time for socializing but apparently you're the girl to know. Guess I got lucky sitting next to you.'

Luck didn't have anything to do with it, thought Karin.

'We'll see, Mr Gold,' she said. 'The night is still young.'

The benefit was buzzing and so was Erin. She had spent the first half of the evening with her mouth hanging open as a throng of socialites and stars poured along the red carpet. She had met Daniel Craig and Ewan McGregor and felt woefully underdressed in her Next shift, surrounded as she was by the acres of silk and chiffon worn by all the glamorous female guests. She had been running on adrenaline since eight o'clock. As Karin had predicted, Erin had received literally hundreds of phone calls about everything from Strawberry Hill's Ordnance Survey coordinates for a helicopter landing, to whether there was a fruitarian option on the menu. Talk about in at the deep end: three weeks ago the only event Erin had ever organized had been Richard's twenty-first party in the upstairs of a pub in Exeter; now she was having to run a dinner for 800. She was exhausted, but it had barely got under way. The guests were tucking into their desserts – well, the men were, she smiled, watching the twiglet-slim wives play with the chocolate on their spoons. And if coffee was being served, that meant that the catwalk show was about to begin. At least that was one part of the night's schedule that Erin didn't have to worry about. Madeline Barker, Karin's head of production, was in charge of supervising and coordinating the runway, so Erin knew she could take a five-minute breather.

She crept backstage which, in contrast to the sedate dining area, was a riot of bodies in motion. Tall, skinny models, pouring themselves into primary-coloured bikinis, dressers flapping around with tit-tape, high heels and jewellery. Hairdressers fussing with gels and clips and sprays, make-up artists in a cloud of bronzing powder, their fingers black with kohl. In the corner, seemingly oblivious to all this chaos, reading a dog-eared novel, was Alexia Dark, the supermodel Erin recognized from the cover of this month's *Vogue*. In the centre of the action was Madeline Barker, wearing an expensive midnight-blue Lanvin dress. She pulled on her cigarette in between gesticulating wildly at the models.

'Hi Maddie, how's it going back here?' asked Erin, clutching her clipboard to her chest and feeling about four stone too fat.

'Oh, hi honey,' said Madeline. 'Chaos, chaos, chaos, as always.' She broke off to grab a stunning redhead who was naked except for her tiny pair of white bikini bottoms. 'Not that one, Jemma! You're in the forest-green tankini, darling.'

Madeline dropped her cigarette into a half-full flute of champagne and turned back to Erin.

'Have you seen Karin anywhere?' she asked. 'It's not like her not to be taking total control. We're on in five minutes and I want her to check she's happy with everything.'

'I passed her a couple of minutes ago,' replied Erin. 'She seems to be engrossed in conversation at her table.'

'Engrossed in Adam Gold, more like,' smiled Madeline.

'Who's he?' asked Erin.

'Ah, the latest victim,' chuckled Madeline, then glared at another model. 'No Alana! You're behind Mischa, get in line. And what is that necklace supposed to be? A Hoover hose?'

Sensing she was getting in the way, Erin headed back into the main room and went to stand by the side of the stage where she was in shadow. From there she could stand and watch both the catwalk show and the glamorous guests in front of her. She felt like Alice in Wonderland, tiny and confused surrounded by beauty and colour in the magic garden.

Suddenly the lights came down and a loud disco beat started

pulsating around the room. Everybody put down their coffee cups and looked intently at the stage, which had erupted in a sea of flashing bulbs and colour. The red-haired model in a deep green bikini strutted onto the catwalk, her hips swaying seductively in time with the music. She paused at the end of the runway, flashed a brilliant smile as the audience erupted in applause. Behind her another goddess emerged, her buttocks peeking cheekily out of a pair of metallic lamé boy-shorts, her breasts barely covered by a strip of mesh fabric. A lone wolf whistle from the crowd said what every man in the room was thinking. The music kept pounding, the girls kept coming. And then finally Alexia Dark stalked onto the catwalk, her black hair flying behind her like a banner, the shimmering lights bouncing off her jewelled bikini and showering her bronzed body in iridescent light. What a finale! thought Erin. What a party!

'Oi!' shouted a voice as Alexia Dark was making her final strut back to the stage. 'Oi you!'

Erin located the voice. It was coming from table twelve, a collection of footballers and their wives ten feet away from where Erin was standing. A girl, no more than eighteen, in a plunging scarlet dress and elaborately coiffed blonde hairdo was waving at Erin and clicking her fingers in the air like a flamenco dancer. Erin recognized her as Natasha Berry, glamour-model girlfriend of Ian Adams, the new Manchester United striker.

'You! I need a drink,' slurred the girl, shaking an empty glass.

Erin left the comfort of her shadow and scuttled to the table in a crouch, not wanting to block anyone's view of the catwalk show as the models all came down the catwalk one last time.

'I'm not taking drinks orders, I'm afraid,' yelled Erin over the music. 'You'll have to ask the waiter over there.' She pointed to a handsome dark-haired boy who was distributing coffee and petit fours on the next table.

'I want a kir royale,' said Natasha, who appeared not to have heard. Erin rolled her eyes, knowing it was pointless to argue, and went over to the waiter, a handsome student called Carlo she had met earlier.

'Sorry Carlo, but I think the *lady* over there wants a cocktail. Can you get her a kir royale before she takes off with all that finger clicking?' The waiter smiled and nodded, quickly turning in the direction of the bar. As he went, a shrewish-looking blonde from his table shouted, 'Hey! You forgot my latte!'

'Sorry madam,' said Carlo, 'I'll bring you one straight away.'

The music was now reaching a crescendo and Karin Cavendish had risen from her chair to take a modest bow in the spotlight.

What happened next, Erin could see unfolding as if in slow motion. Carlo was making his way back through the sea of tables, his outstretched arm carrying a tray balanced with a flute of kir and a tall coffee, when a man pulled out his chair to stand just as Carlo was walking past. For a second Erin thought that Carlo might be able to sidestep the man, but he was concentrating so hard on keeping the hot coffee from falling that the glass of kir tipped over, falling in an arc onto the next table. Erin heard an enraged cry. An elegant blonde now had kir royale all the way down the front of her white dress, like some vast unsightly birthmark. She cursed and Erin immediately recognized the word – a Russian obscenity – and grimaced. It was Karin's precious table of high-spending Russian wives. Karin hadn't missed the commotion; she leapt from her chair and was racing over. Erin got there at the same time. The blonde was now speaking in a fast stream of angry Russian. Erin could understand every word, but it didn't take a Russian degree to tell what was happening as she snatched up her jewel-encrusted clutch bag. She was about to leave and take all her friends with her. Karin put a reassuring hand on the woman's shoulder, but she was clearly in no mood to be pacified by somebody she could not communicate with.

'Let me speak to her,' Erin whispered to Karin.

'What?' snapped Karin, glaring at her. 'Speak to her? What do you mean . . .'

Karin tailed off in surprise as Erin started speaking in fluent Russian.

'It would be such a shame if you have to leave now,' she said quietly in the Russian's ear. 'You are the most important woman here; without you we really don't have a party.'

The woman looked bemused, then pleased to hear one of the organizers speaking to her in her mother tongue.

'Why don't you come with me?' coaxed Erin. 'We have another outfit backstage and you will look fabulous. Look, nobody has seen what's happened. Everybody is watching the show.'

She led the blonde, who had now introduced herself as Irina Engelov, backstage, leaving Karin looking completely dumbfounded.

Shit, shit shit, thought Erin, desperately looking round at the racks of bikinis. Of course there were no spare outfits – it was a bloody swimwear show! She could hardly send Irina back out in a hot pink swimsuit. She spotted Madeline talking to a group of models.

'Quick, Maddie, you've got to take off your dress,' said Erin urgently.

'What?' said Madeline. 'I'm a bit busy at the moment, Erin. The show's still on.'

'Do as I say and I'll explain later,' pleaded Erin, handing Madeline a towelling robe.

Madeline looked at Erin, and, seeing the desperation in her eyes, quickly nodded.

'Okay, but I'd better bloody see it again,' she grumbled, wriggling out of the blue dress. 'It's Lanvin, you know.'

'Maddie, you've just saved the day,' said Erin, grabbing the dress.

She squirted it with some perfume she found on a dressing table and slipped it onto a coat hanger, then sprinted around to where Irina was waiting.

'Size eight, this season, you'll look amazing!' said Erin in Russian, breathing a sigh of relief as Irina pulled on the dress. Irina looked down at herself, simply nodded and walked back to her table as if nothing had happened.

Erin grabbed a glass of champagne and drank it in one.

Molly had gate-crashing down to a fine art. She instructed their taxi driver to drop her and Summer behind a long row of Bentleys and Aston Martins a hundred metres away from the entrance of Strawberry Hill House, then let the car vanish into the cold night before they began to walk down the drive. Their breath made white clouds in the dark air, and Molly's exposed skin prickled in goosebumps, but she had learned years ago to dispense with a coat for a night on the tiles; acres of visible flesh for popping paparazzi were worth far more than keeping warm. She glanced at Summer who looked like some sexed-up Little Red Riding Hood in a white woollen cape floating over a long, deep burgundy dress, her creamy round breasts spilling over its corset. For so many years, Summer had seemed like baggage. Having a daughter aged her, so from a young age Molly had urged her daughter to call her by her name rather than 'mother' so that people wouldn't suspect she was her child. But ever since Summer had blossomed into such a gorgeous young woman, she had become a definite asset. She could take her daughter to any party in town and men would be buzzing around them like wasps at a picnic. But Summer was more than bait to attract the big fish. Since Japan, she had a new confidence, a new glow that could potentially catch her a really big prize, maybe even a prince – and if she did, that would open doors for Molly. *Because where there's a prince, there's gotta be a king*, she thought with a sly smile.

'We *do* have tickets, don't we?' asked Summer, feeling nervous as she saw the two burly bouncers at the door.

'Don't worry, darling,' smiled Molly, adjusting her dress to show a little more cleavage. Not having a ticket had never presented a problem to Molly in twenty-five years of partying. A confident swagger and a generous flash of skin counted far more than any bit of embossed card.

'Time to come back inside,' smiled Molly to the older guard, stroking his lapel as if it was made out of the softest silk. 'I just needed to step outside for a moment.'

And they were in, gliding across the threshold without so much as a grunt. Molly still frowned, however. She had been expecting to be met by a swell of people milling around the communal areas, but there was quiet all around the entrance hall, just a few black-tied waiters clearing glasses in the flickering candlelight.

'Mum, I think people are still eating,' hissed Summer. 'What do we do now?'

A little annoyed at having misjudged the time that dinner was to finish, Molly grabbed her daughter's hand and pulled her towards the large French double doors that led to the main hall.

'Don't worry,' she said, 'we'll slip in at the back and find a seat.' Summer stood hovering at the door, cursing her mother for getting her into yet another embarrassing situation. She knew everyone at the dinner tables would be with their friends and that interlopers would be spotted immediately.

'Come on, I think the auction is about to begin,' hissed Molly, scanning the tables for empty spaces. They crept to the back of the room until they found two seats. Table eighty-three. The eight other faces at the table turned to look at them with quizzical expressions. Molly turned to the gentleman on her right. He was portly, around sixty with a ruddy complexion and a sweep of white hair pulled over like a 1940s comedian.

'I hope you don't mind us taking a pew for a moment,' she said softly, flashing her cover-girl smile. 'We're with the charity. We've been rushed off our feet backstage and wanted to pop out and see the auction – do you mind?'

'Not at all, not at all,' the man blustered. 'You must be parched,' he added, reaching for a bottle of red.

Molly took a sip of the fruity wine and smirked at her daughter.

Summer looked up as applause rippled down the room. Tom Archer, Britain's sexiest Oscar-winning actor, was walking to a podium that had been set up at the end of the catwalk.

'The theme of tonight is compassion,' said Tom, when the cheering had died down. 'Not partying or dinner or catching up with old friends, or even the wine, although I must say it is rather splendid.' The crowd chuckled appreciatively as he lifted his glass. Behind the actor, images of climate change flickered onto huge projection screens: melting glaciers, incinerated rainforest, chimneys pumping out black smoke. Molly used the moment to glance around the room. She recognised a least a quarter of the faces. There was the Cipriani crowd, the White Cube crowd, the San Lorenzo crowd, the Russians, the WAGS; it was an impressive turn-out – not even the Serpentine Gallery party had this sort of pull. *How the hell had that cow Karin Cavendish managed it?*

Tom Archer kicked off the auction with the first lot – a week on Necker Island, with the bids beginning at £25,000. It quickly climbed to £50,000, then £100,000.

'Come on, ladies and gentlemen,' shouted Tom Archer, his hands stretched into the air. 'It's gorgeous out there!'

Molly knew how gorgeous Necker Island was. She had been five years ago, in with a group of friends who were staying as guests of Gunter Strauss, a wealthy German industrialist she had met in Annabel's. She had fucked him on a pedalo while his wife had been playing tennis. She remembered his greedy lips kissing her inner thigh as the Caribbean sun had burnt down on her bare breasts. He had told her she had the best body he had ever seen as his fingers touched every inch of her hot flesh. As she remembered, Molly's hand stretched up unconsciously to stroke her neck. But that was fine for a bit of fun and a free holiday when you were young and carefree, she thought, looking around at the tables. But what happens when you get older?

She looked at all the men sitting at the tables with their wives – wives not mistresses. These were women who had passed the

47

finishing line, women who had closed the deal. No wonder they all sat there with self-satisfied smiles as they sipped their wine, flaunted their diamonds and discussed which villa to visit that summer. The younger wives were the worst. The old birds might have more jewels, but the smiles on the young ones were brighter, smarter. They knew that the law was now on their side and if their husband fucked the secretary, they could slam him for half his assets and move on to the next poor sap while their breasts were still pert. Molly looked down and sighed. At forty-three, she was determined not to stay single for a moment longer, especially with men like Adam Gold in the room.

Tom Archer had now auctioned off a week in the Goldsmiths' Mexican retreat, a fortnight at Michael Sarkis's de-luxe Mustique home and a weekend in Tuscany for a private yoga session with Sting.

'Okay, now we've got rid of all you flash bastards who have just come to book another holiday,' said Tom to laughter. 'It's time to dig deep for some real charity.' A montage of medical equipment, ambulances and water pumps flashed up on the screen behind him, and the auction sprang to life. The bidding was so frantic, the room sounded like a trading floor on Wall Street. 'I do prefer the charitable lots to those holidays in exotic places. Less vulgar,' whispered an elderly neighbour who had been introduced to Molly as Judith Portman, wife of a retired Lazard's banker.

'Totally agree,' smiled Molly. 'Why buy a fortnight at Michael Sarkis's house when, if you know him, you can go there for free?'

Summer saw the old lady's face cloud and quickly jumped in. 'She's joking, of course. Obviously charity is our life – and those ambulances really do save lives.'

A loud cheer went up.

'Two Red Cross ambulances sold to Adam Gold for a hundred and twenty-five thousand pounds!' said Tom, bringing down the gavel. 'Thank you very, very much.'

Molly's ears pricked up and she craned her neck to scan the crowd. There he was, sitting near the catwalk. Even from a distance, Molly could see the broad shoulders, his handsome square jaw dipped modestly as he accepted Tom Archer's praise. Her gaze flicked to the woman besides him. Karin Cavendish. *Damn her.*

'Next we have five hundred acres of rainforest in Mozambique,' said Tom Archer.

'Where shall we start . . . ? Ah, our first bid of five thousand from our cautious hostess, Karin Cavendish. Any advance on five?'

'Oh, I want this,' said Judith, waving her pink hand in the air.

'Do I see six thousand at the back?' said Tom, 'Yes, six it is!'

Adam Gold looked over and smiled at the old woman as Karin countered the bid. Just then, Molly's finger soared skywards.

'Molly! What the hell are you *doing?*' hissed Summer, nudging her mother sharply.

'Getting Adam Gold's attention,' whispered Molly.

'Ah, and I see lovely Molly Sinclair has bid eight thousand pounds for this glorious stretch of rainforest. Well done, Molly!' announced Tom, as the heads of the audience swivelled towards Molly, who quickly lowered a strap of her dress to show off a little more curve. For a second Molly bathed in the glory, knowing every man's eyes were on her plunging neckline. Adam Gold smiled at Molly from across the ballroom and Molly's eyes locked with Karin's.

'Any advance on eight thousand?'

To Summer's relief, Judith Portman's hand stretched in the air. 'Nine thousand pounds from the lady next to Molly,' said Tom. 'I see we've got a little duel going over this fine lot. Excellent stuff, ladies.'

Suddenly, as if it had a life of its own, Molly's hand jumped into the air again.

'Ten thousand pounds! Ten thousand from Molly!' said Tom excitedly. 'Any reply from your neighbour?'

Molly turned nervously to Judith.

'No, no, you've worked so hard tonight, darling,' said Judith, reaching over and patting Molly's hand. 'The rainforest is yours. I'll make do with a couple of water pumps in Nepal.'

Molly's hands felt clammy and her heart was racing.

'I'm going to have to rush anyone else wanting the Mozambique rainforest . . .' said Tom, waving his gavel in the air.

Karin looked over at Molly, a thin, triumphant smile on her lips. Molly felt her heart race, her mouth suddenly dry.

'Judith, please, you have the rainforest,' said Molly desperately.

'Going . . . going . . . GONE!'

The gavel came crashing down. Molly smiled but her eyes weren't laughing as her stomach felt as if it had plummeted to the floor.

'I do hope you've enjoyed yourself,' said Karin, turning to face Adam. Sticking to her game plan, Karin had managed to practically ignore Adam Gold all the way through dinner, allowing all the other female guests on their table to flirt outrageously with him. But now she had seen Molly Sinclair making her move – she didn't remember seeing *her* name on the guest list – Karin decided that it was time to up the ante. While she had no intention of sleeping with him that evening, she wasn't going to let him go home with anyone else either. Especially not Molly.

'It's been a triumph,' said Adam, raising his glass of champagne towards her in salute. 'Thanks for inviting me. Looks like the auction made around two million bucks as well.'

'You've been counting?' said Karin.

Adam smiled and his eyes twinkled. 'I'm always counting,' he said.

Karin looked away as the jazz band launched into a tune on the stage.

'So did you find this place?' asked Adam, his eyes drifting around the room and up to the gilded ceilings. Karin watched him discreetly. He had the casual confidence of someone completely assured of his position in life. 'Buildings like this remind me why I've moved to London,' he said. 'Back in New York we throw a party at the Frick and think, "Man, this place is awesome!" But this place, it's the real thing. Well, Gothic Revival, first time around, anyway.'

'Mmm, you know your stuff,' she said, nodding. 'It belonged to the son of our first prime minister who went crazy adding turrets and extra wings, turning it into Sleeping Beauty's castle.'

'And you clearly know *your* stuff,' he smiled back. 'How about you give me the guided tour?'

Smiling inwardly, Karin allowed Adam to lead her out of the room, his warm hand pressing against her bare back until they had walked out of the rear of the house. Outside the sky was black and cold and there was an intimate stillness that made Karin feel slightly exposed.

'So, why did you move to London?' asked Karin, standing with her back to the house, knowing that with such a backdrop she must look like some splendid romantic heroine. 'To turn all our listed buildings into apartment blocks?'

'You are quite a minx,' he said, smiling suggestively. Karin looked away.

'Well, property developing only makes up about forty-five per cent of the business of the Midas Corporation. We have interests in investments, manufacturing, export/import . . .'

'So why are you here?'

'Don't you want me here?'

'I'm merely curious,' she replied, her teeth chattering as she did.

Adam took off his jacket and placed it around her bare shoulders. Karin could smell expensive cologne and warm cigar smoke. 'London is the new financial capital of the world,' he said seriously, gently rubbing her cold arms through the jacket. 'There doesn't seem to be a more exciting place to do business right now. Plus, my company has interests in London, Moscow and Dubai. The East is the big emerging market and I want to build in India, China and Macao. London is at the heart of all of it.'

'Yeah, right,' she smiled, her eyes meeting his. 'Admit it's the tax breaks and not the time zones and I'll buy you a beer. I read the business papers, Mr Gold. I know why London is flooded with men like you.'

'And what's a man like me?'

'Successful, ruthless, arrogant,' she said.

'Don't be mean to me, Karin Cavendish,' he said softly. 'After this evening, you're probably the woman I know best in the whole city.'

'I find that hard to believe,' she replied, trying to sound more aloof than she felt. She could see the look in his eyes; the look of someone who wanted her. *Well, you're not going to have me, Adam Gold*, she thought. Not tonight anyway. She had to make him wait. Make him long. A gust of wind whistled through the gardens and whipped her hair up around her face.

'We'd better go back inside. The guests will be wondering where on earth I've gone.'

'Okay,' said Adam, 'but can I make a request?'

'What's that?'

'I sort of like it when you're mean to me.'

Erin felt physically shattered. She'd been on her aching feet for fifteen hours, but the excitement and adrenaline were still coursing through her body like an electric current. Everything had seemed to go smoothly, the show was spectacular, even Irina had been happy; so happy, in fact, that she had ended up making a £400,000 bid for the diamond bikini.

'It will be perfect for Nikki Beach next summer,' she had purred to Erin on her way out, kissing her on both cheeks and saying goodnight in Russian.

She wondered anxiously what Karin had made of it all. The last three weeks she had been barked at, abused, pushed to the very limits of her ability. It had been twenty-one days of fetching, carrying, sorting, running – she had been little more than Karin's slave. And for what? So 800 fabulously wealthy people could get pissed, flirt with their friends' husbands and show off how rich they were by buying holidays that they would never go on or jewellery they would never wear. She wanted to hate this world but, realizing her time in it would soon be over, she felt a pang of regret. Karin's universe was like a Scott Fitzgerald novel and she did not want to let it go, certainly not to return to Cornwall and unemployment. She allowed herself an illegal swig of Evian and went to find Karin; she had a message from Adam Gold's helicopter pilot that the winds were getting up and that they needed to leave soon.

'Erin, right? Karin's PA?' said a tall, dark-haired man collecting an overcoat from the cloakroom.

'That's right,' she said distractedly. She was still scanning the room looking for Karin.

'Adam Gold. I was on Karin's table. I was just looking for her to say thank you and goodnight.'

Adam Gold! She looked up. *Christ, he was handsome*, she thought, unable to tear her eyes away from him. Businessmen weren't her usual type and this guy must be at least forty, but still . . . his eyes had the sexiest glint she had ever seen.

'Ah, um, Mr Gold. Actually I was looking for you,' said Erin awkwardly, 'I have a message from your pilot.'

He smiled so the corners of his eyes crinkled. 'Nice work with the Russians, by the way. I thought you handled it brilliantly.'

'And to think I thought my Russian degree was wasted serving drinks,' she smiled.

Adam paused for one moment, his eyes searching hers. Erin could feel her face begin to flush.

'How do you like working for Karin?' asked Adam.

'It's great,' said Erin cautiously. '*Was* great. It was only a temporary gig. Tomorrow's my last day really.'

Adam smiled that crinkle-eyed smile again, making Erin feel a little weak. 'Oh, well, that's convenient. I'd hate to poach anyone from the hostess.'

Erin took a breath, but nothing would come.

'You speak languages?' he asked her.

Erin nodded. 'Russian, French, and a bit of Italian.'

'Are you organized?'

Erin barked out a laugh and spread her hands to indicate the party. 'After this week, I should hope so!'

'Listen, Erin, I need a PA. Mine came over from New York with me but she's missing her family and wants to go home. Goddamn lightweight,' he grumbled.

Erin nodded in sympathy, which she immediately decided was a mistake.

'So are you interested?'

'But you don't even know me,' said Erin, totally gobsmacked.

'How do you think I made the *Forbes* four hundred?' he said bluntly.

'Um, property?' guessed Erin, wincing.

'By trusting my instincts,' he replied flatly.

'So you're offering me a job?' she said, unable to stifle a small, incredulous laugh.

'You've impressed me,' he said, the eyes crinkling again.

'I can't type.'

'I got that covered. You just have to do whatever I say,' he said with a small smile. 'Seriously, it's running my diary, making travel arrangements, fielding calls. All sorts of shit I could be here all night describing. It's long hours and hard work, but I pay well and you might see a little of the world.'

'Pay?' ventured Erin. She was the worst money negotiator ever, her boyfriend Richard always teased her about it.

'How does seventy sound?'

'A day?' squeaked Erin weakly. It wasn't that much more than she'd got behind the bar at the local pub in Exeter.

'A year, Erin,' said Adam. 'Seventy thousand a year, plus my PAs usually get a car.'

Erin stood looking at him for a moment, feeling as if she was going to burst out singing.

'When do I start?'

6

'Oh God, oh God, you're too sexy! I'm not sure I can make it to the bedroom,' panted Harry Levin, his tongue licking Molly's neck like a hungry wolf. They had only just burst in through the front door and already Harry's hand had plunged down Molly's halter-neck to grab at her hard brown nipples. His free hand was undoing the belt of his trousers and he had slipped off his shoes, rendering him at least three inches shorter. *Insoles*, sighed Molly, trying not to flinch as his teeth bit the tips of her breasts like a randy teenager.

She had picked up her latest paramour – cosmetic surgeon to the stars, no less – at the end of the Stop Global Warming benefit, when it was so late that the waiters had begun stacking up tables. To Molly's great annoyance, Adam Gold had left halfway through the jazz band's set, before she had even had time to introduce herself. There hadn't been a great deal number of other single men at the party, although she had counted four ex-lovers, all married, all with their wives and all who had chosen to ignore her. She didn't want to waste the night, not when she looked so hot. Her Cavalli dress was cut so low at the back you could see the dark tip where her spine met her ass. So when Harry Levin was pointed out to her as Harley Street's premier tit man, she knew that she'd go home with him.

'Spank me,' growled Harry, when they had made their way up his sweeping staircase, tearing at each other's clothes as they reached his bedroom. Welcoming the opportunity to inspect his five-storey Hampstead home further, she let him bend over the mahogany sleigh bed, slapping his skinny white arse while she looked around the room.

'You've been a very bad boy,' she purred theatrically, noting the walnut-panelled walls and fifty-inch plasma television over the exquisite marble fireplace.

'Harder!' groaned Harry, clutching his dove-grey duvet in pleasure. Mmm, that bed linen was definitely Pratesi, noted Molly as she smacked him harder, observing the telltale scalloped edges of the pillowcase. She also spotted a Picasso sketch on the wall above the bed and the many silver-framed photographs of Harry: Harry skiing, Harry on a yacht, Harry looking tanned, happy and rich. This one was definitely promising.

He rolled over to face Molly, his dextrous fingers pulling down Molly's tiny chiffon thong in one movement. His eyes widened when he saw her totally bald bush; Molly had waxed it off earlier that day after discovering some tufts of grey.

'I fucking love that,' he mumbled, sinking his face between her thighs. She got onto the bed, long hair splayed across the pillow, one leg artfully bent at the knee, her arms thrown back over her head as if she was posing for a *Playboy* spread. His hands were all over her, and after a couple of minutes of licking her nipples, leaving her breasts cold and wet, he fumbled around with a condom as he prepared to enter her. His cock was small, but he thrust himself in so hard it was like a bullet. She ran her long fingers down his back, but Harry was beyond subtleties: his ass was bobbing up and down like a cork at sea.

She shut her eyes and thought of Adam Gold, but not even that could make this sexual encounter more enjoyable. *Christ, let's get this over with*, she thought, making a few half-hearted groans and digging her nails into his thrusting arse as she prepared to fake orgasm.

'Now! Now!' he shouted before collapsing onto her, his head on Molly's chest.

'Incredible,' he whispered, 'just fucking incredible.'

Molly lay motionless, her eyes fixed on the ceiling as she tried to work out whether it was a Lalique or a Murano light-fixture above the bed.

She stroked her hand across the top of his head, wondering if she could get Harry Levin to cough up for that five hundred acres of Mozambique rainforest she'd won at the auction and not yet paid for. At the very least, she was sure he would give her a good price for that tummy tuck she'd been meaning to get.

7

Erin had only had been at the Midas Corporation a matter of hours but already she felt lost. As Adam's PA, she needed to know every aspect of his business, and she was quickly finding that the scale of his empire was vast. She knew that he was a property developer, and while real estate did appear the core of the business, that was only the beginning. The property portfolio alone was mind-boggling – from luxury residential developments in Manhattan and Macao to prestige office blocks in nearly all of the world's financial centres – but on top of that, Midas owned a dozen hotels, a copper mine in Kazakhstan, a ski resort in Maine, two huge retail villages in Connecticut and Florida and a private jet company leasing out executive aircraft to the super-rich. And that was all she'd managed to find since she'd arrived at 7.30 a.m. It was now dark outside and she was still finding new files and reports. The intercom buzzed suddenly.

'Erin. Can you come in please?'

As it was her first day at work, Erin had tried her damnedest from the moment she had got into the luxurious office block behind Piccadilly, but she still felt as if she was groping about in the dark. Adam already had an executive assistant, Eleanor Bradley, a fiercely efficient New Yorker who had worked with him for seven years and sat outside his door like a Rottweiler. Erin's position seemed to be more like a social secretary: taking calls, making appointments, accepting or declining party invitations and arranging for errands that Eleanor was too busy and important to carry out. She had hardly seen Adam all day and had no idea if she had performed her duties to his satisfaction. Padding into his office from her desk as fast as her brand new three-inch heels would carry her, she smoothed down her long-sleeved cotton dress from Debenhams, feeling even more nervous than she had when she'd met Hector Fox at the benefit dinner. Adam's large corner office was an overwhelming space. With its masculine grey walls, stark architectural photography and dark antique furniture, it reeked of power, money and testosterone.

'Ah, take a seat, I have a question to ask you.'

She perched on the edge of a padded velvet and mahogany chair, clasping her clammy hands together and hoping she looked efficient.

'Erin, why are you still here?' Adam looked up at her from behind his wide wraparound mahogany desk with a straight expression.

Erin's eyes lowered to the floor with embarrassment. She'd been told she had to be in work for 7.30 a.m., ready for Adam's arrival at 8 a.m., but she had no idea how late she was expected to stay. For a £70,000 salary, she suspected it was probably a twenty-four-hour job, but when was she supposed to sleep?

'I wasn't aware that I should be somewhere else, Mr Gold,' she stammered. 'There doesn't seem to be anything in the diary for tonight.'

'Precisely,' he smiled, 'which is exactly why you should go home.'

Erin felt her eyes linger a little too long on his strong tanned hands. She also noticed that his eyes were a rich, intoxicating brown. She wished she could think of something to say, but she found her brain fog and her throat clam up.

Adam let his smile linger, as if he was aware of his young PA watching him and was enjoying the moment. 'So how was it?' he asked. 'I hope it wasn't too painful a first day.'

Erin smiled. 'I loved it. Everyone seems really nice.' *You seem really nice,* she wanted to add. 'Is there anything else you need me to do before I go?' *Please say yes.*

Adam leant back in his black leather chair and folded his arms behind his head. 'I don't suppose you could dig me out Karin Cavendish's phone number, could you?'

She thought she saw a flicker of pleasure stretch across his face as he noted her disappointment.

Erin nodded. 'I'll bring it through straight away,' she said, rising. *What did you expect?* she thought, scolding herself. Men like

Adam Gold would only consider women like Karin Cavendish. He was hardly going to be interested in her, was he?

'How was your first day, then?'

Richard Pendleton was already home by the time she got back to the flat, standing in the little kitchen cooking chilli con carne. Not for the first time she wondered why he was back so early. In the four weeks she'd been staying at his flat, Richard had never once worked late, let alone clocking up the two-in-the-morning marathon sessions he'd constantly complained about when she'd been down in Cornwall. Still, she shouldn't grumble; this week he'd been the most attentive he'd ever been since they first got together eighteen months ago. Not that Richard had ever really been particularly devoted, especially since he had moved to London the previous autumn. He was always taking about 'his own space', even though they lived two hundred miles apart and he had almost blown a gasket when she had asked him if she could stay for a few weeks while she was working for Karin. Now those weeks had become a month, she had been expecting him to start making noises about how his Earl's Court apartment was too small for two but, ever since she had landed the job at Midas, his mood seemed to have softened. Maybe he was getting used to her. The kitchen was a small gallery kitchen with smart wooden units and a little window that looked out onto a tiny manicured patch of lawn that the estate agents had dared to call a 'delightful' and 'mature' garden. She went to stand next to him by the oven and he spooned some sauce into her mouth.

'Mmm, that's actually edible!' she teased. 'Not bad for a pillar of the establishment.'

Richard was still in his pinstriped suit trousers and a white shirt, looking considerably older than his twenty-five years. Erin had noticed that, since he had begun work, he had adopted a rather superior expression, and the arrogant, offhand mannerisms of a man who believes himself to be a cut above. *Leave him alone Erin,* she thought, *you're just stressed and tired.*

'So come on,' urged Richard, 'what was Gold like?'

'Oh Richard, I'm knackered,' she replied, sinking onto a bar stool and kicking her heels off. 'These early starts are going to kill me.'

'Well, that's international business, darling. The man works across several time zones. I bet he was still in the office when you left him, wasn't he?'

'How did you guess?' she said flatly, pouring herself a glass of wine from the open bottle next to the cooker.

Richard ladled the chilli onto two plates and led the way into the main living area that had a couple of sofas at one end and a table and four chairs at the other. Erin had started eating when she looked up to see Richard was clearly still waiting for answers.

'Why are you so interested, anyway?' asked Erin, tearing off some pitta bread and dipping it in the sauce. 'You've never shown this much interest in my writing.'

'I'm hardly going to be interested in those silly fantasies, am I?'

She raised her eyebrows and Richard backtracked furiously. 'Sorry, sorry. Out of order. I'm just excited for you now, that's all. I mean, to be so close to such an important businessman. I bet you're going to hear all sorts. Hey, maybe you could get us a few share tips,' he winked.

'That sounds illegal, Richard,' she scolded. 'I'm sure your senior partner won't like you saying things like that.' Richard's cheeks flushed.

'Actually, speaking of our senior partner, I was telling him today about your new job and he was very impressed indeed. He called Gold a genius. I mean how much do you know about the company?' But, before Erin could reply, Richard ploughed on, keen to show his recently acquired knowledge.

'Well, apparently the Midas Corporation isn't just a property development company at all,' he gushed, clearly pleased with his research. 'In fact it's a pyramid of companies.'

'How do you mean?' asked Erin.

'One small company at the top of the pyramid owns or has controlling stakes in a massive number of other companies, and whoever controls the parent company effectively controls everything beneath it. In this case, Adam Gold owns a hundred per cent of Midas Investment Group, the parent company, which makes him very rich and very, very powerful indeed.'

'Well, I could have told you that without the economics lecture,' said Erin.

'Ah, but one of the guys at work was saying Gold's got to be really, really fishy to be worth over a billion in such a short space of time . . .'

'Maybe he just has the Midas touch,' said Erin sarcastically, suddenly feeling a need to jump to Adam's defence.

Richard shrugged. 'Maybe. Anyway, the important thing is that Charles, our senior partner, was asking who does the Midas Corporation's legals in London. I mean, White, Geary and Robinson offer a very comprehensive service across corporate, property, tax and litigation requirements, you know.'

'Richard,' said Erin crossly, putting down her fork. 'You sound like a used-car salesman.'

Her boyfriend stiffened at the suggestion. 'Come on, Erin, you know how much I want to be taken on in the CoCo department when I qualify. If I can bring in some of Adam's Gold's business, I'll be home and dry.'

She looked at her boyfriend, really quite baby-faced underneath it all. A little boy dressed up as a City hotshot, wanting to please the big boys. She almost felt sorry for him. 'Listen, Richard, I've only been there a day, but I'll try and find out who the company uses and whether they're happy with them. That's all I can do.'

Richard pushed a kidney bean around his plate and looked a little sheepish. 'Well . . . actually, there *is* one other thing you could do,' he said, looking up at her with pleading eyes. 'The firm are having an end-of-financial-year party in a few weeks and . . .'

'What, Richard?'

'Well, I told my boss that you'd bring Adam.'

8

'Are you still in bed?'

Molly muttered a silent curse. She was indeed still in Harry's emperor-sized bed and, lifting a corner of her black silk sleep mask, she saw it was 11 a.m. Reluctantly, she uncoiled herself and stretched. She knew the day was out there waiting, if only she could crawl from under this lovely cosy goose-down duvet. In fact, Molly had barely left Harry's Hampstead home since the night of the benefit a week ago, only venturing into the outside world to pick up some essentials from her apartment – and for Harry to take her out to dinner every night. *Naturally.*

'Oh darling, of course I'm not in bed,' lied Molly, swinging out of the bed, her toes sinking into the thick double cream carpet. 'Although I know you like to think of me in bed every minute of the day, don't you lover?'

Harry gave a low chuckle down the phone. 'Well, I was just calling to say that I've been invited to a very old friend's party tonight,' he said, 'and I want you to come with me.'

'How do you know I've got nothing better in my diary?' teased Molly, standing in front of the full-length mirror and patting her pancake-flat stomach.

'Well, how about I make it worth your while?' he asked. 'Why don't you go shopping this morning and pick out something nice to wear for the party? We can meet in Bond Street at one-ish to go and collect it.'

'Dress, bag and shoes?' smiled Molly.

'I didn't think you'd be a cheap date,' he said, his tone playful.

Molly grinned. 'I'll be in Gucci.'

She showered quickly to shake off her grogginess, throwing on some jeans, a white shirt and her cowboy boots and pulling her hair back in a ponytail. She inspected herself in the mirror: pretty hot, even if she did say so herself, but still she didn't feel quite ready for the hustle and bustle of spending someone else's money. *I wonder . . .* she thought, and walked over to Harry's walnut chest of drawers. Harry was super-neat, with everything in its own place. She rummaged around among his neatly rolled-up silk socks until she found what she was looking for: a small plastic bag containing about an ounce of cocaine. Molly's eyes lit up. She pulled the seal open and dipped a long fingernail inside. The powder was fine and translucent like ground pearls; it looked as expensive as the rest of Harry's possessions. Expertly, Molly tipped a small amount on the bedside table, lined it up with her credit card and snorted, feeling the crackle of coke taking hold. Oh yes, that was good. She pulled on her leather biker jacket, her body twinkling. Now she was ready to go shopping.

'So who is this mysterious friend we're meeting?' asked Molly as they flew down Park Lane in Harry's forest-green Ferrari. 'I like to know whose party I'm going to before I get there.'

'Marcus Blackwell, vice president of Midas,' said Harry, gunning the engine and changing lanes to dodge a Bentley.

'Midas? Adam Gold's company?' said Molly in surprise.

'That's right,' said Harry smugly, 'we were at university together. I was a med student, he was doing maths, if I remember rightly.' He glanced sideways to drink in Molly's figure, barely concealed by the tiny gold lamé shift dress he'd bought her earlier that afternoon.

'I haven't seen Marcus properly for years though,' he continued. 'He's British, but he went to work on Wall Street fairly soon after he graduated. He hooked up with Gold and has been his right-hand man ever since. He's done very well for himself.'

'Hey, you didn't do too badly either,' smiled Molly, expertly massaging both his ego and his cock, her right hand stretched over the gearstick into Harry's lap.

'I guess not,' gasped Harry, trying to keep the Ferrari on the road.

The Midas Corporation drinks party was to celebrate the launch of their flagship London development 'Knightsbridge Heights'. Molly had read about the luxury apartments in the *Evening*

Standard. Apparently, everyone from celebrities to oil sheiks had been clamouring to buy into one of the capital's most desirable slices of real estate, and the party was being held in the building's stunning black marble lobby. By the time Harry and Molly walked in through the black and gold revolving doors, it was already throbbing with the cream of society.

'So how much does one of these apartments go for?' asked Molly, looking around enviously. It was really a spectacular place in which to live. The centrepiece of the lobby was a vast black marble fountain that spewed out water as from a whale's blowhole. The atrium stretched all the way to the glass ceiling hundreds of feet above. Along the back of the building was a bank of sliding doors that opened out onto a lush garden, stocked with exotic plants and lit for the evening with guttering torches.

'I think they start about three million pounds and then go skywards,' said Harry knowingly. 'And I hear ninety-five per cent of them have been sold already. That's the beauty of Midas's residential business. They target the very top of the market. It's pretty much recession-proof up there.'

They eventually found Marcus Blackwell at the entrance of the Winter Garden. He wasn't a particularly good-looking man, thought Molly, his closely cropped dark hair had receded and his eyes, although brown and twinkly, were too close together, giving his face a pinched expression like a vole's. That said, he was considerably more attractive than Harry, thought Molly. Considerably.

'Harry,' said Marcus, 'how are you? It's been too long.'

'Ten years at least,' grinned Harry. 'But now you're back in London maybe it won't be another decade. What about lunch in the next couple of weeks?' he added.

'Sure, sure,' nodded Marcus with a distinct lack of enthusiasm. 'Get your secretary to call mine and we'll sort something out.'

'Fantastic, I'll do that.'

'Marcus, this is my girlfriend, Molly Sinclair,' Harry said.

Molly reached out to shake his hand, holding on to it just a little longer than necessary.

'This place is amazing,' she gushed. 'You must introduce me to Adam. I've heard so many good things about him.'

'Everyone seems to want to meet Adam tonight,' replied Marcus. Molly thought she detected a grain of irritation behind the cordial smile. Interesting, she thought, filing it away for future use.

'He's just out here, showing one of our investors how many flowers half a million pounds can buy.'

Outside, in a courtyard surrounded by trees and flowerbeds, there was a raised pond with another fountain cascading foaming water. Standing with his back to it was Adam Gold, surrounded by admirers, holding court. He was wearing a dark suit with a pale blue shirt – ordinary, conservative. But from her first glance, Molly knew he was the sexiest rich man she had ever seen – and she had seen many. She felt an immediate flutter of lust and excitement as they approached. She was wearing stilettos but he was still at least two inches taller than her; he possessed a natural confidence that matched her own and, although he didn't have Molly's cheekbones or poise, she knew instantly that they would make the most beautiful couple in town.

'I think we were both at the Stop Global Warming benefit dinner the other night,' said Molly, flashing her best cover-girl smile. She searched Adam's face for a flicker of recognition as he moved forward to shake her hand. Surely he had noticed her?

'I don't think we met,' said Adam in a polite but distracted manner that made her cheeks smart. He touched her arm to indicate that he had other people to talk to. 'If you'll excuse me,' he smiled before leaving their group to go and air-kiss a glamorous blonde, leaving Molly's mouth hanging open. The *bastard*.

Karin threaded her way through the lobby of Knightsbridge Heights with the confidence of someone who knew she looked fantastic. For a party this important, Karin had pulled out all the stops, paying a visit to Après Mode, her favourite boutique in Paris. Après Mode was a treasure-trove of 1960s Balenciaga, YSL and other classic labels and she had selected, with the help of the boutique's owner Madam Vervier, a former couture directrice, a primrose-yellow Ossie Clark chiffon dress. But choosing a dress had only been a minor distraction; Karin's life had gone into overdrive in the ten days following the benefit dinner. The papers had splashed the event's red carpet pictures all over their front pages, her phone had rung off the hook with interview requests and the three Karenza stores had reported a fifteen per cent uplift in sales. Karin, however, had barely had time to breathe, let alone bathe in the glory. Instead she had dashed to Paris Fashion Week and a suite at the Plaza Athénée where she had shown her label's autumn/winter collection to press and buyers. It had been a remarkable success. Even Anna Wintour, the singular editor of American *Vogue*, had come back-stage to congratulate Karin. It was there she had taken the call from Erin Devereux, inviting her to a drinks launch at Knightsbridge Heights. She had snapped her mobile shut with a smile: finally, Adam was chasing.

'Honey, you look drop-dead!' oozed Diana, air-kissing her and handing her a drink. 'Where did you get it? You must have spies in every boutique in the Western world. I'm so jealous, you must tell me.'

Karin just smiled mysteriously and linked her arm through Diana's as they joined the main throng of the party.

'So. Tell me all about Paris,' said Diana.

'I don't think you want to talk about Paris, do you?' said Karin knowingly.

'Is it that obvious?' replied Diana glumly, dropping her happy party girl demeanour. Her shimmering black Versace dress suddenly looked funereal.

'Very obvious, darling. Very.'

Karin had invited Diana as her *plus one* because Diana was depressed. Her vulgar husband Martin had just disappeared to Aspen with his ex-wife Tracey and their seven-year-old twin girls Chloe and Emma. He hadn't even bothered to telephone Diana in the last two days.

'I shouldn't have allowed him to go, should I?' said Diana mourn-fully.

Karin turned to her friend, her face serious. 'Of course you shouldn't have allowed him to go,' she said. 'Divorced wives only have two settings: desperate and spiteful, often at the same time. If she was dumped, she'll do anything – *anything* – to get him back. If *she* ended the relationship, she still wants to be number one and will play with him like a fish on a hook. Either way, she definitely wants to screw up your relationship with Martin.' Diana looked stricken as she considered the implications of Karin's words.

'Well, Martin was the one who filed for divorce from Tracey . . . do you think that means that she'll . . . ? Oh God . . .'

Despite her outward dizziness, Diana was a realist at heart. She knew exactly what her husband was like and she had gone into the relationship with her eyes open. Theirs wasn't so much a marriage as a merger. She was the class, he was the money, and men like that came with a price: infidelity. Diana had trained herself to imagine Martin with other women, so the pain would be less brutal when his adultery was unveiled. But this was worse, much worse. Now when she closed her eyes, Diana imagined him with Tracey, tucked up in the bar at The Little Nell, Aspen's most glamorous hotel, drinking Bourbon, Tracey's recently enhanced breasts bursting out of her Chanel ski-wear. Then they would retire to the penthouse for a night of energetic sex. But it wasn't just sex with Tracey. They had history and they had the children to bond them back together. No, it wasn't just sex – it was danger.

Karin could see the crushing look of insecurity on Diana's face and felt a stab of guilt. 'I'm sorry darling. I was too blunt. But I do worry that Tracey has never been off the scene since Hotbet.com floated.'

Diana nodded. 'I know, but how can I say anything? She's the mother of his children.'

'But they're not a family any more,' replied Karin. She held Diana's hand and looked into her welling eyes. 'Look, honey, I've seen this happen with divorced friends a hundred times over. One minute mum and dad are playing happy families on the ski slopes pretending they don't hate each other, the next minute they're back together for the sake of the kids and his bank balance.'

Diana's regal features twisted in confusion. 'So what should I do?' she pleaded.

Karin took a sip of her drink. 'Remind Martin why he married you. Remind him that, without you, he is nothing. Look around you, at this place, at these people. Tracey might have his kids, but that little scrubber can't give him this, can she?'

Karin took the glass of champagne out of Diana's hand and swapped it for a glass of water. 'Take this. You get so morose when you're drunk. Don't worry, honey, we simply need to show Martin just how valuable you can be to him.'

Karin looked across the crowded lobby and had an idea. 'And I think I know just the man who can help us.'

Even though Summer Sinclair was twenty-four years old, she had never been to a rock concert. She had lived in London and Tokyo, moved among the rich and famous and felt at ease in some of the world's most exclusive nightclubs and restaurants, but she had never once been to a live gig. Squeezing her way into the upstairs room at the Monarch, she began to understand why. It was horrible. Claustrophobic, head-splittingly loud and so hot that the air felt solid in her lungs. Summer had to literally force her way between lank-haired surly teenagers to get anywhere near the stage. Her carefully chosen Jimmy Choo ankle boots were getting scuffed on discarded plastic glasses and the soles were sticking to the floor. It was hideous; why did people come to these things willingly? But then the music started.

For a second Summer flinched as a wall of sound hit her. A swaggering rock god had walked onstage holding his guitar. A single distorted chord rang around the room and, when he was satisfied he'd got the crowd's attention, he jumped into the air and The Riots blasted off. Summer could hardly believe it. Charlie was so unrecognizable from the handsome preppy boy at the shoot that she almost wondered if she'd got the right gig. But it was definitely him, his groomed hair replaced by a tousled surfer-boy look and a three-day stubble, the stuffy suits of the wedding shoot replaced jeans, T-shirt and a lorry-load of attitude. *He was so sexy!* The songs were amazing too – from shouty rock anthems to ballads that pulled at Summer's heart strings. *This was fantastic!*

On stage, the drummer yelled at Charlie to slow down. But he wanted to finish and get offstage. Deep in the crowd, through the glaring lights and sea of faces, Summer Sinclair's face shone out at him. He charged through The Riot's set list and ran off backstage, ignoring the pretty girls begging the security guard to be let through.

Please don't let her leave, he thought, rushing out into the crowd to find her.

'Hey. You came.'

Summer was just zipping up her jacket ready to face the cold night outside. She turned and smiled.

'Shouldn't you be backstage taking coke and drinking whisky?' she asked, her head cocked in mock innocence.

Charlie laughed. 'Me? I'm really just a square middle-class boy, but don't tell this lot that,' he grinned.

They propped themselves up at the bar as Charlie ordered two lagers, at the same time accepting assorted back-slaps from excited fans.

'I think they loved it,' whispered Summer as one pimply youth told Charlie he was *wicked*.

'But what did *you* think?'

Summer wanted to tell him that his sexual presence seemed to fill this stage, that his heartfelt lyrics of love and loss had made her want to cry. But she couldn't. She just didn't know how to *be* around Charlie.

'You were brilliant,' she said simply.

'Yeah, well,' he said, looking at the floor, 'playing the Monarch is a big step up for us. It's one of the best places to play in London for an unsigned band because there's always A&R people hanging about. Plus it's got this incredible history. Everyone's played here. Oasis, Coldplay, Chilli Peppers. Playing here is either the beginning or the end of the road for The Riots.'

Summer was still staring at her lager.

'Are you going to drink that or just look at it?' smiled Charlie.

'You'll never believe this,' she said, 'but I've never had a pint before.'

'Good God! Where've you've been living? Mars?'

Her cheeks flushed with awkwardness. 'No, in my mother's universe.'

Charlie nodded. 'Ah yes, someone told me after the wedding shoot that your mum was Molly Sinclair. So what was it? Champagne in your baby bottle?'

'Something like that.'

He took a long slurp of beer that left a white frothy moustache on his lip. 'Fuck. What must that be like, to have a supermodel as a mother? I bet your dad loved it,' he winked.

'Actually, I don't really know my father.'

Charlie bowed his head in embarrassment. 'Oh, I'm sorry.'

'It's fine,' said Summer, surprised at easily she could talk to Charlie. 'My mum lived in New York for a couple of years before I was born. She had an affair with this rich guy, Upper East side, rebel son from a good family, you know the sort. Anyway, she got pregnant and he dumped her. Seems like it wasn't in his family's masterplan for him to settle down with some crazy model. My mum came back to London and never heard from him again.'

'Don't you ever want to find him?'

Summer shook her head defiantly. 'After he abandoned us? No way. Anyway, I guess you don't miss what you've never had.'

By the time Summer had finished the pint of lager, she felt light-headed and happy, and found herself growing more and more attracted to Charlie. It crossed her mind what Molly would think

68

of him; when he had bought their drinks, she had seen him anxiously rattle around a few pound coins in the palm of his hand. She snorted. Molly would go *spare*.

But she wasn't here looking for romance, she told herself. She was happy to be chatting to him, enjoying his company; most of all, she wanted Charlie McDonald to be her friend. It embarrassed her to think how few of them she had. She blamed it on her four-year hiatus in Japan, but the truth was that her nomadic youth had left her with few school friends and she rarely met anyone beyond her mother's party circuit.

'Can I buy you a drink?'

Summer looked up, expecting to see some spotty youth hitting on her, but it was a forty-something-year-old man in an expensive-looking jacket and jeans and the question was directed to Charlie.

'Rob Harper,' said the man, offering his hand. 'I manage bands.'

'Oh, wow, Rob Harper,' said Charlie, 'good to meet you, man. Yeah, I'll have a lager.'

Summer could tell from Charlie's response that he had heard of him. What she did not know was that Rob was one of the most influential band managers in the country, looking after three or four platinum-selling artists.

'So what did you think?' asked Charlie, turning on the swagger.

'I liked you,' said Rob in a controlled voice. 'In fact, we need to talk.' Charlie flashed Summer a panicked expression and she immediately got the message.

'I'm just off, Charlie,' she said gently, throwing her bag over her shoulder. She didn't want to leave but she certainly didn't want to play groupie gooseberry.

Charlie touched her on the arm. 'I can meet you in a minute?'

Summer shook her head. 'Good luck,' she mouthed.

Charlie took a beer mat off the bar, tore it in half and fished a pen out of his pocket.

'Write your number on that,' he said giving her half the mat. And she stepped out into the cold night, knowing he would call.

9

Karin stood by the fountain in the garden of Knightsbridge Heights waiting for Adam. The night had turned chilly and most of the guests were inside drinking and dancing. She knew he would seek her out eventually, quietly confident that she had made a lasting impression at Strawberry Hill House. Of course, Karin did not need to meet Adam Gold at the launch to get to know him better; she was a woman who liked to be prepared. No sooner had she received her invitation to the Knightsbridge launch than she was trawling the Internet for every story, interview and news piece on the Midas Corporation in *Forbes*, *Fortune* and the *New York Times*. Knowledge was a power that she was prepared to use every bit as ruthlessly as her sexuality.

The headlines she found spoke for themselves:

GOLD DEVELOPMENT THE BIGGEST IN SE ASIA

MIDAS SHARE RISE BREAKS HANG SENG RECORD

ADAM GOLD MAKES ANOTHER KILLING

The more she read about Adam, the more she felt they were kindred spirits. She recognized a drive, ambition and entrepreneurial spirit in Adam that she felt in herself. His background was one of wealth: his grandfather Aaron Grogovitz, a Hungarian emigrant who had settled in New Jersey in the 1930s and changed the family name to Gold, had made a fortune developing property in the post-war years. A devout Jew, the only thing he priced above family was his religion. So when his son David, a handsome college graduate on whose shoulders Aaron pinned the entire hopes of his empire, declared that he was to marry pretty classmate – and gentile – Julia Johnson, Aaron cut him off without a penny.

According to most accounts, David didn't seem entirely distraught, happy to raise his family running a small real-estate agency in Yonkers. His son Adam, however, was a different animal altogether, having inherited every ounce of his grandfather's drive and ambition, he won a full scholarship to Yale, but dropped out in the first year – why waste time in a library, he reasoned, when there were fortunes being made on Wall Street? Luther and Katz, Adam's first employers, were a small New York investment house muscling in on the junk bond market championed by Michael Milliken, and their traders were making a lot of money very, very quickly. After Milliken's arrest in 1987, Adam got out while the going was good, sinking his $10-million fortune into the business that was in his blood – real estate. He bought buildings in Tribeca for cash, converted them into designer lofts and sold them at a premium to wealthy traders. But his business really took off in 1992, when he bought landmark Manhattan buildings for peanuts out of the rubble of the property crash.

Suddenly Adam Gold was richer than the bankers, businessmen and celebrities to whom he sold £20-million apartments, richer than the CEOs who occupied his office blocks. His Manhattan home was one of the most talked-about townhouses in 'The Grid', the name given to the most exclusive blocks in the Upper East Side, as well as properties in Nassau, Lake Como and Dark Harbour in Maine. At forty-five, Adam Gold was eligible with a capital 'E' and speculating who would get him down the aisle had become a sport in the American society pages.

Karin was still lost in thought, turning all this information around in her head, when she heard a whisper in her ear.

'Earth calling Karin . . .'

'Adam,' she smiled, turning to kiss him lightly on the cheek. 'Sorry, I was miles away.'

'Literally, I hear. I thought you were in Paris for the collections.'

She nodded. 'For work not pleasure. My label shows there, plus I have to attend a trade fair to look at new fabrics for next season.'

'Premiere Vision?' asked Adam, gently taking her arm to steer her further down the garden.

'You know it?' asked Karin surprised. 'I don't meet many men who know so much about the fashion industry.'

'I spend half my life with interior designers,' he shrugged. 'The gap between fashion and interiors is shrinking all the time.'

'Umm, I guess we're both selling a lifestyle to the same sort of people.'

Now he had led Karin to a quieter part of the Winter Garden where the background noise of the party had faded to a hum. She wondered what he was thinking. Was he sensing the same crackle of chemistry between them? Was he thinking about how long they could wait before they should end up in bed? She looked at him shrewdly. His face certainly wasn't giving anything away; it was impassive and thoughtful, like a chess grand master waiting for her to make the next move.

'Well, I think the apartments are incredible,' said Karin quickly. 'I heard a rumour that you've kept the best apartment for yourself.'

He nodded. 'I could show you if you like, then you can make up your own mind.'

Karin felt as if they were in some elaborate Regency dance, both skirting around one another, slowly observing and sizing each other up, each trying to stay three moves ahead of the other.

'I should really go and find my friend,' said Karin with some reluctance. 'She's a little depressed and I'm worried she might throw herself into the fountain if I don't stop her.'

Karin was scanning his face, willing him to look crestfallen at her refusal, but he merely nodded. 'Maybe some other time, then.'

Karin returned the nod, determined not to show her own disappointment. Finally Adam smiled. 'You know, you're still the only woman I've had a decent conversation with in London,' he said, as if it was a private joke between the two of them.

'I didn't know you were keeping count,' smiled Karin, feeling a small flame of triumph.

'So would you like to go for dinner?' he asked.

It was Karin's turn to make her chess move. 'I'm very busy for the next week or two,' she said.

'Yes, so am I,' he shrugged. 'I'm in Venice for the carnival and Miami for business, but I'm sure we can find a window.'

'How odd. I'm going to the carnival too,' she replied as casually as she could.

'Oh, that's excellent. I was hoping you would give me the grand tour of London, but perhaps I can show you around Venice instead.'

'Perhaps. I do know Venice very well,' smiled Karin.

Adam was shaking his head and smiling. 'Are you always this difficult?'

She grinned. 'Only when I'm having fun.'

'Molly Sinclair. You don't look as if you're having a good time.' Molly turned round to see Marcus standing behind her. She had been leaning against the glass doors of the winter garden listening to a trickle of water falling into the circular pool. She was still fuming from her brief encounter with Adam Gold; that cocky shit had barely looked at her and he was constantly in an impenetrable throng of businessmen. To make matters worse, she'd spotted him cosying up to Karin Cavendish in the garden. She'd taken it out on Harry, ordering him to fetch her jacket from the Ferrari.

'Well, I'm having a much better time now,' she said, turning on the charm.

'Where's Harry?' asked Marcus, looking around. 'I've hardly had a chance to say a word to him all night.'

'He's off talking to people,' she said with a dismissive wave of the hand. 'I'm sure he's found someone more interesting to chat to.'

'Well, I find that hard to believe,' said Marcus. Molly examined his expression, trying to decide if his last comment was flirtatious or merely polite. Marcus Blackwell could be useful, she thought.

Marrying well was never just a case of two star-crossed lovers meeting by chance – not in the real world, anyway. It involved a lot of careful planning and manoeuvring. It was an art, thought Molly, an art she had studied for a long, long time.

'You never did show me that apartment you promised,' said Molly, touching Marcus's arm.

'It's all locked up for the night.'

'Oh, come on. You're the boss around here. Surely you have a key?'

Marcus nodded and patted his pocket. 'The reason I know the show apartment is locked is because I locked it myself.'

He put his hand lightly on her waist to steer her through the crowd to a private lift. Marcus slotted a card into the wall and the doors hissed open. They stood silently as the lift took them up to the fifteenth floor.

'Wow,' whistled Molly as she stepped out onto carpet so thick it almost covered her shoe. It was really was quite impressive what £10 million bought you in real estate.

Molly made her way slowly through the flat, Marcus silently following behind, lapping up her effusive compliments. And there was much to admire: floor-to-ceiling 'his-and-hers' plasma screens in the master bedroom, a walnut kitchen with white resin walls, climate-controlled closets and a polished bamboo floor in the bathroom. The look was cool minimalist with luxurious flourishes. Each apartment even came completely fitted out with bespoke cutting-edge Italian furniture. And then there was that view, high over Hyde Park.

'You'll see best from the balcony in the master bedroom,' said Marcus slowly. Molly looked at him, then kicked off her heels and walked across to open the doors. She didn't go out onto the balcony, just stood in the doorway, letting the cool night air ruffle her hair.

'Is it embarrassing to admit I had your calendar on my wall at college?' said Marcus behind her. Molly smiled; she knew she had him. Marcus was your typical Master of the Universe in the boardroom, but his devotion to work had starved him of passion. No regular girlfriend, possibly a few hookers. He was ripe for the picking.

'Come over here,' she said, wetting her lips with the tip of her tongue, 'The breeze is lovely.'

Marcus walked over hesitantly. His eyes were hungry but nervous.

Molly gently took his hand and placed it on her breastbone, sliding it down her dress until his fingers brushed her hard, erect nipple. 'Look what you did to me,' she whispered, leaning so close that her bottom lip brushed his ear lobe.

'Molly, Harry is my friend,' said Marcus, the words catching in his throat.

'I don't want Harry,' she purred, brushing her lips across his neck as she spoke. Her fingers traced down the line of his shirt buttons until she found his zip. 'I want you,' she whispered, 'I've wanted you from the second I saw you.'

Suddenly their mouths were together, Marcus hurriedly undoing his trousers and pulling his boxer shorts off as they shuffled towards the bed. Pushing Molly back onto the expensive linen, Marcus hiked up her dress and roughly pulled down her panties, dipping two fingers into her wetness.

'Now, don't wait,' she said, her voice shuddering. She wrapped her legs around him and guided him into her inch by inch, slowing him, taunting him, until he was fully inside her. Marcus was groaning in pleasure, reaching down to spread her legs wider, lifting her buttocks off the sheets so his cock could reach deeper and deeper.

'Oh God, yes, harder,' she begged, arching her back as Marcus thrust faster and faster into her, before he erupted, crying out, his face twisting, his nostrils flared.

He held on to her for one moment, then rolled to the side; they were both gasping.

'Can I call you tomorrow?' asked Marcus finally, as Molly sat up on the edge of the bed, pulling her panties back on.

'*I'll* call *you*,' she said with a dirty smile, before smoothing down her short gold dress and moving towards the door. Three minutes later, she was back at the party, where Harry was frantically searching for her, clutching her jacket.

'There you are darling,' she said, kissing Harry on the lips. 'I've been looking for you everywhere.'

10

The weather in Venice was remarkably good for late winter. A strong sun dazzled the city, the colourful landscape of ice-cream coloured buildings and red-brick palazzos looking even more striking against a clear blue sky. Karin and her friend Ileana Totti, heiress to her family's luxury goods company, were in the lobby of the Danieli Hotel catching up.

'So you lied to Adam Gold that you were going to be in Venice for carnival?' laughed Ileana, taking a sip of her Bellini. 'I never knew you were so devious.'

'It was a *white* lie,' said Karin. 'I am in Italy, aren't I?'

She had spent the last two days visiting a fabric manufacturer in Bologna. 'I mean, I didn't honestly expect him to want to hook up in Venice. He said he was only coming for a couple of days. Now he wants me to come with him to some masked ball.'

'What a drag,' said Ileana, teasing Karin with a hint of sarcasm.

Karin chuckled. She had tried to sound disgruntled, but they both knew she had been delighted when Erin had called her two days after the Knightsbridge Heights launch to arrange a Venetian rendezvous with Adam.

'So will you sleep with him tonight?'

'Illy!' said Karin, feigning shock. 'He hasn't even been in touch to say when or where we're meeting. It might not even happen.'

'Well, call him then!'

'No.'

'*Mia cara*,' purred Ileana, playing with the large canary diamond on her finger, 'you've just faked a trip to carnival. Now is not the time to play hard to get.'

'You're right,' smiled Karin, imagining herself naked in bed with Adam. 'I don't need games – he's already in the bag.'

'I know he is, darling,' smiled her friend, and they clinked glasses.

After she had said goodbye to Ileana, Karin took a shiny walnut and chrome motor launch over the Grand Canal to the Cipriani to check in. When there had been no message from Adam waiting for her on arrival, she had felt a slight rumble of anxiety. *Don't panic*, she reassured herself, *He'll call. Why wouldn't he?* By 4 p.m., however, that confidence had evaporated, to be replaced by an unfamiliar sense of insecurity.

'Signor, can you check again?' asked Karin, calling down to reception.

'Signora. I assure you il Signor Gold has not left a message. I will let you know if he does,' was the polite but firm reply.

Karin paced around her suite, a sumptuous, spacious room where marble and velvet managed to feel modern rather than dowdy. She couldn't settle, throwing down a book after just a few lines, flicking the TV on and off. Earlier that week she had requested a local costumier send over a selection of gowns for the party which had been laid out on the bed. She tried to distract herself by pulling them out of their heavy plastic wrappers. There were two glorious period dresses, one scarlet brocade, one a thick jade silk, both with low scooped neckline, a big bustle and layers of lace under a thickly gathered skirt. But even the beautiful clothes couldn't distract her from Adam and she flung them back on the bed angrily.

Karin looked out of the window; the sky was beginning to darken, low clouds glowing rosy on the Venetian horizon. She would give Adam until 5 p.m., and then that was it. Or maybe 6 p.m.

She ran herself a hot bath, letting herself sink into the suds and willing her anxieties to melt away. Surely she hadn't misread the situation so badly? After all, he had contacted *her* to meet in Venice, not the other way around. And yes, it was through his PA, but that was how rich men dated, just another window in a busy diary. Besides, if he wanted some bimbo model, he could have settled down years ago. And yet here she was, successful, sexy and clever, exactly the kind of woman Adam Gold needed – even if he didn't know it yet. *Ah, fuck him*, she thought, jumping out of the bath and stomping back into the bedroom. *I'll meet up with Illy. She'll be more fun, anyway.*

She was just wrapping a bathrobe around her when the suite's buzzer went. She opened the door to find a bellboy holding an envelope. 'This have just arrived for you, signora,' he said in broken English, trying hard not to look at Karin's curvy wet body.

Back inside, she tore it open and a stiff white invitation peeked out from gold tissue paper.

You are invited to dinner, drinks and dancing at the Palazzo Sasso. 8 p.m. Dress: Masked ball.

She noticed some black inky squiggles on the back. *See you later. Adam.* Karin jumped on the bed and whooped.

Molly was meeting Marcus at the Ivy. The restaurant was one of Harry's favourite places for supper and she was half hoping to bump into him, as she still hadn't quite got round to breaking the news that it was over between them. The morning after the Knightsbridge Heights party, she had given him one last mercy fuck, cleared all his coke from his sock drawer and disappeared. But, instead of getting the hint, Harry had left a dozen increasingly soppy messages on her answerphone, his latest communication informing her that he had booked them into the Paris Ritz for that weekend. While she was tempted to make contact, if only to slip into the fluffy peach robes at her favourite French hotel, she exercised restraint. Overlapping lovers didn't usually bother Molly; it wasn't unusual for her to have two or three on the go if they were particularly generous or useful. But Harry and Marcus were friends. She had *principles*, for God's sake!

The taxi waiting on the street tooted its horn once more. Molly tutted and painted on a final slash of lip gloss, then stood back to check the black Alaïa dress that clung to every curve in the mirror. Then she grabbed her bag and ran for the stairs. She was just closing the front door when she saw a scruffy young man standing at the bottom of the steps.

'Excuse me,' he said.

'I don't want one, thank you,' said Molly tartly, double-locking the door.

'You don't want what?' asked the man.

'A *Big Issue*,' said Molly. 'And this is a residential street, so I'd be grateful if you moved along.'

Molly had walked to her taxi but he was still standing there.

'No, I just wanted to ask: is this where Summer Sinclair lives?'

'And who is asking?' asked Molly, rather perplexed.

'Charlie McDonald. I'm a . . . a friend,' he said cautiously.

Charlie? The name didn't ring any immediate bells.

'We arranged a date on Wednesday, but I lost her number,' Charlie added. 'I just remembered she said she lived on Basset Road. That lady with the dog thought she lived here,' he said, pointing vaguely down the street.

Summer arranged a date? thought Molly, confused. *Where was she on Wednesday?* Then she recalled with a shudder something about a rock gig in Camden. Something to do with a male model from the bridal shoot. She gave him a second glance. Hmm, well, he was certainly good looking enough to model underneath that stubble and dirty leather, she thought. But even so! Had she not taught Summer anything over the years? It was rule number one: no creatives. Not unless you were talking musicians like Rod Stewart. Creative people just didn't make money. It was so typical of sweet, simple Summer to let her head be turned by some long-haired poet with holes in his jeans.

'I'm so sorry, Charlie, but you've had a wasted journey,' said Molly sadly. 'She lives here alright, but she's hardly ever here. Spends most of the week at her boyfriend's house in Mayfair.' She smiled kindly. 'But I'm her mother, Molly. I can pass a message on if you like.'

Charlie mouth was firm, but his eyes told of his disappointment.

'It's okay,' he replied with a shrug, 'I was just passing.'

She climbed in the taxi and pulled away. Molly looked through the rear window, watching Charlie McDonald get smaller and smaller until he had disappeared out of sight and out of Summer's life forever.

The Palazzo Sasso was like some Shakespearian fantasy. An enormous labyrinth of rooms with high painted ceilings, arched windows and ornate plasterwork, all lit by enormous fat lamps hanging from the walls that sent a flickering yellow light around the ballroom. Entering the room alone, Karin was immediately glad Adam had chosen this place to meet. She had been to so many fantastic parties all over the world, but this room looked so sexy, mysterious and theatrical that it was impossible not to be impressed. There were fire-eaters, jugglers and a string quartet that could just be heard above the hum of the crowd, the whole atmosphere pulsing with decadence. All the guests were in full costume for *Carnevale;* there must have been enough velvet in the room to stretch from Venice to the moon. The men were either in black tie with capes or in authentic period dress of doublet and hose, the woman straining in fitted corsets and flowing skirts. Everybody's faces were obscured by masks made from papier-mâché or thick brocade, making it impossible to spot Adam, but the sensation of being alone, hidden, was exciting, almost a sexual thrill for Karin. God, she had to find Adam – and quickly. She moved through the crowd, passing from the main ballroom into the tangle of anterooms, soaking up the delicious atmosphere, listening to the babble of different languages. Finally she came across a smaller room, filled with people, crackling with excitement. Walking closer, she understood why she had been given a handful of casino chips on entry; it was a roulette table. She found a place at the table, put all of her chips on red and held her breath as the ball bounced around the wheel.

'Red, twelve,' said the croupier and pushed over a pile of chips. With a growing confidence, she moved half of her stash onto zero.

'No more bets,' said the croupier as the ball began to rattle round the walnut wheel. Karin dropped her cool and clapped with excitement as the ball came to rest on zero. A respectful hum ran around the crowd.

'Go for broke,' said a man standing next to her. 'After all, it's not real money is it?'

Carried along by the moment, Karin moved all her chips onto number twenty-nine, watching, waiting her heart pounding as the white ball swirled, rattled and slowed.

'Red, thirteen.' There were hoots of excitement as the croupier scooped up all Karin's chips with his rake and pushed them towards the end of the table. Karin looked down the table to see the victor. His eyes met hers and he smiled. He was wearing a gold mask with a long curved nose, but she could see the bottom half of his face and that square jaw was unmistakable. Adam. *The bastard.*

'Thirteen. Lucky for some,' laughed Adam, leading Karin back into the ballroom.

'Lucky for you, you mean.'

'Don't be so competitive,' smiled Adam. 'Not when there are more important things at stake.' They reached the edge of the dance floor just as the sound of Mozart soared into the air. With a curt nod of invitation, Adam took Karin in his arms to dance.

'When you said we should see Venice, I didn't think it would be from behind two papier-mâché slits,' smiled Karin, enjoying the feeling of closeness as they whirled around the room.

'I like the idea of masks, don't you?' said Adam. 'The idea of being someone else for the night? It has so many possibilities. That's why the Venetian lords threw big balls for carnival – they wanted to allow their guests to adopt a different party personality to the one they usually had.'

'So who are you tonight?' asked Karin playfully. 'The King of Roulette?'

'Casanova,' he joked, leaning his mouth close to her ear.

'I thought you said *different* personas.'

The air was thick with chemistry; a thick wall that both separated and pulled them together. Karin was enjoying putting Adam on the spot. She was naturally direct, challenging and cool. It worked in business and she also found it drove certain men crazy.

'Don't believe everything you read in the *New York Post*,' scolded Adam.

'You're forty-something and unmarried – people draw conclusions.'

The music stopped and Adam took a flute of champagne.

'I've never married because my parents had a wonderful marriage and I've spent my whole life comparing my relationships to theirs,' he said more seriously.

'Well, not everybody wants marriage,' said Karin quietly.

'You've never tried it?' asked Adam.

'My first, only, husband died last year in a boating accident,' she said. She wasn't sure if she had needed to tell him quite yet; but she knew he'd find out. And besides, it made her seem more sensitive, more mysterious and certainly less predatory than a single, unmarried woman in her thirties.

'I'm sorry. I didn't know,' he said softly, reaching up to touch her face. They both looked away, out onto the dance floor.

'It's quite incredible,' she sighed. 'So decadent.'

'I love Venice. It reminds me of Manhattan.'

'You're kidding!'

'Seriously,' said Adam. 'They're both islands built around commerce; Venice was once the wealthiest city in the world. There's an old Venetian saying that a man without money is a corpse that walks.'

'I'm sure thousands of New Yorkers think that every day,' said Karin dryly.

He laughed. 'Not just New Yorkers.'

They fell silent again, watching the masked dancers revolving around the floor.

'Actually, there was something I wanted to talk to you about,' said Adam, still looking at the ballroom.

Karin felt a little leap of excitement in her belly.

'It was something you said at the Knightsbridge party. That we both sell lifestyle statements,' he continued. 'I've been to your stores and I think your corporate identity is really strong.'

Karin felt the delicious bubble of anticipation pop. '*I think your corporate identity is strong*'? she thought furiously. Had he brought her all the way to Venice to talk business? Whatever happened to 'I think you're the most beautiful woman I have ever seen' or 'I think we could be great together.' She'd even settled for *I think you have great tits.* She'd gone to enormous lengths to be here and that was the best he could do? Did he have any idea how difficult it was to get a room at the Cipriani during the carnival?

She took a deep breath: *Calm down, Karin,* she told herself. *You're a businesswoman, start behaving like one.*

'Well, thank you for the compliment, Adam,' she said coolly. 'So what did you want to talk about?'

'I have a team of creative people advising the Midas Corporation,' he said. 'I would love you to do some consulting for the residential division. I think you could really add some class.'

But Karin was only half listening. A tall, slender man in black tie had caught her eye across the dance floor. His harlequin mask could not disguise his handsome features; a long straight nose, a wide mouth and a strong jaw. He boldly walked across to Karin and extended a hand. 'May I have this dance?' he said with a heavy Italian accent.

'Eduardo Ribisi, is that you?' she laughed.

'*Sì,* Karin *carissima,* it is I!' he said, whirling his cape dramatically.

Karin grinned. 'I didn't recognize you at first, although you can hardly blame me with that mask.' She looked at Adam. 'If you'll excuse me for a few moments . . . ?'

The music swelled as Eduardo took her in his arms and swung her across the dance floor with expert grace.

'So who is he?' whispered Eduardo playfully.

'Someone who has just made me very cross,' said Karin, unable to shake her annoyance.

'Karin, darling, you come to Venice for passion and laughter, not for this sad little face,' he said, touching his finger on her down-turned lip.

Over Eduardo's shoulder, she could see Adam still standing there, his eyes following them.

'Do you want to go back?' asked Eduardo.

'Not yet. Just hold me.'

Adam was stony-faced by the time she returned. 'Who was that?' he said flatly, taking a canapé off a tray and biting into it rather harder than necessary.

'Just an old friend. He's from a very old Italian family. Practically royalty if Italy still had a monarch. Very charming. Now what were you saying about me consulting for Midas?'

'Oh, we can discuss in London,' he replied dismissively. He fell quiet as they slowly walked around the palazzo to explore its dark corners, finally finding a quiet courtyard that opened onto a canal, the water lapping up against the marble floor.

'Eerie, isn't it?' he whispered.

'Have you ever seen *Don't Look Now?*'

He laughed, moving closer to her so their fingers brushed.

'Shall we go?' he asked. She nodded and he led her out of the palazzo, down a tangle of narrow streets and into St Mark's Square where the launch to the Cipriani was located up a little carpeted gangway.

'You at the Cip too?'

'Palazzo Vendramin, next door.'

No other guests boarded and they sat in silence at the uncovered rear of the boat, watching the green water of the Grand Canal splash and foam around them. The Venetian skyline never failed to make Karin smile, the tall tower of St Mark's stretching up into a midnight-blue sky peppered with stars. Suddenly there was a whoosh and a spider's web of colour lit up the sky. Carnival was famous for its firework displays and, for the rest of the journey across to Giudecca Island, the sky was studded with gold and crimson stardust. There would not be a more magical spot to be alone with Adam Gold for the first time, Karin thought to herself, letting her hand slip onto the seat next to his.

'The view from my suite is just like this,' said Adam quietly, touching her fingers with his. Karin offered up a prayer and made a mental note to call and thank Eduardo for his brilliant perform-ance. The brother of an old school friend, she had known him since he was a teenager. Now twenty-nine, the gorgeous Venetian playboy was also still in the closet, too afraid of his staunch Catholic parents to tell them the truth about his sexuality. But he had been more than happy when Karin had phoned him earlier that day to play her suitor. 'I'm going to that party anyway,' he had giggled, 'And it won't be hard to pretend I am madly in love with you, *carissima*.' He had played his part beautifully. The psychology of rich men was fairly easy to understand. They wouldn't stand for something to be taken from their grasp.

The boat chugged to the dock at the Cipriani and the captain helped her onto dry land. Karin and Adam walked down the dark, leafy path into the hotel, where they could hear the tinkling of a piano and the good-humoured murmur of guests leaving the bar.

'Could you handle another drink?' asked Adam.

'I could, but aren't we going to frighten everyone in the bar?' she smiled. They were still wearing their heavy cloaks with the elaborate Venetian masks pushed back off their faces.

'My suite or yours then?' smiled Adam. Karin's stomach flip-flopped as she attempted to look nonchalant.

'Yours, but just for a few minutes,' she said, and they began to weave through the fragrant gardens of the Cipriani towards the exclusive quarters of the Palazzo Vendramin.

Adam unlocked the heavy mahogany door and let his guest into the suite, walking over to the long shutters and opening them without turning on the light. Karin followed him The view was every bit as impressive as Adam had promised, the milky glow of the moon adding to the magic. He moved behind her and his lips brushed her neck. She had hoped to deny him a little longer, to make him chase her, but it was impossible. The sexual charge between them was too strong. His fingers untied the ribbon of her cape, which fell to the floor, a pool of velvet.

He kissed her on the mouth, his warm hands cupping her face, moving down her back, quickly pulling at the zip. Her dress fell away from her in one movement and she stood there totally naked, save for the mask on the back of her head.

'For someone who wants to start designing panties, I thought you might be wearing some,' he said, his voice gravelly.

'Do I have to practise everything I preach?' she said softly, her hands moving inside his clothes. She began to undress him, but he gently held her hands still, reaching up to pull her carnival mask back down over her eyes. In the dark, the black mask obscured almost everything and her skin tingled with the thrill. She felt herself being lifted and lowered onto the bed, her groin aching, every nerve tingling with heightened sensualness. She groaned loudly as she felt her left nipple between Adam's moist lips, then shuddered as two of his fingers pushed into her, sliding back and forth across her clitoris as she arched her back in pleasure. He withdrew and for a few moments she felt nothing but ripples of pleasure and the cool breeze breathing in through the window. Then he parted her thighs with his hands, still damp from her juices, lifting her knees to her chest so his thick cock could sink deep inside her. And, as they rocked together, their sweat-sheened bodies moving in perfect rhythm in the moonlight, she cried out with a sweet mixture of passion, pleasure and triumph.

11

'I have to say, Erin, you've really pulled it out of the bag this time.' Richard adjusted his bow tie in a self-satisfied manner and smiled over to his girlfriend. It was true that Erin was attracting a number of admiring glances from Richard's colleagues at the White, Geary and Robinson annual dinner – not that there was a huge amount of competition, she thought. The Park Lane Hilton was awash with bottle-green taffeta, burgundy velvet and ill-fitting cummerbunds, so Erin's silk peacock blue DKNY evening dress made her look like a supermodel.

'Glad you like it,' said Erin, stroking the fabric. 'It cost six hundred quid. I don't think I've spent more than that on anything except rent.'

'Bloody hell!' whistled Richard. 'Have you won the lottery and not told me?'

Erin had received her first pay-packet earlier that week and, after nearly fainting at the size of it, had decided to go to Knightsbridge on a shopping spree. At first she couldn't believe how much designer clothes cost. It was ridiculous! Still, she had to admit it was worth every penny: the blue was stunning against her alabaster skin and it clung to every new curve. She had lost eight pounds since she had left Cornwall; working for Adam meant there wasn't time to eat. Richard disappeared to check the sitting plan and returned with two flutes of champagne.

'Fuck me!' he whispered gleefully, 'we're only sitting on the managing partner's table!'

'I take it that's a good thing,' said Erin, laughing at his boyish enthusiasm.

'Erin, Charles Sullivan is only one of the highest-earning lawyers in the City,' he hissed, 'bills millions for the firm. Millions!'

He was beginning to sound like David Attenborough describing some lesser-known species of the Amazon rainforest.

'Well, I hope he's a good laugh if we're sitting with him for dinner.'

'A good laugh?' Richard spluttered. 'Erin. We're talking invaluable networking opportunities here. One good word from him and I can pick and choose which department I go to when I qualify. I tell you, it's a job well done here, Erin. Thank you, Adam Gold. Speaking of which, where the bloody hell is he?'

As if hearing Richard's words, Adam walked into the room. His presence was like a shock of sex appeal in the otherwise sober company of the lawyers and their partners. The cut of his dinner jacket seemed a little more sharp, his shirt more crisp, his tan glowing among the papery English complexions. All heads and eyes swivelled to look at him. Erin felt a bolt of pride as he came up to her and Richard.

'Sorry I'm late. I was caught in the office. Had a few calls to make to New York. Shall we go in?'

'Thanks for coming,' whispered Erin as they strolled into the dining hall, 'I really appreciate it.'

'Well I hope he's going to buy you something very nice for this,' said Adam, nodding his head in the direction of Richard.

Adam was seated between Erin and Charles Sullivan. Charles was a powerfully built man with a shock of grey hair and a deep voice. In the legal world, he was something of an ageing matinee idol. Erin enjoyed watching the interplay between two successful businessmen. Charles Sullivan was clearly angling for work, gently promoting the firm at every opportunity, but he avoided anything direct, choosing safer subjects of conversation like shooting and golf. Richard, however, was less subtle, leaning over Erin and barging his way into the conversation wherever possible.

'I assume you've moved to London because you intend to float the business on the stock exchange,' asked Richard with an air of authority.

'And why would you assume that?' asked Adam, with just the hint of amusement in his voice.

'Well, with the introduction of REITs, isn't every property company to go public?'

'What's a REIT?' asked Erin.

Richard rolled his eyes. 'A Real Estate Investment Trust. Property companies convert to REIT status to become tax efficient.'

'Well, thank you for the lesson, Richard,' said Charles, his smile loaded with warning. 'But I hardly suppose Adam is going to let us in on his plans for Midas, is he?'

'It's also a little more complicated than that,' smiled Adam politely.

Erin could see that he was trying to stop the direction of the conversation without wanting to be rude. Richard, however, was like a small dog with a big bone, yapping and jumping, wanting everyone to see how clever he was. Erin looked at Richard with a sinking feeling of *what?* Disappointment? Embarrassment? When she had first got together with Richard, she had been in her final year of her degree and he was beginning the legal practice course in preparation for his traineeship. All her friends at Uni had considered him to be quite a catch, but at first she hadn't really seen it. It wasn't that he was particularly good-looking – there were certainly sexier men at college – but slowly she saw that Richard possessed a self-confidence, a worldliness and a purpose lacking in most of the men she met at the students' union. Richard talked about the future and his place in it when most students mumbled about indie bands and scoring 'a quarter' and she quickly found his considered opinions on politics and economics incredibly attractive. He was a real man, not some lank-haired teenager. She was also seduced by his family, who owned a big red-brick rectory in Worcestershire. She loved the sense of having a big, close-knit family; there were his mother and father, Brian and Margaret, and three brothers, who all worked in the city. But at the same time, on her rare visits home with Richard, she had felt inadequate, as if Richard was out of her league. She'd asked him once what he had seen in her.

'Fantastic knockers,' he'd said with apparent sincerity. 'Whatever happened to that tight black T-shirt you used to wear?'

She'd laughed it off at the time. But here and now, sitting next to Adam Gold, the scales were slowly falling from her eyes.

'I'm just going to the bathroom,' she whispered as Richard swirled his teaspoon around in his coffee with the air of a prime minister listening to his cabinet.

'Yeah, sure, honey,' he said absently, waving his hand. 'Take your time.'

The bathroom was quiet, with only a few cubicles occupied, so Erin had the mirror to herself as she dabbed some blusher on her cheeks. Then she noticed another woman standing a few feet away, just watching her. It unnerved Erin a little. The woman had a long, horsey face and the glassy look of someone who had drunk too much. Finally Erin nodded to her. 'Hello,' she said, wondering perhaps if she had met her before.

The blonde stepped towards Erin, a little unsteady on her feet. 'Richard Pendleton's girlfriend, yes?' she said with an accent Erin could only describe as phoney-Sloaney. 'It's good to finally meet you.'

'Really?' Erin was surprised that Richard spoke about her with his workmates and she suddenly felt a little guilty about her uncharitable thoughts at the dinner table.

'Well, never particularly wanted to meet you before, no,' said the woman with a twisted smile. 'But obviously now I'm curious.'

'Curious about what?' asked Erin, feeling a sudden fluttery sense of foreboding.

'Why, curious about you,' she laughed malevolently. 'Richard's little girlfriend tucked away in Cornwall.'

Erin didn't want to be rude to any of Richard's colleagues, but this woman was clearly hostile for some reason. 'Is there a problem?'

The woman laughed. Erin noticed that her lips and teeth were stained purple from the wine. 'No, no problem, not any more. Not now you have the ear of Adam Gold. This firm would kill to get a slice of the Midas legals and there's no way they would have got Gold here tonight without you. So Richard is officially Charles Sullivan's blue-eyed boy. No wonder he's gone running back to you.'

'Running back to me?'

The blonde's sneer was slowly dissolving, her lip wobbling. 'Last month he told me that he loved me,' she said, her voice cracking. 'He said he loves me because we're a good match. He said you live in Cornwall and that it wasn't working and it was never serious. He told me himself.'

Erin felt her cheeks burn hot. 'You've been seeing Richard?' she said incredulously.

'For six months. And then you deliver Adam Gold on a bloody platter and Richard decides to "give your relationship another go".' The woman's words were dripping with spite and bitterness. Erin almost felt sorry for the silly, vengeful cow.

'Don't waste your tears on Richard Pendleton,' said Erin, taking a deep breath to compose herself. 'Because you know what? I won't.'

She turned and walked into a cubicle and sat on the toilet seat, pressing her thumbs into her eyes and willing herself not to cry. For a moment, she actually thought she might laugh, but then the tears came, dropping onto her knees. What she had said to the blonde woman was true: it wasn't Richard she was crying for; she could see now he was a self-seeking, pompous prick. But she still felt worthless. Gullible. A fool.

It had always been that way she thought sadly, remembering when she was fifteen and she had really fancied Michael McGavey from the next village. They had flirted for weeks in school, taken long walks on the cliffs and kicked pebbles into the sea with their shoes. When Becky Lewis announced her parents were away in Tenerife and she was going to have a sleepover party – boys and girls – Erin couldn't believe her luck. She had gone into Newquay to buy a new dress and she and her friends had giggled with anticipation over what might happen over the course of the evening. Michael had been less friendly that night. Becky had smiled at him and plied him with her dad's beers. When the games and the horror movies had finished, he'd gone into Becky's bedroom while Erin had lain frozen in her red sleeping bag listening to the sounds of muffled first-time sex. Some girls didn't care if you fancied a boy. Some girls thought that if they fancied that boy too, then it was all that mattered. Even if they were your friends, they would still have him. Because they were prettier and wittier and because they could.

Adam can't see me like this, she thought stubbornly. If she could just reach the cloakroom without seeing anyone, she could slip away unnoticed.

'There you are. I've been looking for you.'

Richard had taken his jacket off and his dicky bow was hanging around his neck. He looked bloated with self-satisfaction and more than a little drunk. He looked around the lobby smugly, where a few people were already beginning to collect their coats.

'What a good night – and isn't Adam great? I think I made an impression there. Do you think he'll request me personally when he instructs us? Anyway, it looks as if Charles is going to swap my final seat from probate to tax. I mean, what good will fucking probate do me? And I'll be sitting with one of the heavy-hitting partners too.'

Erin stared blankly at him. He had completely failed to register she was upset.

'Well, you deserve it,' she spat, 'after you've been working so *hard* over the last few months.'

'Ooh,' he said sarcastically, 'what's got into you?'

'I've just been speaking to some blonde in the toilets who was telling me exactly why you've been putting in such long hours at the office. You must have been exhausted, you poor thing.'

Despite Erin's obvious sarcasm, Richard still hadn't completely twigged her meaning. 'Some blonde? Who?'

'Long face, short skirt, says you're great in bed apparently. I said we must have been talking about another Richard Pendleton.'

'Bella?' he croaked. 'Oh, she's just another trainee. Worked with her in the CoCo department – as you know the hours could be incredible sometimes, but . . .'

'You bloody liar!' she said, jabbing a finger into his chest.

Richard's face whitened. 'Look, what's she been saying?' he stammered, his earlier confident bluster now completely dissolved.

'The real reason you didn't want to come down to Cornwall or have me to stay at weekends. Quite a handy arrangement for you, wasn't it? Her up here and me tucked away two hundred miles away.'

'She's making it up,' he said, trying to sound indignant. 'She's a bit, you know, la-la,' he said, twirling a finger at his temple.

'Save it Richard,' she spat, pulling her coat on. 'I'm not interested any more.'

'Look, okay,' he said, grabbing Erin's arm and lowering his voice, 'so we had a little fling. You know how difficult the long-distance thing between us is. And, yes, Bella and I were both working long nights and one thing led to another. But it's long over and she can't accept it.'

He began shaking his head, his mouth twisting up sourly. 'I can't believe the little tart told you.'

'But it didn't stop long ago, did it, Richard?' said Erin, shrugging off his hand. 'It stopped the second I became useful to you.'

'Erin, stop it,' he hissed, noticing that people were beginning to look at them. 'Let's go home and talk about this.'

They both saw Adam Gold coming out of the ballroom at the same time. He was pulling on his cashmere overcoat when he saw them.

'Erin, Richard. I have to go,' he said, glancing at his gold Patek Philippe. 'Thanks for a great evening.'

Richard, still pale, went to shake his hand. 'It was an absolute pleasure, Adam. Thank you for coming.'

Adam smiled, although his brow furrowed. 'Erin, can I grab you for one minute?' he said, pointing towards the door.

She followed him, trying to compose herself, aware that her eyes were still stinging from crying.

'Are you okay?' he asked.

'Absolutely fine,' she forced a smile. 'Probably had a bit too much to drink.'

At that moment a rogue tear slipped down her cheek and she turned so that her back was to Richard, still hovering in the lobby.

'Erin, what's the matter? What's happening?' whispered Adam, shooting a ferocious glare in Richard's direction.

'It's nothing Adam, honestly,' replied Erin, struggling to suppress the sobs she felt welling up.

'Tell me.' It was an order.

'Okay. My boyfriend is a liar and a cheat,' she said as matter of factly as she could, gulping in air between the words. 'While I was in Cornwall, he was cheating on me. All that time.'

Adam touched the sleeve of her coat gently and turned to look at Richard. Behind him, they could see Charles Sullivan waving a balloon of brandy in the air as he said goodbye to guests. He saw Adam and began to move over towards them.

'Do you want to teach Richard a lesson?' whispered Adam.

She blushed. 'He deserves it,' she said, laughing despite the tears. 'What are you going to do?'

'Just watch.'

They walked towards Charles and Richard. Erin's heart was beating so furiously she thought it might stop, and her mouth was dry with anticipation. She recognized the look on Adam's face, the 'smiling assassin' expression he had when he was just about to close a good deal.

'Adam! Not going already?' said Charles, slapping him on the shoulder. 'Well, I have to say, it's been a pleasure. Let's stay in touch – you know what they say about your people phoning our people . . . ?' he said winking at Erin. 'I gave you my card, didn't I? It goes without saying that the firm would love to do some work with the Midas Group.'

Adam pulled the business card Charles had given him from his pocket and held it in the air. 'Thanks, Charles. I have your details.'

The managing partner smiled, scenting big new business.

'And as you know,' continued Adam, 'I am looking around for a new law firm for the Midas Group. We farm out a high volume of contract work,' he said temptingly. 'We spend a lot of money on our legals. A *lot* of money.'

Charles was beaming now.

'Only there seems to be an issue of trust.' Adam turned to look evenly at Richard whose face suddenly seemed frozen in fear. 'You see, if my assistant can't trust your trainee, I'm not sure *I* can trust White, Geary and Robinson.'

Charles Sullivan had gone a violent shade of pink and was looking at Richard as if he were about to throttle him. 'But . . . Adam, Mr Gold, I'm sure I . . . that is we, can . . .' spluttered Charles.

'Oh, and Richard,' added Adam in a low voice, 'I hope you haven't been billing all that late-night extracurricular work you've been doing to a client account? That would be fraud, and I believe that sort of thing is very frowned upon in the legal profession.'

There was a collective silence. Charles Sullivan now had purple spots on his cheeks and Richard looked as if he was about to cry.

As Adam turned and led a smiling Erin towards the revolving doors, he flipped up the collar on his coat and grinned. 'I've got a feeling your ex-boyfriend is about to be debriefed.'

'Erin, come home, this is ridiculous.'

Jilly Thomas was a placid woman most of the time, but when her granddaughter was in trouble, she was as fierce as a pit bull.

'Gran, I'm not coming home,' said Erin down the phone, 'it's just a setback.'

'But where are you going to live?' It's just like that terrible Michael McGavey all over again, and look how long it took you to get over him.'

Erin sighed. 'I'm a big girl now, gran,' she said. 'It's going to be alright; I like it in London.'

'Are you sure you don't want to come home? We're always here for you, you do know that, don't you?'

'I'm sure. And yes, I know that and it makes me very happy.'

Jilly was silent for a long time. 'Well, you're missing all the gossip. Did you know that Janet was pregnant? Same age as you and about to have a baby. Isn't it lovely? Due just before Christmas.'

Erin smiled into the receiver. Suddenly she didn't want to go home at all.

12

As the British Airways flight from Zurich landed at Heathrow Airport on a clear March Monday morning, Molly turned to Marcus, asleep next to her, and smiled contentedly. Right now, life felt good; really good. She had a rich, generous, well-connected man wrapped around her little finger. He was showering her with gifts and compliments but, more importantly, she felt sure he was going to lead her to the real prize: Adam Gold. Yes, her relationship with Marcus was progressing at speed, but she had never thought of Marcus as the goal; he was merely a stepping stone to the real money. Marcus was wealthy, but Molly's standards were higher, much higher. In fact, Molly ranked men according to the kind of plane they owned. A Citation or a Challenger would do, but preferably a Learjet or a Gulfstream V or, at the very top of the tree, a custom-built Boeing 737. It was a long time since she had travelled by commercial airline on a romantic weekend, but Marcus was a useful pit stop and, she had been pleased to discover, he was actually quite good company. In the two weeks following the Knightsbridge drinks party there had been three Mr Chow suppers and as many all-night sex sessions at his pied-à-terre in Chelsea or his country house in Buckinghamshire. Finally, Marcus had invited her to St Moritz to ski. Not that they ever made it to the slopes; the closest they got to the snow was dislodging some powder from the roof as they had sex in the penthouse suite at Badrutt's Palace.

She glanced at Marcus's profile, dark against the morning light that was pouring through the aeroplane window. Square patrician forehead, nose, slightly broken, firm chin. Fucking him wasn't hard work at all. Not like Momo, the overweight oilman from Brunei. Not like Giles, the peanut farmer's son from Georgia, or Jeff, the gnome-faced Hollywood producer she had met at the BAFTA party who had wanted her to piss all over him. Or even Harry, poor tiny-cocked Harry, who was still calling despite the fact that Molly had not returned any of his phone calls. No, Marcus was definitely a find.

A Midas Corporation car picked them up at the airport and dropped Molly at home, where she deposited her bags and freshened up before she set off for work. *Work!* The very thought of going in to Feldman Jones Productions made her groan. Although she only went into the events planning company two days a week, they were the longest two days of the week by far. She really didn't know why she bothered with it sometimes. But rent was expensive, coke was expensive and the prices of 'it' bags had shot through the roof. And in return for rolling into Feldman Jones Productions a couple of days a week, she had a ten per cent share in the company. *Thank you and good night.*

'Where is everybody?' Molly sauntered in and sat down at her desk, dropping her Bottega Veneta bag by her chair and rifling through a mountain of post had that accumulated since her last appearance in the office. It was 11.30 and Feldman Jones' office – on the top floor of a pretty pale blue mews-house in Westbourne Grove – was empty except for a couple of work-experience girls manning the phones.

'Becca and Jenna are at the venue for tonight's party,' said one nervously, 'and Lindsey and Sophie went to a meeting in the City first thing this morning.'

Molly nodded, enjoying her moment in charge. 'Great. Well can you get me a strong black coffee? And when you've done that, can you go through those files over there? I want you to dig out any pitch documents we've done for Filey Walker.'

Molly was surprised just how together and authoritative she sounded. She certainly didn't feel it. She felt dead on her feet; not enough sleep by a long chalk. Just then, Sophie and Lindsey walked in; the moment they saw Molly their expressions clouded.

'Ah, Molly, there you are.' Despite her butter-wouldn't-melt Home Counties accent, Sophie Edwards-Jones had a core of steel. Feldman Jones Productions was her life. She had grown it from a fax and phone in her kitchen to being one of the top events planners companies in the country.

'Yes, here I am,' said Molly brightly, pointedly ignoring the atmosphere. 'Sorry I'm a bit late but the traffic from Heathrow was a bitch.'

'So you've been away?'

'Yes,' said Molly, flicking a sheaf of hair over her shoulder. 'Back to Badrutt's Palace. Gorgeous as ever. Didn't I tell you?'

'No, you didn't tell us actually,' Lindsey Feldman's voice was harsh. She was a five-foot-two-inch dynamo who didn't take any shit and was the perfect foil to Sophie's silver-spoon polish. 'If you had told us, we might have had something to say about it, seeing as we had a pitch with a client this morning that we needed you to be at.'

Molly looked bemused. 'We had a meeting? With who?'

'Callanders, the stockbrokers, remember?' said Lindsey with a hint of sarcasm. 'Want us to do their Christmas corporate event? Two thousand guests? We did discuss this, Molly. It was rather embarrassing when you didn't turn up.'

'Callanders. Oh shit. Yes. I completely forgot. As I said, my flight didn't get in until nine thirty. Then I had to pop home to freshen up.'

Sophie stared at Molly for a long moment. 'Can we just have a chat in the meeting room, Molly?'

Molly pushed her chair back and walked after the women, seething. *How dare they talk to her like that in front of the workies?* Making her feel as if she was a teenager caught smoking behind the bike sheds. The nerve! Molly sat down truculently and Lindsey got straight to the point.

'This can't go on, Molly,' she snapped.

'Jesus, Lindsey. I miss a meeting. I'm sorry,' said Molly, rolling her eyes at the ceiling. 'I can take the client out again if it means that much to you.'

'It might well be too late for that.'

'Oh don't worry, we'll get the pitch,' said Molly. 'We always get the pitch.'

'If we do it will be no thanks to you, Molly,' said Lindsey abruptly.

Sophie held up a hand, stopping the argument mid-flow. 'Molly. We might as well cut to the chase,' she said. 'This arrangement just isn't working. You're hardly in the office, you don't come to pitches, and when we hold an event you spend the whole time socializing.'

'Socializing! Isn't that what you want me to do?'

Sophie nodded. 'It was what we *wanted* you to do when we started, but things have changed.'

It was true Molly Sinclair had been a definite asset when Feldman Jones had launched – she had high-class contacts and clients were flattered to see a supermodel at pitches. She certainly added an undeniable sheen of glamour to a party too. But she was simply not doing what they had brought her on to do – attend pitches, charm the CEOs, bring in new clients. Put simply, she was baggage.

'Molly, we want you out of the partnership.'

Molly felt her blood run cold. She didn't exactly enjoy working at Feldman Jones, but being a partner in a company gave her credibility. It also gave her a salary. Okay, it wasn't much, but she relied on it. A woman like Molly could expect swish nights out and holidays to be paid for by some rich guy in return for a blowjob in the shower, but even she had overheads to pay. She hated to admit it, but she needed this job.

'You can't do that,' said Molly, struggling to appear calm and confident, 'I'm a director of this company.'

Sophie smiled. 'Yes we can. We've already had a lawyer look into it. Don't worry, you won't be out of pocket, we'll get a valuation and buy out your shareholding for a fair price.'

'But you need me,' said Molly, a waver of panic in her voice now. 'You need me to bring in the business.'

Lindsey couldn't suppress her smirk. 'Molly, you haven't brought in any business for over a year, and Feldman Jones Productions generates its own business now. We have a fantastic reputation and we need everyone to be pulling their weight.'

'I do pull my bloody weight!' said Molly indignantly.

Lindsey couldn't resist a jibe. 'The only thing you pull, Molly, is the clients.'

Molly jumped to her feet and strode to the door. 'I will enjoy watching this tinpot company crash to its knees when word gets around that I have resigned,' she said haughtily.

Sophie smiled. 'I think we'll manage,' she said.

'Oh and Molly?' Lindsey called after her. 'Could you clear out your desk? We don't want the drug squad round again.'

13

'Don't we have any more girls to see?' sighed Karin, snapping the portfolio shut and dismissing the fifteen-year-old Estonian blonde with a regal wave. As the skinny model shuffled out of the Karenza office, Karin looked at the pile of model cards in front of her and rubbed her eyes. Karin and her head of merchandise Kirsty Baker had been casting for the Karenza spring/summer advertising campaign all afternoon, and not one girl had been even remotely right.

'What about Gisele?' said Kirsty, flicking through a copy of American *Elle*.

'Can't afford her.'

'Kate?'

'She's everywhere. Plus we can't afford her.'

'Daria?'

Karin threw down the pile of model cards in irritation. 'We're not fucking Gucci, Kirsty. The commercial rates for the very top girls are fifty grand plus *a day*. This is a three-day shoot, plus travel days, plus agency fees. Then you've got the photographer and crew, location costs, the advertising agency's bill plus the cost of running the ads in the magazines. Christ, we're talking upwards of a million pounds.'

In fact, Karin was beginning to think that was the only answer, although her instincts were totally against it. Despite the prohibitive costs, she was wary about using a well-known face for the first Karenza campaign. She wanted the ads to showcase the product, not the model. Yes, they needed a girl who oozed glamour and beauty, but they also needed the girl to make it seem as though it

99

was the Karenza swimwear that was giving her those magical attributes, not the other way around. Put simply, they needed showstopping cinematic visuals and an exotic siren smouldering on a Caribbean beach, not some emaciated teenager in a photographic studio in Hoxton.

Karin stood up and stalked around the office impatiently, twisting her spiked heels into the cream carpet. She had come a long way in seven years since she had started the company from her old Chelsea apartment, but she wanted more, much more. She didn't want to own a tiny niche of the fashion world, she wanted the whole thing – and she had a plan. While all her friends from Briarton had gone to Florence to take art history courses to equip them for dinner party conversation, Karin had headed straight for the Polimoda, Italy's famous fashion college. Karin had lapped up every lesson and had quickly formed a strategy. Her decision to go into swimwear had been considered and calculated. Womenswear was too competitive, too brutal, too much of an up-hill struggle. Shoes were a closed shop with Blahnik, Choo and Louboutin dominating the top of the market, and while accessories were the golden goose of fashion – the mark-up on a designer handbag was huge and more importantly one size fits all. No wonder accessories was where the luxury goods companies LVMH, Gucci group and Club21 made their mouth-watering profits. Instead, Karin had spotted a gap. Society was getting richer and people were getting more greedy. They didn't just want luxury goods – the bags, the shoes, the cars – they wanted the full luxury lifestyle. Karin had watched as her friends took a dozen holidays a year in an ever-growing list of exotic locations but, despite the constant talk of holiday wardrobes in the glossy magazines, these women rarely dressed at all during the day, staying in a swimsuit from dawn till dusk. Swimwear was sexy, it was glamorous, it was *her*.

'Dammit, why are all these silly little girls so skinny and pale?' said Karin impatiently, flipping through the model cards once again. 'They just look like children.'

'That will be because they *are* children,' said Kirsty with a smile. 'Models start at twelve these days, you know.'

'But we're not selling clothes to children,' snapped Karin. 'Our customers are women, real-life women with hips and tits, not these broom-handle freaks!'

Karin knew what women wanted. They didn't want revealing wisps of lycra, they wanted to feel like Ursula Andress emerging out of the sea in *Dr No*, they wanted to feel like Sophia Loren wearing a turban in *Arabesque*. Classy, sexy, in control. So she created a collection of classic pieces that made great bodies look even hotter. She then carefully drip-fed them into the market, only allowing Karenza to be stocked in exclusive corners of the market like Harrods and Harvey Nichols. She wooed important fashion editors, sending them top-of-the-range bikinis every season and was rewarded by flattering articles about the hot new jet-set swimwear label that *everyone* was wearing. But it was Sebastian who had encouraged Karin to open her first shop. She had met him two years after her first collection had debuted, and they were engaged six months later. She didn't need anyone to help her think big, but Sebastian was supportive – and, more importantly, he was connected. A school friend of Seb's from Eton had offered her the lease on a small shop on Walton Street and, not being able to afford an expensive interior designer, Karin copied the look of a pal's Cape Cod beach house, all fabulously pared-down with white floorboards and white walls. It was low-key luxe for people who didn't want to shout about their wealth. It was perfect. Now she had three shops and a £20-million-pound annual turnover and Karenza was Europe's fastest-growing swimwear company, but for Karin's fierce ambitions it was not growing fast enough. It needed more visibility as a major luxury. She needed a print campaign in the major glossy magazines. She smiled a small, sad smile. She knew Sebastian would have approved.

Kirsty was waving a black-and-white photograph of a skinny brunette with long legs in Karin's face.

'She's hot. What about her?'

'Too thin. Looks cocky,' she said, tossing the photo on the pile dismissively.

'Or her?' asked Kirsty, pointing at a toothy blonde.

'No way! Check out that mouth. She looks like a rabbit.'

'She did do the Prada show last season,' offered Kirsty weakly.

'Kirsty! The girl fronting this campaign represents our brand,' snapped Karin. 'She is our face and body. I want our potential customers to look at our campaign and think, "I can be that sexy and chic and gorgeous". Even if she's fat, I still want her to think that three hundred pounds is money well spent if she can be magically transformed into the gorgeous creature in our campaign.'

'I thought you didn't want any fat and frumpy housewives wearing Karenza designs,' said Kirsty sulkily.

'That's not the point,' replied Karin briskly. 'We need someone hot. Someone who can fill a bikini like she's been poured into it, not some six-foot stringy teenager. We want a *woman*.'

She spun round her Eames chair so it faced the window overlooking the street. 'She's got to be out there somewhere.'

Dan Stevens, one of Europe's hottest fashion designers, was crossing Regent Street when he saw her. He was already late for his next appointment – his last meeting at Vogue House had gone on forever – but something about this girl, standing on the other side of the road, made him stop and look. Even from fifty feet away he could see her right-angle cheekbones, her poker-straight pale blonde hair and her dancer's posture. Dan frowned; why didn't he know this girl? He worked with top models and actresses every day; he thought he knew all the beautiful women in London, but he had never seen this one before. Surely she *must* work in fashion? He thought, she was too stunning, too stylish to be a civilian. He quickened his pace to catch up with her and, drawing level, tapped her on the shoulder. She was dazzling. How many hours had he spent retouching photographs of stars with bad skin, all those smoker's lines around the mouth, or the eyes deadened from drugs and parties. This girl, though: wow. Those enormous, slightly startled lavender-blue eyes, her incredible bone structure: she was a knockout. Not for the first time in his career, he wished he was single.

'Hi! I, ah, I just wanted to introduce myself. I'm Dan Stevens, I'm a photographer. Are you a model by any chance?'

Dan Stevens. Holy shit! Summer's mouth dropped open. She'd only come shopping to cheer herself up because she hadn't had a go-see in a week and here she was being stopped by one of the world's hottest photographers. You couldn't open *W* or *US Vogue* these days without seeing his name on a cover story. Molly would be *really* impressed.

'Oh, I know who you are,' she smiled, butterflies fluttering round her tummy. 'And yes, I'm a model, although you won't have heard of me.'

'Good,' said Dan. 'Are you busy for the next hour?'

'Just spending money I haven't got,' smiled Summer.

'In that case, could you come with me to my next meeting? There's someone I really think you should meet.'

Dan Stevens walked through the door grinning from ear to ear. Karin, however, did not think he had much to smile about. He was two hours late for the casting – she couldn't abide lateness – and she met his grin with a stony face. Dan knew he was getting off lightly: Karin Cavendish in hell-hath-no-fury mode was a fate you wouldn't wish on an enemy. But she was in no position to make a point; she was very, very lucky to have secured Dan's services for the campaign. If she hadn't given Dan his first break, setting him up an appointment to see her fashion editor friend at *Elle* when he was a struggling nobody, she would never had the kudos to book him. But Karin's irritation immediately melted away when she spotted the petite blonde girl trailing in nervously behind Dan. The girl was exquisite. Long pale blonde hair hung at either side of a perfectly oval face with a cute upturned nose, full lips and lovely almond-shaped eyes.

'You're a little late for the casting,' said Karin, holding out a hand. 'Can I see your card?'

Summer stood in the doorway, nervously playing with the strap of her handbag. 'I'm sorry, I don't have one with me,' Summer replied politely, a little intimidated to be face to face with Karin.

'She wasn't sent for the casting,' said Dan quickly. 'I found her shopping on Regent Street. I've taken some quick Polaroids and – here – I really think you should take a look.'

Karin quickly studied the Polaroids, a crucial tool for casting. Pictures in a model's portfolio were so retouched that it was often impossible to tell whether she photographed well or not. But these Polaroids were amazing. She really was beautiful; in the flesh and on film.

'How tall are you?' asked Karin, still looking at the photographs.

'Five eight,' lied Summer.

'Five seven,' said Karin coolly, scribbling it on the bottom of the Polaroid.

She looked up at the girl again; she looked familiar but she couldn't place where she had seen her before.

'Have I met you before?' she asked.

Summer felt uncomfortable. She didn't want to mention her

mother. It always sounded as if she was cashing in on Molly's fame.

She shook her head. 'I don't think so.'

Suddenly the penny dropped: seeing that long hair swishing about was a dead giveaway. Now Karin saw it – the nose, that wide, luscious mouth, that long curtain of platinum hair. She felt herself stiffen with displeasure. The platinum hair suddenly looked a little too brassy, her generous breasts just a little too large.

'You're Molly Sinclair's daughter, aren't you? You came to my benefit dinner.'

'Really?' asked Dan, congratulating himself for spotting talent.

'Really,' smiled Summer, flushing.

'Well, thanks for coming in. Goodbye,' Karin said quickly, gesturing towards the door with her eyes.

Summer's heart plummeted and she slowly turned and left. She was gutted: Dan Stevens hadn't even spoken out for her.

'Are you not even going to get her to try a swimsuit on?' said Kirsty after Summer had left. 'She was lovely.'

'A pretty girl, yes,' offered Karin brusquely. 'But she's too small and too curvy.'

'Karin, she's fantastic!' laughed Dan incredulously.

'She belongs on a *Sports Illustrated* cover!' snapped Karin.

'I thought you wanted the campaign to be sexy?'

'If the girl is too obvious it'll look tacky.'

'Well I can't believe she hasn't fronted a big campaign before. The second I take to her into *Vogue*, every magazine and fashion company is going to want her. Her day rate will skyrocket.'

'You're going to take her to *Vogue*?' asked Karin, her eyes narrowing.

'US *Vogue*. I see them on Monday.'

Karin's mind went into business mode, thinking three moves ahead.

'What agency did she say she was with?'

'La Mode agency,' said Dan.

'Never heard of them,' sniffed Karin, but she was secretly pleased. A small, unknown agency would give her Summer for peanuts, just to ingratiate themselves with a fashion house. It could save Karin thousands and, if Dan was going to champion her as he was suggesting, this girl could be the next big face – and Karenza would have her first.

'I wonder what she'd be like brunette?'

Karin snatched up her phone. 'Jane? Can you send the model back up?' she asked the receptionist. As they waited for Summer to come back up, Karin opened her desk drawer, removing a pair of scissors which she gave to Kirsty.

'Can you just cut me some of your hair?'

'What?' replied Kirsty, startled.

'Your hair. I *need* it,' said Karin tartly, her eyes locking with Kirsty's. 'Come on, it's important. Just two or three inches will be fine. It will grow back, for goodness' sake.'

Kirsty gingerly snipped at the bottom of her brown bob and handed the segment of hair to Karin.

As Summer came back into the room, Karin walked purposefully towards her. 'I want you to go to Joel at Real Hairdressing,' said Karin, handing Summer the brunette locks. 'Tell him I sent you and tell him to make your hair that colour. When he's done it – and not before – come back here and maybe we can start trying on some swimsuits.'

Kirsty and Dan looked at each other and smiled.

14

Jilly was worried. After that snake Richard had gone off with the office floozie and Erin had moved out of his apartment, Jilly had fully expected her granddaughter to return to Cornwall immediately. After all, she had no home, no boyfriend, some job answering telephones twelve hours a day; what on earth could be keeping her in London?

'I just don't understand it, lovey,' she said down the phone line. 'London's expensive, it's lonely. Why don't you come home?'

Erin had to admit Jilly had a point. She'd been in London six weeks and here she was, living in a single room in a Bayswater hotel costing her a hundred pounds a night. She hadn't any friends to stay with after she'd left Richard's – she could hardly have asked Adam to put her up for a few days while she found somewhere new to live – and working so hard at the Midas Corporation, there seemed neither the time nor the opportunity to make any new friends. It wasn't quite the glamorous life either of them had imagined for her; then again, there was something about Midas that made her fizz with excitement, and it wasn't just her £70,000 pay-packet. She wasn't quite ready to leave just yet.

'When you spent four years at university getting a Russian degree, it wasn't to spend your life making somebody else's travel arrangements, was it?' said Jilly. 'Come home. Finish your novel. That's you've always wanted, isn't it?'

Erin felt an enormous rush of guilt at the mention of her novel. Jilly could almost read her mind; Erin hadn't written a word since she had been in London. But she'd started another career now and she couldn't very well admit defeat so soon and go running home just because Richard was such a rat.

'Let me give it a week,' said Erin. 'This hotel arrangement is purely temporary. If I haven't got settled in a week, we can talk again.' She put down the receiver and resolved that she had to find somewhere immediately, if not sooner.

'Now the next property I'm going to show you is really special,' said the estate agent with an encouraging smile. Erin groaned inwardly. It was the fourth flat in as many days that this estate agent had shown her. He had kept phoning her up at work, promising her he could find her something amazing, but everything he had shown her so far seemed decidedly overpriced or poky.

Perhaps this flat would be the one, Erin thought hopefully, as they pulled up outside a huge Victorian building in a shady street in Canonbury, the prettiest part of Islington. It certainly looked good from the outside, with rich, honey-coloured brickwork and large well-tended flowerpots sitting on the wide windowsills.

'Incredible isn't it?' smiled Ryan Hall, the agent. *It's her who's incredible*, he thought. *I've got to close the deal on this one*. Ryan had been desperately seeking out impressive properties all week, just so he could see Erin again.

'It used to be an old cotton factory,' he said, striding up the path. 'Lay derelict for years until it was redeveloped a few years ago.' He jangled the key in the lock and gently touched Erin's shoulder to guide her in.

'I'd live here if I could afford it,' said Ryan, hoping she get the hint and invite him around. 'A girl like you deserves a place like this.'

As they walked inside, Erin nodded in agreement. There was a large lobby with a marble floor and an old-fashioned grille-front lift – a relic from the building's industrial days. She had always dreamed of living in a place like this. Erin crossed her fingers as they rode up to the second floor. *Please be nice*, she whispered, *please be nice*. She desperately needed to find somewhere to call her own or she'd be back on that Port Merryn clifftop before the end of the month.

'Our agency looks after the entire building,' continued Ryan as he opened the door to apartment eleven. 'I've only been with

Thomson Bailey three months but my boss tells me that apartments in this building hardly ever become available. Once you're here, you don't want to leave.'

For once, Erin thought Ryan Hall might be telling the truth. It wasn't a huge space, a corridor painted soft sage green with high ceilings and curly cornices led into a big living space already kitted out with squashy cream sofas and billowing velvet drapes. There was a small open-plan kitchen, a bathroom with just enough space for a shower, and a large bedroom with a sleigh bed and – she gasped – French doors which led out to a tiny balcony.

'It's fantastic,' smiled Erin, unable to hide her glee. 'You should have shown me this place first.'

'Then I wouldn't have had the pleasure of your company all week,' smiled Ryan Hall honestly.

'How much did you say this one was?' she asked.

'Five hundred a week,' said Ryan, flicking a piece of fluff from his shoulder.

Erin felt her heart clank to the ground. It was almost twice what she had been planning on playing; over half of her salary after tax.

Just then, Ryan's mobile began to ring furiously. 'Make yourself comfortable and think about it,' he whispered.

'Yes, er, hello darling. Just got caught up. I won't be long,' Ryan hissed into the phone, quickly moving down the corridor and out of the front door.

Erin smiled to herself: the girlfriend. Clearly Ryan's sledgehammer seduction techniques worked on someone. She wandered back into the hallway, trying to add up her outgoings in her head, when suddenly there was the clatter of the lift door opening followed by raucous laughter. Seconds later, a head appeared round the door.

'Oh hello. You must be looking round,' said an Irish accent.

'Yes, I am,' said Erin, a little surprised. She took a moment to look at him. He was late twenty-something with a crop of dirty blonde hair, a mischievous smile and lively eyes that looked a little glassy and drunk.

'Sorry. Just being a good neighbour and all that,' he said, slightly slurring his words. 'I saw the door open, so I was just checking it hadn't been burgled or anything.' He vaguely extended a hand but then thought better of it and used it to prop himself up in the frame of the door. 'Anyway. I'm Chris Scanlan.'

'No, not a burglar, just looking round,' smiled Erin. Chris Scanlan

108

was dressed in a suit, she noted, but not one that suggested he worked in the City, more like a student dressing up for a wedding. He was standing next to a petite pretty girl with long dark hair who wrapped her arm proprietorially around his waist. She looked a little drunk too.

Chris Scanlan pointed to the door of number twelve. 'I live there, by the way. Are you going to take it? I'm not drunk and noisy very often, honestly,' he added.

'I like it, but it's a little pricy for me,' she whispered, hoping Ryan Hall couldn't hear her. 'And,' Erin smiled, 'I think the all-night parties might be a bit much.'

'Talking of all-night . . .' smiled the little brunette, tugging Chris Scanlan's hand towards his flat.

'Well, it's definitely a great place to live,' said Chris over his shoulder, before he was yanked inside and the door was slammed.

What a prat, thought Erin. Do I want to pay all that money to live opposite some womanizer with balls bigger than his brains? She'd had enough of that with Richard.

'So. Do you want overnight to think about it?' asked Ryan Hall, appearing in the hallway slightly flustered. 'Although I have to warn you, I'm showing three people round tomorrow morning.'

Erin turned around to look at the flat lying invitingly behind her. All cosy colours and soft lighting. And she thought of the Bayswater hotel costing her a hundred pounds a night.

'How about I make a offer of four hundred a week?' she said, smiling as sweetly as she could. 'I can supply excellent references. I actually work for Adam Gold, you know, the property developer?' said Erin hopefully.

But Ryan Hall didn't need any more incentive. He was already thinking that, if he could get a nice low rent for this very pretty girl, then she might somehow owe him a favour. Like dinner at Lola's.

'Tell you what, I'll put in a few calls and we'll see if I can wave my magic wand,' he said with a wink.

Erin drove all the way back to her single bed in Bayswater, hoping that Ryan Hall would do just that.

15

Alexander Delemere, fifth Lord of Stowe, thought his cock was about to explode. Molly Sinclair sat astride him, grinding her hips into his, the muscles of her pussy tightening exquisitely around his shaft, dipping her body so she lowered a sweet brown nipple into his mouth. Molly leant back, her spine arched, her rounded breast pointing skywards.

'Yes, yes,' she screamed, feeling the sweet pulse of orgasm swell around her body. 'Hell yes!' shouted Alex in reply, before collapsing on the crumpled linen of the hotel sheets.

'Good Lord,' he whispered, as Molly slid herself off his cock and lay down beside him to light a cigarette.

She propped herself up on a pillow and looked at Lord Alexander Delemere through a haze of grey smoke. Ever since Marcus had come on the scene, Molly had cut down her current list of lovers, but Alexander Delemere was one fix she was not prepared to give up, no matter how serious things were getting with Marcus. It never ceased to amaze Molly how good sex with Alexander Delemere could be. Age was not an issue when it came to Molly's lovers: but enjoying sex, not having to fake orgasm, certainly was. Men over sixty were so soft – their crepe-textured skin, their blancmangey buttocks and their baggy balls could be quite off-putting unless she was drunk, but Alex was in fine shape for a man his age.

They had been meeting once a week at the Basil Street hotel ever since Evie Delemere's christening, and the pattern was always the same. They would meet for a quiet lunch in Mayfair in dusty restaurants so far off the social scene they might as well have been in Scotland. Alex would have fish or pheasant. They would take a black cab to the Basil Street hotel where the concierge would pretend each time not to know them. They would undress, have sex, a little conversation, each time getting to know one another a little better. Sometimes Alex would present her with a gift. He was not a generous man. So far she had received an obvious red satin camisole that was too big, a box of chocolates and a small butterfly-shaped brooch with coloured stones that Molly thought were rubies but later discovered were merely crystal.

She was realistic enough to know that at this point she was no threat to his marriage, and that although Alex seemed to crave her body like some infatuated teenager it was going to take a good deal more than a handful of fucks in a Mayfair hotel to break up his marriage to Lady Vivian. He was old money, and that meant golden handcuffs and traditional values. But Molly wanted to keep this iron in her fire to see what would happen. And there were worse things to be than the mistress of one of the richest men in the country, after all.

She watched him get out of bed and put on a towelling robe.

'Shall I order a little room service?'

Molly shook her head. 'I assume you have to be going soon.'

'You assume correctly,' he replied, glancing at his watch. 'Although I might ring down for a pot of tea.'

Molly had to suppress a smile. *Rock and roll.*

He sat back on the edge of the bed and Molly knelt behind him to give his shoulders a rub.

'How's Evie?' she asked playfully. 'As gorgeous as her granddad?'

Alexander turned to face her. 'Do you have to remind me of my advancing years?'

She wrapped her arms around his body, her fingers probing between the fold of his robe. 'You're only as young as the woman you feel Alex.'

'Since you ask, Evie is a delight. Donna on the other hand . . .' He paused. 'I'm sorry, she is a friend of yours, I'm being rude.'

Molly sat back on the bed and took a drag of her cigarette to stop herself smiling. Do-gooder Donna was no friend, just someone useful. 'Please, be my guest and continue,' she said, lying back on the pillow.

'It's just her plans for the estate,' he said, pacing around the floor with visible irritation. 'I assume you've been?'

Molly nodded. The Delemere estate comprised two main parcels: the main house, a vast Queen Anne mansion often described as an 'architectural national treasure,' where Alexander and Vivian lived, and a smaller manor house on the edge of the grounds, where Donna and Daniel resided and where Donna had spent the best part of last year renovating the barns to create the Delemere farm store and spa.

'She spent the better half of two million pounds on her little alternative health and farming fantasy. *Two million pounds*,' continued Alexander, his eyes blazing like dark coals. Molly knew that, while she could reduce him to a purring kitten in the bedroom, Alexander Delemere had not built up one of the country's foremost industrial empires by being soft.

'That she is spending my son's money as if it were water is one thing, but the fact that she has hoodwinked my wife into this New Age mumbo-jumbo folly is another. They are partners now apparently in this ridiculous New Age business. Vivian,' he paused, seemingly embarrassed to utter his wife's name, as if it might summon up her physical presence in the room. 'Vivian is now insisting she use our money, *my* money to expand.'

Molly didn't like to point out that the Delemere shop and spa was probably a very good business investment where London's social elite flocked to buy overpriced sausages and organic cheese or pick up an expensive facial. Organic 'natural food' destinations were hot, but she suspected Alexander didn't want to hear that point of view. 'It is a rather absurd notion,' agreed Molly, pulling a sheet around her body. 'Then again, Donna has always been – how can I put this politely? – on the make.'

'Really,' said Alex coolly, suspecting she was a sympathizer. 'What makes you say that?'

'Oh nothing,' replied Molly, taking a lengthy drag of cigarette. 'Just things I hear.'

She really had his attention now.

'Well, if you ever hear anything else, please let me know immediately,' he said thoughtfully. 'I will not have that woman go through my son's money, my wife's money, *my* money as if it were her own. I won't have it.'

The doorbell rang. It was a bellboy with tea.

'Mmm . . . why don't we have our Earl Grey in bed, Alex?' purred Molly. 'Shame to let it get cold.'

16

Summer Sinclair stood waist-deep in the warm Caribbean waters, hands placed provocatively on her hips, and pouted. Her skin glistened with grains of pinky-white sand, the sun had toasted her a pale bronze, while hair and make-up artists hovered in the background to ensure that Summer stayed the right side of casually sea-drenched.

As Dan Stevens snapped away with his Nikon camera, Summer wondered whether she was doing a good enough job. This was by far the sexiest shoot she had ever done, and for the first hour she had felt completely self-conscious; she had spent hours preparing for the shoot. No other model she knew did homework, but Summer had pored over *Sports Illustrated*, old Pirelli calendars, *Vogue* and *Harper's Bazaar* editorials, photography books from David Bailey and Helmut Newton, scrutinizing poses of the great, sexy models past and present: Gisele, Cindy Crawford, Jerry Hall; angle of head, the facial expressions, the hair and make-up. She had spent her entire life in the shadow of her gorgeous mother but today, standing in the bright Anguillan sunlight, she felt like her own woman.

'Okay. Let's take a break,' shouted Dan Stevens, looking up from his camera. 'Summer, put something else on and we can try another setup.'

Karin looked at her watch and stalked over the sand to Dan. 'Well I'm due back at the hotel. Don't start before I've returned.'

'The light is going to start going soon, Karin,' complained Dan, looking irritated. 'We have to get a move on.'

'I'll be twenty minutes,' she mouthed, walking to the huge white hotel in the distance.

Mike, the genial photographer's assistant, handed Summer a towelling robe and she looked over at Dan anxiously.

'Is everything okay?'

'You look gorgeous, honey.'

'Have you got the shot?'

He shrugged and then laughed.

'That's a no,' Summer smiled, feeling a little deflated. She bet Molly would have captured the magical image that would be used in the campaign after seven hours of shooting. She always used to boast that when she worked with photographers like Bailey, they'd get the picture in the first dozen shots.

'You're doing great,' said Dan kindly. 'Go and get changed and when we start again we're going to nail it, okay?'

She walked over the hot sand to the trailer that had been set up at the edge of the beach. Tessa Samuel, the stylist, was sitting on the steps sipping an iced tea and listening to her ipod. She was a leggy brunette, with the high cheekbones and broad mouth of a former model, and wearing a white bikini top and a pair of denim shorts cut high up her legs.

'Dan wants me in something else. What do you suggest?' asked Summer.

Tessa walked into the trailer and began flicking through the racks of swimsuits, bikinis and kaftans. 'What does Kaiser want you to wear?' she said sulkily.

'Kaiser?'

'Karin,' smiled Tessa. 'She told me this morning in no uncertain terms that *she* was creative director of the shoot and would be choosing all the outfits.'

'What are you here for then?'

'Dunno. Decoration,' she smiled, playing with her gold hooped earrings. 'I've been like a spare part all bloody day. Still suits me getting paid to do nothing.'

'Well, she's gone back to the hotel, so I think you'd better pick something out,' replied Summer, taking a cup of water from the cooler.

'That's right, she's got her boyfriend coming, hasn't she, lucky bitch,' sniffed Tessa. 'Have you ever met him? Sexy as fuck. Too good for Kaiser.'

Summer laughed. 'I've seen Adam. Never met him, though. Men like that scare me a little. Too good-looking. Too rich. *Too much*. I'm sure Karin can handle it though.'

'A man can never be too sexy or too rich,' said Tessa, her fingers speeding through the racks. She pulled out a tiny white bikini and handed it to Summer.

'Try that. You've got the body for it.'

Summer stripped off and poured her curves into the bikini. 'It's a bit small,' she said, struggling to fasten it. 'Can you help me?'

'Your tits are massive,' grumbled Tessa, pulling the white strip of Lycra tight across Summer's back.

Summer breathed in, the fabric like a straitjacket across her chest, and walked out of the trailer, feeling fat and uncomfortable.

Karin hadn't wanted to miss a second of shoot time, but she knew she had to freshen up before Adam's arrival. She'd almost jumped for joy when she had told Adam about the shoot in Anguilla and he had suggested coming along so they could tag a few days in St Barts at the end of it. But the fact that Summer Sinclair was also going to be there had made her feel a little nervous. The young model was looking fabulous. Too fabulous, thought Karin, considering Adam's imminent arrival. Her eyes, an iridescent lavender in the bright Caribbean sun, exuded the right amount of both sensuality and innocence. Her incredible body – her slim hips and round, voluptuous breasts – was sexy and womanly. She was a goddess; perfect for the campaign. Karin knew that thousands of women would want to look like her. But the last thing she wanted was *Adam* to want her.

She picked out a sheer printed Ossie Clark kaftan, chic and sexy, showing the outline of her perfect figure underneath. She wasn't going to try and compete with Miss Sexpot down on the beach; she had her own brand of potent sexuality.

Taking a seat by the plunge pool of her suite, she heard the door clatter open and a bellboy put Adam's expensive-looking leather suitcase on the bed.

Adam followed behind him; he walked onto the balcony and wrapped his arms around Karin's waist. He looked good, in cream trousers and a Hermès belt, leather flip-flops and a pale blue Lacoste shirt. He had the smooth olive skin that tanned in seconds and had already caught some sun across the bridge of his nose.

'Fancy a dip?' he smiled, walking over to the minibar and pouring himself a vodka miniature.

'Tempting,' she smiled, walking back into the room, 'but I've got to be at the shoot.'

'Of course. I can't wait to see the master at work.'

She knew it was the truth and threw him a dazzling smile.

He opened his case and changed his T-shirt.

'Marcus said that the model is Molly's daughter,' he said, climbing into the golf buggy that was to take them to the beach.

'Small world, hey,' replied Karin, putting her hand on his knee.

'Apparently Molly was angling to get a lift in the jet and come over.'

'Well I'm glad *that* never happened,' said Karin tartly. 'She'd have been sneaking off to take coke every two minutes and no doubt taking her daughter with her.'

Adam laughed. It was a throaty, knowing chuckle. 'I'm not sure what you have against the poor woman. You make out as if she's Keith Richards or something. She doesn't seem that bad at all. In fact, Marcus seems to really like her.'

'She likes Marcus's position in your company. She's a fortune-hunter, plain and simple. She likes the drinks invitations to your house, the little weekends in St Moritz courtesy of Marcus's bank balance. He should be careful.'

'Marcus can look after himself. Anyway. Is she hot?'

'Who?'

'Molly's daughter.'

Karin turned and frowned. 'What? Hot like Molly?'

'I didn't mean it like that.'

'Well, you can see for yourself,' said Karin moodily as they rounded the corner and the white strip of beach, fringed with palm trees and a sweep of emerald ocean, came into view.

Summer was back in the surf by the time they had reached the beach and walked over to where Dan was peering into his camera.

'Look at me like you wanna have sex with me, Summer,' shouted Dan, his tousled head bobbing up to watch her.

'Dream on, Dan,' laughed his assistant Mike, adjusting the silver bounce board at right angles to Summer.

Summer stretched out on the beach, where the waves were breaking on the shore, letting white surf swirl under her and tickle her stomach.

'Is this okay?'

'Gorgeous,' shouted Dan.

Summer looked up. She could see Karin and Adam walking towards the shoot from the hotel. Adam looked directly at her and smiled as Summer suddenly felt very exposed and naked. Shit, he was good-looking, she thought, fiddling with her bandeau top to pull it up a little higher. She felt self-conscious enough on shoots as it was – she had never learned to fully relax in five years of modelling, but it was easier when she wasn't surrounded by good-looking men.

'Dan, I told you not to start without me,' snapped Karin, fanning herself with a magazine.

'There's only another hour of good light.' Dan was peering into his camera, not bothering to look up.

'Why is she wearing that thong with a bandeau?' Karin asked, looking around for Tessa. 'They're not a set.'

Tessa came running clumsily over the sand with an armful of swimsuits. 'Do you want to change it?'

'Of course I want to change it. Get the chocolate-brown tankini.'

'It looks good to me,' smiled Adam, who had his arms folded and was watching the action intently.

Karin looked at Summer lying in the sand like a wanton sea siren. In the tiny white thong, her buttocks rose out of the sand like two perfectly ripe peaches. She had to admit she looked sensational.

A big wave swooshed onto the shore and Karin heard a ping.

'Argh!' screamed Summer, as her bandeau top popped off and was swept away along the beach.

Tessa scampered after it as Summer lay rigid on the sand to stop her breasts being exposed to everyone.

Dan Stevens kept peering intently into his camera. 'Summer, honey. Can you just relax your expression and let's keep shooting?'

'But my top!' she said with a half laugh.

Karin saw immediately what Dan was thinking. 'Yes. Just trust him.' The image in front of them, Summer, almost naked and glorious, was more potent.

Her mind whirled into action. She could see the billboard in her mind, crystal clear. A potent image, a provocative shout-line. This campaign was going to be sensational. It was going to cause a stir. It was going to make Summer a star, she thought with a grimace.

Shooting wrapped at six.

Adam treated everyone to a lobster supper at the clapboard seafood restaurant on the seafront and, as darkness fell, everyone adjourned, drunk and happy, to the Beach Barbecue that the hotel threw every Wednesday. A steel band played a Bob Marley medley. Dan was helping himself to a second dinner, piling a huge mountain of jerk chicken onto a plate, Mike the photographic assistant was chatting up the make-up artist.

The beach was swarming with guests from the hotel. A bonfire crackled, its orange flames leaping into an ink-black sky.

Karin sipped a little rum punch and felt smug. Summer stood alone at the water's edge, dipping her toes into the cold, foamy surf, glad it was over, daring to think it had been a success.

'You were really great today.'

Summer stopped listening to the waves on the shore and looked up to see Adam. 'Sure I didn't look like a porn star?'

'Have you seen any porn magazines recently? Believe me, they don't look like that shoot this afternoon.'

Summer could feel herself blush in the darkness and looked over to the bonfire to avoid his gaze. 'We've only just met and we're talking about porn,' she laughed nervously. 'Believe me, I'm not that kind of girl.'

'And I'm not that kind of guy,' he smiled.

'So we can call it quits.'

'We'll never mention the p-word again.'

'Or I'll tell my mother you're a bad influence.'

'And I don't want to get on the wrong side of her,' laughed Adam. The silence hung like a charge in the air and it made Summer feel suddenly uncomfortable.

'I'm going back to the hotel. It's been a long day.'

She had already started walking away from him. When she looked over her shoulder, back at the surf, he was still standing there watching her and lifted his hand to wave.

From this distance she felt safer. She smiled as a happy buzz hummed around her body, scolding herself immediately for feeling it.

Karin had changed into a long white strapless jersey dress. A long silver turquoise pendant fell between her collarbones and her hair was swept up into an elegant chignon. Excluding Summer, she was the most beautiful woman at the party. Including Summer, she was the most stylish. She had still kept her eye on her model all evening. She'd seen Adam watching her on the shoot and had been on red alert ever since, even though Summer, she begrudgingly had to admit, seemed a sweet girl.

Despite her sex appeal, Summer seemed to lack that predatory gene that constituted her mother's make-up, although it was Karin's mantra never to trust anyone.

Dan Stevens lolloped up to Karin, visibly drunk and waving a balloon of rum.

'What do you think my chances are with Summer?' he slurred.

'You're a married man,' laughed Karin, secretly hoping he might entertain Summer for the evening and diffuse the threat.

'Well, I need a distraction to keep me in check,' he smiled. 'Why don't you make a speech?' he added.

'What for?'

'A war cry. To thank everyone. Brainwash everyone into the Karenza message.'

Dan had a point. Karin did want to thank everyone properly. Everyone had worked their asses off. The campaign was going to be as good as anything Lauder or Gucci had ever done, but she had done it on the cheap. And she wanted to impress Adam.

She scanned the beach for everyone. There were only ten or so of them in their party, but she couldn't see anyone. More importantly, she had lost sight of Adam and Summer.

She felt sudden unease and checked the crowd again. 'Have you seen Summer?' she asked Dan urgently.

'I think she's gone back to the hotel.'

Yeah right, thought Karin, striding across the sand. She walked to the barbecue, which had stopped cooking. The chefs were dancing in the area around the band, which had been turned into a makeshift dance floor. There was a huge throng of people on the beach now.

Honeymooners slow-danced in other arms, kids twirling their arms ran and in and out of middle-aged couples, who held hands and moved awkwardly to the sounds of Bob Marley's 'One Love'. Adam and Summer weren't there or by the bar.

A few people had milled out further along the sands, where the beach blurred into blackness, and Karin walked towards them. After a few minutes of walking across the cold sand, she saw a couple ahead of her by the edge of the water. It was silent out here now. All she could see of the party was the orange furry glow of the bonfire.

An icy chill shivered down her spine as she marched over. She could make out Adam from a hundred metres, recognizing the navy shirt he had changed into. But the other woman. It was hard to identify her as she was naked except for a pair of briefs. She stood like a statue at a distance, watching the woman splashing in the surf, tempting Adam to join her.

Forcing herself to move closer, her hands curled into a tight fist. The long brown mane of the girl's hair swished away from her face so Karin could make out who it was.

Tessa.

Karin was twenty metres away when they saw her approach. Tessa ran over to a little pile of clothes sitting on the sand, her breasts like two round tanned tennis balls bouncing in the air as she fled to grab her T-shirt.

Adam turned round and looked straight-faced.

'We were just going swimming. Are you coming in?'

Karin felt a lump in her throat. She quashed every urge to stop a scream coming out of her mouth, but took a deep breath and smiled thinly.

'I wouldn't want to spoil your fun,' she said tartly.

'Karin, wait,' said Tessa still pulling her T-shirt on.

'Get out of my sight, you little tart,' snapped Karin. 'You're fired.'

Tessa grabbed her shorts and sandals and ran off along the beach.

Karin exhaled and waited a moment before she said anything.

'It wasn't how it looked,' said Adam, running his hand through his hair.

'Of course it wasn't,' said Karin sarcastically.

'She just wanted to go skinny dipping.'

'You've humiliated me, Adam,' she said coolly. 'I hope she was worth it.'

'Nothing happened,' he said, moving towards her. 'I had all my clothes on.'

Karin snorted. 'I bet that's what Bill Clinton told Hilary.'

Adam was shaking his head. 'I came to Anguilla to have a good time. With you.'

'That's not how it looked two minutes ago.' She could feel an aggressive wobble in her voice and suddenly Adam's expression went from sympathetic to defensive.

'Can we let this go?' he snapped, his eyes looking moody. 'It's not even as if we're exclusive.'

The comment was like a slap across a sore cheek.

'Exclusive?' She had never dated an American before. Did exclusivity have to be spelled out? Written in blood in a contract? 'Forgive me for getting the wrong end of the stick, but flying out halfway across the world to be with someone sounds pretty exclusive to me.'

She looked out to the inky-black sea, feeling a tear pricking at the back of her eye. She bit her lip to stop it escaping and turned to him shaking her head. 'Do you know what? Forget it. If that's how you feel, then I shouldn't care about what's happened as much as I do.'

Adam stretched out a hand towards her. 'Kay. I'm sorry. Let's talk about this. I do care about you.'

'Clearly not enough,' she said steadily and began to walk back to the hotel, determined to keep her pride.

17

Working for the Midas Corporation had taken over Erin's life. In an average day she might take a helicopter to a development site, set up meetings in Miami, Kazakhstan and LA or spend hours locating a specific type of vintage wine or rare sculpture – all at Adam's whim. She had become on first name terms with the PA of every business giant and, after Adam had insisted on giving her a clothing allowance – he had politely suggested that she smarten up her image – she was starting to feel completely at home in the high heels and designer suits she now wore to the office. Erin's life had changed beyond all recognition, and she was beginning to really enjoy herself. It was true she simply didn't have time for a social life, but then who needed to be sitting in a loud, smoky pub when you travelled private?

As usual, Erin was exhausted by the time she reached the front door of her new apartment block. At least it was still early, she thought, glancing at her watch: 8.30. It had been a hard day; a hard week, in fact. Adam had returned from Anguilla a couple of days early with a sexy hazelnut tan and a very bad temper, and he had been making her life a misery ever since, picking at every detail. He had gone ballistic at the finish on the limestone flooring in the Chelsea Marina development and had demanded that the whole thing be redone. Erin had barely been off the phone for six hours straight.

'Alright you?'

Erin had spotted Chris Scanlan standing at one end of the hallway, sifting through his post, and had tried to walk softly over the marble tiles in the hope of not being seen or heard. No such luck; he turned and grinned.

'Hard day at the office?' he asked with a sympathetic look. She couldn't work out if he was making fun of her.

'You don't know the half of it,' she said, walking briskly to the lift. 'I wish I could say I'm going to drown my sorrows with a glass of wine, but I just haven't had time to do any shopping.'

Chris grinned at her mischievously. 'Well, you certainly have the right neighbour, Miss Devereux.'

She was surprised he knew her surname. No doubt been nosing around the post.

'In what way?' she replied defensively.

'Didn't I tell you what I did for a living?'

Erin shook her head. Ever since she had moved to Peony House, any contact with her neighbours had been limited to a few cautious hellos.

'President of Moet et Chandon?' she asked, looking at his slightly shabby suit. She surprised herself by having noticed it; a month before she wouldn't have been able to tell Savile Row from a shell suit.

'Close,' he said, entirely seriously. 'I am the food and drink editor for the *Herald*. I dare say I can rustle something up from my cellar.'

Erin felt her face flush with embarrassment. 'Oh, I didn't know,' she stuttered, 'I really wasn't trying to scrounge a bottle of wine from you.'

'Come on. You know you want to,' he teased. 'Anyway. I hate it in London when you don't even know your neighbours well enough to borrow a cup of sugar.'

Judging by the number of women she had seen going in and out of number twelve, Erin wasn't entirely sure if she was safe going round to borrow a bowl of sugar. On the other hand, she would just love a chilled glass of Sauvignon right now.

'I'll even throw in a bowl of risotto,' he added.

Erin hesitated. How much she would love right now just to curl up on her sofa underneath a blanket with a hot drink, quiet music and just rest. But she was hungry and she knew that her fridge was full of wilting vegetables that she had bought with moving-in enthusiasm, but had never had the energy to cook.

'Okay,' she nodded. 'Thanks, that sounds good.'

Chris's flat was smaller than Erin's. Just a big room that doubled as a lounge and a kitchen that was surprisingly tidy. There were two big grey sofas, a heavy oak coffee table with a few empty wine glasses and a bookcase bursting with books. The kitchen area looked like Harrods' food hall, stuffed with olive oils, vinegars and exotic fruit and vegetables. Chris ran over to the stove where a big pan was simmering and stirred frantically.

'You do surprise me, Chris Scanlan,' said Erin with a smirk.

'Why?' he asked, looking up from tasting a spoonful of the rice.

'From where I usually see it – my front door – you seem to live off pretty girls and cigarettes. But this – well, it's a picture of domestic bliss.'

'I think there's a compliment in there somewhere,' he said cynically, picking out a bottle of white. He poured two big glasses, and handed Erin one.

'I assume it's the high-powered job makes you all uptight and prickly. What do you do again?'

She told him and took a sip of the wine. It felt good on her lips, like grass and gooseberries. 'And I am not uptight and prickly,' she said, spilling a droplet of wine on her skirt.

'Course you're not, Prickles,' grinned Chris, then picked up a black, coal-like lump and started shaving it into the steaming risotto.

'What's that?' asked Erin, drinking in the deliciously earthy smell.

'Hey, don't admit you just said that to your billionaire jet-setting boss,' replied Chris, handing Erin a bowl. 'They're truffles. King of the mushrooms.'

She looked at him, raising an eyebrow. 'Aren't they an aphrodisiac?'

'You're not my type, Prickles, so stop panicking and just enjoy it.'

Erin did as she was told. The truffles melted on her tongue like a musky butter. 'Wow – they're fantastic! I could get used to those.'

'Easy, Tiger,' smiled Chris. 'They cost a fortune. You'll have to marry your rich boss if you want truffles as your teatime snack.' She felt a warm rush at the mention of marriage to Adam. *Stop it*, she scolded herself.

'So why are they so pricy?'

'Well, you wouldn't believe the trouble it takes to get that to your plate,' said Chris. 'About ten years and a lot of paranoia. Truffle hunting is shrouded in so much secrecy. In some areas of Italy, only the father of the family knows where the truffles can be found, and the secrets are passed down from generation to generation.'

'Gosh, sounds like the basis for a thriller,' said Erin.

'Hmm, maybe that's the answer to my literary impasse,' said Chris.

'How do you mean?'

Chris looked a little sheepish. 'Well, I am writing a book. Actually I've written two, although neither of them have ever been near a bookshop.'

'Really?' asked Erin. 'What sort of thing? Cookbooks?'

Chris shook his head. 'Horror.'

Erin nearly choked on her risotto. 'Horror? How . . . odd,' she said lamely. 'You are a dark horse.'

'Hey, don't knock horror, young lady. It's one of the biggest commercial genres in the industry. Look at Stephen King.'

'Well, yes. Precisely,' she teased.

'Anyway, I've just been binned by my agent but –' he drained his wine glass with a flourish '– I will continue. Stephen King only got his break when his wife rescued his notes for *Carrie* out of the dustbin, and the rest is history.'

Erin was shaking her head and laughing. 'Actually I'm writing a book too,' she said, greedily scraping the last of her risotto from the bowl.

'Look who else is full of surprises,' smiled Chris. 'I didn't think you would have time to put pen to paper with all the international jet-setting.'

'Stop being cheeky. I am a lowly PA with a dream,' she said smiling. 'But you're right. I've got an agent but no time,' she added, realizing she hadn't even opened her laptop for at least three weeks.

'I tell you what, Prickles,' said Chris, putting his feet up on the coffee table. 'Let's have a competition. By the end of the year, let's see if one of us can get a publishing deal.'

'Okay!' said Erin, suddenly enthused about her book once more. 'And every competition must have a prize.'

Chris flicked the rim of his glass. 'I've got it – whoever gets the first book deal has to take the other out for a meal of their choice in any restaurant in the world.'

'That's not fair!' complained Erin, 'you can go anywhere for free!'

'Hey, don't assume that I'm going to win.'

She blushed. He was cute. 'Okay, you're on. But out of interest, where would you like to go?'

'I've never been to the French Laundry in the Napa Valley,'

replied Chris seriously. 'Thomas Keller is one of the world's best chefs.'

'Napa Valley,' spluttered Erin. 'I was thinking more like that gastro-pub at the end of the road,' she smiled.

'Well you'd better get on with winning, then!'

They clinked glasses and, as she let the wine slither down her throat, a light giddy feeling washed over her.

She extended a hand to Chris and he shook it. 'It's a deal. But there's one more thing.'

'Name it.'

'Don't call me Prickles.'

18

At 7 a.m., the morning after her showdown with Adam, Karin had packed her bags and left for the airport. She didn't leave a note; she just wanted to be out of there. Waiting in the queue at check-in, she called Christina Levy. Years of experience in these matters told her that Christina was a woman who believed that no crisis was insurmountable and that anything could usually be solved by a therapeutic trip to Hermès or a weekend in a Mediterranean hot spot. As luck would have it, Christina wasn't in London, but escaping the grim British winter on her husband's 250-foot yacht, the *Big Blue*, currently anchored in St Barts' Gustavia Harbour. Within minutes, Karin had bought a flight ticket to St Barts, and by lunchtime she was on board the *Big Blue*. Well, she reasoned, as she stretched out on the top deck with a cocktail, if she was going to drown her sorrows, she might as well do it on one of the most luxurious yachts in the Caribbean.

'I knew Adam Gold was too good to be true,' said Christina, sitting back on a day bed in a tiny white bikini, stroking the rim of her cosmopolitan. 'He's disgustingly handsome, but his manners are appalling. Skinny dipping with a stylist on your photo-shoot? I mean, who'd believe it?'

Karin knew her friend was trying to make her feel better, but she was still fuming. She felt tricked. Humiliated. Adam's lavish gifts, the nonstop attention, his cute 'Let's play hookey and spend a few extra days in St Barts' spiel – well, it obviously counted for *shit*. The second her back was turned he was like a dog on heat.

'Still, I guess you knew that he might not be the settling down kind of guy,' said Christina, trying to sound kind. 'So many

127

successful men are commitment shy these days. Divorce laws can be so punishing, you can almost see their point, can't you?'

Perhaps, thought Karin, but she wasn't defeated yet. Every instinct in her body told her never to see or speak to Adam Gold again – he was a two-timing shit who clearly didn't give a damn about her feelings – but she hated being beaten. Karin was always the hunter, the femme fatale who made her man beg for more, but now Adam had clearly shown her that he was the one with the power, the one who could take or leave the relationship, and she hated feeling so out of control. But damn it all, she still wanted him. And she wanted all *this,* she thought, looking around the top deck of the *Big Blue* and letting the soft, salty Caribbean breeze blow against her skin. She wanted the best – and Adam Gold could give it to her.

Christina caught Karin's wistful expression, and clapped her hands.

'More drinks!' she said sternly, summoning the waiter with a wave. 'I think that's enough moping about Adam, sweetheart,' she said. 'You are here to forget about him, not to spend hours obsessing about him. Listen, there are bigger, better, *richer* out there, Karin. Adam only just made it onto the *Forbes* list this year, for goodness' sake, and unless the Midas Group has a seriously good twelve months, he might not even stay on it.' She shook her chestnut mane over her shoulders and laughed. 'When I suffered at the hands of Flavio's *betrayal*, what did I do? I fought back.'

Christina's actions after her fiancé, tycoon Flavio Mendes, had run off with her best friend Maria two months before the wedding, were the stuff of Belgravia legend. Within weeks, Christina had hooked up with Ariel Levy, whom she had met at the Royal Academy's Summer Exhibition party. At Christina's behest, Ariel had acquired Flavio's company in a hostile takeover and Flavio's standing in the business community had dropped like a stone. He had tried to claw his way back, but every investment he made seemed to turn sour. It was whispered that Christina had been instrumental in making sure they did. Now Flavio and Maria were rumoured to be living in a three-bedroomed apartment in Alicante, while Christina had the run of twelve homes around the globe, use of a yacht, a private jet and two helicopters. For someone who had been a mediocre model, failed singer, and an actress with a nonexistent CV, Christina was a world-class operator in the art of men and marriage.

Karin looked around her and suddenly felt depressed. She wondered if it had been a good idea to come to St Barts after all. Karin might have a fat inheritance sitting in the bank and her company might be turning over millions of pounds a year, but compared to this – walnut decks, helipad, Picassos in every state-room – her life seemed decidedly parochial. She wanted this lifestyle so badly, she could feel the pain knot in her stomach. She felt lonely, wretched, powerless. She wanted to get off the yacht, quickly.

As if reading Karin's thoughts, Christina lifted her lithe tanned body off the white day bed and threw on a fine silk kaftan, which slithered down over her bronzed curves.

'What you need is a distraction,' she announced, motioning to the waiter, who sprang forward with her Hermès crocodile Birkin and jewelled flip-flops. 'We're going to Nikki Beach for lunch and then we'll do some light shopping,' she said, walking down the steps to the middle deck. 'Whatever you fancy: Ariel's treat.'

'Did I hear my name?' called a baritone voice from the far end of the deck. Ariel Levy was sitting at the table reading the *Wall Street Journal*. He had thick, grey curly chest hair, a small head with thinning hair and a powerful aquiline nose. He reminded Karin of old pictures of Aristotle Onassis.

'Karin needs cheering up. We'll only be a few hours,' said Christina, bending over to kiss Ariel's cheek. 'Do you want to have a late supper on board or shall we go down to Le Yacht Club?'

'I'm sure we will do whatever you choose to do in six or seven hours' time,' he said flatly, rustling the pages of his newspaper. 'Have a lovely time, ladies.'

'What's wrong with him?' whispered Karin as the girls climbed into the tender that would take them to shore.

'Just his grouchy, lovable self,' smiled Christina. 'Can't get enough of me, that's his problem.'

Nikki Beach was on the other side of the island on St Jean Bay, just across from the Eden Rock hotel where Karin had stayed many times for the St Barts New Year celebrations. They settled into a couple of white directors' chairs and ordered mineral water and salads.

'Who can I commission to do some nudes?' mused Christina.

Karin smiled. Her friend's conversation was like a butterfly flitting from one flower to the next, never settling too long on anything.

'And we are talking what? Photographs?'

'Of course,' said Christina sharply. 'I haven't the patience for anything else. Anyway, it's Ari's birthday soon. When we were first married I had a set of myself done by Helmut Newton, but now he's dead I need another genius who can capture me in the same way.' She ran her hands across her body. 'Although I must get some work done first, of course. I'm feeling a bit blobby.'

Karin gave a low laugh. 'You have an amazing figure.'

'Do you think so?' she replied eagerly. 'I'm doing this incredible work-out at the moment.'

'Oh yes? Which one?'

'I'm fucking the gardener,' giggled Christina.

Karin coughed on a crouton and Christina had to slap her back. 'Tina!' she spluttered. 'How? When? WHY?!'

Karin was genuinely shocked at Christina's confession – it was so completely out of character. Her friend had often told her about what she called 'Christina's Charter', which had only two rules. Rule one: the way to get a rich man is to give incredible head. Rule two: the way to keep a rich man is never, *ever* screw around. Christina was nothing if not pragmatic and, as a learned scholar of the minutiae of international divorce law, she had decided that fidelity was the foundation of a successful marriage.

'So – which gardener? Town or country?' asked Karin, referring to Christina's vast Mayfair home, one of the few detached private residences in W1, the Surrey mansion they had recently bought from an oligarch, or their vast shooting estate in Yorkshire.

'Our Surrey place. You know, I find it so fucking boring out there, but then he came along, *Jamie*, and now I can't keep away from the place ... Honestly, Kay, Ariel is so uptight these days. I'm not sure he can cope with a business that size,' she said. 'Anyway, he's making me feel so stupid and awkward these days, that the arrival of Jamie on the scene is such a release.'

Karin laughed out loud, beginning to feel a little bit better.

'And, honey, you'll find a way to fix it too,' said Christina, putting her hand over her friend's, the diamonds on her fingers sparkling in the sun. 'You'll fix the situation with Adam, if you want it to be fixed.'

Karin nodded. Christina was right; she had spent a lifetime getting what she wanted and, at thirty-one, at the height of her power, the height of her beauty, she wasn't going to let that situation change any time soon.

They stayed at Nikki Beach for a couple of hours until the cheesy Europop and self-satisfied Eurotrash spraying Cristal into the swimming pool started to grate. They moved on to Cartier, where Christina enquired about the possibility of a custom-made piece. Legend had it that, many years ago, Mexican actress Maria Felix had gone into Cartier in Paris with her pet baby crocodile and requested its likeness be fashioned into a diamond and emerald necklace. Christina had decided that she wanted something just as personal and unique, although she couldn't decide if she wanted a brooch in the shape of her chihuahua Kiki or a tiara in the image of a dolphin in honour of the *Big Blue*. By the time they reached the harbour's edge in Gustavia, the turquoise water had already deepened to cerulean in the late afternoon sun.

'Have I had too many cocktails, or am I seeing things?' asked Christina, looking unusually puzzled.

Karin had noticed it too. The *Big Blue*, which only hours before had taken centre stage in the sweeping crescent of Gustavia Harbour, was no longer there.

'Shouldn't it be where it was?'

Christina looked perplexed. 'Maybe Ariel's got bored and they've taken it round the bay,' she said, dipping her hand into the Birkin to pull out her phone. 'Let me call him.'

She angrily pressed a few buttons and cradled the phone to her ear.

'Dammit, it's going straight to voicemail. Where *is* he? This is fucking ridiculous!'

Karin instinctively knew something was wrong from the wobble in Christina's voice, a feeling that was confirmed when a black Mercedes pulled up beside them at the dock.

A stocky man holding an attaché case climbed out. 'Mrs Levy. Good afternoon,' said the man.

'And who are you?' asked Christina haughtily.

'Barry Rosen. I'm a colleague of your husband's. I have been instructed by Mr Levy to give you these,' he said, handing her a large brown envelope before turning back to the car. He opened the rear door and pulled out a suitcase that Karin immediately recognized as her own.

'I do believe these are all your belongings, Ms Cavendish?' he said politely, placing the case on the dockside. 'Mr Levy says he is terribly sorry to inconvenience you, but he has booked you into the Eden Rock hotel in St Jean, for which he will naturally pick up the bill.'

'What the *hell* is going on?' said Christina, her voice beginning to quaver. 'Where the fuck is the boat? Where the fuck is Ariel?'

'I'm afraid you'll have to contact your husband for those details,' said Rosen, before climbing back into the Mercedes.

'Where is he?' screamed Christina as the car pulled away. 'Where's my fucking boat?'

She tore open the envelope and scanned the contents, letting out a long guttural cry of despair as the truth sank in. Christina's legs buckled and she crumpled to the ground like a wounded animal.

Karin pulled the sheets of paper from Christina's trembling fingers and put an arm around her friend's shoulder to comfort her as she read them. There in black and white was confirmation that the lifestyle she had so coveted could collapse like a house of cards. Divorce papers. The *Big Blue* wasn't coming back.

Even though her body was telling her it was still the middle of the night, Erin could tell from the light pouring through a crack in the curtain that it was morning. She got out of bed, threw back the curtains and apricot light flooded into the room; the first bright sunny morning of the year. She took a deep breath and smiled. There was nothing like sunshine to remind her of home and, although she badly needed rest after her exhausting week, the lure of a perky spring morning was too strong; she knew she had to get out of the flat. Knocking at Chris's door, she was mildly disappointed when a woman had answered, but Chris had been good enough to offer her use of his bicycle and a dog-eared A–Z and she felt a small thrill of excitement at the prospect of exploring London on two wheels.

She bumped the bike down onto the street and swung into the saddle, feeling suddenly full of energy as she pedalled away. Her legs were still strong and fit from the daily walks she used to take in Cornwall, but this time the view was very different. No cliffs, hawthorn bushes and crashing waves. Instead it was red buses, black cabs and street-corner newspaper vendors. Everywhere she looked there were people: families popping into the deli, tired-looking workers coming back from late-night shifts and giggly girls in party clothes from the night before. She coasted down Rosebery Avenue, past the stately Inns of Court, by-passing the West End, bloated with shoppers and tourists, and made her way along the river, watching the boats tug up and down, the steely water twinkling in the sunshine. She kept pedalling until she found herself in Battersea, right by the crumbling power station. This part of town had never registered on her radar before now, but as she stood there by the river, she could feel the energy of the place, the air of expectation that surrounded an area in the middle of a regeneration as developers injected life back into the old buildings. She had always thought you had to be a writer or a painter to create, but here, in the heart of the metropolis, she could see that creativity was being driven by commerce. It was the developers and the businesses that were forcing this organic city to grow, building new places where people would live, work, eat and fall in love. Jilly was wrong to dismiss London as a faceless, impersonal wasteland where only fat-cat corporations could prosper. Here Erin could see little cafés, bars, boutiques and small businesses springing up, their owners full of excitement and expectation and she felt herself energized by the place.

She wheeled her bicycle a little bit further along the towpath and took a few random turns down backstreets, remembering a favourite game of when she was little – getting lost. Finally, she stopped outside a long row of black railings where she chained up the bike. There was a thick wedge of privets behind the railing, which made Erin instantly wonder what was behind them. She followed the railings until she found a rusty gate. Feeling a little naughty, she pushed it open and poked her head inside.

It was a beautiful old red-brick building. Its walls had been scrawled with graffiti, the windows were covered with chipboard, the drainpipes covered in moss. But the building itself was wonderful; proud and Gothic and just a little eerie, as if it had been an old workhouse. She looked up at the roof, which was missing half its slates, and thought that all those rooms hiding in its eaves would have magnificent views of the river and the Albert Bridge. She took out her mobile phone and used its little camera to capture the building's image. It was perfect for a Midas Corporation boutique development. She would find out who owned it and report it to Adam immediately. That would put a smile on his face.

19

Karin Cavendish was not at home to Adam Gold. She did not answer her mobile, screened her calls and refused to accept the huge bouquets and neatly wrapped gifts he sent to her home and office. Adam had started bombarding Karin with phone calls the second she had left Anguilla, but she had made him wait. On the third day after she'd returned from St Barts, she finally took his call.

'Well?' she asked.

'I want to make it up to you,' said Adam.

'You're going to have to do something special.'

Karin had agreed to have dinner at Adam's Knightsbridge duplex, but had maintained a frosty and aloof manner throughout the filet mignon and asparagus tips, concentrating instead on watching the London skyline spread out in front of them. Karin knew she was playing a dangerous game, but she wasn't going to take Adam's behaviour lying down: she simply couldn't. If she sat back and accepted it without a grumble, where would it end? Even if she did get him up the aisle, Adam would still assume she was the dutiful, unquestioning consort, prepared to turn a blind eye to absolutely anything. No, she would be giving him carte blanche to fuck anything that moved – and she had no doubt he would take full advantage of it. Of course, they both knew he could have any woman in London he chose, but Karin had a sneaking suspicion that Adam would respect a woman who played hard to get and who put her foot down. So she had carefully selected an outfit of skinny jeans, high heels and a fitted McQueen jumper and she had been encouraged to see that Adam had pulled all the stops out. His chef had prepared a fabulous supper of meltingly rare beef followed by a pistachio soufflé and the wine was an excellent Chateau Lafite '83. The lights were low, the music soft. Unless she was much mistaken, this was his way of saying sorry. But Karin wanted to hear Adam say it out loud.

'So, what did you want to talk about?' she asked with faux innocence.

Adam shrugged, breaking off a corner of Poilâne bread and swirling it around a small, shallow dish of olive oil.

'I want to talk about Anguilla,' he said.

'I thought that conversation was closed,' she said coolly, enjoying her moment.

'It is,' said Adam. 'I don't want to talk about that, I want to talk about you.'

Karin was taken aback. 'Don't you mean you want to talk about *us*?' she said.

Adam looked at her, gauging her, assessing her. 'Anguilla was my first proper brush with the Karenza brand and I was impressed,' he said, 'very impressed.'

'Are you referring to seeing a Karenza bikini up close? Oh sorry, I forgot; Tessa wasn't wearing one.'

Karin immediately regretted saying it, but she couldn't help herself.

A silence prickled between them, but Adam wasn't going to be deflected by Karin's sniping. He carried on, ignoring her comment. 'As you may know, the Midas Group acquired a building in St Tropez last year,' he continued. 'It's a prime location right by the port and we've spent the last nine months developing it.'

'Residential?' asked Karin, immediately interested, her business instincts sensing an opportunity.

Adam shook his head. 'No, a hotel, which opens next month, under management by the Sarkis Group of Hotels. However, twenty-five thousand feet of the ground floor is being kept aside for retail. A couple of luxury brands are taking units there, plus a yacht charter company, all pretty high end. However, one of the best units has just become vacant; you know what I think it would be perfect for?'

Butterflies were fluttering around Karin's belly. 'Karenza St Tropez.'

Her breathing had quickened now. She had long realized that if

135

she was going to launch the swimwear brand on a global scale, she had to expand internationally. She was stocked in Fred Segal in LA, Neiman Marcus in Miami and a select handful of other concessions in upmarket shopping districts, but a store would give her brand identity much greater impact.

'It's something I've already considered,' said Karin, trying to keep the excitement out of her voice, 'either a Malibu, Palm Beach or St Tropez outlet. But I would need to look into financing, and location obviously is key. It is possibly a little early for expansion so, if we are going to do it, we need to hit the bull's-eye first time.'

Adam smiled. 'I think you'll find there is no better retail location in St Tropez. It is also a small unit, so you shouldn't be over-stretching yourself.'

She looked out at the twinkling London skyline, adrenaline coursing through her like a sexual thrill. Karenza St Tropez! It was perfect! But she was damned if she was going to show her enthusiasm to Adam.

'Well, it's a big decision . . .' she said, toying with the stem of her glass. 'Somewhere like Palm Beach would possibly be better as a first international outpost – more year-round appeal. St Tropez is a ghost town out of season.'

Adam went into sales mode. 'But Palm Beach means expanding into America – that's a big step. Too big, possibly for now. I would have thought St Tropez is a better initial fit. Granted you'll only be in business for six months of the year, but for those months the market will be brisk and the target audience perfect. Plus it's close to London so you can keep tight control on it.'

His eyes flirted with hers. 'Why don't we fly down this weekend at least and have a look at it?'

'Adam, slow down, please,' said Karin, excited but still wary. She stood up and took her wine to the window, staring out into the dark night. She was tempted, really tempted. Business wasn't about remaining static, it was about moving forward – and now was the time. Worldwide sales were brisk; her financial director Ed Sassoon had been urging her to find other sites while turnover in both Karenza UK stores was so healthy. Not that Karin was afraid of the expansion, either. She wanted Karenza to grow from a niche swimwear line into the ultimate jet-set brand as soon as possible but, for that, she needed serious investment. Jimmy Choo had pulled it off, while Erès had been bought out by Chanel after thirty years. Well, Karin Cavendish wasn't going to wait thirty years. She looked into Adam's eyes. 'I really must look into the company's financial position before we continue this conversation,' she said, suddenly the in-control businesswoman. 'Karenza is wholly owned by myself and I want it to remain that way for the foreseeable future.'

'In that case, don't you want to hear me out?'

Karin eyed him suspiciously. 'What are you proposing?'

'That I take a small percentage of the business in return for the St Tropez outlet. I can get Marcus and our team to work out a fair shareholding . . .'

'You have got to be kidding!' she said fiercely. 'You could be potentially getting something as valuable as Gucci – and for what? The price of the rent on a beach boutique? I really don't think so!'

She saw that Adam was chuckling. He beckoned her back to the table. When she was close, he curled his hand around her waist and pulled her onto his knee. She tried to move away, but he was strong, nuzzled his lips into her neck. 'This isn't always how I conduct my business negotiations,' he murmured into her neck.

'Well, I have made my position clear,' she said, trying to remain firm, but a small smile beginning to curl on her lips.

'You're no pushover, are you?' he said, releasing her.

'I thought you'd have worked that out by now,' said Karin, holding her head high as she sat down opposite him and poured herself another glass of wine.

'So we'll leave it that I'm turning down your proposition, shall we?' she said, dabbing the corners of her mouth with a napkin.

'It was worth a try,' he smiled. 'However, the offer still stands.'

She tilted her head in question. 'I want you to take the unit,' he said.

'Adam, I am not giving you a share in the company,' she responded tartly. He held up his hands in surrender.

'Look, take the unit. Have it rent-free for the year. It will do the development good to have the Karenza brand on the site. And, if you ever bring out a men's range, just remember to keep me in shorts,' he grinned.

Karin almost burst out laughing, but knew she had to contain herself. She subtly pulled at her top to give a flash of cleavage and flicked a curtain of raven hair over her shoulder.

'It's a very generous offer,' she said finally, 'but one I can't accept.

You may remember telling me when we first met that you never mix business with pleasure.'

Adam stood up and walked round behind her, putting his hands on her shoulders, letting his fingers slide under the thin jersey of her jumper. 'So you see yourself as pleasure, do you?' he breathed huskily into her ear.

She let Adam's hands glide deeper and deeper under the sheer fabric while maintaining a cool, professional voice. 'I'll consider the St Tropez store carefully but, if I accept, I insist that we pay you the full market value.'

'How about we look a bit more into that pleasure you were just talking about?' he purred. 'And then maybe we'll see if we can't come to some arrangement. Full market value is an awfully high price to pay.'

She turned to face him, pushing her fingers between the buttons of his shirt. As they kissed, Karin opened her eyes and smiled. She knew that she had played it perfectly.

20

They were going to Nobu Berkeley Square for lunch. For a second, Erin had felt nervous when Adam had suggested it, but she was sure she hadn't done anything wrong; and anyway, would he really take her to a swish eatery if he was planning to fire her? Think positive, she told herself, as she applied her make-up with extra care that morning; he probably just wants to dictate a letter. But she had worn her new Diane von Furstenberg wrap dress all the same.

As they walked into the restaurant, all heads turned. Erin was getting used to the reaction; the presence of a New York billionaire still set tongues wagging six months after his arrival in London. The difference today was that she wasn't trailing six feet behind him, carrying an armful of papers and folders, mobile locked to her ear, harassed and stressed. Today, Erin was by his side. And it felt good.

'Would you like me to order for you?' asked Adam as they settled into the banquette seat. 'The yellowtail sashimi is particularly good.'

The only Japanese food Erin had ever had was Prêt à Manger sushi, although her tastes had been on a definite upward curve since the truffles in Chris's flat. She could now tell her cosmopolitans from her caipirinhas but, looking at the menu, she still had no idea what sashimi was. Or yaki for that matter. She wanted to tell Adam that she didn't want anything raw, but she knew that wouldn't exactly give the idea of sophistication she was striving for. 'Yellowtail it is then,' she smiled, hoping it wouldn't make her sick.

'I really should have taken you out for lunch before,' said Adam, summoning the wine waiter, 'but I don't need to tell you how busy we are.'

Erin willed herself to say something funny or witty or clever, but instead all she could do was sit there.

'I don't know what your career plan was before you started at Midas,' he continued, 'Something about interpreting or translating, wasn't it?' Erin nodded. She hadn't told him about her novel. While Adam was always banging on about the importance of using the best creatives – by which he meant interior designers or architects – she doubted he would hold much truck with authors. Writing a novel was hardly Wall Street.

'I know working for Midas fell into your lap, but I really think you have a long-term future with the company – if you want it, that is.'

Erin blushed at the praise.

'You're bright, resourceful and you have a good eye.' He pointed a finger in the air to emphasize a point. 'That building in Battersea you brought to me was a gem. It will make a nice acquisition for Midas's senior apartment division. There's a growing demand from the over-fifty-fives who want design-led properties in city centres.'

Erin thought of Jilly and her group of friends living in trendy apartments opposite the Thames and giggled. 'The retired people I know live in cottages and make Cornish pasties. I can't see them popping out for cappuccinos.'

'Rule number one, Erin,' Adam said seriously. 'Don't think about what people want or need now. You have to be predictive. Remember that the new generation of pensioners grew up listening to the Beatles. Old people are pretty cool now. You've always got to guess what people are going to want in five years, even ten years.'

She'd read enough about Adam by now to know that was exactly how he had made his money. People had laughed at him after the 1992 crash for going into property, buying up skyscrapers and developing disused warehouses in unfashionable parts of town like Tribeca, but he'd been able to cash them in as they became trendy.

'I want to learn from you, Adam,' said Erin, hoping she didn't sound too gushy. 'I'd love to get more involved.'

'What do you like about property?' he smiled, taking a tuna roll between chopsticks. 'What do you like about our business?'

She had come out for lunch, not an interview, but she couldn't choke now. She took a sip of green tea and thought back to the moment when she had found the Battersea building and the adrenaline rush it had given her.

'It's creative,' she said, her face flushing slightly, 'and kind of romantic too. You come across a building. Maybe it's neglected, or no one wants it, or maybe *everybody* wants it and you have to head the competition off at the pass. You develop it, nurture it, and then, just as you've got it how you want it, you have to let it go.'

Adam was smiling to himself and nodding. 'I've always thought the process was a little like a love affair, too.'

His green gaze met hers and Erin felt a flutter of excitement. 'You won't know this,' said Adam, 'but Eleanor handed her notice in to me this morning. She's going back to New York.'

'Eleanor leaving!' said Erin. 'But I thought she was devoted to you.'

'Well, it seems "was" is the word,' he smiled. 'Apparently I worked her so hard she didn't socialize, never went to parties or bars and consequently she never met anyone. But then a couple of weeks before she was due to come to England, she fell in love with some guy who works for FedEx who kept coming into the office to pick up my packages.'

'You can't begrudge her that,' laughed Erin.

'Of course, I'm happy for her. Anyway, that leaves a vacancy as my executive assistant.' He paused and stared at her while Erin felt her heart stop.

'Me?' she asked quietly.

'Erin. This is a considerable step up from what you're doing now. This isn't just diary dates and RSVPing to parties. You have to be my eyes and ears. You'll be making decisions that affect the company. You know that some CEO's exec assistants have MBAs from Harvard? Well, you've got my faith.'

Erin's head whirled. Adam made it sound like an honour. He made her feel special. He made her feel wanted. Erin looked at Adam and she wanted him right back.

'I won't let you down,' she said.

21

Clutching a handful of retouched photographs from the Anguilla shoot, Karin took her freshly squeezed raspberry juice out onto her bedroom's roof terrace to decide which of the glorious images of Summer Sinclair she was going to use for the Karenza swimwear campaign. For the first week of April it was unusually warm. The air smelt fresh, of grass, spring flowers and promise. It was the perfect morning to plot, plan and think, if only there wasn't that terrible clatter coming from the guest bedroom.

This is the last time I play Good Samaritan, thought Karin crossly, swatting the photographs down on the wrought-iron table. Out of the goodness of her heart, Karin had allowed Christina to move in. It was only a temporary arrangement, she had made that clear – or at least she thought she had. Karin tutted and tried to read her copy of *Vanity Fair*, but she just knew she was about to get summoned at any moment.

'Kay! *Kay!*' Christina's shrill voice cut through the peace. Used to a maid, chef, butler and masseur at her beck and call, Christina was seemingly unable to grasp the fact that Karin was not hired help. She was constantly bombarded with requests, demands and criticisms of her lifestyle: 'What do you mean you don't have a chauffeur? You drive *yourself*?' 'What's the thread count on these sheets?'

'Karin,' said the voice, more irritable now.

'What do you want?'

'I need you.'

Sighing, Karin got up and stalked back through her bedroom and onto the landing, where Christina was standing in a pair of ivory silk pyjamas, one sleeve rolled up. She looked pathetic and helpless and Karin instantly regretted her irritation; after all, Christina had been through a lot since they had returned from St Barts. Ariel was petitioning for divorce on the grounds of adultery, and Jamie Bacon, their new organic gardener, had been cited in the papers. Christina was stunned – it was the only time in the seven-year marriage she had been unfaithful and she'd been caught out royally first time. She knew that British divorce law was not apportioned on blame, but she didn't want to take any chance with the settlement.

'What's wrong?' said Karin. 'Do you want to borrow a dressing gown? I'm afraid you'll have to put up with La Perla.'

'I don't want a dressing gown,' said Christina tartly, 'I want you to go and get a camera.'

'A camera, whatever for?' asked Karin, following Christina into the guest bedroom, which was crowded with Goyard trunks and shoe boxes, couture dresses spilling over every surface. She grimaced at the mess. She *hated* mess.

'I want you to take a photograph of *this!*' said Christina dramatically, rolling up the sleeve of her ivory silk pyjama top to expose a slim, tanned arm. Just below the shoulder was an ugly lilac and blue bruise.

'Urgh! What's that?' asked Karin.

'A huge fucking bruise! What does it look like?' snapped Christina, pushing it in front of Karin's nose. 'Go on, get the camera out. I need a picture.'

'Whatever for?' asked Karin, examining her friend's skin more closely.

'Evidence,' replied Christina flatly.

'Did Ariel do this?' whispered Karin, frowning. 'He didn't hit you, did he?'

For a moment Christina refused to meet her friend's eye. 'Not exactly,' she replied.

'What do you mean, "not exactly"?'

Christina sat down on the bed, crushing a number of expensive silk gowns as she did. She looked up at Karin and pouted. 'He didn't exactly hit me, no. But he could have!'

Christina saw her friend's disapproving look and shrugged. 'Look, I went round to the house yesterday to pick up some more things. I mean, *everything* is still there. My riding boots, my Norma Kamali vintage jump suit, that pretty little yellow diamond Graff necklace I wanted to wear to dinner tonight. Everything!'

Karin pursed her lips. Her home wasn't a hotel.

'Anyway, I get there and he has only changed the fucking locks! Consuela wouldn't let me in either. Said Ariel had strictly forbidden it. Can you believe the nerve of the woman? I sorted out her visas, for Chrissakes. She would still be in Manila sweeping shit off the street if it wasn't for me.'

'But why's he changed the locks? Has it turned nasty already?'

'Not half as nasty as it's going to get,' snapped Christina. 'I think it's because I sent all his suits to the Salvation Army. If you know any men with a forty-four-inch chest and a thirty-inch leg you should tell them to get down there.'

'Yes, but what's all this got to do with the bruise?' said Karin glancing at her Cartier Tank. It was 10.30 a.m. Adam was due in thirty minutes and she still hadn't put on her make-up.

'I was forced to enter through a window,' said Christina grandly, as if she was giving evidence in court. 'Consuela always leaves one open when she is cleaning. I mean, imagine the humiliation of it. Anyway, as I was climbing in, I banged my arm on the ice machine. But, as far as my lawyers are concerned, Ariel did it when I was trying to collect some belongings. He *assaulted* me.'

'But he didn't,' replied Karin. 'I'd be an accessory!' She understood Christina's tactics but was making her sweat a little in return for all the jibes about her chauffeur and sheets.

'He *could* have done,' repeated Christina. 'Oh, you've got to help me Kay, I can't take chances. We have a pre-nup. The courts might not take any notice of it but, if they do, I'm fucked. One million for every year we've been married? Jesus! That'll buy me a three-bedroom maisonette in South Ken if I'm lucky. I'll have to have the prix fixe at San Lorenzo,' she added, shuddering.

'So what's the bruise got to do with anything?'

'Everything,' she whispered. 'My lawyer told me that a recent case has revived the concept of blame in divorce. It can affect the payout. At the moment it's my word against his, and I've got photos to prove it.'

Karin scooped her hair up into a ponytail, shaking her head. 'There's a Polaroid camera in the dressing room for the shoes; do it yourself if you must. Listen, I'm going to Adam's friend's house tonight. Will you be here?'

'I'm tempted to give Jamie a call. I feel so uptight, I could do with a release, but I had better keep my nose clean,' she said with a wink.

Karin laughed and Christina wandered off in the direction of the dressing room.

Karin sat at her carved mother-of-pearl dressing table. She rubbed some tinted moisturiser onto her face, added a little blusher on the apples of her cheeks and a slick of lip gloss. She wondered idly how Christina's life would change. One minute she was in a detached house in Mayfair with a staff of seven, a private jet at her disposal and nothing to do except plan the next extravagant party. The next minute she was in Karin's spare room, forging criminal injury, and sneaking around after a twenty-two-year-old labourer. She was sure that Christina would land on her feet, although she also suspected that Ariel would play dirty to hold on to his fortune.

The doorbell ding-donged. She slipped on a pair of Tod's loafers, picked up her holdall, carefully packed for a weekend in the country – trainers, jodhpurs, silk dress, and a tiny coffee-coloured lace teddy she had picked up in Paris – and ran down the stairs. Adam was standing at the door holding the car keys to his Aston Martin. He smelt of pomegranate cologne, soap and shaving foam.

'Are you ready, honey?' he asked. 'I said we'd be there in time for lunch.'

'I just have to get my coat,' she said, running to the concealed closet in the hall for an acid-yellow leather jacket, perfect for the bright, fresh morning. As she turned back towards the front door, she saw Christina coming down the curving staircase. Her dark, wet hair was scraped back off her face, her damp body glistening like diamond dew, covered only by a minuscule white towel that stopped at the top of her thighs. She tiptoed over to Adam to give him a light kiss on the cheek.

'You two have a fabulous time,' she smiled, before springing back up the stairs, sending a coquettish smile over one shoulder.

Adam was grinning like a Cheshire cat while Karin picked up her holdall and walked to the car without another word, vowing that she'd have that bitch out of the house as soon as she got back to London.

Standing in front of the dressing-room mirror in the master bedroom of The Standlings, Marcus Blackwell's Buckinghamshire farmhouse,

Molly was in an whirl of indecision about what to wear for lunch. Adam Gold and Karin Cavendish were coming for the weekend and she wanted every detail to be just right. She had changed outfits half a dozen times, trying to anticipate what Karin would be wearing; Molly's outfit had to trump her, but only in a very subtle way. With Marcus out at the local golf club, she had tried on the entire contents of the increasingly large wardrobe she kept at the house. She decided on a elegant scooped-necked dove-grey jersey top with bracelet sleeves, perfectly offset by a pair of deep indigo jeans so tight and sexy they made Molly's long legs look even longer. Her hair was left long and tousled, and she finished off with a handful of gold jangly bangles and some chocolate-brown loafers. It was a look that said modern, off-duty chatelaine.

Walking over to the long windows overlooking the grounds, her eyes were drawn out into the distance, where the Chiltern Hills beckoned and a pale blue sky stretched out, cloudless, above a sweep of russet trees. Even though Molly had only been dating Marcus for a couple of months, she felt quite at home at The Standlings. Their relationship was progressing quickly and, ever since she had been fired from the PR company, she had practically moved in, complaining to Marcus about 'being cooped up all day in Kensal Rise'. With time on her hands and a need to impress her new boyfriend, Molly had discovered quite a talent for keeping house. Although she had taken to describing The Standlings to friends as 'the manor', in reality it was a substantial eighteenth-century red-brick farmhouse with ten acres of grounds. Marcus had bought the place from a wealthy elderly couple three months earlier, and it was badly in need of some TLC. Declaring the farmhouse far too chintzy for the vice president of a luxury property development company, Molly had persuaded Marcus to embark on a programme of renovation and redecoration, which, of course, she would supervise personally. Kitchen planners from Mark Wilkinson had already visited, and they had decided on Tuscan-style units, granite worktops from Germany, and an island in the middle of the room on which Molly fantasized about having sex with a handsome live-in French chef. Still, that was all to come, and the unrenovated Standlings would have to make do for this weekend. Not that Molly had left anything to chance. She had commissioned her favourite West London florist Orlando to create huge centrepiece blooms of red roses and lilac rhododendrons all over the house, which made the house smell as if it had been dipped into a bottle of cologne. A local caterer had just delivered huge bowls of salads, freshly prepared lobster ravioli and tiramisu, all of which she fully intended to pass off as her own, and bottles of Cristal were chilling in the fridge.

She was just sitting down at the farmhouse table, sipping a small tumbler of vodka-tonic to kick-start the day, when she heard the grumble of Marcus's Maserati on the driveway and stood up to see Adam's black Aston Martin following close behind.

'Molly. Good to see you again,' said Karin, trying to inject some warmth into her voice as she slipped off her jacket and looked around the farmhouse.

'I thought you weren't getting here until one,' smiled Marcus, embarrassed at just beating his guest home.

'Oh, Adam drives so fast I thought we were going to take off,' she smiled.

Karin had to admit Molly had done a good job in the lounge; if you liked that English country house sort of thing, of course. Ruby-red velvet curtains and squashy chocolate-brown sofas blended with antique cabinets and beautiful lamps with bronzed sculptured bases. More quaint than luxurious, thought Karin; certainly not the sort of place Karin had in mind for Adam: that would be a very special property indeed. Something Grade I listed, perhaps, in the Cotswold triangle, with an arboretum, trout fishing, possible previous royal occupiers. She would enjoy the search when the time came – *if* the time came. Karin had felt needled all the way up to Buckinghamshire, unable to shake off the image of Christina parading herself in front of Adam like the Venus di Milo – how *dare* she? And he didn't help matters, lapping up the attention. Still, she felt better now, as she eased herself back into the soft leather of the sofa, feeling comfortably superior. Sitting next to Adam, his hand lightly placed on top of hers, she felt like the prom queen with her king. She had never considered Molly a serious player in the social stakes and, watching her sitting beside her latest conquest, Marcus, in her too-tight jeans, only confirmed Karin's opinion while bolstering her own credentials. Marcus was a decent enough bloke – intelligent, yes, sober, a little dull, but he was an also-ran; one of life's runners-up. The second tier country house, the vice presidency, his pleasant but nondescript looks. Karin felt a little sorry for him, wondering how long it would be before Molly traded him in for a better model.

'Is it true you have Christina Levy staying with you?' asked Molly with faux concern. 'Awful, what's happened to her.'

The St Barts story was circulating like wildfire around London – a cautionary tale for anyone getting too comfortable or careless in their relationship.

'Oh, I thought she looked pretty good for a woman who has just been dumped,' smiled Adam, taking a sip of chardonnay. Karin's good mood suddenly evaporated. She felt her back stiffen, removing her hand from his, and darted a look to Molly. Karin was convinced she had just suppressed a smile.

'Speaking of which, Molly, how are you shaping up after leaving Feldman Jones?' she asked with equal concern. 'Lindsey can be such a cow. I'll spread the word around to avoid using the company.' Like hell she would.

'Yes, Marcus told me about this,' said Adam. 'Are you okay?'

'Oh, it's fine,' said Molly, waving a hand. 'Lindsey and Sophie were getting greedy, that's all, they didn't want to split the pot three ways and I was ousted. It happens in business.' She directed a smile at Adam. 'And I have a pretty good track record. I'll find something better.'

'What about the Midas Group?' asked Adam casually. 'I think our PR department could do with being bolstered by someone with an events bias.'

'Really?' said Molly, brightening visibly. 'That would be great.'

'Is it a good idea to work so closely with Marcus?' asked Karin tartly.

Adam scoffed. 'The only thing Marcus has to do with our events is turn up. Even then you're not too keen, are you?' he laughed.

Marcus shrugged. 'I haven't got a problem with it if Molly hasn't. And it might stop you spending all my money on the house,' he said, smiling at Molly.

Karin felt her guts twist. The thought of having Molly working so closely with Adam was intolerable. Events! What was that? Late-night corporate schmoozing with booze and drugs and goodness knows what other aphrodisiacs.

'But I thought you were more of a figurehead at Lindsey's company,' said Karin. 'Did you actually do any events planning?'

Karin wanted to kick herself. It had come out snippy and ungracious. As Molly turned to smile sweetly at Adam, Karin knew that she had to be careful and clever.

'I think there's enormous overlap with what I did at Feldman Jones and could do at the Midas Group. Corporate entertaining has become so competitive and it's vital to compete if you want to send out the right company message. I've worked with the best caterers, planners, florists in London and—'

Adam held a hand up and laughed. 'Stop! Stop! I'm here for lunch, not to interview you. Let's hook up in the week to iron out the details. Now, did somebody mention lobster ravioli?'

Karin look a deep swallow of her wine and could taste only bile. Men could be so bloody stupid.

Molly felt dizzy with pleasure. Three glasses of wine had gone to her head, lunch had been a success and even Karin had commended her on the tiramisu.

'A little something I whipped up this morning,' Molly had replied. 'I can give you the recipe.'

But the thing putting her on such a high was the job offer and the look on Karin's face when Adam had suggested it. *Well, honey, that was just the start of it*, thought Molly, as she poured out four espresso coffees into her tiny Wedgwood cups. *A few intimate private meetings with Adam and he'll forget all about you.*

'Oh, bugger,' said Marcus, slapping his pockets, his eyes looking around the room, 'I think I left my mobile at the golf club. I'd better go back and get it. Why don't you all take the horses out for an hour?'

'Sounds good,' nodded Adam.

Karin threw an arm round him. 'You ride? Is there nothing this man can't do?'

'Disgusting, isn't it?' laughed Marcus. 'Expert skier, ruthless businessman, and didn't you row for Yale?' he grinned.

'Guilty as charged,' said Adam immodestly.

'Do you mind if I give the riding a skip?' replied Karin. 'I've got a stiff shoulder from a Pilates class. I might go and read in the bedroom. The view is so pretty.'

'Fine. Let's all meet back here in an hour.'

The stables at The Standlings had been a pleasant discovery for Molly when she had first visited. She had never suspected that

Marcus was a keen rider, but he had proudly explained that his mother had been a national standard eventer who had brought up her children to love all things equestrian. Marcus, however, had spent twenty years living in Manhattan ('the nearest I got to a horse was the jockey statuettes outside the 21 Club,' he had joked), so as soon as he arrived in England, he had sought out a property with stabling and horses. Now was her chance to take advantage of it, thought Molly, as she rushed to the master bedroom to pull on her riding boots. She looked at herself in the mirror and felt a rush of anticipation. She felt so horny. Sitting opposite Adam all lunch had almost made her wet. He was without question the sexiest man she had ever met and it was quite incredible that he was absolutely loaded as well. The presence of Karin had only served to heighten her desire, not quash it, firing a competitiveness that was almost a sexual thrill in itself.

She strode to the stables with a spring in her step. There was a small yard, strewn with hay, and she could hear the neighing of Marcus's chestnut gelding Olympia. Molly walked inside and her face fell. In the stable, tacking up and preparing to mount the horse, was not Adam but Karin.

'Oh, hello,' said Molly flatly.

'Expecting somebody else?' said Karin archly. 'Oh, yes. It was Adam wasn't it?'

'And what is that supposed to mean?' asked Molly, her disappointment turning to anger.

'Oh, has the strain of making lunch taken the edge off your razor-sharp mind?' said Karin flatly. 'You'll work it out.'

'I'll have you know I worked very hard on—'

'Oh give me a break,' mocked Karin. 'I'd be very surprised if you could boil an egg. I'm not entirely sure how long you can keep us this Martha Stewart charade up, but at least Marcus seems taken in by it. By the way, what happened to poor Harry Levin after you got him to pay for all that Mozambique rain-forest?'

'Leave Harry out of this,' said Molly thinly.

'The Standlings was a more attractive proposition than a discount tit job?'

Molly was staring at Karin with undisguised rage. 'You rude bitch,' she whispered.

Karin shrugged. 'Astute rather than rude, I think you'll find.'

Molly took two steps towards Karin, making her flinch. The

150

horse caught the movement and tossed its head, snorting. 'Ooh, feeling nervous are we, Karin?' smiled Molly, taking another step. 'I don't think you liked Adam's suggestion that he and I start working closely together.'

'Don't you mean waitressing at a few of the firm's parties?' scoffed Karin. 'No sweetheart, I'm not really worried about that.'

'You should be,' said Molly, her eyes narrowing. 'You really should be.'

The overt challenge made Karin catch her breath and fired up her fury. 'Don't even think about threatening me, you opportunistic whore,' spat Karin, unable to keep her cool.

'You're just a washed-up, gold-digging little coke-head. It might take Adam and Marcus a little while to see it, but we both know what's under that sweet smile.' She moved down the stables towards Molly, slapping a riding crop against her thigh.

'This little setup with Marcus is the very best that an old hag like you is going to ever get, so I'd hang on to it, darling,' she said. 'Don't think that you can trade it up for something shinier, because you can't. He's mine.'

'Oh yes?' said Molly coolly, putting her hands on her hips and standing her ground, the two women now facing each other, eyes locked. 'For someone who's not threatened, you sound awfully rattled.'

'Rattled?' laughed Karin smugly. 'I don't think so. In the meantime, a word of advice . . .' She smiled sweetly and pointed the whip at Molly. 'Don't ever think about crossing me, Molly, because, if you do, I will become the biggest bitch you've ever seen.'

They stood there, neither woman moving an inch, until suddenly Olympia whinnied and stamped, breaking the deadlock.

'Coming, sweetie!' called Karin, still not taking her eyes off Molly. Then she turned on her heel and walked back to the horse, taking the reins to lead him out of the door.

'Oh, and Molly?' she said, turning and throwing the riding crop so that it went skittering across the cobbles to land at Molly's feet. 'I think you might be needing that more than me.'

22

Adam Gold personally received about 5000 items of post a week. Gifts from clients, promotional items from companies keen to get the Midas Corporation using their goods or services, letters begging for money, letters begging for jobs, even crazed paternity demands from women Adam had never met. It was Erin's job in her new role as Adam's executive assistant to sift through this mountain and dig out the possible gold: speculative brochures and particulars of property for sale that Adam might be interested in looking at. In a single day she would come across lighthouses, stately homes, rows of terraces in inner-city slum areas, even billboards and telegraph poles, all up for sale, all wanting Adam Gold's attention.

It had not taken Erin long to work out the sort of things Adam would be interested in. Acres of wasteland in strategic locations, interesting architecture, hotels with heritage. If it was struggling to gain planning permission, so much the better: Adam had the planners in his pocket. That particular morning, Erin was leafing through a high-end estate-agent's brochure, flipping past more of the same – Edwardian terraces, new-build faux-farmhouses, bland country estates – when suddenly she stopped. It was gorgeous. A perfectly formed Georgian terrace. It instantly reminded her of Peony House, only a pocket-sized version. She quickly read the particulars. The location was hardly Belgravia: it was in a little pocket in Crystal Palace. Erin felt elated, excited. And slowly an idea began to germinate. She had spent the last four months sitting outside the office of one of the greatest property developers in the Western world. She had listened. She had learned. She had met scores of businessmen and -women who had started with next to nothing and had built up a development fortune. Property. It was the way to make money for people in a hurry. And Erin was starting to get itchy feet.

Jeremy Sergeant, head of auction sales at Rachman Estate Agents, had been having a bad day when Erin had called. His girlfriend of seven months, Miranda Coulston, was having a hissy fit because Jeremy was taking his mother instead of her to the Rachman annual party. This meant that Miranda would not get to meet – and, as she saw it, seduce and possibly marry – George Rachman, the super-loaded, very single owner of the business. Not that Miranda was expressing it in those terms. 'You can forget about ever seeing that Myla lingerie you bought me,' was how she put it. And she had already called him three times that morning to remind him. When Erin walked into his office, however, wearing a Marc Jacobs skirt so short that it made him swallow his morning latte rather too quickly, Jeremy's day began to improve.

He had fixed the appointment immediately when she had called him, introducing herself as an executive from the Midas Corporation. Sergeant knew all about Adam Gold – who didn't? Midas was one of the biggest players in London now and, to anyone with an interest in property, Adam Gold was a superstar. Jeremy was actually feeling a little nervous about meeting someone who worked alongside him.

'Good of you to see me,' smiled Erin with a confidence she didn't feel, handing him one of the generic Midas Corporation business cards she kept in her top drawer. 'Let me get straight to the point,' she said, after he had shown her into his office. 'I work very closely with Mr Gold but, as you can imagine, he delegates a lot of the smaller acquisitions.'

Jeremy Sergeant smiled to himself and nodded. She was awfully young, he thought, but terribly pretty. Typical of the Americans to surround themselves with gorgeous little ball-breakers like this one. He offered a cup of tea and then settled back in his Eames chair to admire the view. Erin snapped open her briefcase and took out the auction brochure.

'So, how can I help you?' he asked. 'Will a representative of the Midas Corporation be attending the auction on the fifth? As I'm sure you've seen, there's a lot of fabulous property with bags of potential. Longton Ness, for example . . .'

Longton Ness was the jewel in the crown of the auction, a Grade I listed, fifty-bedroom Palladian stately home in Oxfordshire. It was the ancestral home of the aristocratic Montague family, but they were being forced to sell it off in lots to meet crippling death duties. Jeremy had been running a sweepstake in the office on who would buy it. Jeremy had £100 on Gupta Roy, the Indian steel magnate said to be shopping around for a country estate. But you could never discount the stately home being bought up by a developer to turn into more luxury apartments.

'Obviously, I can't reveal all the Midas Corporation's plans this early,' said Erin smoothly, although inside her stomach was churning. 'But there are certainly a number of lots that have taken Mr Gold's fancy,' she continued, taking a delicate sip of tea.

Jeremy smiled. With the Midas Corporation in the room, bidding on the properties could go crazy. Thirty, maybe even fifty per cent more than the guide price. He smiled at the amount of extra commission he could make for himself. Enough to take Miranda on that week to Reethi Rah in the Maldives that she was always banging on about. That'd get her lingerie out.

Erin picked up the brochure and opened it to the page marked with a Post-it note. 'The property that had immediately caught our attention is this one,' she said, pointing at the miniature Peony House. Jeremy looked puzzled.

'Hmm, not a typical Midas acquisition then?'

Erin laughed politely. 'No, this wouldn't be for commercial development. Adam is keen to acquire a property to be used as company apartments for Midas junior personnel coming over from New York.' She felt sick at telling the lie, but if there was one thing that she had learnt from her short time at Midas it was that you sometimes had to be economical with the truth to get what you wanted.

'Oh, I see,' said Jeremy, smiling. 'And with the new East London line . . .'

'Precisely,' said Erin, filing the brochure back in her briefcase to stop her fingers from trembling.

'The thing is this, Jeremy. We want this property quickly. We have the interns coming in October, and there is obviously considerable renovation needed on it to make it habitable.'

Jeremy nodded.

'So what I am proposing is that you take it out of the auction, accept the guide price now and we can complete within, say, four weeks.'

Jeremy steepled his fingers in front of his lips. 'Well, I was expecting this SE19 to go for considerably more than the guide price,' he said cautiously. 'The area is something of a hot spot, what with the improved transport links and so on. At auction it could go for—'

'You would be doing the Midas Corporation a considerable favour,' interrupted Erin. 'In fact, we're having a cocktail party at The Sanderson on the fifteenth. It would be lovely to see you down there; we can talk about how our two companies can work more closely together in future. I know Adam is looking for an agent for one of the Canary Wharf developments.'

Jeremy's eyes lit up like a Roman candle. Some of the Midas developments were worth millions: hundreds of millions. If he could be responsible for brokering a deal like that, he'd be made partner in no time.

'I suppose Belvedere Road is really a very inconsequential lot,' he said slowly. 'It's a probate property; I'm sure I can persuade the vendors to take it off the market for a very quick sale.'

'You understand that we'll only pay the guide price?' said Erin, holding her breath.

Jeremy waved a hand. 'Fine. Let me make a few phone calls and we can get this ball rolling. And can I just ask? Could I bring a plus one to the party?' he said. Miranda had always said how she'd love to meet Adam Gold.

23

Molly waited until 7.30 p.m. before she made her move. She left her small cubicle in the Midas Events Department and rode up to the executive floor, where Adam, Marcus and the Midas top brass had their offices. Marcus had left the building a couple of hours earlier for a business dinner with one of their main contractors, but Molly had learnt from Adam's mousy assistant Erin that Adam would be working late. Molly's first job at Midas was to plan Adam's birthday weekend, to be held in Monte Carlo during the grand prix, and it was the perfect excuse for regular tête-à-tête with her boss.

As the lift hissed open, Molly found herself surrounded by shadows. Most of the lights were off, with the odd grey glow of a computer screen adding an eeriness to the scene. Molly walked down the long corridor towards Adam's office, her heels tapping lightly on the polished floor. She had taken particular care over what to wear that morning. A pair of slim tailored black crêpe trousers skimmed every curve, her four-inch slingback Manolos exaggerated Molly's long legs. Her fitted shirt was unbuttoned just a shade too low for the office, and worn without a bra, so that when Molly had grazed her fingers over her nipples during the short journey in the lift, they had stood to attention like hazelnuts. Molly knew she looked good, powerful and sexy, like a Guy Bourdin model.

As she got closer, she could see a shaft of light coming from Adam's office and, peering through the crack, she could see him bent over his desk, reading a document under a blade of lamplight. He looked up as she tapped lightly on the door.

'You're here late, Molly,' he said, putting down his pen. She noticed him rake his eyes over her body as he motioned her to sit. 'I'm just finishing up here myself.'

'I've been making some calls to Monaco. It's taken me all day to get through to some people.'

He motioned to a decanter of bourbon on a table by the window. 'Drink?'

She nodded, willing him to make it a good measure.

'So, how's it going?' he asked, handing her a tumbler. 'As I'm sure you've discovered, the team have solid business PR backgrounds, so I'm really glad you can bring some flair to our entertaining.'

'Well, parties are what I'm good at,' smiled Molly, sliding back in the chair and crossing her long legs. She liked this; the pair of them sitting in half light, Adam's desk a barrier between them like the chessboard in *The Thomas Crown Affair* when sexual tension crackled between Faye Dunaway and Steve McQueen.

She looked up and he was staring at her. 'So?' he asked, a slight smile on his lips.

She picked up the see-through folder she had been carrying. 'I wondered if you had a few minutes to go over the plans for your birthday party in Monte Carlo, but if you have to dash off . . .'

He glanced at his watch and shrugged. 'No. It's fine, I have a few minutes.'

To Molly's annoyance, Adam meant what he said. If he had initially appeared interested in the curve of her breast underneath her thin shirt, now he wanted a swift summary of the menus, schedules and whether he could get into the royal box to watch the grand prix. Molly leant even further forward in her chair so her elbows rested on Adam's desk, hoping he could get a glimpse of her deep cleavage. She glanced up and saw the scene reflected in the darkened window behind them, his back strong and muscular underneath his white gleaming shirt, her cheekbones accentuated by the lamplight. *Oh, we look so good together*, she thought, a smile playing on her lips. *We fit.*

'You're in a hurry. We can do this tomorrow,' she said, hoping she could goad him into offering another drink.

Adam leant back and pulled his jacket off the back of the chair. 'You know what? Let's do that,' he said, as Molly's smile instantly disappeared.

'I said I'd go round to Karin's, and I'm sure you're seeing Marcus.

He has the most dull dinner guests at the Savoy tonight, so he'll be glad of your company.'

Molly stood up quickly, irritated but not beaten. Men usually fell like dominos when she was looking this hot, but if Adam Gold was going to play hard to get, then fine. She would bide her time. There would be other moments like this, of that she was sure. But still, she didn't want to waste the moment.

'It's probably out of place for me to stay this,' she said carefully as he slipped his diary and laptop into his briefcase. 'But I'm glad you've come along for Karin after everything that's happened.'

Adam smiled. It was a mischievous 'I'm-not-sure-I-believe-you'-smile, but a smile all the same.

Molly pressed her point. 'You obviously know about the death of her husband Sebastian last year,' said Molly gravely.

'Of course,' he nodded.

'It was such a difficult year,' said Molly, shaking a tumble of hair from her shoulders. 'I mean the loss of a partner is bad enough, but then having to cope with that whispering campaign? Well, that's got to be tough for even the most strong-minded of people.'

Adam's eyes narrowed and she knew she had got his attention. 'Whispering campaign?'

Molly pretended to look flustered. 'Oh, I . . . I'm sorry,' she stuttered. 'As I say, it's none of my business. I'm sure Karin will tell you in her own time.'

'Molly, tell me,' said Adam, looking cynical. 'What whispering campaign?'

Molly paused. 'About how Seb fell off the yacht.'

Adam raised an eyebrow. 'But he was drunk. The man sounded like an alcoholic.'

'Yes, but people said the most wicked things,' said Molly softly.

'Just tell me, Molly,' snapped Adam.

'People were saying that she pushed him off.'

Adam laughed, although it sounded hollow in the empty office.

'That's just fucking ridiculous,' he said with a half-smile. 'I think someone, somewhere has an overactive imagination.'

Molly's expression remained earnest as she continued. 'You're right, there was clearly nothing in it. I did hear that a *Vanity Fair* journalist was sniffing around the story for one of those society crime stories they like doing, but I don't remember seeing it run, so there obviously wasn't anything to find.'

'No, no, of course not,' said Adam. Molly's eyes searched Adam's face, which suddenly looked a little more anxious.

'Poor Karin,' said Molly quickly. 'But, as I say, it's good she's found you. She deserves a break after all that.'

Adam smiled, but his thoughts were clearly elsewhere as he gathered his things and showed Molly out of the office.

'Have a lovely time tonight!' said Molly cheerfully as she turned and stalked off down the corridor, swinging her hips as if she was on a catwalk. If Adam could have seen her front, he would have seen a wide smile break out across her face.

Erin could hardly believe how easy property developing was, particularly when you were creative with the truth. After leaving Jeremy Sergeant in the Rachman offices, Erin immediately made an appointment at the bank. The Midas Corporation banked with one of the large multinationals, and Barty Clark, the firm's client manager, ran through the spectrum of options for buy-to-let mortgages.

Erin needed a £400,000 mortgage to cover buying the property and the renovation costs. The problem was, despite her small inheritance, she didn't quite have the twenty per cent deposit required by the bank.

'I know you work very closely with Mr Gold,' said Barty, peering over his glasses at Erin. 'Will he be making any input in your project?' he enquired.

'Adam is my mentor and is very supportive with me,' she said, trying not to grimace.

Barty nodded slowly then, seeming to make a decision, ticked a few boxes on the application form. 'Congratulations, Ms Devereux,' he smiled, 'I'm sure you'll make a great deal of money on this venture. I look forward to helping you invest in it.'

Erin walked out onto Lombard Street with a sigh of relief. It was amazing how many doors the name Adam Gold opened. At this rate she would be able to buy the real Peony House by the end of the year. A sense of unease rattled around at the back of her mind, but she tried to squash it immediately. Adam had faith in her. He'd told her so, and to be a success in business you needed confidence and front. The rewards were worth it. She smiled and wondered if there was time to pop into Gucci before she headed back to the office.

24

The Midas Corporation had worked a miracle. By giving Molly a purpose, it had turned her into a power-suited, arse-kicking businesswoman. Efficient, driven and no-nonsense, she strode around her office in spiked heels and pencil skirt, barking orders and watching with a satisfied smile as her minions jumped. Midas – or Marcus, to be precise – had put her in charge of organising Adam's birthday party on board the 245-foot company yacht *The Pledge* during the Monte Carlo Grand Prix. It was a huge job and, to the surprise of everyone, not least of Molly herself, she had thrown herself into it with an energy she usually reserved for pursuing men. Even though the cosy catch-ups with Adam she'd envisaged hadn't quite come off, Molly suddenly felt as if life was full of possibilities – and she was actually enjoying herself, bossing people around and keeping an eye on every last canapé. And Molly knew where every last honey-glazed fig skewer would be at any point, just as she knew exactly how many bowls of Krug would be on every table. Molly had found that her attention to detail was second to none when she knew that Adam would be judging her; she was going to make his party fabulous or she was going to die trying.

'Adam wants a full rundown of where we're up to with planning,' said Molly to Erin, 'so I want to know which guests have confirmed and who is staying where. I need all the schedules from the limos to the fireworks. I need to know *everything*, Erin.'

It was Saturday lunchtime, the day before the race, and Molly and Erin had been there since the previous night, checking that every last detail was perfect. Erin Devereux was scribbling into her notebook at high speed, keen not to miss anything that came out of Molly's mouth. The girl irritated Molly – she was too strait-laced, too eager to please when Adam was around – but she had decided that, as Adam's executive assistant, Erin could be useful, so she had taken a softer line with her. 'Do we have final numbers on the confirmations, darling?' asked Molly with an over-wide smile.

Erin looked in her big leather-bound journal. 'Sixty-three,' she said, 'but I don't know where they're all going to stay. Rooms at the big three hotels in Monaco have been booked for months.'

Molly smiled, happy to show off. 'Don't worry,' she said, tapping her nose, 'I have my ways. Twenty people will be at the De Paris – that's the top tier of friends who aren't staying on the yacht. The yacht can sleep twenty, tops, but the Hermitage is beautiful too and we have another twenty there. And I've got a couple of villas on stand-by in Roquebrune. Adam said it's not a milestone birthday so he didn't want to make too much fuss, and I advised we keep it small and exclusive, manageable. I think he'll prefer it that way,' she added smugly. 'Okay, so read me back the schedule.'

Erin cast her eyes down the list. 'We have the drinks reception which starts seven p.m. Saturday. Sunday, there's brunch on the yacht from ten thirty. Two o'clock, watch race. Seven p.m., cock-tail party. Midnight, everyone moves to Jimmy'z nightclub.'

Molly walked to the window, nodding her approval and mentally adding the other 'off-piste' events she had also scheduled. A table had been booked for lunch at the Moulins de Mougins, the smart restaurant in the tiny gastro village a thirty-minute drive away. Reflexology was available at Les Thermes Marins, the delicious spa whose floor-to-ceiling windows overlooked the harbour. Molly smiled, satisfied the event would be a success.

'Are we sure we'll be able to keep everyone to the timetable?' asked Erin, who was just as keen for this party to go without a hitch.

'Yes, well, there will be a bunch of other yacht parties,' said Molly confidentially. 'But to be honest I think everyone is going to want to come to Adam's.'

She smiled to herself. She was sure of it.

Down the road in Menton, Summer tried not to feel as if she'd been short-changed. She was only three miles from Monte Carlo, but Menton was a world away from the glitz and glamour of the neighbouring principality. She looked around the dingy hotel room and sighed. She supposed she should have been grateful; after all, she was here to see her friend, not the celebrities. Sarah Simpson, a bubbly blonde party girl who had been Summer's flatmate in Japan, had just returned to London, where she had landed a job fronting a reality show about the rich and famous called 'On Heat'. As a way of catching up, Sarah had invited Summer to come along to the first weekend's filming at the Monaco Grand Prix. Having been brought up on Molly's glamorous stories of Monte Carlo – Princess Grace, the Red Cross Ball, the De Paris – Summer had jumped at the chance, but the Menton Auberge was not exactly the Hermitage. One room served as bedroom, lounge and kitchen, there was no air-con, and the only window opened onto the eight-lanes and diesel fumes of the Cannes–Milan autoroute. Just then, Sarah wandered in from the bathroom, wearing only bra and knickers.

'One of us is going to have to get lucky tonight,' said Sarah pointing to a very small sofa bed underneath the window. 'Because two of us are never going to fit on that thing.'

Sarah pulled a Cavalli cocktail dress from her case and hung it on the curtain rail.

'I can't believe the production company have put me up in this dump. You wouldn't get Cat Deeley putting up with this shit,' she sniffed, pinning up her hair carelessly. She was unkempt, thought Summer, but she was sexy. She was far more suited to TV presenting than modelling: curvy, boobs, full lips and slanting grape-green eyes. Plus Sarah had a definite look – unpinned, sultry sex kitten – rather than the bland chameleon looks that so many of the big models had right now; models were, after all, a blank canvas onto which you could paint the client's desires. Sarah was the real thing. Maybe a little too real.

'So, tell me about this party tonight,' said Sarah, flopping into a chair and lighting a Gauloise.

'Shouldn't you be working?' asked Summer.

'Nah. The researchers are already scouting out places where we can film, people we can talk to. People like your mum's friends, in fact. So I suppose I am working really.'

Summer smiled thinly. She was not exactly looking forward to spending another night out with her mother, even if it did mean they would be moving among the richest of the rich. Molly had, of course, been delighted when Summer said she was going to Monte Carlo. Even for someone with Molly's front, it had been simply too awkward to ask Adam if Summer could join the select number of guests for the birthday weekend, but the drinks reception was more of an open-house invitation and Summer and Sarah were on the list for the soiree on Adam's yacht that evening.

'It's fine for us to go to the party,' said Summer nervously. 'But I'm not sure Adam and Karin will be happy about a camera crew coming onto the yacht.'

'Relax,' smiled Sarah. 'Who mentioned anything about a camera? We're there to mingle, baby.'

Summer looked at Sarah and smiled ruefully. There was a look in her eye that she recognized only too well: social ambition. Sarah didn't want to go home with a showreel. She wanted to find a boyfriend. A rich boyfriend. Her friend was turning into her mother.

Karin was enjoying Monte Carlo already. She had been several times before, of course: twice to the grand prix, once to the annual music awards and a couple of times to the Red Cross Ball. But today felt special. Today she was here with a powerful connected billionaire, staying in the master suite of one of the sleekest yachts in the harbour. Previously, she had just been a yacht-hopping guest among thousands in Monaco's packed harbour. Today she felt a special sense of belonging; she felt as if this could become a habit.

Perhaps it was their dramatic entrance that had begun her good mood. Adam's jet had flown into Nice Airport that morning and they had got a helicopter straight to Monte Carlo's heliport. A sports car was waiting for them and they had then zipped through the narrow Monegasque streets, the breeze whipping Karin's hair around. Now, pausing while she dressed for the evening, she looked out of the picture window of their suite at the stern of the yacht and sipped a glass of chilled champagne with a soft smile on her lips. The sun was lowering in the sky, casting Monaco in an apricot light. It looked just perfect.

'Pretty good weekend to have a birthday, huh?'

Adam had approached Karin from behind, wrapped his arms around her and clinked his own champagne flute against hers. Karin was only wearing her bra and pants and his hand trailed up and down her taut stomach.

'Did you have to make this a work thing?' said Karin sulkily.

They could hear Adam's banker clients drunk and guffawing at the bow of the yacht.

'Oh baby, I wish it was just us too,' said Adam, kissing her on the neck. 'But *The Pledge* is officially the company yacht . . . and you know what it's like: when it's your own business, you can't switch off.'

'So who's the blonde?' asked Karin, pulling away from his embrace and moving over to top up her glass, trying to sound as nonchalant as possible.

'Just a banker baby,' smiled Adam. 'Don't give me a hard time'

'I'm not, I'm just curious. She's definitely not your typical banker.'

'She's called Claudia Falcon,' said Adam, unbuttoning his shirt. 'Heads up Hudson Capital. She's helping us with an acquisition.'

'Oh yes?' asked Karin, her business sense kicking in. 'Of what?'

Adam smiled and tipped his head back to drink his champagne. 'I thought you didn't want this to be a business trip.'

Karin moved back to his side and ran her fingers through his chest hair. 'I'm just interested in your company, honey.'

Adam slid his hand around the thin curve of her waist. 'You know, I've never had a girlfriend who gave two shits about my company – other than for the parties.'

'I'm not like other girlfriends,' she smiled.

'No. You're tougher. Cleverer. Sexier, and I adore that about you.' He came towards her and planted a soft kiss on her neck. Her nipples immediately stood to attention. She moaned.

'You don't mind us having the party on the yacht, do you?' he mumbled into her hair.

She stepped back and looked at him, puzzled. 'No. Why would I mind?'

Adam looked into her eyes, a serious expression on his face. 'I just thought . . . about what happened with your husband last year.'

It was the first time she and Adam had ever discussed the night of Sebastian's death. She hadn't wanted Adam to see her as a widow, which she did not consider to be particularly sexy. Moreover, she didn't want him to think she was an unlucky charm. Men like Adam wanted to be surrounded by beautiful, blessed people; money men were some of the most superstitious people on earth.

'It was a terrible, horrible accident, but it doesn't mean I won't ever step foot on a yacht again,' said Karin coolly, turning away from him and walking over to the wardrobe, where she started flipping through the rail of clothes, her hand stroking the acres of silk, chiffon and tulle. She felt his presence behind her and then a hand on her bare shoulder.

'Karin, you can talk about this, you know,' he soothed. 'Why do you always have to behave like some robot, as if you have no feelings?'

'Oh yes, and what about you?' she snapped, pulling away from him. 'It's not like you've got where you are today without being tough.'

He laughed. 'Tough and emotionless are not the same thing, honey. There's nothing clever about admitting to yourself, to me, how hard things have been. Losing Seb, that must have been hard, but then having people talking afterwards, well . . .'

Karin felt a sudden chill. 'What do you mean, "people were talking"?' she said. 'What were they saying exactly?'

Adam flushed slightly, uncharacteristically embarrassed. He cleared his throat. 'They were saying . . . that it wasn't an accident,' he said solemnly.

Karin dropped the red silk Cavalli dress she had been holding to the floor. Her face had drained of colour. 'They've been saying that?' she said quietly, her voice trembling slightly. 'Do they think that I had something to do with it? Who has been saying it?'

Adam went over to her and put his arm around her shoulder, but she shrugged it off violently. She looked at his face, desperately trying to read it. What had he been told? What did he believe? What was he thinking about her?

'Molly told me you'd had a tough time after Sebastian's death because there had been a whispering campaign against you.'

'She's a liar,' said Karin angrily. 'How can anyone have been talking about me? I didn't do anything. I *loved* my husband.'

'I know,' said Adam softly, 'I know, but if other people have been talking, then we have to face it . . .' She caught a look in his eye. Was it pity or suspicion? Either way it scared her. She felt fury wash over her. She could see exactly what Molly was doing and loathed her for it, because she knew that it might work. She lifted another dress from the rail, but then threw it down in frustration, tears finally welling under her eyes.

'Seb was drunk and high and he fell off the boat,' she whispered, staring down at the dress on the floor as she spoke. 'His business was failing, he was on self-destruct. I was at the night-club on shore with about twenty-five other people. Dozens of witnesses know that. But I wish I had been there; God, I wish I had, but he was alone.' A tear dropped onto the carpet and she looked up at Adam. 'Molly is trying to poison your mind against me. Can't you see that?'

Adam let out a small, low laugh. 'Honey, stop overreacting. She didn't tell me out of spite.'

'Oh *please*! Can't you see why she told you?' shouted Karin, losing all control, her grief turning to anger. 'The woman is a trou-blemaker. You're her next victim and she doesn't want me in the way to stop it.'

As soon as the words came out of Karin's mouth, she knew she had made a huge mistake. She cursed herself. Had she learnt nothing over the years? Women like Molly were cunning and clever and they pushed all the right buttons, while men were always completely blind to their scheming. But striking back at her only served to make Karin look bitchy and paranoid. She could see she was right; Adam was shaking his head, a disap-pointed look on his face.

'I'm gonna take a shower,' he said.

Karin sat on the bed and nodded, looking out at the sunset again, which was now draining to dark. Suddenly her hold on this fabu-lous life didn't seem quite so strong.

Molly and Sarah were getting on famously. Lying back on the top deck of *The Pledge*, they were drinking cocktails and giggling like old friends.

'Tell me again about that time you met Rod Stewart,' laughed Sarah, knocking back her fourth Martini which, she had to admit, did taste so much better with a twist of lemon; Molly knew so much good stuff. Molly was also having a great time, having found an audience for all the anecdotes about the rich and famous she had accumulated over the years, but which impressed nobody in her circle of friends. She also found Sarah spunky and great fun; she wished her own daughter could be more like her.

'Oh, Molly, I need a rich man,' moaned Sarah, throwing her arms in the air dramatically. 'I'm sexy, I'm available, where are they all?'

'Well, you're not going to find one like that,' laughed Molly.

'How do you mean?' said Sarah, sitting up and paying attention.

'Think rich, get rich, my dear,' she smiled knowingly, raising her glass for emphasis.

'Okay, so how do I do that? In fact, how do I know who's even rich?' asked Sarah, swivelling her head to gaze up and down the rows of yachts sandwiched together along the quayside.

'Everybody's rich here, darling,' smiled Molly. She was beginning to feel drunk and a bit frisky. Having ensured that every last detail for the party was in place, Molly had finally passed the hands-on organizational duties to one of the junior members of the Midas events team. Having worked hard, Molly felt it was definitely time to play hard, and from where she was sitting she could see ten of the world's top thirty biggest motor yachts. It was the world's greatest playground.

'But who's everyone?' insisted Sarah, her words a little slurred.

'Oh, Eddie Jordan, Flavio Briatore,' began Molly, pointing to their yachts and quickly pointing out a dozen more from her impressive database of wealth. 'See the big ones at the end?' she said, pointing to the far end of the marina. 'They will belong to people like Paul Allen, the Microsoft billionaire: he has one of the biggest yachts in the world – and one of the biggest bank balances, of course. And the others –' she swept her arm back down the harbour '– well, they're all still pretty rich. Darling, Monaco is just one of the biggest melting pots of rich men in the world. Americans, Russians, Greeks, they all come.'

'And who's the best?' asked Sarah eagerly.

Molly laughed. 'I prefer the oilmen.'

'Oilmen?'

'O-I-L,' smiled Molly. 'Old, ill and loaded.'

Sarah pulled a face. 'Ooh, I don't think I could manage an old man,' she said, shivering. 'What about the real oilmen, all the Russians and Arabs?'

'Well, Russians tend to go for other Russians – models usually. Plus they almost always have wives because they marry young. The oil sheiks from Brunei, Saudi, the Emirates and so on are generous but don't expect a relationship. Plus, they usually have five or six wives. Americans? Well, take your pick. Movie types are either sexually uptight or kinky. Miami guys are total druggies or total playboys. New Yorkers – they're fun but, baby, you'd better take good care of yourself.'

Sarah was waving her hand in the air for another Martini. 'What do you mean, "take good care of yourself"?'

Molly leaned in conspiratorially. 'Gary, an investment banker I once dated, used to check my bikini line every time we made love. He loved me clean-shaven and if it was beginning to look a bit chicken-plucked down there, he would run a mile.'

Sarah brayed with laughter, spilling her cocktail. 'So what did you do?'

'Got a waxer on speed dial.'

Sarah sighed heavily. 'It's time I met some decent men. London is shit for it.'

'Well, maybe you're looking in the wrong places,' smiled Molly.

'How about you show me the right places to look then?'

The older woman laughed. 'You're on. But don't say I didn't warn you.'

Sarah looked up as she heard a clatter of flip-flops moving along the top deck towards them.

'Summer,' she squealed, 'come and join the party. Your mum is just about to take me yacht-hopping.'

Summer looked at them and felt a little stab of jealousy. Sarah had her hair long, blonde and loose like Molly's; they were both in tiny dresses that skimmed mid-thigh, drinking and giggling. They looked like sisters.

'Come on, sweetheart,' said Molly, standing up and slipping on her silver flip-flops. 'We're going to go across to Abdul's first. He always has the best caviar.'

Summer turned to her friend. 'Sarah, shouldn't you be getting back to your shoot? It's almost eight o'clock already.'

Sarah waved a hand in the air, then had to quickly put it down again to steady herself. 'Oh don't fuss, Sum. I'm only going to be half an hour. Anyway, I'm scouting locations. They'll understand.'

'Are you coming?' Molly asked Summer, a hint of impatience in her voice.

Summer could see Molly was coked-up, she knew those eyes well, and she shook her head. She knew where this night was going. Molly responded with a narrowing of the eyes, a look that said 'killjoy'.

'Well, if you must stay here, don't spend all night giggling with

168

that frump Erin. Go and find yourself a man; there're some loaded bankers down the front. No point in wasting the whole trip.'

As Molly and Sarah staggered off arm in arm, Summer called after them, 'What should I tell Marcus if he asks where you are?'

'As Sarah says, we're going to be half an hour. Don't wait up!'

Summer rolled her eyes. Some things never changed.

'Look at us, gambling widows,' smiled Diana, settling back into a chair in Le Bar Américain in the Hôtel De Paris. Karin picked a pistachio nut from the table in front of her and offered a thin smile. After the scene with Adam on the yacht, she had felt glad to retreat to the De Paris, opposite the casino, for drinks with Diana and Christina.

'This is exactly why I hate grand prix weekend,' sniffed Christina. 'Not only does the noise of those cars zooming round the track give me tinnitus, the men just turn into total bores. I tell you, Ari used to say he was popping into the casino, and fifty grand later he'd still be there. Deaf and poor: that's where grand prix weekend leaves you.'

'So who was that blonde at the tables?' asked Diana, sipping her Bloody Mary.

Karin pulled a sour face. She didn't want to be reminded; her day was going from bad to worse. After their spat, she and Adam had hardly said two words to one another during the cocktail reception on board *The Pledge*. When one of the party of bankers had suggested a trip to the casino, Adam had pointedly asked Claudia Falcon to accompany them to the leather-lined salon privé of the casino. With everyone watching, Karin had had to ask for a lift to the casino bar. It had been humiliating.

'It's a bit strange, isn't it?' said Christina. 'I've never seen them let a woman join the table before. It's usually all boys together.'

'Well, she's practically a man,' sniffed Karin. 'She's MD of some investment bank. Real ball-breaker by the sounds of it. Helping Midas finance some brownfield site or something.'

'Well, watch it,' warned Christina. 'You don't want Adam to . . . Shit.' Christina's face had suddenly turned as white as paper.

'What's the matter?' asked Diana, twisting around to follow her gaze.

'Emily Kent has just walked into the bar.'

The name didn't sound familiar to either Karin or Diana.

'Joshua's maths tutor,' murmured Christina distractedly. 'Joshua was falling behind with his schoolwork so I got someone to help him out. What on earth is *she* doing here?'

Karin looked around to see a slim, nondescript brunette standing at the entrance of the bar as if she was looking for someone. She didn't look anything like the average De Paris guest. Mid-twenties, a floral summer dress hovering at her knee, her face freshly scrubbed and free of make-up, her light brown bobbed hair pushed back off her face. She looked more like a librarian than a grand prix goer – and her face fell as she spotted Christina rising and walking towards her.

'Emily. What a surprise!' said Christina, kissing the air lightly in the direction of her cheeks.

'Likewise,' replied Emily, her eyes still scanning the room. 'I thought you gave the grand prix a wide berth.'

'Yes, well, here I am.' She paused. 'And who told you that? Ari?'

Emily nodded awkwardly as a thought popped into Christina's mind. *But surely not,* she thought, *that's just not possible.*

'So who are you here with?' asked Christina, trying hard to sound casual.

'Just a friend,' stammered Emily. 'And how's Joshua? I haven't seen him in a little while.'

'Really? I wasn't aware that Ari had stopped tuition.'

Over Emily's shoulder, Christina could see through the glass door of the bar and into the foyer of the hotel where, at that moment, she saw Ari walk in through the revolving doors towards reception.

'If you're looking for my husband, sweetie, he's just walking in,' said Christina. Emily had the look of a rabbit caught in a trap.

'Christina. Look, I . . . I'm sorry. I thought he had told you. We didn't realize you'd be here this weekend.'

'Why would he tell me, you stupid bitch?' hissed Christina. 'That bastard's filing for divorce on the grounds that *I* have been unfaithful, and all the while he's fucking the maths tutor.'

Guests in the bar were beginning to look round. Karin leapt from her chair and put her hand on Christina's shoulder. 'Tina, it's not worth it,' she muttered as Christina shook her hand away.

'You little whore!' growled Christina. 'What right have you got to parade yourself in front of everyone, in front of my friends?'

Emily moved for the door. 'I think I had better go,' she said quietly.

Christina laughed cruelly. 'The fucking maths tutor? This is more of a mystery than Pythagoras's theorem. What on earth does he see in you?'

Emily turned back and looked at Christina with surprisingly cold eyes. 'I'm not you,' she whispered.

Christina laughed again. 'That's right. And don't think a mousy frump like you is going to replace me, sweetheart!' she shouted.

Emily casually held her wrist up and jangled a string of diamonds.

Christina stopped cold. She immediately recognized it: a Tiffany tennis bracelet worth at least £30,000.

'Christina,' smiled Emily as she turned from the room, 'I think I already have.'

Erin had been expecting to hate Molly's daughter. After all, Summer was younger than Molly, considerably more beautiful and, having spent twenty-something years in Molly's shallow world, she was bound to have the same expectant arrogance, the same hard-faced ambition. But when Summer arrived on *The Pledge* earlier that evening, Erin had liked Summer immediately. She was modest, funny, polite, and had a smile that was warm and genuine. Plus, unlike most people she had encountered in Adam's world, Summer spoke and listened to Erin as an equal.

Summer had a body made for sin, that much was obvious, the simple white jersey dress she was wearing could not disguise her spectacular figure. But even though she looked like every man's fantasy, she was quite clearly a girl's girl, chattering to Erin about shoes and ice cream and rom-coms. It was just like going down the pub with one of her best friends. In Summer's company, Erin felt herself properly relaxing for the first time in months.

'I expect you come here every year, don't you?' asked Erin. The two girls had retreated to the top deck for cocktails as Adam had joked that Erin was only 'half on duty'. He wanted to her to relax and enjoy the party, but to be there to sort out any complications. And Erin was glad Adam had been so generous as they had a spectacular view of the harbour.

'Oh no, this is my first time,' said Summer, 'My mother always wants to drag me to these sorts of places, but thankfully I've been out of harm's way in Japan for the last four years.'

'*Dragged* to these sorts of places? What's there not to like about yachts and champagne?' laughed Erin at Summer's objections.

Summer gave a half-smile and put her flute of Krug down on the walnut deck. 'Hang on,' she said distractedly, 'my mobile is going.' She looked at the screen. It was Sarah.

'Summer! You'll never guess where I am!' gushed Sarah as Summer made a face to Erin. 'I'm on Larry Nelson's yacht! It's that white and blue one right at the end of the dock. It's *so* big. And the men here are lovely! Why don't you come over?'

'Are you still with my mother?' asked Summer, slightly concerned.

'No. I think she's gone. But it doesn't matter, because I've met everyone. Sum, I've just met this guy who plays for AC Milan but he's injured.' Sarah was giggling hysterically and slurring her speech.

'Sarah, come back to the yacht,' scolded Summer.

'Oh, don't be such a party-pupper . . . piper . . . pooper,' slurred Sarah. 'Anyway, I won't be long. Just another ten minutes.' She began giggling and was clearly talking to somebody away from the phone.

'Sarah? SARAH?' said Summer, but the phone had gone dead. She looked at Erin apologetically. 'Look sorry, that's my friend Sarah, I think I'm going to have to go and get her.'

Summer had switched into responsible mode. She had done it a thousand times before, when Molly had been coked out of her face at a party and needed a taxi summoning to some remote spot on the outskirts of London, or when a friend had called to say her mother was passed out cold in a bar.

'Who the hell is Barry Nelson?' asked Erin.

'One of the richest men in the world.'

'So why don't you leave her to it?' asked Erin. 'I'm sure she's enjoying herself.'

Summer glanced at her watch and frowned. 'Hmm, I would, but she's supposed to be in the Casino Square in twenty minutes. She's presenting a programme about the lifestyles of the rich and famous. It's the first night of filming tonight and she sounds totally out of it.'

'Do you want me to come and retrieve her?'

Summer smiled that warm smile and nodded. 'Would you?'

At 325 feet long, *Bratsera* was too big to dock at the harbour and instead had to join the other mega-yachts moored offshore like a flotilla of super-rich invaders. Erin and Summer took a tender to the yacht. As they approached, they felt dwarfed by the sheer size of the five-deck monster, towering over them like a floating office block. It was so large, it even had its own helicopter landing pad; the girls could see some of the crew playing basketball there as they climbed aboard. As soon as they stepped onto the first deck, the girls were handed cocktails from silver salvers. There were at least sixty people on the main deck, circulating and drinking champagne. 'Who are all these people?' hissed Erin from behind her hand.

'Oh, billionaires, heads of state, Euro-celebrities; just your average Saturday evening party,' smiled Summer.

Several women – all tall, slim and glamorous – were wandering around in bikinis.

'. . . And there might be a few hookers as well,' she added.

It was, however, far too crowded and dark to see Sarah.

'Oh, where the bloody hell is she?' groaned Summer, as they threaded their way through the crowd. It was 9 p.m.: Sarah was so late for the filming.

'Wait here. What does Sarah look like? I've got an idea,' said Erin, and disappeared towards the back of the ship. Standing at the side of the party and scanning the faces, Summer recognized Barry Nelson, the yacht's owner, leaning against the rail in a pair of cream chinos and an green open-necked shirt. He was quite plain-looking, but there was an undeniable halo of power and confidence around the man, she thought. Amazing what $20 billion in the bank will add to a man's allure.

Erin reappeared with a smile on her face. 'I've just been sweet-talking those crew guys we saw playing basketball. One of them saw a girl who looked like Sarah going into a stateroom on the third level. Come on.'

The third deck was just a long row of doors and, after a brief knock, they peeked behind the first. Nothing beyond a beautifully panelled cabin with the finest cream linen sheets on the king-sized bed. The same at the next door. On the third, they found her.

'Fuck. It's you.' Sarah was sitting on the end of the bed in a pair of coffee-coloured lace panties and bra. Her hair fell loose and tousled on her shoulders and her eyes looked glassy. She was wavering from side to side, trying to pour brandy into a tumbler. 'What are you doing here, Summer? I know I said come, but you'd better clear off.'

Summer took the bottle from her friend's wobbling hand. 'Why would we do that?' she asked.

'Johnny will be back any minute.'

Summer picked up the dress that had been flung over a Biedermeier chair and handed it to Sarah. 'Get dressed,' she instructed, 'we're going back.'

Sarah flung the dress down and bared her teeth. 'Don't you fucking understand?' she slurred angrily. 'Johnny is Johnny *Galanos*. The Greek ship guy. He's bloody loaded and he's dead fit too.'

'But Sarah, you're supposed to be filming right now!'

'Oh, we can do some tomorrow,' said Sarah vaguely, waving her glass in the air. Suddenly Sarah froze. 'Oh shit,' she said, and bolted in the direction of the bathroom. 'I'm going to puke.'

Erin had been standing at the cabin door watching it all. She pulled at Summer's arm. 'Come on, don't bother with her. She's wasted. Let's go and find her producer and tell him his star presenter is a dead loss.'

25

'Where the fuck is that silly cow?' Simon Garrison, the producer/director of 'On Heat' was angrily stalking around the square, a mobile phone clamped to his ear as he tried to call Sarah for the fifth time in as many minutes. This was the nightmare scenario for Simon. A very expensive, very impatient crew, standing around in one of the most expensive square footages in Europe were ready to roll, and their presenter was AWOL. He was ready to kill.

'Simon?' The director turned to face a beautiful girl with incredible lavender eyes.

Summer had identified Simon immediately from Sarah's description earlier that day. 'Always wears a baseball cap,' she had said, 'thinks he's Steven fucking Spielberg.' Along with the navy Yankees cap, Simon also had a couple of days' worth of stubble around his chin, intelligent eyes and a deep furrow between his brow to indicate he was very, very hacked off.

'Not now sweetheart,' he muttered, gesturing to his mobile, 'bit busy at the moment.'

'No, you don't understand, I'm a friend of Sarah's,' said Summer with an apologetic smile. Simon immediately snapped the mobile shut and turned to Summer.

'Well, where the hell is she?' he demanded, looking behind Summer hopefully.

'Not here, I'm afraid,' shrugged Summer.

'I can see that,' snapped Simon impatiently. 'It's nine fucking thirty and she was supposed to be here half an hour ago. Please tell me she's on her way. Tell me.'

'Actually . . .' The look on Summer's face said it all. 'Actually she's really ill. Food poisoning, I think. Someone is just putting her in a cab back to Menton.'

Simon went pink. If it had been a cartoon, steam would have come out of his ears.

'Menton?' he shrieked, 'what frigging good is she to me in Menton? We've only got about ten minutes of film so far and most of it is shit!'

Simon's researcher, a pretty blonde girl with her hair in a pony tail, coughed discreetly and offered a solution.

'Maybe we can just get a lot of colour?' she suggested. 'You know, film everyone going into the casino? Try and get into Harry's and so on. Do we really need a presenter on film all the time?'

Simon looked as if he was thinking about it and then shook his head. 'No, I wanted the grand prix segment to kick off the show. This is the start of the season. If we ever needed the presenter, it's here.'

'Maybe we could do more filming with her tomorrow?' asked the researcher.

'Has to be tonight,' said Simon, rubbing his eyes. 'We've only got permission to film in some locations today. Plus, there's a massive party going on tonight at the Sporting Club. Diddy is going to be there.'

Simon turned to Summer. 'Just how ill is she? Is it worth me going round and kicking her arse in a cab?' he asked hopefully. 'We've got a make-up artist if she's looking too green.'

Summer winced. 'Sorry,' she said. 'Last time I saw her she had puked about half a dozen times. I don't think a dab of foundation's going to fix it.' She didn't like to add that her friend was also so loaded it would probably take her until this time next week to come down.

Simon swore under his breath. He'd suspected something like this might happen. Sarah Simpson had been a royal pain in the arse from the start: constantly late for production meetings and a complete diva to boot. What they really needed was a no-name presenter who would do exactly what she was told. Suddenly a light went on in his head and he looked Summer up and down. 'You're another model, right?'

'I saw you in *Elle* this month,' said the eager-to-please researcher, 'in that Karenza swimwear advert.'

Summer flushed a little. It was only the second time she'd been recognized. 'Yes, that was me,' she smiled shyly.

'Ever done any TV? Any presenting?' asked Simon hopefully.

'No, sorry. I've only ever done print work.'

Undeterred, Simon muttered some instructions to the cameraman, who trained his lens on Summer. Simon leant over to watch the digital image playback.

'Talk to me,' said Simon, looking intently at the picture. 'Tell me what you've done this evening.'

'Oh no, come on, this isn't my sort of thing . . .' Summer could feel her cheeks redden and had no idea what to say.

'Just relax,' coaxed Simon. 'Tell me where you've just come from.'

Summer shrugged. 'I've just spent two hours on Adam Gold's yacht, aka HMS *Gold-digger*,' she smiled. 'Lakes of Krug, herds of Cavalli, hundreds of innocent ostriches slaughtered to make handbags for old women whose faces don't move.'

She could see Simon's face beaming behind the camera. This girl was dynamite. When she started talking, that gorgeous face lit up and the megawatt smile flashed, words flowing fluidly. He couldn't believe that this shy, polite girl in front of him had transformed into a glorious witty live-wire. She was just what he needed.

'Why the fucking hell have you never done telly before?' he asked, smiling.

Because it's always the pushy girls like Sarah that get put forward for the TV gigs, she thought.

'Dunno. Why do you swear so much?' she replied playfully. Simon laughed.

'Well, right now would be a good time to shut the fuck up because I'm about to make you an offer you can't refuse. Luckily for you, the commissioning editor of the channel is in town and I'm going to get him down here to see what he thinks of these clips; but if he thinks what I'm thinking, I don't think we'll have any problems.'

Summer's head was reeling. 'Sorry,' she asked, 'what exactly is this offer I can't refuse?'

'Fuck me, girl!' laughed Simon, 'I'm asking you if you fancy being a household name, a star of the small screen, the next big thing. I'm asking you if you would like to replace your deadleg friend and take over presenting the show?'

*

The Villa La Vigie was one of the most beautiful properties on the whole Côte D'Azur. A primrose-yellow jewel perched on a hill just outside the principality, it had once belonged to Karl Lagerfeld and had also featured in the film *Tender Is the Night*. With its mani-cured, sweet-smelling gardens bursting with bougainvillea, it summed up the Côte D'Azur elegance. Tonight the villa was the venue for one of the most exclusive bashes of the grand prix weekend. Lynn Hanson, wife of the Texan billionaire William Hanson, was hosting a twenty-fifth wedding anniversary party and the entire villa had been swathed in silver and white especially for the occasion. Karin and Christina walked out into the gardens and smelt the honeysuckle-infused air. It was a beautiful warm night and the Italianate gardens had been lit by flickering torches, but not even the sound of a famous Italian tenor singing heartbreaking melodies from the candlelit temple at the bottom of the lawns, or the free-flowing grand cru champagne could lighten Karin's mood. She was feeling as if her world was falling around her ears. It was now way past midnight and there was still no sign of Adam, or anybody else from the Midas party, in fact. She had phoned Erin to find out where everyone had got to, but had been put straight through to message. Besides which, she thought with a shiver, if Adam didn't want to be found, his assistant wasn't going to be able to do much about that, was she?

'Are you sure this was where everybody was coming?' asked Christina, craning her long neck to survey the crowd.

'Not everybody, no,' said Karin. 'Lynn and Bill's is strictly invi-tation only. Molly has arranged for "everyone" to go to Jimmy'z, but when I spoke to Erin earlier, she said Adam was coming along here.'

'He can't still be at the casino, can he?' said Christina, waving to someone in the distance.

Karin shrugged, not wanting to tell Christina about their fight. She had enough problems, without alerting the most predatory woman in gold-digging history to a possible target.

'I suppose if he's losing money, he'll be there until he wins it back,' she said vaguely.

'Well, I hope Ari does well at the tables,' said Christina.

Karin looked at her friend quizzically. 'After what happened tonight?'

The two women had walked to the edge of the gardens, where

the scent of honeysuckle was even stronger, and beyond them lay the crescent of Monte Carlo, twinkling like a Utopian playground.

'Do you remember when I had to break into the house and bruised my arm?' asked Christina, running her finger around the rim of her champagne glass. 'Well, the diamonds weren't all I took from the safe. Ari keeps copies of all his offshore accounts in the house. I have details of every numbered account he possesses in Switzerland, Bermuda, the Isle of Man and Jersey.'

Karin whistled. 'You wouldn't use them though, would you?'

'I could have the Inland Revenue go crawling so far up his ass they could see his dental work,' said Christina with a thin smile.

'But Tina, you can't mean to send him to jail for tax evasion?' asked Karin.

Christina shrugged and took a sip of Krug. 'Well, I guess he could go to jail. But I think he's smarter than that. This is a business, pure and simple, and Ari will understand that all information has a price.' Christina looked at her friend with steely eyes. 'I would have preferred not to use the information. I would have preferred that he gave me a decent settlement without the need for a courtroom. But no, Ari decided he would have his PR company spin lies about me all over the newspapers, making me out to be a whore, when all the time he was screwing Emily Kent.'

Karin could sense her friend's deep-seated anger as Christina continued. 'Ari could have settled it like a gentleman, but he tried to play dirty. Well, now the rules have changed and now it doesn't matter if we have a pre-nup or if I fucked the gardener or if he fucked the man in the moon. I think he'll roll over and beg for me. And now my price has just doubled.'

'So what do you want?'

'I want to see what price he puts on his own freedom. I think we'll start at one hundred million.'

The women smiled at each other and Karin clinked her glass against her friend's. 'I'll drink to that.'

Just then Karin's mobile rang. It was Erin. 'Hi Karin. So sorry for not getting back sooner. My phone was out of juice.'

Karin tutted. 'Well, Christina and I have been stuck at the Hansons' party for the last hour with no sign of Adam or anybody. Can you tell me exactly what he said again?'

Erin sounded awkward. 'I think there's been a bit of a mix-up.' She stuttered, 'I didn't actually speak to Adam; it was Molly who told me he would be at Villa La Vigie. She said it was on the schedule.'

Like hell it was, thought Karin as she snapped her phone shut.

Molly! That bitch was pulling every trick in the book to get her out of the way. Karin looked at Christina and remembered what she had said about playing dirty. *Two can play at that game*, she thought, and smiled as a plan began to form in her head.

'These women look good,' said Simon, pointing at three tall blondes who had just got out of a cab outside Jimmy'z. 'Summer – go grab them!'

Talk about a baptism of fire, thought Summer, picking up her microphone and pulling down her dress. Silverland Media hadn't been allowed to film inside the exclusive nightclub and instead were trying to catch people on their way in and out.

She trotted up to the entrance where Ferraris were being valet-parked. A cameraman was following close behind Summer until she suddenly stopped walking. 'Shit, it's my mother,' she whispered.

Somewhere between the drinks on the yacht and here, Molly had changed into a black micro-mini dress that showed off her long legs to perfection. She was wearing a pair of very high, very strappy sandals and Summer had to admit she looked incredible; you'd never guess she was forty-three.

Molly spotted her daughter and strode over. 'Where the *hell* have you been?' she began then, spotting the microphone, gave Summer a sideways look. 'And what on *earth* are you doing?'

Summer flushed and shrugged, feeling like a little girl caught playing dress-up with her mother's best clothes. 'I'm . . . ah . . . it's a long story.'

'Try,' said Molly sternly, turning to wave her two friends inside.

'Well, Sarah had to go home ill,' said Summer, twisting the microphone lead in her fingers. 'I went to tell her producer. And they asked me to fill in.'

She smiled hopefully, for one moment thinking that perhaps her mother might congratulate her. Instead a black cloud swept across Molly's face.

'Television?' she hissed, grabbing Summer's arm and pulling her to one side. 'What have I told you all these years? Modelling, then movies. Not TV. TV's cheap, it's small-time. You will never meet a decent man in the ITV canteen.'

'But it's a good opportunity, mum,' said Summer, cursing herself for sounding like a teenager.

'No, the good opportunities are inside that club,' snapped Molly, gesturing towards the entrance. 'Look, over there.' As she spoke, the crowd parted to let Prince Albert pass inside.

'Listen, Adam is on his way over from the casino with a group of rich players. Real men with real prospects. Why are you wasting your time pretending you're Davina bloody McCall?'

Summer flushed again, but with the TV crew hovering in the background, she somehow felt stronger. 'And why are you wasting your time on Adam when he'll be coming with Karin?' she hissed back. Molly's mouth dropped open. She looked as if she had been slapped.

Summer pulled her arm away from her mother and walked back towards the club, beckoning the cameraman as she went.

'I'll come in later,' she said over her shoulder. 'I've got work to do first.'

That ungrateful little bitch, thought Molly as she took a seat at one of the reserved tables by the dance floor. *After all I've done for her. Well let her play her little games. I've got bigger fish to fry.* Molly smiled as she remembered Summer's comment about Adam. Of course Adam wasn't coming with Karin, she smirked to herself. She clicked her fingers to summon the wine waitress and ordered an extortionately priced bottle of vodka and champagne for the table. She'd find someone to pay for it later.

But two hours later there was still no sign of anyone from the Midas party and, although Molly had kept herself entertained flitting from one old acquaintance to another, she was beginning to get bored and anxious.

'Well, well . . . Here's somebody I haven't seen in a long time,' said a voice behind Molly.

She turned and groaned inwardly. 'Gunter. How are you?'

Gunter Strauss was a German industrialist. Rich and flash, he liked to dip in and out of the circuit when his fierce wife in Düsseldorf would allow him. Molly had met him at the Red Cross Ball five years earlier and he had invited her to Necker Island six months later. Gunter slid into a seat beside Molly, his long face twisted in a leer.

'Here for the race, Molly?' he asked.

'No, actually,' she said, turning away from him slightly. 'I'm working with Midas Corporation this year.'

'Ah, Adam Gold,' nodded Gunter, 'I was just going to meet him.'
Molly looked at him, surprised. 'Meet him where?'

Gunter smiled and ran a hand lightly up Molly's bare thigh. 'On
his yacht. He's moored a couple of berths down from mine. I saw
him at the casino about an hour ago. Said I should drop by for a
drink.'

'So he's not coming to Jimmy'z?' said Molly, pursing her lips.

Gunter shook his head. 'It appears not. But how about we go
for that drink together? Then I can show you my yacht. I believe
I have a bigger one than Gold's,' he smiled lasciviously. 'Why don't
you come and measure up?'

With a mounting bar bill, Molly had no intention of staying at
Jimmy'z if Adam wasn't coming along. If she could get Gunter to
settle it and get a lift down to the harbour, then all the better. She
could dump Gunter once she got to Adam's tub.

Gunter's car was a blue BMW with cream interior. Molly got
into the passenger seat and sank back into the soft leather as Gunter
gunned the engine and sped off, leaving rubber on the road. Monaco
was tiny and the drive from Jimmy'z to the harbour was short, but
it would never do to be seen tottering down the narrow streets to
the yacht, especially not when there were so many prestige cars to
travel in. But Molly knew immediately that they were going in the
wrong direction, heading out of the small town into the hills of
Roquebrune.

'Gunter, I think maybe you have had too much to drink because
the harbour is that way,' she said, feeling her nerves begin to jangle.

'I just want to take you for a spin,' said Gunter, smiling. 'You
like my car, don't you?'

'Well yes, but I would like to go back to the harbour now,' said
Molly more forcefully.

They were out of Monte Carlo now. They had taken a turn off
the coastal road and Gunter was slowing the car into a viewing
bay at the side of the road. They could see the orange lights of
Monaco to their right. Out in front of them, beyond the pine trees
clinging onto the cliffs, the Mediterranean spilled out jet-black
towards the horizon.

'I love Monte Carlo, but sometimes it gets a bit crazy, no?' said
Gunter, sliding his hand onto her bare thigh again. 'Sometimes you
just need to be alone . . .'

Molly twisted away from him, illuminated only by the car head-lights spilling out onto the soil in front of them. She knew why they had come out here. His wife was probably on their yacht, waiting for him, and Gunter wanted some fun beforehand. Six months ago she would have given him what he wanted, a little sexual buzz to end his evening, but tonight she was angry. She had been tricked away from Adam and she wasn't in the mood to be playing the likes of like Gunter.

'Can we go back, please?' said Molly loudly, removing Gunter's hand from her thigh. Gunter just chuckled and unclicked his seat belt, moving closer to Molly.

'Now, tell me you haven't gone all chaste on me?' he sneered. His lips were close to her neck and she could smell a £500 bottle of bourbon on his breath. 'Because that would be a real waste.'

'Get off me!' she spat, quickly rolling away from him and grabbing the car door. It was locked. Gunter's fat, sweaty hand was back riding up her thigh so his fingers were touching the rim of her panties.

'I've missed you, Molly,' he whispered, 'I've missed you sucking my cock. No one can suck cock better than you, Molly. I want you to remind me how good you are.' He was almost on top of her now, groping at her breasts and fumbling with the zip of his trousers.

'Get the fuck off me,' she screamed, but Gunter was strong, pushing her down with his weight, guiding her hand to his cock, tugging roughly at Molly's panties.

'Please, Gunter. I don't want to. I'm with someone now and I have to get back to the yacht.'

Gunter was smiling malevolently now. He had pinned her to the seat and hissed in her ear, 'Oh yes, you're quick to take my hospitality, aren't you, Molly? Quick to come and stay in my villas. Quick to get me to pay your bar bills, to accept the ride home in my car. But it's not all "take, take, take" in this world, darling. Sometimes you have to give something back.'

He tore at her panties, and she heard them rip away. Molly knew it was no good trying to overpower him so she relaxed her body and forced a thin smile onto her lips.

'Well, I don't want to be seen as ungrateful,' she whispered, twisting her hips towards him and spreading her thighs until she could see his eyes widen and glint with lust. Smiling like a little boy at Christmas, Gunter moved away from her to pull down his trousers properly. At that moment, Molly bent her legs and kicked against his chest as hard as she could.

'You fucking bitch,' snarled Gunter, slapping her hard across the face. Molly felt her head vibrate and her skin sting, but the anger numbed her pain. This bastard was getting between her and her prize. A desperate rage possessed her. She flung her body forward, and grabbed the handbrake of the car, clicking it off. The car jerked forward and began to roll.

'You crazy whore!' screamed Gunter, scrabbling desperately to untangle himself from his trousers and to find the brake before the car toppled off the cliff. Given a brief breathing space, Molly punched the car's central locking button and yanked open the door. Gunter howled and grabbed at Molly's legs, failing to prevent her escape, but flipping her out of the car, sending her spinning into the soil, dirt flying in her face. She rolled away from the door, one shoeless foot slipping on gravel, terrified that Gunter would follow her and continue his violence.

Her heart leapt again as she heard the car engine roar into life, and she flailed backwards, landing by the side of the road. She lay there, hoping she was hidden by the brush as the blinding head-lights swung across her face. The car stopped and the window buzzed down. She looked up and could see the shadows of Gunter's face in the light of the dashboard, his eyes angry, his lips in a snarl. 'You pathetic fucking whore,' he said, and flung her shoe out of the window. It landed just in front of Molly's face, coughing up a little cloud of dirt.

Her heart was beating so fast that she had to shut her eyes and breathe deeply to calm herself down. As the rear lights of Gunter's BMW faded into the night, Molly slowly, shakily pulled herself to her feet. Her throat was dry. She felt a tear sting at the back of her eye as she looked at her knees, grazed and bloody from being thrown on the ground. She bit her lip and shook away her emotion. At least he had paid for her bar bill, she thought defiantly. *At least he had paid for the bar bill.*

She was surrounded by complete darkness, but she could just make out the line of the road. The lights of Monte Carlo did not seem too far away. She took off her other shoe and started walking.

26

Overnight, Summer's life had changed. The executive producer of
'On Heat' had been delighted with the segments Summer had shot
in Monaco and now wanted her on board for every production
meeting. Her arrival back from Monte Carlo also coincided with the
appearance of the Karenza spring/summer advertising campaign. It
was nothing short of sensational: Summer's body, naked except for
a tiny white thong, the sheen of Caribbean water on her skin sparkling
like diamonds, her skin so tanned and polished it looked as if she'd
been dipped in molten gold. Best of all, the ads were everywhere:
Vogue, Harper's, Elle, Marie Claire, even on selected crash-inducing
billboards around London. AdWeek called it the sexiest campaign
since Brooke Shields told the world what came between her and her
Calvin's, and the Advertising Standards Authority denounced it for
its 'gratuitous sexual content'. That was enough to turn a great ad
campaign into a public event. The *Daily Mail* ran an angry editorial about the damage Summer's body was doing to impressionable
young minds, while the *Sun* ran a centre-spread image with a 'Who's
That Girl?' headline. Summer had arrived and she was on a high.
Even Sarah Simpson had taken the news of her replacement by
Summer surprisingly well. She'd met an Italian at the casino and she
was considering relocating to Milan to be with him.

Molly, of course, was delighted, and decided to take her daughter's
success into her own hands. She fired La Mode agency and put in
a call to IMP, who had taken Summer onto their books, immediately being snowed under with offers. The fashion industry were
like sheep; if there was a hot girl in a hot campaign, then everybody wanted to use her. Molly's interest in Summer's career wasn't

185

entirely altruistic, however. Two days after Summer appeared in the *Sun* centre spread, Molly's agent Eric Snowdon gave her a call for the first time in years. 'Remember what Twiggy did for Marks and Spencer?' he said. Apparently *Playboy* were also interested. The fee was huge but Molly reluctantly told Eric to turn them down. She gave him some faux-modest flannel about being too long in the tooth, but the truth was Molly was embarking on another career now. True, there were some men who liked seeing their girlfriends in *Playboy*. But not many. Not Marcus, not Adam, and certainly not Alex Delemere.

Molly was already at Le Caprice, flicking through a copy of *Tatler*, when Summer arrived to a flurry of platitudes from the maître d'. She put down the magazine to embrace her daughter and kiss her fondly.

'It's so nice being able to do lunch,' gushed Molly as they sat down. 'And table seven,' she whispered, referring to the restaurant's most sought-after spot.

'Shall we get a bottle of wine?'

'Actually yes,' smiled Summer, who usually stuck to water at lunchtime. 'We have something to celebrate.'

'Yes, we do,' said Molly, already speed-reading the list of champagnes. 'I've been doing some thinking and I've decided to become your manager.'

Summer felt a blur of conflicting emotions all at once: flattered and excited that her mother thought that much of her, but insulted and mildly panicked that Molly would now be controlling her life even more than before. Summer didn't need a shrink to tell her that the thing she had really enjoyed about the Karenza campaign was that she had done it all herself without any interference from her mother.

'But I already have an agent,' said Summer quietly.

'Different things, darling. IMP are fabulous and you need them for shoots, but they've got hundreds of other great girls on their books who are essentially in competition with you. I, on the other hand, will proactively steer your career in the direction I think you should take.'

'Which is what?' said Summer suspiciously.

'Darling, you could be the new Heidi Klum.' She stabbed her fork into her tomato galette.

'Heidi's the cleverest model out there. She knows she's not the most cutting-edge girl on the circuit, but does she go crying into a copy of *Spoon* magazine? No. She's designing for Birkenstock and jewellery houses, making millions with Victoria's Secret. And she still makes the cover of American *Elle*. Modelling's not everything, darling. It's just the start.'

Summer took a breath. 'Thanks for the offer, Molly. But don't you think you're too busy with the job at Midas?'

Ignoring her, Molly pressed on. 'I don't know why you are bothering with this presenting business. It's not really the right image.'

'Heidi Klum does TV.'

'She also gets to be executive producer,' said Molly sagely.

Summer felt herself bristle. Filming in Monaco had been the most fun she'd ever had working. Already she had been to a production meeting at Silverland Media and had spent an hour bouncing ideas around, brainstorming episodes and even coming up with ideas for other shows she could be involved in. She had loved it and she was not going to let Molly sabotage it.

'Mother, I'm not going to—'

'At least you'll be going to the right places with this TV thing, I suppose,' interrupted Molly. Summer looked surprised at her mother's turnabout. 'Because my number one priority is to find you a boyfriend.'

Summer sighed. So Molly hadn't changed her tune, after all; she just wanted to get her married off to some fat hairy millionaire.

'I mean, have you even had a date since you've been back in London?' asked Molly.

Summer shrugged. She had had plenty of men offer to take her on dates, alright. They stopped her on the streets, at the gym, on photo-shoots, but she liked to keep her distance. For a moment she allowed herself to think about Charlie McDonald, wondering if he had ever got his record deal. Molly grabbed her daughter's hand across the white starched tablecloth.

'Darling, you are the star of the sexiest ad campaign of the summer and you should be capitalizing on this. Plenty of good men have become available recently, and we all know they don't hang around for very long. I'm going to set you up on a date.'

Summer couldn't help but giggle nervously. 'I thought you wanted to be my manager, not my pimp.'

Molly threw down her fork. 'Don't be ridiculous! I'm your mother and I want the best for you. I always have.'

Maybe Molly was right. It was a long time since she had had any fun; she could do with some male company. No, it wouldn't do any harm to go on one date, would it?

It wasn't exactly a blind date. Molly had taken Summer out for dinner to Cipriani and had invited half a dozen friends, who spent the entire evening knocking back Bellinis and talking excitedly about where they were spending the summer. It was like an episode of 'On Heat', Summer thought to herself with a smile. She found herself seated next to Ricardo Lantis, a second-generation Panamanian businessman whose family had made millions in supplying food to supermarket chains around the world. He looked in his early forties; skin tanned, expensively dressed in a blue open-necked shirt, a hint of black chest hair. Ricardo had a permanently serious expression, but lively green eyes and his powerful charisma made up for his rather average looks. Molly had whispered that he had a house in Belgravia and a sprawling estate on Mykonos, where he held the 'most decadent' parties every July.

'It's impossible to think why we have never met before,' said Ricardo to Summer as his lobster linguine arrived.

'It's probably because I've been living in Japan for the last four years,' she said. 'It's been strange coming back. Things seem to have changed completely.'

'Well, you must let me show you around,' he said, pouring her a glass of Chablis. 'London is so underrated, but it is far more exciting than Tokyo, Paris, New York, or wherever your modelling exploits have been taking you.' He paused, 'Your mother's been telling me all about your glittering career.'

Summer wondered how well he knew her mother. She was intrigued by Ricardo, but found him a little intimidating, with his stories of international business. He told her he had studied law at Harvard, but he quit his studies at the age of twenty-four when the lure of the family business – one of the biggest wholesale food businesses in the world – became too much to resist. Now Ricardo was a multimillionaire and commuted between Panama City and London twice twice weekly. On top of that success, he had climbed the Matterhorn, competed in a triathlon and was a black belt in tae kwon do. He was the archetypal alpha male; just the sort her mother approved of.

When the dinner party disbanded, Ricardo proposed leading a

party in the direction of Annabel's, but Summer made her excuses – she had a meeting at a cosmetics giant in the morning – a possible campaign, said her agent.

'Oh come on, darling,' hissed Molly, who was clearly taking advantage of the fact that Marcus was in Dubai on business.

'I can't, mum,' said Summer. 'Tomorrow is business.'

As they waited in the street for their drivers, Ricardo asked Summer for her number.

'How about we do dinner on Thursday?' he said, handing her a card. 'I'll send the car to collect you at eight. You can text me your address beforehand.'

As she pulled away in a taxi, Summer sank back in the seat with a satisfied feeling. Her mother certainly seemed pleased for once, and Ricardo was interesting company. Not drop-dead gorgeous but, yes, he was certainly attractive. She closed her eyes and began to look forward to Thursday.

27

'Don't look now, but there is somebody very yummy staring at you *just* over there,' whispered Candy Woodall, tipping back her Chardonnay spritzer.

'Where?' giggled Erin, trying to look around the wine bar without making it too obvious. Erin and Candy – Marcus Blackwell's PA – had come out for a rare girls' night out after work and the wine and gossiping had gone straight to Erin's head.

'*There*. The one who looks like Jude Law,' said Candy a bit too loudly, pointing a discreet finger in the direction of the bar. Erin's eyes scanned the bar. It was hard to see in the dim light; this bar was trying very hard to be French brasserie, with sea-green mosaic walls, a long walnut and bronze bar and too much candlelight. Her eyes followed Candy's now frantic pointing and she finally saw him, sitting on a bar stool. He was very handsome, with nut-brown hair, green eyes and a smart white shirt.

'Crikey,' Erin gulped, 'I think I know him.'

'Well go over there and talk to him!' said Candy, making 'shoo-ing' gestures with her hands. 'He's been looking over at you for the last five minutes.'

Erin felt herself blush. She wasn't exactly on first-name terms with him; they had met for about three seconds earlier that week when he had come in to see Adam with some colleagues from Dennon Associates, a firm of architects. But she remembered him: the smile he'd given her when she'd handed him a coffee had kept her on a high all week.

Candy pushed a ten-pound note in her hand and gave Erin a gentle shove in the direction of the bar. 'It's my round, but you're buying,' she smiled. 'I want another spritzer and you want his phone number.'

Still blushing furiously, Erin made her way to the bar, wishing she had taken more care dressing that morning. Rushing for the tube, she had resorted to cast-offs from her Cornwall days: a white shirt and a black cheesecloth skirt, saved from falling off her now-narrow hips by a wide leather belt. Taking a deep breath, she found a space at the bar next to him but pretended not to notice him, instead waving her tenner at the barmaid to get her attention.

'I know you, don't I?' said a voice to her left. Turning, she saw the man from Dennon was smiling at her. His eyes were the clearest green she had ever seen.

'I think you had a meeting at Midas this week, didn't you?' she said.

'Yes, I'm Julian Sewell. You're Adam Gold's assistant, right?'

'Um, yes, I am. I mean, that's where you probably know me from and yes, I'm Adam's assistant. Erin Devereux,' she gabbled. It was so long since Erin had any male attention, she had forgotten how to flirt. It wasn't as if Chris took her seriously and, much to her daily disappointment, Adam didn't even seem to notice she was female. Erin stood there awkwardly as the handsome stranger looked her up and down. Why wasn't she wearing one of the sexy little numbers she'd spent a bloody fortune on over the last couple of months, she scolded herself.

'Devereux. That's an unusual name.'

'I think some distant relatives were Huguenots,' she smiled.

'A sexy French name. I like it.'

Erin blushed furiously. 'So. How did your meeting go?'

Julian laughed. It was a lopsided smile and, as the corners of his eyes crinkled, Erin's heart did a somersault. 'Don't expect much will come of it. We're only a boutique practice and the Midas Corp tend to use the starchitects.'

'Starchitects? What are they?'

'You know. The biggies. Architects as famous as their buildings. Richard Rogers, Norman Foster, Frank Gehry.'

'As you can tell, I've not been in the business long,' she said with an embarrassed smile. 'I don't know the lingo.'

'Well, then,' he said pulling up a bar stool for her. 'I appear to have been stood up by my friend. How about I buy you a drink and you can tell me what you've been doing all your life.'

28

It was six o'clock and Molly was desperate to leave the office, go home and have a hot bath. She applied a second coat of Chanel's Vamp polish to her nails and wondered how she could while away another forty-five minutes. It wasn't that she didn't enjoy having drinks at Claridges, it was just that she didn't much enjoy having to do work at the same time. The meeting she had scheduled there was with some guy called Jasper Goodman, about the Midas Christmas Party. It would no doubt be deadly dull, but she supposed it had to be done. Adam had indicated he wanted it to be the biggest, the most extravagant festive corporate bash, but quotes from all the party planners that Molly had contacted were nothing short of extortionate. Not that Midas were strapped for cash, but Molly wanted to impress Adam, to prove herself an indispensable new asset to the company, so when Jasper Goodman, MD of a new company called HangDog Productions had called promising to do the job for no fee, she had agreed to meet him immediately.

Deciding her nails had had enough TLC, she went down to Claridge's a little early; there was always a chance there might be some Euro prince hanging out there. She took a seat in the bar, ordered a cocktail and had just begun flipping through American *Vogue* when an outrageously handsome man appeared at the door, smiling.

'I bet you're Molly Sinclair,' he said. He was around thirty, tall, lean, in a slim-fitting navy suit, with dark blond hair and a curl to his lips that made it look as if he was thinking something filthy. Molly felt as if she was going to come just by looking at him.

'You don't mind if I have a beer, do you?' he smiled as he

squeezed in next to her and signalled to the barman. 'I don't usually drink when I'm presenting to clients, but I've have a day from hell and you look as if you wouldn't say no.'

'To what?' flirted Molly, her eyes holding his.

'To me having a beer,' he grinned, his hand brushing hers as he pulled a ring-bound folder from out of his attaché case. 'Now, shall we get started?'

Molly found it hard to say no to anything at the best of times, especially if it involved drink, drugs or men, and she had a feeling she was going to agree to whatever Jasper Goodman asked her.

When he took a sip of his beer, leaving a trace of froth on his mouth, Molly was desperate to kiss it off. For the next half an hour, Jasper took her through the costings for three options of Christmas party: a Bollywood banquet at Hampton Court Palace, an Alice-in-Wonderland themed bash at Shepperton Studios, and a recreation of Lapland in Battersea Park, complete with reindeers, real snow and Asprey baubles in the goody bags. The cost of suppliers seemed very reasonable compared to other quotes she had received and, as Jasper's company would do it for no fee, it was definitely the most cost-effective pitch she had seen to date.

'So, what do you think?' he asked cautiously.

Molly paused, looking at Jasper's worried expression and enjoying the power. 'I won't beat around the bush, Jasper, I'm impressed by the pitch but, as you'll be aware, Midas are a huge, high-profile company, and everyone wants to be seen to be organizing our party.'

'That's why we're doing it for no fee,' said Jasper eagerly.

Molly nodded. 'Well, I'm going to show my boss first thing in the morning and we will make a decision on who we are going to go with immediately after that. Good enough?'

'Excellent. But how do you rate my chances: "good", "poor" or "middling",' he asked, the flirtation thick in his voice. 'I know I could definitely get my teeth into this one.'

'At the current time, I'd say your chances were good,' smiled Molly as she paid the drinks bill. And getting better all the time, she added to herself as she felt Jasper's hand on the small of her back, gallantly steering her towards the exit.

'I don't suppose you have any literature on the company, do you?' asked Jasper suddenly when they were out on the street. 'I think I could tailor something even more tightly towards your boss if I knew a little more about the company.'

Molly smirked. 'Well, when you think Midas Corporation, you just have to think very up-market, very luxurious, very sexy,' she smouldered. 'But I do have some brochures in the office. It's just around the corner, if you'd like to . . . ?'

They went up through the big granite lobby of the Midas Corporation and took the lift to Molly's tiny office. The floor was quiet. Just a solitary cleaner sweeping a vacuum over the floor.

'Nice offices,' whispered Jasper respectfully.

'Well, this is what we do. Chic offices, smart apartments.'

Molly handed a sheaf of brochures to Jasper and they walked back into the darkened corridor. The hum of the Hoover had now gone, leaving just the crackle of sexual chemistry between them.

'And what's in here?' asked Jasper, opening the door to one of the meeting rooms. The blinds were open, the room shadowy-black, with the cityscape sparkling below them.

'You're very forward, aren't you?' said Molly quietly, as Jasper shut the office door behind them.

'Forward? You ain't seen nothing yet, sweetheart,' he murmured, coming up behind her so she could feel his soft breath on her neck. Molly knew that she often had a strong effect on men, projecting raw sex appeal in a way that could catch men off balance. It was rare for her to meet a man who had the same effect on her, but Jasper Goodman was one. Their mutual desire was palpable in the air as she relaxed into his body and felt his hands on her. Oh, how she wanted him; she felt dizzy with lust. She was sick of tired, balding, middle-aged men. She wanted someone young and hot and hungry, and Jasper was all those things.

She turned to face him and he immediately pushed her back onto the long walnut table.

'I don't usually do business like this,' he mumbled, his firm hands riding up her thighs. 'But I guess you could call this fringe bene-fits,' he said as he spread her legs, peeled down her panties and gave her his very special service.

29

'Bonjour madam, c'est bien de vous voir.'

Karin air-kissed yet another guest at the launch of her St Tropez store and silently congratulated herself on the evening's success. She had decided against a big, extravagant party on the grounds of both cost and space, and instead had invited a small, carefully selected crowd for cocktails. So milling around the new Karenza outlet on the harbour were the wealthiest villa owners from the hills beyond St Tropez, visiting celebrities and high-rollers currently staying at the Byblos, and the fashion editors from *The Times*, *Elle*, *Le Figaro* and French *Vogue*. It was an eclectic mix, but everybody seemed to be having fun. As numbers were small, she had served the best vintage champagne and fine canapés prepared by the head chef of the Artemis.

Karin had never doubted her ability to throw a good party; what had surprised her was pulling off the Herculean task of opening her first international store in the space of two months. She was exhausted, but exhilarated. She had been working ninety-hour weeks to be in time for the start of the Riviera's summer season, and it had been worth every minute. It was only a small boutique, 500 square feet, but its location was perfect and it had been fitted in cool pale oak floorboards, cream walls and lots of glass and mirrors to create a pared-down luxurious space. As a concession to the Riviera's jet-set traditions she had framed blown-up black-and-white prints of Gianni Agnelli on his yacht and Bardot waving from Pampelonne Beach. The stock was presented like works of art on polished brass racks, which only served to make the swimsuits seem more exclusive. Karin had created a jewel of glamour right at the heart of Europe's most glittering destination.

'I can't bloody believe you've pulled it off,' said Diana, who had come over from London for the grand opening. Karin had insisted: Diana was constantly quarrelling with Martin and badly needed some glitz in her life.

'It's amazing,' said Diana, wide-eyed. 'You've had about two weeks to organize all this and look, everyone's here.'

'Everyone except Adam,' said Karin tartly.

She had been furious when Adam had called her at the shop earlier that day to say that he couldn't make it. He had apologized profusely, muttering about some urgent meeting with a contractor. After three months of dating, Karin was used to Adam cancelling their arrangements at the last minute, but this was one date she wanted him to be at. The fact that Christina had also bailed out of flying to the Côte D'Azur had definitely unsettled her, but Karin was trying to pass it off as coincidence. She had no real reason to suspect that her best friend was sleeping with her boyfriend, except that Karin saw signs of Adam's infidelity everywhere. Every cancelled supper was a secret assignation with a model or society girl. Every urgent phone call to his mobile was a rival trying to steal her man. That Saturday night of the grand prix weekend, when he had turned up drunk in their cabin at 5 a.m., she hadn't believed him when he said he'd been at the casino all night. Karin was jumping at shadows, and she barely recognized herself. It wasn't that she had never trusted a man before, but this was the first time she really cared.

'Allow me to introduce myself,' said a soft voice behind her. Karin turned to find a slight, olive-skinned man with dark slanted eyes looking at her.

'Victor Chen,' he said. 'I think we might have business to discuss.'

The car that had been sent to collect her from the shop wound its way up into the hills behind St Tropez, around hairpin bends, until the port was just a shimmering crescent of blue water studded with yachts the size of white dots. Karin felt elated. It had been the first day of trading at the Karenza St Tropez outlet and it had been a fabulous start. The wife of a multimillionaire Russian restaurateur had bought one of each type of swimsuit in a size thirty-six. The fashion editor of *Le Figaro* had rung to say she was doing a major piece for their Saturday magazine, and there had been a flood of customers walking out with the crisp, white Karenza cardboard bag tied with a forest of green ribbon. Best of all, they had all been exactly the right sort of customer: slim, beautiful and rich.

It had been a good day, but Karin could not help feeling a little apprehensive about this evening's meeting. Victor Chen was spoken about in hushed tones in the business community, a mysterious semi-recluse who had grown a large family inheritance into a huge global conglomerate that included department stores in the Far East, an American discount chain and an Asian cosmetics line. Karin had recently read that he was one of the Far East's richest men and, rumour had it, was currently expanding into China where he was almost certain to become even richer. But what did he want with Karin, and why had he come to the launch of a small boutique?

Finally their destination came into view. A magnificent white-washed villa hanging on the side of a hillside, large, sprawling and impeccably kept. The car stopped in front of a large underlit fountain and a uniformed servant opened the door for Karin as she sucked in the jasmine-scented air.

'This way Mrs Cavendish, if you please,' said a tall elderly man in an impeccable butler's uniform, leading the way into the villa.

Victor was from Hong Kong but owed his Western features to an English grandfather. Only his pale olive skin and narrow black eyes hinted at his Asian roots. His build was slight, almost effeminate, and he was wearing a black silk turtleneck and a pair of cream slacks. Karin thought he looked a little like a Bond villain.

'I am so glad that you have decided to come,' said Victor, his voice soft and precise. 'I am sure it has been a very hectic day for you. I have had word that you have done very brisk business indeed; congratulations are in order.'

Victor led Karin into an enormous drawing room, which was even more impressive than anything in Christina and Ariel's portfolio of homes. The walls were covered in the softest sand-coloured silk, high ceilings were painted with frescos, and a dramatic oil painting, which Karin recognized as a Caravaggio, hung over the medieval fireplace.

'Would you like a drink and we can go out onto the terrace?' asked Victor, gesturing to the open French windows. Karin took a seat at a round marble table at the end of the terrace, with a view of the dark sea and a clustered wooded hillside, and sipped her wine. A cool breeze cut through the balmy air and made the flares around the garden flicker. They made a little small talk, and Karin discovered that Victor was divorced with two children, a fourteen-year-old boy at Eton and a sixteen year-old daughter at school in Switzerland. His age, however, was hard to decipher. She would guess that he was around fifty, but his supple, unlined skin suggested younger.

Two white-uniformed waiters came to serve supper, a plate of finely slicely buffalo mozzarella with asparagus and juicy plum tomatoes glistening with drizzled balsamic vinegar.

'I hope you had a good time at the cocktail party last night,' said Karin. 'What did you think of the range?'

'I was impressed,' said Victor seriously. 'Your swimwear is elegant, timeless; sexy, not trashy. Possibly not the perfect fit with St Tropez,' he said with a smile. 'But I expect you are wondering why you are here – while I am sure you will be a delightful dining companion this evening, I have a proposition for you.'

Karin stiffened and Victor caught the movement.

'I am interested in your company, Mrs Cavendish.'

Karin took a deep breath, feeling slightly giddy. After only seven years in business, she did not imagine that it would be ripe for a takeover by one of the world's biggest retail conglomerates. In bed at night she would do calculations about how much she considered her company to be worth should the day come when someone made an offer for it. Today had been a big day for Karenza swimwear, but it was shaping up to be momentous.

She inhaled sharply to regain her composure. She had learned to be a shrewd negotiator over the years, and to show emotion was to show weakness. 'And why do you think I would be interested in your offer?' she asked. 'Indeed, in any deal which would involve me sacrificing my control?'

'Because you are ambitious for your brand,' said Victor. 'And at the moment you are standing still.'

He held up his hand to stifle her protests. 'You are a creative woman, Mrs Cavendish, but your marketing is naïve. Yes, you have had some success, fashioning yourself into a brand ambassadress, going to parties in your pretty dresses to remind everyone of your sexy little swimwear brand, but it is little more than guerrilla marketing.'

She felt her skin prickle. The cheek of the man.

'Mr Chen, in seven years I have built my business from fabric on a kitchen table to a multimillion-dollar business,' she said, struggling to control her voice.

Victor laughed low and softly. 'It is not a criticism, Mrs Cavendish. You are a talented entrepreneur but few entrepreneurs can grow their company beyond a fifty-million-dollar business without outside investment and help. Don't be afraid of accepting help, or skills that complement your own.' He paused to let this sink in.

'You have a luxury product that can be commercialized on a much greater scale. How many women can afford to spend five hundred dollars on a swimsuit?'

Karin shrugged her shoulders. 'I spent twelve months persuading the best factories in Italy to produce my swimwear. It is the best. That is why women are willing to pay five hundred dollars for a bikini.'

'But how many super-rich women are there? Hundreds? Thousands? The swimwear market is set to explode in the Middle and Far East. You will have access to hundreds of millions of women.'

Karin's eyes sparkled. The scale of the business Victor was proposing made her head swim. Victor continued in a low, even voice.

He swirled some champagne around the bottom of his glass and stayed silent so they could hear the crickets in the long grass in front of them. 'I have had one of my analysts tracking your brand for some time and we feel that in partnership with the right group you can capitalize on that demand and become the leading swimwear brand in the world. We could grow from East to West and finally roll out into America. I understand that you are launching a lingerie line next year, which also interests me. With my help, I think we can turn your brand into the next Victoria's Secret.' Victor looked at Karin in the flickering light. 'It is a billion-dollar brand, Mrs Cavendish.'

A billion-dollar brand. The very thought of it made her struggle to catch her breath. In a rush, she thought of the *Big Blue* and Christina's Gulfstream and all that De Beers jewellery she had always promised herself. But what sort of compromises would that sort of expansion entail? Victor was certainly suggesting a move away from the luxury brand she had spent years cultivating. For a second she wished that Adam could have been by her side to debate it.

But where was he when she needed him? Off on some 'business conference' with Claudia Falcon, or even Christina, no doubt.

'Obviously it's a conversation we can potentially take further after I have discussed it with my people,' said Karin finally.

Victor nodded and watched silently as Karin finished her dessert: poached white peaches steeped in Calvados and honey that melted on her tongue. It was now dark and Victor got up and moved behind her chair to pull it out. His old-fashioned manners were quite endearing, but the stillness of the villa unnerved her.

'That was a most pleasant dinner,' he said. 'How long are you staying in town? Perhaps we could go to dinner at La Cavassona tomorrow to discuss things further?'

'I'm sorry, I am taking the first flight out of Marseille tomorrow morning,' replied Karin.

Again, Victor nodded silently. 'I am scheduled to be in London a week today. Perhaps we could meet then. Do think about it, Mrs Cavendish,' he said. 'Many of the top fashion brands have been a marriage between the very best creative and business talent. Partners in life as well as business,' he added.

As he spoke, he moved closer, gliding forward like a cat. 'Do you want my driver to take you home, or do you want to stay a little while?' he asked smoothly. 'I probably have the finest wine cellar in the Côte d'Azur.'

Victor brushed his hand against her cheek. She smarted inwardly, but let his finger slide down her neck and over her dress, until his soft fingertips rested momentarily on her nipple hidden under the flimsy fabric.

She pulled away with a small cold smile and Victor nodded respectfully. Karin Cavendish had always been the mistress of her own destiny, she had always prided herself on making the right choices. Now here was one standing right in front of her. A billion-dollar opportunity. And suddenly she knew what she wanted. She wanted Karenza to be the biggest, most luxurious swimwear brand in the world, and it would be soon.

30

'Get your coat. We're going straight out.'

Julian Sewell had appeared at Erin's front door at twelve on an early summer afternoon, then whisked her away on a magical mystery tour in his open-topped car. Erin felt as if she had stepped into a Cary Grant movie, which was quite an improvement considering she had never expected the date to happen. True, they'd had a good time that night in the Piccadilly wine bar. Julian's friend hadn't turned up, and Candy had slipped off when Erin wasn't looking, so Erin and Julian had sat at the bar talking and laughing and getting increasingly drunk until it was gone midnight and the barman had told them it was time to close. She'd desperately wanted him to invite her home, but he hadn't. He said he'd call, but that was what men said, wasn't it? Until that very moment, when he was standing in front of her in blue jeans, a white short-sleeved shirt and *that* smile, Erin hadn't really expected to see him again.

'Are you coming, or am I going to have to come and give you a fireman's lift down to the car?' shouted Julian as Erin rushed around finding her shoes and bag and keys. Erin still couldn't quite believe he had called; men like Julian Sewell, – handsome, successful, sexy men who probably had model girlfriends tucked away in their designer lofts – weren't interested in her. If they chatted you up it was because they were drunk. If they took you to bed, they didn't remember your name the next morning. But here he was, as large as life and so handsome that she almost burst out laughing.

'But where are we going?' asked Erin as she ran down the steps.

He handed her an *A–Z* as they walked towards a soft-top vintage Mercedes SL.

'An alfresco lunch.'

'Where?'

'Open the page, any page and decide where,' he smiled, lighting a cigarette and wedging it between his lips.

Erin closed her eyes, flipped open the *A–Z* and pointed. Dulwich village.

Julian drove them all the way into southeast London with the roof of the car down, so the sun warmed their faces and the breeze ruffled their hair. They parked the car in the village and walked into the park with a creaky wicker hamper Julian had produced from the boot. They found a spot on the grass, laid out a blanket and spread the picnic out; there were two types of carved ham, three types of pickle, a ludicrously comprehensive selection of cheese, along with crusty bread, ripe strawberries and a bottle of chilled Veuve Clicquot.

'Sorry, I forgot to bring any glasses,' said Julian as he popped the cork. 'D'you mind using straws?'

Erin laughed, feeling more happy than she could remember. 'Oh, I always use a straw,' she said, 'it's the only way to drink champagne.'

Erin lay back on the rug and looked up at Julian. She wanted to know everything about him: what his favourite music was, who he'd like to be stranded on a desert island with, how many girlfriends he'd had. Particularly the last one. She already knew a lot about him from their night at the bar. He was thirty, which she used to consider old, but working with oldies like Adam, Julian just seemed mature, experienced. A graduate of Manchester University, just like Norman Foster ('my absolute hero'). Julian had told her, without a hint of irony, that architecture was his life.

'So is that what you want to be, then: a starchitect?' she asked, biting into a strawberry.

'I guess,' he smiled, breaking off a piece of bread. 'I mean, it would be amazing to be like Frank Gehry. He turns his hand to everything from jewellery to concert halls, and the really cool thing is, whether it's a bracelet or a suspension bridge, you can tell it's his.'

Erin smiled; he had the same passion for his job that she saw in Adam. He had the same magnetism, too, but Julian's was a different kind of sex appeal – softer, more obtainable perhaps. Julian was definitely more classically handsome. Definitely. In fact, it was all she could do to prevent herself from reaching out to touch him, to run her fingers over the hint of pale brown stubble on his chin, to feel his tanned skin and those long lashes that framed his eyes. She took a deep breath and tried to concentrate on what he was saying.

'. . . But even if I stay working at our practice forever, I'll be happy,' he went on. 'I just want to design. Both my parents are architects, so I guess I'm doing what I know best.' Julian plucked a long stem of grass and began to play with it. 'What do your parents do?' he asked suddenly.

Erin licked the strawberry juice from her lips and rolled over to look at him, propping herself up on her elbow. She rarely discussed her parents with anyone. She'd barely even told Chris the story, and he was her closest friend in London. But there was something about Julian that made her want to open up to him, mentally and physically. She wanted him to know everything.

'My dad was in the fashion business, but nothing very glamorous like a designer. His company actually made jeans,' she said, looking a little embarrassed. 'My mum worked for him sometimes, doing the books and things, but mainly she was a housewife. Anyway, my dad's dead. I went to live with my gran when I was six.'

Julian looked confused. 'Why didn't you live with your mum?'

'Because she's missing.' She paused, knowing it was a first date and it all seemed completely inappropriate to discuss, but he had put his hand on her head, stroking her hair with his fingertip, and she knew it was okay to talk.

'Missing?' asked Julian quietly.

'My dad committed suicide after his business went under. My mum had always been a bit of a depressive and it just got worse after he'd gone.'

Julian nodded, encouraging her to go on.

'We lived in London then, but spent a lot of time at my gran's in Cornwall. One day, the summer after my dad's death, we were in Port Merryn and my mum said she had to pop back to London for the night. She never came back. Police found her car a week later near Beachy Head but they never found her body.'

She glanced at Julian, wishing she hadn't told him, but at the same time glad she had.

'Do you think she's still alive?' asked Julian.

Erin shook her head. 'She's dead,' she said categorically. 'I know it sounds weird but, even before her car was found, I just couldn't feel her around any more. Anyway, I know if she was alive that she would have come back for me.'

She fell silent for a moment. 'I know that might make me sound like a bad person. Believing she's dead, I mean. My gran's the opposite, she won't accept that she's gone. She still keeps a light on in my mum's old bedroom at night, so she can find her way home, I guess.'

She scrunched up her eyes in the sun and a tear ran down the crease.

'You have to believe what is right for you,' said Julian slowly, reaching out to touch her hand.

'Well, it definitely worked out for the best, me getting a job in London. I had to leave Cornwall to escape the limbo,' she said softly. 'Every night I'd see the light and it would make me feel bad.'

Julian began to pack away the hamper and took her hand. 'Come on. We're going to cheer you up. Let's go and hire some bikes from that place by the gate.'

'Good idea,' smiled Erin, rubbing her face. 'Because I want to show you something.'

They put the hamper back in the car and cycled out of the park, out of Dulwich and up the hill towards Crystal Palace. Puffing and grinning, they finally made it to one of the highest points in London and looked down at the sprawling capital spread out like their picnic blanket. Erin could see Canary Wharf and the Swiss Re gherkin, thinking with a sense of pride that two more landmark buildings, currently being built by the Midas Corporation, would soon be rising out of the city's skyline.

'Bloody hell, Erin, what have we come all the way up here for?' asked Julian, braking to take a breather.

'Come on lazy,' she laughed, 'I want to see what you think of a building. A professional opinion, if you like.'

They wheeled the bikes along the pavement for a few minutes, then Erin turned into a leafy side street and stopped at an old white Georgian building set back from the road.

'This old thing? What about it?' asked Julian, shielding his eyes from the sun as he gazed up at it.

'It's mine,' said Erin softly. 'I just bought it.'

Julian looked at Erin, then back at the house. 'You're kidding.'

Erin shook her head. 'It's one residence now, but I want to convert it into apartments,' she said eagerly. 'I'm on a very tight budget, but I think there's a real opportunity here. The building is pretty, the area is up and coming. The smart estate agents and the gastro-pubs are moving in, prices are rising.' She spread her arms. 'It's all here.'

'Wow. Get you; you're a real little Adam Gold prodigy, aren't you?'

Julian leant his bike up against the wall and walked up to the house, running his hands over the brickwork like a sculptor feeling clay.

'I realize it's a bit shabby now, but I just know I can make this work,' said Erin, trying to sound more confident than she felt. Ever since she had completed on the property purchase she'd been wondering whether she'd been too rash. 'But I have a massive mortgage, so I need to get planning permission straight away. I can't afford for it to be unoccupied for too long. And I have to get an architect to draw up plans before I can apply for planning permission.'

'Well, if it's an architect you need,' he said, standing back and peering up at the roof, 'I know a pretty good one.'

'So do I,' laughed Erin,' but I bet he's expensive.'

'Oh, I'm sure we can come to some agreement,' he replied.

He moved closer towards her and put his hands on hers, moving his face in close. 'Shall we start talking terms and conditions?' he whispered as sunlight poured through the trees around the house and dappled them with light.

'Well, I think this is a very good start,' she smiled, as he moved his lips towards her for the sweetest, most sensual kiss.

Erin pulled away, her head feeling light and dizzy. She looked at the house, then at Julian. 'Consider yourself hired,' she said.

31

Molly had just grabbed her jacket from the back of her office chair and was dashing for the lift when her phone rang. It was Adam. 'Molly, can I just have a word with you upstairs for a minute?' he asked.

'Oh Adam,' she breathed, 'I have a meeting Mayfair in half an hour, is there any chance it can wait until tomorrow?' She was due to meet Alex for their fortnightly rendezvous and she knew Lord Delemere well enough by now to know he hated her being late.

'Now, Molly,' replied Adam, and the phone clicked dead.

Cursing, Molly slicked some gloss over her lips, undid a button on her blouse and went upstairs. She entered Adam's office and sat down in the black leather swivel chair opposite him, crossing her legs and giving him a lazy smile.

'I won't keep you long,' said Adam flatly. His stiff back and sober expression immediately put her on her guard.

'Well, the Christmas party is already looking fantastic,' said Molly, trying to fill the silence. 'I've had a great quote from a company who want to do something really special. I'm thinking a Bollywood banquet; snake charmers, real elephants, a whole sensuous bazaar feel. We're just getting some spread sheets and visuals together and, if you approve them, then we can get the ball rolling.'

'Fine. But that's not what I wanted to talk to you about,' said Adam abruptly.

Molly raised her eyebrows quizzically. Adam looked down at his desk.

'Molly, something has come to my attention that could be incredibly awkward for a number of people, not least myself.'

Molly shifted in her chair. She had a feeling that the late-night cognac and indecent proposal she had envisioned weren't on the cards tonight.

'Something happened in the office on Friday night which was – is – quite frankly unacceptable.'

Friday? What happened on Friday? Oh God! Molly had a flash-back to her boardroom tryst with Jasper, remembering his hands, his mouth, the pure sensual pleasure . . . but there was no way Adam could know about it – was there?

She looked at him and Adam met her gaze, his expression steely, his jaw locked and impassive.

'Molly you know what I'm talking about,' he said slowly.

'No, I'm afraid I don't,' she said lifting her chin defiantly, 'you're going to have to illuminate me.'

'If that's how you want to play it,' said Adam, reaching for a remote control and pointing it at a television at the side of his desk.

The picture flicked onto a grainy black-and-white image. Molly's face was immediately recognizable, thrown back in pleasure as she lay on the boardroom table, her skirt up around her hips, her legs splayed like the arms of a clock, a man's head between them. Adam kept the television on a moment longer than was necessary, then snapped it off.

Molly could hear the sound of her own quickened breathing filling the silence. *How could she have been so stupid?* She had been in that boardroom a hundred times and never noticed CCTV. She tried quickly to think of something to say, an excuse, a denial. But it was useless. She had been caught red-handed.

'Molly, we just can't have that sort of thing going on in the office.'

She nodded solemnly and Adam paused.

'I take it Marcus doesn't know?' he asked.

'Of course not,' she said, the words coming out like a croak. 'It was a one-off. I was so stupid, so fucking stupid,' she said, biting her lips in anger.

'I think this Friday should be your last day in the office,' he said flatly.

'What?' she gasped. 'You're joking!'

'Why should I be joking?' asked Adam angrily. 'My events coord-inator fucks someone who isn't her boyfriend, my vice president – my friend – on my boardroom table. Why should I be joking?'

She could feel her heart pounding so loudly she was sure Adam could hear it. Right now Adam Gold had the power to destroy her whole life, to wipe out the entire existence she had become so comfortable with. The Standlings, the parties, the Maserati. Everything.

'But I thought I was doing a good job, I thought . . .'

She looked up at Adam, her eyes pleading. 'You're not going to tell Marcus, are you? Please Adam, I beg you.' Her voice was beginning to crack and real tears spilled down her cheeks.

Adam glanced away for a moment, shaking his head. 'I won't. For now.'

Molly breathed a sigh of relief.

'But my loyalties are to him, Molly,' continued Adam. 'And if I get even a whiff that you've screwed around on him again, not only will I tell Marcus about your little extracurricular activity, I'll get you blackballed from so many companies in London, you won't be able to get a job in this town shovelling shit.'

'Thank you, Adam, it will never happen again, I promise you.'

'Don't thank me,' said Adam, looking at Molly with disgust. 'Just get out.'

'What do you mean, you haven't told Marcus?'

Karin was furious. How could he not tell him? Men could be such *idiots*. She and Adam were sitting at the best table in a fabulous new chic French restaurant in Chelsea, and he'd made her evening by telling her he had just fired Molly, but then gone and spoiled the whole thing with some sort of weird twisted male logic.

'But what would it solve, honey?' said Adam, filling her glass with water which she drained almost immediately. 'If she's telling the truth and it's a one-off, then there's no point telling him. Marcus has had a run of bad luck with women, but he seems to really like Molly. If she's a serial cheat, well then he'll find out soon enough, but I'd rather it didn't come from me.'

Karin couldn't believe it; how had Molly been able to secure Adam's silence? *With sex*? No, he wouldn't do that – would he? She tried to put that thought out of her mind. What irked Karin the most was that it had taken such a huge amount of planning. Molly was such a slacker, Karin knew that she wouldn't bother to fact-check or take references on anything. If she had, Molly would soon have discovered that HangDog Productions didn't actually exist and that Jasper Goodman, the man she'd fucked on the board-room table, wasn't a gung-ho party planner with an impressive CV and a Rolodex of society contacts. He was Jonathan Gooding, an out-of-work actor and sometime escort who would do anything for money and who had deceived Molly Sinclair beautifully. *Damn it! If only Adam had told Marcus.* After Molly's conniving in Monaco, there was nothing Karin would like better than to see the dreadful woman out of the picture. Well, almost nothing.

'Don't let Molly Sinclair put you in such a bad mood. She always seems to rile you,' said Adam as the waiter placed their food in front of them.

'I just have a lot on my mind,' said Karin truthfully.

'I hope this isn't still to do with me not coming to St Tropez, is it?' asked Adam, raising a crystal wine goblet to his lips. 'Karin, this refinancing is crucial. It was the only time I could get all the guys from the bank together.'

She shrugged, smiling. 'You know I'm not one of those demanding women who insists their boyfriend be there for every minor life triumph.'

'Hardly minor. Karenza is now an international brand.'

'Not before time,' she said, raising her glass to his.

She swilled the contents of her glass around before she put it back on the table and looked at Adam intently. 'I met Victor Chen in St Tropez. He wants to buy the company.'

Adam put his knife and fork down. 'A serious offer?'

'As serious as these things are. He wants to take the company mass prestige, move production out to the Far East, bring down prices, increase stock. Basically he's proposing to have Karenza in every department store from Manchester to Manila.'

'Well, that's one business model for the company,' replied Adam. 'Although I suspect you may have other ideas?'

A waiter came to fuss around them, refilling Adam's glass with the restaurant cellar's best white wine, and filling Karin's with still water.

Karin paused again. 'He also tried to sleep with me,' she said.

'What?' snapped Adam, prompting a nearby waiter to lift his head to see what was going on. 'Where? At the shop?'

'No. He invited me to his villa for dinner.'

Adam glared at Karin, his face a mixture of anger and jealousy, which was exactly the response Karin had been hoping for.

'And you *went*? I turn my back for a moment and you're running off to some guy's fucking villa to *talk*.'

'Adam. It was to talk business. You know how it works.'

'Of course I know how it works,' he spat. 'He wanted to screw you and he tried to seduce you with promises of a global business.'

Karin flashed him a wry smile. 'And you know how it works so well because . . . ?'

Adam looked at her, fuming. Then he shook his head and snorted with laughter. 'Touché, Karin Cavendish,' he said.

Karin leaned over and touched his sleeve. 'Adam, I didn't sleep with him. And I don't want him to buy the business. But what I do want is fast expansion: roll out the lingerie, add another dozen shops within two years. I want to keep the company high-end, but sell on a much larger scale – do that and the private equity companies will be falling over each other for a buyout.'

Adam was mulling this all over quietly. 'You'll need external investment,' he said.

Karin nodded. 'But I'd rather not go back to Victor Chen.'

Adam looked at her critically. 'I've offered once. I believe the response was that you wanted complete control.'

'I still do,' said Karin honestly.

'Honey, that's not the way it works,' he said, trying hard not to sound patronizing.

'Look, Adam, Victor was good for one thing,' said Karin, ignoring his curtness. 'He's made me think about cutting my costs.'

Adam smiled. 'Ah, I sense a plan coming on.'

Karin leaned forward conspiratorially. 'As you know, the lingerie range launches before Christmas. The designs are done, but they haven't gone into production.'

'You're thinking about moving it out to the Far East, aren't you?' nodded Adam.

Karin shrugged. 'Maybe I've been too much of a snob.'

Adam repressed a snort and Karin smiled at him. 'I've been looking at samples and there really is very little difference between product made in Italy and China. Knickers are made to come off, so does anybody really care where they come from? I'm going to cancel the order with the Italian factory and go elsewhere. '

'I thought you said provenance was everything.'

'Let's just say I won't be compromising our reputation.'

Adam met her gaze. 'What do you want, Karin? My investment?

You know Midas is about to float. I'm not sure now is the right time for me.'

'This is pocket money for you, Adam,' she said flatly. 'I want to issue non-voting B shares in the company in return for a five-million-pound cash injection.'

'Non-voting?' queried Adam.

'I know what I'm doing,' she replied, her voice steely. 'Do you want to make money or not? In two years' time, you'll be bought out for ninety million dollars minimum.'

'You drive a hard bargain, Karin Cavendish,' smiled Adam, his eyes pooling with lust.

'It's what you love about me,' she smiled, running the tip of her toe up his leg.

'Just promise me you didn't fuck Chen,' he said, motioning the waiter for the bill.

'I didn't have sex with him,' Karin whispered in the quiet, rarefied atmosphere of the restaurant.

'Come on. Let's get out of here,' she smiled wolfishly, as they both got up from the table. 'There's something we should do.'

32

As Summer had no idea of where Ricardo Lantis was taking her for dinner, she had dressed neutrally in a pair of black pants and a dark green silk vest. It was conservative for her and she felt a little old, but she didn't want to be too sexy either. On the dot of eight, a black Bentley convertible came to pick her up. The driver introduced himself as Samuel and politely asked, as it was a warm night, if Summer would like the top of the car down. Summer had grinned but declined the offer, preferring to sit in darkened anonymity as they wound through the streets of London, finally gliding to a stop in a grand residential street in Belgravia.

'This is Mr Lantis's house,' said Samuel, indicating an impressive Georgian house as he opened her door. Rather apprehensive, Summer walked up to the polished black front door and knocked.

An olive-skinned woman of about forty answered. She was too smartly dressed for a housekeeper, thought Summer. She was polished and haughty and a little frightening.

'I am Dita. Good evening,' she said, stepping back to allow Summer to enter. The cream walls of the hall were lined with framed photographs of Ricardo in all sorts of exotic locations – on the ski slopes, on a yacht, driving a sports car – and in each, his arms were around all sorts of glamorous blondes, brunettes and redheads.

'Would you like a drink?' asked Dita. She beckoned to a butler who was already pouring a glass of champagne.

'You must think I am terribly rude,' smiled Dita, pressing the glass into her hand. 'I haven't introduced myself. I am Ricardo's cousin. I am afraid Ricardo has just called to say he is going to be a little late. Work is his life,' she sighed. 'If something needs doing he will not stop until it's done. Why don't you go through and meet the others?'

Others? thought Summer, following Dita into a magnificent drawing room. Beautiful tapestries and art lined the walls and at one end was a walnut bar stocked with expensive-looking liqueurs in decanters. Stretched across the plump ivory sofa were two slim, beautiful girls, who were chatting and drinking from crystal tumblers. A third girl, with waist-length black hair and a backless dress was giggling as she tried to play the black grand piano. They all looked up as Summer entered, but none of the girls seemed surprised to see Summer.

'Hi. I'm Tasha,' smiled the prettiest of the three, 'that's Rachel and Becki.' Tasha was about Summer's age. She had long wavy chestnut hair swept up into a high glossy ponytail and a body that could carry off skin-tight black leather trousers and a fitted white T-shirt that had a diamanté palm tree on the front. For a second Summer wondered if they were Ricardo's sisters. Or even *daughters.*

'Are you coming out with us tonight?' asked Tasha brightly.

'With Ricardo?' said Summer cautiously.

'Sure,' laughed Tasha. 'Actually he's just called, did Dita tell you? We're meeting him at the club now. There's no point leaving here for an hour or so, so make yourself comfy and we can all get to know one another.'

Summer was beginning to wonder what she had got herself into.

Sitting in a VIP booth of the Athenaeum, a cavernous basement club made to look like a nineteenth-century opium den, Summer wondered when it would be polite to make a getaway. It was almost midnight. They hadn't left Ricardo's house until 10 p.m. and Ricardo himself had only showed up an hour later, when he'd given her ten minutes of chitchat about working late and how fantastic she looked before he had begun to circulate around the rest of the VIP area. Summer wondered how she had managed to get the wrong end of the stick. Suddenly, the loud Euro-pop stopped and the DJ played a cheesy fanfare. A waitress walked towards their table with a jeroboam of Cristal, putting the huge, £5000 bottle of champagne in front of them with a flourish. Summer cringed. She had seen this ritual before at Les Caves du Roy in St Tropez, but on home turf it seemed an even more vulgar display of wealth. Tasha, however, seemed delighted, clapping her hands and holding out her glass as the waitress struggled to open the huge bottle.

'Are you coming back to the house later?' she asked Summer, her eyes sparkling.

'I'm not sure,' said Summer. 'Will Ricardo's cousin be there?'

'Who?' asked Tasha.

'Dita.'

'Oh, Dita's not his fucking cousin!' laughed Tasha, running her hands through her ponytail. 'She's his . . . hmm . . .' Tasha paused and frowned, putting her finger to her lips. 'She's his fixer.'

'What, like a concierge?' asked Summer, taking the drink Tasha offered.

'Of sorts,' smiled Tasha a little patronizingly.

Summer looked over at Ricardo sitting squashed in a booth with Rachel on one side, Becki on the other. She noticed that Ricardo had his hand right at the top of Becki's thigh, her short skirt having ridden up so that Summer could almost see her knickers. Summer felt her cheeks flush, feeling stupid.

'Dita is a *madam*?' she said, realizing she sounded like a prude.

'Easy tiger,' laughed Tasha. Discreetly she opened a pill box, tipped a small pyramid of coke onto the back of her hand and snorted it. She shook her head, ponytail swishing in the air.

'Dita isn't a madam, silly. But she kind of helps Ricardo. I mean, when you're that successful and rich, you don't have time to sort out a social life, do you? Think about it.'

'Well, he found the time to ask me to dinner,' replied Summer moodily.

'You're upset about tonight, aren't you?' said Tasha, offering her the pill box. Summer shook her head. She was feeling light-headed enough, drinking on an empty stomach.

'What did you think tonight was going to be? Hearts and flowers and some candlelit dinner for two?'

Tasha rested her hand on Summer's knee. 'I'm sorry, honey, I didn't mean it to sound that way. Ric obviously likes you, but tonight he wanted to party a little bit. He's probably had a really hard day. But listen. Stick with him, yeah? He's so much fun, and so generous. He's offered to pay for this fashion design course I've been desperate to do.' She lowered her voice. 'Becki says she heard that if you become one of his favourite girls, he'll pay for your flat, car, holidays everything. It must be true. At

Easter we all went to his chalet in Courcheval which was mental.'

Summer didn't want to be involved with anything mental. In fact she had made up her mind to leave, but she felt in a very awkward position. Ricardo was Molly's friend, after all; she didn't want to embarrass her mother. Just then, Ricardo came over to her, motioning Tasha out of the way.

'Drink up, Summer,' he said, handing her a cocktail. 'What about another glass?'

She sipped the drink politely, but Ricardo noticed Summer's reluctant expression. 'I can see the look on your face and I completely agree with you. It's dull, here. Dull, dull, dull.' He clapped his hands together and Rachel, Becki and Tasha, plus a couple of other girls Summer hadn't noticed before, all stood up, ready to leave.

'Actually Ricardo, I've had a fun evening, but I think it's time I got going,' said Summer as they walked towards the entrance.

Ricardo wrapped his arm around her waist and guided her out to the pavement. 'Come on, honey,' he urged. 'The house is only five minutes' drive away. I have some great cognac.' He moved closer towards her, out of earshot of the other girls, his manner becoming reassuringly more serious. 'Don't you think I wanted a nice dinner tonight, too? I was really looking forward to good food, good conversation, but what can I do when friends come round to the house?' He looked round at the girls and shrugged. 'Next time I'm going to tell Dita that she must send them all home.'

Summer wasn't sure if he was blatantly lying or if he genuinely believed this to be the truth. *Like hell Dita will send them all home. She is the one that invites them in the first place.*

'I'm really sorry, Ric, but I must go,' she stressed as the Bentley had pulled up at the kerb and Samuel had come round to open the rear door.

'Five minutes,' smiled Ricardo. There was something unsettling about Ricardo, but somehow that made him more attractive. She knew she was a little tipsy, but she felt powerless to resist. Summer doubted that anyone ever said no to Ricardo unless he wanted them to.

She got into the back seat, telling herself she would stay twenty minutes and then request that Samuel take her home.

'You don't like clubs.' It wasn't a question.

She smiled weakly. 'I think I've just had enough of them.'

'Not like your mother. Now she can party.'

When Ricardo mentioned Molly, there was a definite tone of affection. 'How about next week, we'll do something quiet, yes? I'm sorry again for tonight,' he said, resting his hand lightly on hers. 'Sometimes you just need to let your hair down, have a few drinks, see some friends. I thought that would be okay with you too, but I was thoughtless.'

'Let your hair down, that's what Tasha said you wanted.'

'She's knows me well, that one. She's an old friend. A very talented designer.'

They pulled up outside the house. A couple of lights were on; Summer wondered if Dita was still up. In fact she wondered whether Dita actually lived there. The taxi pulled up simultaneously and five girls piled out, laughing and shouting.

'Hey, come with us!' said Tasha, grabbing Summer by the hand and pulling her inside the house, following the other girls up a marble staircase in a clatter of heels to an enormous bathroom

Peering inside, Summer was startled to see that the girls were all in various states of undress. Rachel was in just her bra and knickers and was turning on the Jacuzzi, so the sound of gushing water echoed round the room.

'Ricardo, do you mind if we use the sauna?' shouted Becki, running in wrapped in a teeny white fluffy robe.

Ricardo walked to the doorway of an adjoining room. He had kicked off his shoes, undone a couple of buttons on his shirt and was holding a tumbler of amber-coloured liquid. 'Cognac?' he said to Summer, beckoning her into the room. He handed her a glass and walked into a large closet. Summer sipped the drink cautiously, feeling very uncomfortable standing in what was obviously Ricardo's bedroom. *What the hell am I doing?* she thought.

'Shall we go and join the girls? It's playtime,' purred Ricardo, returning wearing a white towelling robe.

'Ricardo, I think . . . I think I . . .' she said, putting a hand on a wall to steady herself. Suddenly she felt dizzy and the room was beginning to swim. She could feel his hands on her arm, leading her towards the spa room. Three girls were now in the Jacuzzi. Tasha was naked and Becki was kissing her mouth and breasts, while Rachel was perched on the side of the Jacuzzi, snorting a line of cocaine.

It was becoming a nightmare.

'Ricardo, I need to go home,' mumbled Summer, finding it difficult to get the words out.

'Relax, Summer! You might just enjoy yourself,' laughed Ricardo, rubbing her shoulders.

'I want to GO!' she said more forcefully, shrugging off his hand.

He stepped towards her, a smile still plastered on his face, but it was somehow cruel and mean.

'Well, you know where the door is,' he spat.

Summer jolted backwards, stumbling on a towel and slamming into the door. She scrambled sideways and made for the stairs, slipping on the marble and twisting her knee, but fear pushed her on through the pain.

'I never had this problem with your mother,' yelled Ricardo after her, as Summer opened the front door and gulped in the night air.

Head pounding, vision blurred, she felt a huge weariness – she just wanted to lie down and rest, but panic was driving her, telling her to get away from the house. She zigzagged down the street, bumping into railings and cars, unable to coordinate her movements. Finally she could see the Berkeley Hotel ahead of her. Surely she could wave down a taxi from there, she thought. A doorman in a grey suit and bowler hat noticed her and put a reassuring hand on her shoulder. 'Madam, are you alright? Can I do anything to help?'

Summer was summoning the energy to speak, when the hotel's doors opened and she heard a familiar voice.

'Summer? What's wrong? What's going on?'

She could barely focus now, but she heard the voice again.

'Okay, Robert, she's a friend. I'll take it from here,' and she felt firm, reassuring hands on her back and she allowed herself to be helped into the expensive leather seat of a large car.

'Thanks, Adam,' she managed weakly. 'I don't know what's the matter with me. But I've just had the evening from hell.'

When Summer woke up, it was dark and still. For a moment she thought she was dead, until she realized she was lying under a soft blanket on a black leather sofa.

'Easy does it,' said Adam softly, handing her a glass of water as she tried to sit up. He was dressed in sweat-pants and a T-shirt and had a bleary, pink-eyed look, as if he'd just woken up himself.

'Where am I? Have I been asleep?'

'Don't worry. You're at my apartment. I was going to take you straight home but you passed out in the car after a few minutes. You've been asleep for a couple of hours.'

Summer felt a rush of emotions: relief, fear, shame. 'Urgh, I feel dreadful.'

'I'm not surprised after spending the evening in the company with that jerk. I think he might have given you Rohypnol.'

Summer sat up suddenly, sending stars across her vision. 'You're kidding!'

'No,' said Adam gravely. 'And it wouldn't be the first time I've heard about Ricardo trying it on with that shit. People call his house "The Brothel". He certainly seems to have one hell of a merry-go-round of women in that place.'

'I feel such a bloody idiot,' said Summer, nervously reaching up to smooth her hair, thinking she must look like a scarecrow.

'We should go to the police,' said Adam firmly. 'If he's drugged you they can arrest him.'

Summer felt a rush of panic. The last thing she wanted was to involve the police. After all, Ricardo was Molly's friend and it was her who had set them up on a date.

'I just want to forget about it,' she replied.

'Listen, if you're worried, I can go with you . . .'

'*Please* Adam. No. I really, really don't want to.'

He nodded, not wanting to push it. 'Well, are you hungry? My chef doesn't arrive for an hour or so, but if you want to take your chances with my cooking I make a mean pancake.'

'Urr, Adam, the way I feel . . .' She glanced at his eager expression and laughed. 'You're not going to let me say no, are you?'

'No,' he smiled.

Feeling a little better now, she followed him through to the kitchen, an impressive open-plan oak and granite design filled with shiny chrome appliances. As he opened the fridge, she could see, the firm muscles of his back through his thin white T-shirt and, blushing slightly, she forced herself to look away. Out of the window, the night sky was turning grey and gold and birds were beginning to sing in Hyde Park. She was glad dawn was breaking; it felt too intimate being in Adam's apartment at night. He was too good looking, too damn sexy to feel comfortable with, remembering the last time they'd been together – alone at the beach party in Anguilla.

She'd tried to deny the chemistry between them then. But here, alone, only yards from his bed . . . *Oh God, Summer, stop thinking that way*, she groaned to herself. She took a sip of water which was ice cold against her lips and looked out at the dawn sky again.

'It's going to be a gorgeous day,' she said absently. 'A heatwave, apparently. I really want to do something.'

Adam turned back from the stove. 'What do you mean "do something"?' he asked. There was a definite flirtation in his voice, and something filled the air between them.

'Oh, you know, take advantage of the sunshine. Something where you can feel nature, like a paddle in the sea or flying a kite.'

Adam smiled again. 'You make it sound good.'

'The simple things often are.'

'So, do you fancy doing something together?' he asked.

She glanced away, feeling a flutter of illicit excitement and guilt. She thought of Karin, and tried to shake it away.

'So?' asked Adam, trying to catch her gaze.

'I'm not sure,' she said slowly.

He touched her lightly on the shoulder. 'I think you need some fun after what you've just been through.'

She gave a little shrug. 'I guess. So what did you have in mind?'

'Wait and see,' he smiled. 'But we might have to drop by your flat for some jeans and sneakers.'

He's only being friendly, thought Summer, *he's just looking after me. Nothing wrong with that, is there?* Nothing wrong at all.

'Okay, I'm all yours,' she said.

33

Erin was annoyed. It was her first morning off since she'd been at Midas and she'd wanted nothing more than to stay in bed with Julian, eating croissants and making love. But Julian had left her flat at 7 a.m. to get to Bath for a mid-morning business meeting and Erin had her own appointment; she'd been summoned to see Ed Davies, her agent, who she had not seen or heard from since Christmas. It was the last thing Erin wanted to do on a fine spring morning.

Davies and Partners occupied a small mews house in a leafy, blossom-filled street in Bloomsbury. The reception was full of shiny pristine books, all lined up in display cases; fat bestsellers next to slick political biographies and fiercely clever literary authors she recognized from the *Sunday Times* lists. For a moment, Erin felt a rush of excitement she had not experienced since the first time she walked into the Midas Corporation building. But, as she walked up the stairs to the agent's office, it was quickly replaced by a feeling of guilt and frustration that she hadn't had time to do anything on her book since she'd been in London.

'Erin. So good to see you again,' said Ed Davies warmly, getting up from behind his big mahogany desk. The room was stuffed with books and manuscripts, reminding Erin of her tutor's study at university. She shook his hand and took a seat opposite him.

'I would have suggested lunch, but I know how busy you are with your new job and so on,' he said with a knowing look.

'Guilty as charged,' smiled Erin.

'Now, then,' said Ed distractedly, turning round to his coffee machine. 'Let's talk about the book.'

Tasmina Perry

Erin had a sudden flashback to school, feeling as if the headmaster was about to tell her off for something she had not done.

'I assume you haven't got any more for me to have a look at today?' he said, taking a sip of espresso.

'I don't suppose you want to hear about how busy I've been?' she said weakly. 'I've just been snowed under.'

She felt herself blush: it was a half-truth. She *had* been busy with her crazy, ninety-hour working weeks, but she'd certainly found time for Julian; plenty of time. Since their first date in Dulwich Park they'd been out for dinner twice, to a late-night cinema preview, and rowing in Hyde Park. Plus writing a book seemed so much less urgent and important now she had bought Belvedere Road.

Ed nodded as if he'd heard it all before. 'Erin, about fifty per cent of my authors also have full-time jobs,' he said flatly, steepling his fingers in front of his face. 'And I don't hear excuses from them because, do you know what? There *are* no excuses. Nobody is forcing you write a book. You do it, even if it means juggling another career, family, friends, because you really, really want to. You don't write books for the money because, believe me, for every John Grisham or JK Rowling there are thousands of really brilliant, talented authors out there writing books for less than ten thousand pounds a time.'

Erin winced. 'If this is a motivational speech, it isn't working,' she said sulkily.

'You write books, Erin, because you have a story burning inside you that you want to share,' continued Ed, his voice soft and assured. 'It doesn't matter whether it's still around in a hundred years, lauded as a classic, or whether it brought pleasure to just one person, the idea is to write a book and see it printed and bound and think, "I did that".'

Ed smiled kindly. 'And I know that's how you feel. Or rather how you *did* feel, because I saw it in your face and I read it in your words when you sent me your manuscript almost a year ago.'

Erin nodded weakly, knowing he was right, but also knowing that, if there had ever been a burning desire to write a story, it now been dulled by a nice salary, a lovely flat, a wardrobe of beautiful clothes and a gorgeous house that was going to make her fortune.

As if he were reading her mind, Ed put down his cup and looked at her. 'In life, Erin, some people do things for love and some people

221

do things for money. Take it from an old man, the people who do things for love tend to be the ones who end up happiest,' he said with a crinkled smile. 'Did I tell you that thirty years ago I worked for an investment bank? It seemed to be the thing to do when you were fresh out of Cambridge.'

Erin was amazed. Sitting here surrounded by books and paper, she couldn't imagine Ed having ever been anywhere or anything else.

'So what happened?' she asked.

'An epiphany.'

'And do you regret it?'

Ed shook his head vigorously. 'Friends I worked with then are now partners in the big banks, buying second and third homes in Tuscany with their very large bonuses. They're rich, and stressed, and for the most part unhappy, because there is always someone richer than them, more successful than them, and it doesn't make them feel good.'

'But you're successful anyway,' said Erin swiftly, knowing that with a roster of big-name authors on the books, Ed Davies was hardly on the breadline.

'The difference is, I would do what I do for free.'

Ed leaned forward on his desk and patted the top of a large pile of manuscripts. 'There are fifty wannabe authors here, all desperate for me to read their scripts, take them on my list, help them live their dream. But I can't, because I already have too many authors who are taking up too much of my time, and that is why I only take on one or two very exceptional writers a year.'

Erin had a sinking feeling in the pit of her stomach. 'Are you saying that you don't want to represent me any more?' she stammered.

'I'm saying I want to see something from you by the end of the summer. Because if you can't find it inside yourself to find the time, I want to find another young writer who can.'

'Can you believe he said that?' said Erin grumpily, biting into a club sandwich. She had arranged to meet Chris for lunch in Green Park and was giving him a blow-by-blow account of her meeting with Ed. 'And I thought you might show a bit more concern for my predicament.'

Chris was lying on the grass with a newspaper over his face to protect him from the sun. 'Well, what do you expect?' said Chris in a muffled voice. 'He's right, isn't he? You haven't done a thing and you're holding back real talents like myself.'

She threw a crust at him, but it just bounced off the paper. She sighed and looked around the bustling park. Cabbage White butter-flies danced in the air, children were running around with ice-cream cones. It was like high summer in Cornwall, she thought, immediately trying to blot the notion out. She hadn't been home in months, and that seemed like just another thing to feel guilty about.

'Anyway, I want to start afresh with a new idea, but I can't think of anything.'

'Worse excuse in the world,' said Chris, lifting an edge of the paper and squinting at her. 'You'll be telling me you're too busy next.'

'Oh, stop nagging me,' she frowned. 'I have my reasons.'

'Oh yes?' he said, sitting up to look at her properly. 'And what secrets are we keeping, Miss Devereux?'

She avoided his gaze. She didn't want to tell Chris about either Julian or her fledgling property development quite yet. Julian felt too good to be real and she was scared that if she said his name out loud he would cease to exist. And she didn't even want to think about the Belvedere Road site, let alone talk about it. Everything seemed to be taking so long. She hadn't even made the planning permission submission yet and already one mortgage payment had left her bank account. Worried that she had bitten off more than she could chew, she didn't want to mention it to anyone until she knew the project was going to succeed.

'No secrets,' she said, blushing. 'But I am busy.'

'In that case I have a proposition,' he said, reaching across and swiping Erin's orange juice.

'Oh yeah,' smiled Erin. 'Going to ask me on a date now? I didn't think you'd got that far down your list.'

'Not yet, sweetheart,' he said with a smile. 'But seriously, I have a week off work in about a month and I've booked a cottage in the grounds of the Cliveden estate in Berkshire to write my book. I've been there to write before; it's National Trust land, really beautiful, really inspiring, right by the river. I always gets loads done. If you fancy it, there's a spare bedroom . . .'

'It sounds good,' said Erin cautiously. It *did* sound good, but then who could predict what might happen in a month's time?

Maybe Julian would want to go on a mini-break or something, and Midas being an American company, she only had two weeks' annual leave.

'But?' asked Chris, his blue eyes meeting hers.

'A week is a long time.'

'Well, how about a long weekend? It'll be fun. You get ducks coming right up to the door to ask for bread.'

She looked at him and smiled. She knew it would be fun. But spending a week with Chris Scanlan writing a novel wasn't really where her heart lay and they both knew it.

'I'll think about it, okay?'

'No skin off my nose, sweetheart,' said Chris, putting the paper back over his face. 'But hurry up before Cameron Diaz jumps in. I've heard she loves ducks.'

She laughed and threw another crust at him. 'I'll think about it.'

34

By lunchtime, Summer and Adam were sailing out of Poole Harbour, the sail of their forty-foot yacht billowing in the strong breeze as they passed Brownsea Island, heading towards the Solent. Adam was barefoot on a walnut deck warm from the sun, his mouth set in a line of concentration as he piloted the boat single-handedly.

'Do you want to take the helm while I put a tack in?' he called, taking Summer's hand.

'Me?' she shouted over the cracking flap of the sail. 'You don't want me in charge of this thing, do you?'

'I take full responsibility,' said Adam, moving behind her and placing her hands on the big wheel.

Summer shut her eyes, enjoying Adam's strong arms around her, not quite believing that only twelve hours earlier she had been trapped in a nightclub with Ricardo. But, if she had felt dreadful when she had got up that morning at Adam's, the salty wind whistling through her ears seemed to have blown anything toxic out of her body.

'Hard to starboard,' said Adam, moving to the side, pulling hard on the rope for the headsail.

'Argh! What do I do? What do I do?' squealed Summer, as the boom swung towards them.

'Don't worry, you're doing fine,' smiled Adam, moving back behind her.

'So is this boat yours then?' she asked when they were back on a straight course. 'You must be a pretty good sailor.'

'She belongs to a friend of mine who lives on the Sandbanks over there,' he said pointing to a spit of land behind them. Summer had heard of Sandbanks, of course. Her mother was constantly talking about all of the most exclusive places in the country to live.

'But I do sail a lot. I have a house in Maine so I take a boat out whenever I'm there.'

'You're going to think I'm an idiot, but you can't do all this tacking thing on that boat we were on in Monaco, can you?' asked Summer. For some reason, she felt okay asking Adam questions like this; she felt safe with him.

Adam smiled and shook his head, reaching into an icebox for a cola.

'No, *The Pledge* is a motor yacht, it doesn't have a sail. It's used more for corporate entertaining than actual sailing. I have a small yacht like this in Dark Harbour, but I'm having a sailing yacht built as we speak in a shipyard in Holland.'

'What's it like?'

Adam's eyes glinted with passion and pleasure. 'She's not even half built, but already she takes my breath away. She's twenty-five metres, a sloop-rigged sailing yacht based on the eighteenth-century French cutters, which just slide through the water, but with the best technology and material that we've got today. An aluminium hull, carbon-fibre mast and boom.'

Summer laughed. 'She sounds beautiful.'

He nodded absent-mindedly out to sea. 'I'd love to race her in the America's Cup.'

'So why don't you?'

'It's the world's most expensive hobby,' he shrugged. 'Your yacht is just the start of it. There's management, crew, transporting the boat all over the world; it's a serious business. You're looking at around twenty million pounds a year to compete seriously.'

'Wow!'

Summer wondered how rich you had to be before you didn't even have to think about your limitations. She was sure it wasn't a good place to be. As Adam said, you had to have your dreams.

After an hour at sea, they sailed into Studland Bay. It was more sheltered and, without the wind of the open sea, the sun burnt down on their bodies.

Adam dropped the anchor as they bobbed a few hundred metres from shore. 'Do you want to go on land? There's a mooring close by.'

'No, I like it here,' she said softly.

She sounded calm, but her heart was racing. She knew she shouldn't have come, but she wanted to be here more than anywhere else in the world. She still felt sick when she imagined Karin watching them, angry and betrayed, but they were having too much of a good time. Adam's fingers felt too good on her skin when he touched her. He had saved her from Ricardo, and swept her away and made her feel alive and safe, sexy and interesting. And a hundred miles away from London, it was just the two of them on the boat, unable to escape from one other. *Not wanting to,* she thought, looking at him squinting in the sun.

He walked towards her and took her face in his hands. 'I don't want to go home yet, either,' he whispered, pulling her in closer. And then they were kissing, pulling at each other's clothes.

They stumbled down the stairs to the cabin, and Summer bumped her head on the low beam, giggling. He pulled off his T-shirt and then hers. There was a light scrub of dark hair on his tanned chest which tickled her breasts as he held her close. She licked his neck, his skin tasting of salt.

'You are so beautiful,' he whispered, pushing her up onto the bed. He cupped his hand around her breasts, and circled her nipple, round and round until she gasped. Not thinking about anything except the need to feel and taste every inch of each other, they scrambled out of their clothes, his thick cock sliding through her wetness until they were locked together, their bodies coming together with a passion as strong and powerful as the sea. And when she came, the sweetest pulse rippling round her trembling body, she cried out, tears streaming down her cheeks, as she finally understood what the fuss of hot, passionate sex was all about.

35

Curled up on the four-poster bed in the master bedroom of The Standlings, Molly swallowed a mouthful of brandy and grimaced. She just couldn't concentrate on the late-night movie she was watching – even the fifty-inch plasma screen couldn't make it more interesting. She sighed and took another sip. The last fortnight had been hell. The humiliation of having to clear her desk at Midas had been bad enough, but then she had been forced to face a week of complete paranoia, terrified that Marcus would smell a rat. Thankfully he seemed to buy her excuse that she wasn't enjoying the job and would much rather get on with the renovations at The Standlings. But Molly was missing London. Working in Piccadilly had given her so much freedom – to meet Alex, go shopping or see friends for lunch on her Midas expense account. She had once boasted about 'the manor' but, now it was all she had, she felt trapped and suffocated. Just then, Molly's mobile chirped. She didn't want the distraction, but Marcus was away on business and would expect her to answer. She put down the brandy and flipped it open.

'Hey there . . .' she purred.

'Is that you, Molly?' asked a woman's voice, its tone soft and apologetic. 'I'm sorry for calling, especially so late. But you hadn't replied to my letters and I wasn't sure if you'd received them.'

'How did you get my number?' asked Molly, instantly recognizing the voice and sitting up straight.

'I called – what's it called? – the Midas Corporation. I saw you in the papers and it said you worked there. That's how I knew where to send the letters. Anyway, I told them who I was and said it was very important I speak to you.'

'You haven't got my phone number for a reason,' said Molly coldly.

There was the sound of soft sobbing down the line. Molly sat there listening, her eyes drifting to the window. It was pitch-black outside and she could see her reflection in the glass, her face shadowed and sinister. She looked like a ghost.

'Okay, so I got the letters,' said Molly, irritation in her voice.

'Did you read them?'

'Yes, Janet,' said Molly numbly. 'I read them.'

'Well, it's got worse, Molly, it's worse than when I last wrote. Your father. I think he's going to die.'

Molly Sinclair had wanted to escape her small village on the outskirts of Newcastle for as long as she could remember. At sixteen she was already tall, beautiful and precocious; a lazy student, she had little desire to do well in the classroom, knowing that her fortune lay in her face and her body. There were no shortage of men in Newcastle's Bigg Market queuing up to buy her drink. One told her he was a photographer and offered to get her started as a model. At the 'studio', a small bedsit in Fenham, the man told her to take off her clothes and lie down on a bed draped with black chiffon. When he'd gone to fetch his film, she'd smashed his camera onto the floor, then run. Did he think she was stupid? She wasn't going to be exploited by anyone.

Molly's luck had changed on her seventeenth birthday. Her new boyfriend, an oil-rigger stationed in the North Sea, couldn't get to the shops to buy a present, so had sent her £500 cash.

'I'm going to London,' she had told her father and stepmother the moment she opened the envelope.

They hadn't shared Molly's vision. 'What's so special about London?' her stepmother Janet had demanded angrily. 'It's not paved with gold, you know.'

She'd show them, she thought, boarding a train for St Pancras.

Molly had a plan: she had read *The Face* and *Blitz* magazine religiously and she knew that Chelsea and Soho were where all the beautiful people hung out. Trying on a pair of PVC pants in Seditionaires, the famous shop on the King's Road owned by Malcolm McLaren, Molly had been approached by a glamorous woman who wanted to know if she was a model. This time, the photographer was real, and within six months Molly had bookings for *Harper's & Queen* and *Cosmopolitan* magazines, a commercial for a cosmetics company and catwalk shows for the top fashion houses. Molly was part of a new era of girls, the next generation from Marie Helvin and Jerry Hall, and her status brought her wealth, fame and fun. She lived in a house in Edith Grove with two other models, Michelle and Lulu, both slightly older and both protective of Molly when she confided in them about her upbringing: the death of her mother, her father's neglect of his only daughter when he'd remarried 'that bitch Janet'. Molly had hinted at domestic violence and abuse, and Michelle and Lulu took her out on the town to help her forget. They spent night after night in The Wag Club and the Limelight, or being wined and dined by rich men at Langan's. Sucked into her new glamorous jet-set world, she forgot Ken and Janet even existed; when people asked, she told them her family was dead. Sometimes she even believed it.

Then, six weeks ago, the first letter had arrived for her at the Midas Corporation. In scratchy black ink, Janet had told her that Ken was ill, having suffered a minor stroke. The second said that hospital investigations had revealed weaknesses in his heart that could spark off an aneurism at any time. She'd hadn't bothered reading the third letter; she had simply folded them all up and put them at the back of Marcus's wardrobe. She had tried hard to forget about them, but at night when The Standlings was very dark and the floorboards creaked, the sight of the wardrobe had begun to trouble her, as if there were ghosts banging inside.

'I'm sorry to hear about it, Janet,' she said finally, knotting her hand in a fist. 'But I don't see what all this has got to do with me.'

'Molly! How can you . . . ? Don't you care? Don't you want to see your father?' said Janet, her voice becoming angry. 'He's having open-heart surgery. We're hoping he's going to be strong enough for it, but he . . . well, he needs it. Without it, doctors say he will only have a few months.'

Molly shook her head. What was all this to her? Why was this woman bothering her again after all these years? She dug her nails into the bedspread, feeling angry for being disturbed and angry with herself for feeling bothered at the news.

'Are you going to come home, Molly? He still doesn't know what he did to upset you, or why you won't see the family . . .'

Molly was silent.

'But none of that matters now,' said Janet. 'It's time for us to be together. Maybe for one last time.'

'We're not really a family any more though, are we?' said Molly, closing her eyes as she said it. 'I don't belong there, I never have done.'

'This is ridiculous, Molly. He's your father. *Your father*!'

'Janet. Please don't bother me again.'

'Listen, he's in Newcastle Infirmary. The operation is a week tomorrow and—'

Molly didn't hear the rest of the sentence. She dropped the phone, went over to the wardrobe to retrieve Janet's letters, tearing them into pieces before she flushed them down the en-suite toilet.

36

For once in her life, Erin felt truly happy. Sipping a champagne cocktail, surrounded by twinkling candlelight, facing the man she felt sure
she was falling in love with, Erin felt as if she were on a set of *A
Midsummer Night's Dream*. Julian had picked her up after work and
taken her for dinner at Julie's restaurant in Holland Park, grabbing
a cosy table for two in the gorgeous open-air courtyard. This was
just typical of Julian, she thought gleefully. Every morning, she would
spend at least half an hour deciding what to wear on the off-chance
that he would show up after work, the top down on the sports car,
to whisk her out for supper or home to her flat, where they would
sit on the tiny balcony drinking red wine or go straight to the bedroom.

The sex, of course, had been sensational. He was both unselfish
and demanding; his hunger for her body made her feel sexy, desired,
grown-up. His touch excited every nerve-ending in her body, and her
orgasms were like fireworks. On those mornings, the Julian mornings, Erin would go into the office with a smile as wide as China.

Adam would tease her, of course. 'Did someone strike it lucky
last night?' he grinned. But Erin had denied everything: she'd had
to. Julian's company were still potential clients and, as Adam's PA,
it would be very poor form indeed to date an employee.

'How about we skip dessert and go back to your place?' asked
Julian. It was only 9.30. Julian winked and motioned the waiter over.

'What about your place?' asked Erin. They had only been to
Julian's Hoxton loft apartment once, but she had loved it. She had
seen sleeker apartments – she saw them every day as part of her
job – but pottering around Julian's place in his oversized towelling
robe, sliding into his free-standing stone egg-shaped bath, or making

tea in the chrome-fitted kitchen, she felt as glamorous as any of the sophisticated designer-clad women she had met working at Midas. More than that, she felt at home.

Julian pulled a face. 'No, not my place. Islington's closer. Anyway, I prefer it at yours, I like being around your things.'

Erin's brief disappointment dissolved as she saw other women glance enviously at her as they left the restaurant and screeched off in the convertible, her hair trailing behind her like a banner. For a second she thought this is how Karin must feel every day of her life.

At Peony House, Julian parked the car while Erin went into the lobby to check her post.

'So you're alive, then?'

Chris was waiting for the lift, looking as if he was just coming back from work, with bicycle clips still fastened around the bottom of his suit trousers.

'So it seems,' smiled Erin, collecting a parcel of Amazon books from on top of her pigeonhole.

'Well, you're in luck, Frankenstein,' said Chris, holding the lift door open for Erin. 'I've been sent a bottle of Petrus by a French importer. Don't ask me why. All I do is take their bribes,' he smiled. 'Fancy a nightcap? You can tell me where you've been hiding for the last week.'

Erin looked embarrassed as she heard footsteps and Julian appeared behind them.

'Did someone say nightcap?' he smiled.

Chris gave a vague nod of the head. 'Oh hello. Yes, I'm Erin's neighbour. And you are . . . ?'

'Chris, Julian. Julian, Chris,' said Erin, rushing to introduce them, feeling her cheeks blush hot. But why should she feel awkward? Okay, so she should have mentioned Julian to Chris before now, but it was hardly a secret, was it? She had just declined to mention it. Chris merely raised his eyebrows and the three of them rode up in the lift silently.

'Are you always nipping over for nightcaps then?' asked Julian when they were in the flat. He had slipped off his shoes and had gone over to the fridge to open a bottle of wine while Erin lit a scented candle and quickly tried to tidy up.

'Don't be silly, it's nothing like that,' she said. 'He writes about food and wine for the *Herald*, so it's kind of research.'

'Is that what they call it now?' he grunted as he pulled the wine cork, pouring them both a glass before they flopped onto the sofa together.

'Don't go getting all huffy,' said Erin, kissing Julian on the neck. 'I've barely borrowed a cup of sugar from him.'

'Well, just see that you don't,' grumbled Julian.

Perversely, Erin was enjoying his jealousy. It was a new experience for her – and she liked it. The room was dark, lit only by the candle, which gave it a sepia glow. Erin's head was fuzzy with claret and happiness.

'So, how are the plans coming along for Belvedere Road?' she asked.

He reached over and stroked her hair. 'Hey, don't spoil a nice night talking about work.'

Erin knew he was right, she really needed to unwind, but, still, she was feeling more than a little anxious about the development. She'd had a phone call from the site manager that afternoon, who had told her that he had six men pencilled in to start in eight weeks' time and there was still no sign of the plans.

'I know,' she sighed, 'but I'm new to all this and I need your help. If you're not confident about getting planning permission by then we'll have to delay it. I don't want men sitting around doing nothing.'

Julian moved closer to her and his lips brushed hers, sending a shiver of desire up her spine. 'Let's talk about it tomorrow, eh?' he whispered, 'I've got other plans for right now.'

She felt his hand on her thigh, pushing up the thin red jersey dress until it was ruched up over her tummy. He bent down to kiss her navel and along the top of her panties, grazing her skin with his teeth, tickling her thighs with his lips. Impatient, Erin reached over her head to pull off her dress and Julian unclipped her bra so that her full breasts sprang out. Julian picked her up, giggling, naked except for her white panties, and carried her into the bedroom, ready to explore every inch of her body with his tongue.

Exhausted and happy, Erin fell into a deep, blissful sleep almost immediately after sex. She did not hear Julian creep out of the bed and into the other room.

Silently he crossed to her desk and sat naked in front of Erin's laptop with the Midas logo on its titanium lid. Accessing Erin's work files would now be easy, if only he had the password. He thought for a moment, then typed in 'ADAM'. Women could be so predictable, he thought to himself. The screen flickered to life. He was in. He smiled and got to work.

37

Five o'clock. It was time. She was never late, he thought, as he gazed out of his bedroom window, a smile briefly lighting up his thin, pallid face. He watched as she jogged past his house and down the street until she disappeared out of view. He knew the route she would take. Towards Hyde Park. He had followed her once on his bicycle and watched as her personal trainer had put his hands all over her while she had stretched, touching her warm body as she rotated her hips, her hair swinging from side to side gloriously like a thick, dark waterfall.

For those few seconds when she ran past his window his life was complete, filling his day-to-day nothingness, giving him a purpose, a reason for being. She was perfect. Lean and fit, strong and sexy like a comic book heroine. She was a drug, a drug that had to be consumed again, and again and again. But those few seconds each day were not enough. Not now. Now he wanted more, much more. It was time to get to know her better. Because they were destined to be together. She would see that. She would see that soon.

38

Sitting in the first-class carriage of the 10.45 to Newcastle, Molly rested her head against the glass, seeing the blur of embankments, tunnels, hedges and ponds, but taking in nothing in particular. She closed her eyes and tried to work out how long it had been since she had been home. She snorted. Home? That place had never been home. Besides, it was all so long ago that it was as if that life had belonged to somebody else. But, over the past few days, that old life had begun to leak back into her thoughts. Since her conversation with Janet, at night her mind would drift to their tiny terraced house; the small living room that came straight off the street and smelt of chip fat and furniture polish, the bathroom with its pink suite and crocheted doilies over the toilet rolls, the beds covered with candlewick eiderdowns. *Some home*, thought Molly with derision, but still she felt its pull. At night, staring into the darkness, it was all she saw.

Guilt was not usually a sentiment in Molly's emotional spectrum, but now it was choking her. Guilt at never having told Summer she had a grandfather. Guilt at all the stories she had told about Kenneth Sinclair being a work-shy, bullying monster, about her stepmother ignoring her and demeaning her, day after day. Yes, Molly had painted a vivid picture, of a poor, dirty, violent past she had clawed her way out of, becoming strong and successful against the odds. Molly, the survivor.

But Molly's stories were a long way from the truth. Kenneth Sinclair was not a wife-beater; he had never hit Molly or deprived her of what little he could afford. No, Kenneth Sinclair's crime was that he was poor. Poor and proud. He was nothing more than a painter and decorator, a family man, a regular in the Crown, a decent working man. Nothing more, nothing less. And Molly had hated him for it.

Newcastle was bright and sunny, the water glinting in slivers as the train crossed the Tyne. Molly strode up the platform and fought for a taxi at the front of the station, asking the driver to take her to Newcastle Infirmary. The hospital was a soulless building, despite the warm weather and a cheerful banner announcing a summer fair the following Saturday. She had last been there when she was thirteen and she had fallen off a wall outside the off-licence, cracking her head. Molly had been hysterical, inconsolable. Not from the pain of the fall but from the fear of the stitches leaving a scar.

She climbed out of the taxi, tipping heavily, and walked into the reception, looking completely out of place in her silk tee-shirt, white jeans and Gucci sunglasses. Glancing at a big information board she found that that the Cardiac Unit was in the Orange Zone, wherever that might be. She walked down the long peach-painted corridor, hearing the sound of her heels tapping on the lino. Her steps got slower and slower as she got closer, dreading the moment. She had no idea what she was going to say; over the past few hours she had tried to think of something, but nothing had come. Finally, a sign above a pair of tatty double doors announced that she had reached the Cardiac Unit. She noticed a few private rooms and hoped her father was in one of those. It was bad enough meeting your family again after twenty-odd years; it would be worse if you had to do it in front of dozens of other ill people.

What would he look like now, she thought as she put a hand on the door. Thinner? Greyer? Maybe his hair would be white. Would there be tubes coming out of his chest? One of those air pumps? She shivered.

'Can I help you?'

A nurse no more than Summer's age was standing in front of her with a serious expression.

'I'm looking for Kenneth Sinclair. I'm his daughter.'

She saw a look of awkwardness and sympathy on the young woman's face, as she put a hand on Molly's shoulder and ushered her into a small room off the main ward.

'I'm so sorry. I thought you might have heard. Mr Sinclair – your dad – passed away about two hours ago. There were severe complications after the operation. The doctors did their best, but he was a very ill man. But I'm sure you knew that.'

Passed away? Molly tried to take a breath but her lungs seemed to suddenly shrink and close.

'He's dead?' she whispered.

'Can I get you a drink. A tea?' asked the nurse.

'He's dead, he's dead.' She repeated it over and over again and again, trying to understand the words.

'We do have a bereavement counsellor on site,' said the nurse kindly.

'He never met my daughter,' said Molly, her eyes staring vacantly at a notice board pinned with posters on flu jabs and leaflets on healthy eating.

'Your family left about an hour ago, I think. I can arrange for a taxi to take you home, as I'm sure you'll all want to be together,' said the nurse patiently.

'A taxi?' Molly looked at the woman blankly, then suddenly jumped to her feet, picking up her handbag and slinging it over her shoulder. 'Yes, a taxi. That would be very kind of you,' said Molly. 'I'm sure I've taken up enough of your time.'

The car dropped her off outside the Metropole Hotel in the city centre. She checked into a suite, and phoned room service to bring her a club sandwich and two bottles of their best red wine. Plundering the minibar, she poured four miniatures of Scotch into a tumbler and drank it in two gulps.

She ran a bath, removed her clothes and answered the door naked to a startled waiter, taking the wine and a glass from him without a word. Sinking into the hot suddy water, the claret slipping down her throat like warm honey, images of her past and present whirled and merged, echoing around her head like an empty hospital corridor. As she drifted into semiconsciousness, her eyelids growing leaden, she didn't notice her shoulders sliding slowly down the curve of the bath, the cooling water edging up towards her ears, her head lolling onto her shoulder as exhaustion and alcohol washed over her. She just didn't notice.

If Summer had ever harboured any ambitions to be an actress, she had not realized it until she was at the Serpentine Gallery party and had overheard a delicious piece of gossip. 'Darling, haven't you heard?' gushed Daria Vincenzi, a gorgeous Italian model with a plummier voice than the Queen. 'Luc Balzac – you know, the maverick French film director? He's making an action movie at Pinewood Studios for like a hundred million dollars and they want to cast a complete unknown for the female lead. Isn't it just the best?'

Summer sidled up to Allegra Fox, the aristocratic face of numerous fashion brands. Allegra was the best connected and least discreet model she knew. If anyone knew the full skinny, she would.

'Oh yes, I had a meeting with Imogen Sanders, the casting director, only yesterday,' she boasted. 'Officially it's open auditions, but Imogen is calling in all the top girls from the big agencies.' Allegra gave Summer a dismissive look to suggest she wasn't in the same league. 'Although, apparently the script is terrible, so it might not be the right move for me right now.'

As Molly had thankfully lost interest in 'managing' Summer's career, she decided to take matters into her own hands, and the next day went into her agency, IMP, as early as she dared. Just off Regent Street, IMP was London's most powerful agency, with some of modelling's biggest names on their books. The office was a slick, open-plan affair, with one big circular table in the centre at which sat the agency's bookers, yelling into their headsets like a fashionable version of King Arthur's knights. Summer's agent, Michael Tantino, had an office of his own. He had just been promoted to head booker – signing the Karenza girl hadn't done his cause any harm at all – and he was delighted to see Summer.

'Summer!' he cried, throwing his arms in the air as she walked in to his sparse chrome and glass office. 'My favourite model in all the world!'

A flamboyant half-Tunisian, half-Spaniard, Michael had skin the colour of butterscotch. His black fitted shirt was left open to give Summer an eyeful of his freshly waxed chest. 'Although I do say that to everyone. How can I help you, honey?'

'Do you have any dealings with Imogen Sanders?' asked Summer, sitting on a orange sofa.

Michael gave a half-shrug. 'Sometimes, darling. Why do you ask?'

Michael winced inwardly. He knew exactly what Summer was referring to, but he didn't want to hurt her feelings. Imogen Sanders was one of his oldest friends and had called him for recommendations on beautiful girls who could act. He had not put Summer's name forward. As head booker, he was fiercely protective of the agency's reputation and had only sent his biggest girls to see Imogen Sanders. The girls who could command $50,000 a day, and the ones who had the seven-figure contracts with the giant cosmetic houses. The cream of the cream. Summer Sinclair was beginning to bring in good money for the agency, sure. And she was hot, no question of that; *GQ* was on the phone every week wanting her to do a cover. But he didn't think she was ready for Hollywood.

'. . . Only I was talking to Daria last night,' continued Summer, 'and she said you'd sent her to see Imogen.'

Michael pulled a face. Summer was such a modest, timid little thing. She might have landed that TV show, but she didn't have the big bubbly personality like Cameron Diaz or the celebrity boyfriend like Jude Law who had sent Sienna Miller's career into overdrive.

'Yes, honey, that's true, but I really don't think the time's quite right for you right now. How about we start you off on this music video I've heard about . . .'

Summer took a deep breath, imagining what Molly would do in this situation. She certainly wouldn't allow him to fob her off. She might not be a 'top girl', but she wanted it. She wanted it badly. And if she was going to be an actress, now would be a good time to start.

'Listen, Michael,' said Summer, mimicking Molly expertly, 'I know they're having open auditions; there was even an advert in *The Stage*, for goodness' sake. This job is not a secret.'

She leant forward and tapped her nail on Michael's desk for emphasis. 'I'll contact Imogen myself if I have to. But if I get the gig I might just be looking for a new agency. I'm sure Models 1 would be very welcoming if I—'

'Okay. Okay,' interrupted Michael, holding up hands. 'I'll call Imogen. In the meantime, there's a casting tomorrow for some pop video for some James Blunt kind of guy. Apparently he's hot. The record company are seeing people tomorrow. They've seen your book already.'

'Okay, give me the details,' said Summer, allowing herself an inward sigh of relief. 'And you won't forget to call Imogen, will you?'

'I won't forget,' teased Michael. He looked at her and felt a little sad. She had big dreams that were getting bigger. She was a good kid. He didn't want her to get chewed up and spat out. She was too good for that.

39

Erin hadn't heard from Julian for nearly a week. She had tried to call him and had left at least a dozen messages with both his assistant and on his answering machine. But so far, all she was hearing back was a yawning silence, which wasn't good news however she looked at it. If he'd been in an accident, surely his secretary would have mentioned it, ditto if he'd been out of the country, which only left her staring down the barrel of rejection. The previous night she had cried until her eyes were sore, wondering what she could have possibly done or said that made him lose such rapid interest. But her broken heart was just the half of it. Not only had Julian disappeared, but with him had vanished his drawings for Belvedere Road. She badly needed those plans to secure planning permission and, the longer she left it, the more of Erin's very limited supply of money was pouring down the drain. Money she had inherited from her father. Her nest egg. At this rate she was going to have to sell the property on again without having done an iota of work on it. She knew her father wouldn't have wanted that.

'Erin! Get Marcus.' Adam usually used the telephone to speak to her, but right now she could hear his booming voice coming all the way from his desk. Marcus came up straight away and there was a heated exchange that Erin couldn't help but overhear.

'Fucking Dreamscape Construction have undercut us on the London Gallery,' said Adam.

Erin's ears immediately pricked up. The London Gallery was perhaps the biggest contract that Midas Construction had been pitching for this year. A major art gallery, to rival the National Portrait, it was part of a vote-winning initiative for the current government, who were playing the caring-sharing 'spaces for the people' card. The project had taken them months of planning, presenting and schmoozing of ministers and advisors.

'How could this happen?' snapped Marcus, pacing around the room. 'Our proposal was fantastic. I'd be fucking amazed if anyone had a design as good or could cost it so low. What the hell's going on?'

Adam pushed his hair back in a gesture of irritation. 'Apparently, the Minister for Culture and Art's office has heard that Midas are doing a very similar, even bigger, project in Paris. They've said – off the record of course – that they'd prefer the company that won the London Gallery tender to make it their number one priority. Basically the Paris development has scuppered our chances.'

'But the Paris thing hasn't even been announced yet,' said Marcus. 'How could they possibly know?'

'Fuck knows,' growled Adam. 'Someone has talked somewhere. Maybe the architect?'

'Sergio? No way. His whole reputation's on the line here.'

Erin could see why they were angry. She knew the architects' fees alone for the London Gallery pitch were in the hundreds of thousands – Sergio Vinchely, a Spanish architect from Seville, was the best in the world. He only took on a handful of major commissions every year and he had done an incredible job.

Erin was as mystified as Marcus and Adam – there had obviously been a leak, but who would do such a thing? Erin stared at her computer screen and scrolled through her documents, running through the possibilities, hoping she could help. And slowly, ever so slowly, she began to get a horrible sinking feeling.

40

'So, Summer, what did you think of the veal?'

Marcus was topping Summer's glass up with an expensive claret and forcing conversation, while Molly watched contently. She was glad to be back in London. Back in a smart restaurant with her rich boyfriend. Back where she belonged. Her trip to Newcastle was something she had been trying all week to put in a box at the back of her mind. Only a dislodged bath plug had saved her from certain drowning in the bath of the Metropole. She had finally woken up in the cold, empty porcelain tub, with a thumping head and alcohol curdling round her bloodstream. She had taken the first train back to St Pancras without contacting her stepmother, not even to find out about the funeral. She had gone back to Newcastle and almost died. It was a sign that she did not belong there. A sign that she had done the right thing by severing all ties with her past.

'The veal was delicious,' smiled Summer politely, hoping nobody would want dessert and delay the agony of the evening.

'Tell Marcus about the film you're auditioning for,' said Molly, snapping herself out of her thoughts. Summer winced. *Please God, not the proud parent routine.*

'Molly,' she said, 'I don't even know if I'll get seen by the casting director yet.'

'She'll get seen,' said Molly, turning to Marcus with a smug smile. 'Of course I had my opportunities in Hollywood too. Did you see Robert Altman's *Prêt-à-Porter*? Bob really wanted me for a cameo but filming clashed with another commitment.'

Summer rolled her eyes. The evening was turning out to be even worse than she'd imagined. Marcus had invited Molly and Summer for dinner at Le Gavroche, having been inexplicably seized by the notion that they all spend quality time together. Even though the food was exquisite and the restaurant sumptuous, Molly was behaving strangely. One minute she'd be morose and thoughtful, the next minute she'd be the charming, gushing parent, to the extent that she was treating Summer like a teenager.

Adding to Summer's awkwardness was that she was sleeping with Marcus's best friend. It was impossible for her to relax. Still, thought Summer, taking another sip of claret to anaesthetize herself, at least Marcus seemed a decent enough man. Molly's boyfriends usually fell into two narrow categories: objectionable and pompous.

It was a game of Summer's to guess the background of her mother's boyfriends. It was easy to spot the playboys, of course, with their perma-tans, extravagant dress-sense and the hungry, hooded lids when they looked at Summer. The inherited money was also obvious; the rebellious sons of old established families, who invariably took the most drugs, and had the worst manners once they had drunk a few glasses of wine. Marcus fell into the third, and rarest category of Molly's paramours. He had the serious, considered manner of someone who had earned his wealth. He looked at Summer with the respectful interest of someone who wanted to know what she had to say, rather than what she would be like in bed.

Summer could also tell a lot about Molly's boyfriends by how her mother behaved around them. Her mother possessed a chameleon-like ability to adapt herself to become any man's fantasy woman. Her physical appearance, her clothes, hair and her make-up would all alter slightly to fit to the man's tastes. Robert Cabot, a hedge-fund banker with a wife in Manhattan, had been treated to pencil skirts, kitten heels and a succession of white shirts, unbuttoned just a little too low. Her hair would be lightened a few shades to a buttery blonde and she would talk about her time in New York, when she had partied with Basquiat. With Stavros the son of a Greek shipping heir, Molly wore Cavalli. Skirts were shorter, heels higher, lips as red and juicy as berries. More friendly, flirty, louder, prouder; more Notice-me.

For Marcus, Molly was definitely a softer, quieter version of herself. Hair in a ponytail, jeans and a Chanel jacket, her conversation was peppered with glamorous people and places. Marcus was a numbers man, who sat behind the desk while Adam wheeled and dealed and travelled and had dinner with the rich and famous. For Marcus, Molly added colour and sophistication to his life.

'Molly tells me you're doing terribly well with the modelling,' said Marcus. 'Apparently brunettes have more fun.'

Summer tugged at a lock of hair. 'Well, it does all seem to have taken off after I had my colour done. I suppose I have Karin to thank.'

'Not really Karin, though, honey, was it?' said Molly quickly. 'Summer was discovered by Dan Stevens the photographer in Regent Street, would you believe it?'

'Speaking of Karin,' said Marcus, giving his dessert menu back to the waiter, 'Adam has invited us to down to the yacht in Capri next week, if you fancy it? I think Karin is in Italy visiting the factories. I'm sure Adam won't mind you coming along, Summer. Have you been to Capri?'

'Ooh, Capri, darling,' said Molly, looking over to her daughter and nodding. 'I'm sure Karin will be glad to see you; after all, it's your image that's getting her cash registers ringing right now. And will there be anybody interesting on the yacht for Summer?' she continued, nudging Marcus gently.

'Mother,' said Summer sternly, averting her eyes. The thought of standing face to face with Karin filled her with dread. How could they make small talk and say how lovely it was to see her again and pretend that she did not know the taste of her boyfriend's mouth or the muscular hollow at the top of his thigh, or the tiny mole on the shaft of his cock.

Marcus laughed, trying to diffuse the tension. 'Rule number one, Summer. Never let your parents fix you up with anyone. My first date was with the daughter of my father's boss. She weighed two hundred pounds and had a fascination with newts.'

'It's a lovely offer, but I can't,' said Summer, adding to her acting skills by feigning regret. 'As you probably know, I'm doing this TV show and we're doing some filming that weekend.'

'Really?' said Molly, raising a sceptical eyebrow. 'What can you be possibly covering of any note next weekend? It's so quiet in London right now. Everyone's buggered off on holiday.'

'I think we might be going away,' said Summer vaguely. 'I never really know what we're filming until the production meeting a few days before.'

Molly flashed her a look that clearly said, *we'll talk about this later*. Marcus, however, was hardly distraught. Summer appreciated the gesture, but it had clearly been for appearances' sake. As he paid the bill and they walked down the steps, it was just going dark. The streets of Covent Garden were unusually still.

'Do you want to wait here while I go and pick up the car?' asked Marcus, rattling his keys.

Molly shook her head. 'This is really a night out with my daughter. You're just tagging along, Marcus, my dear,' she teased, turning to kiss him lightly on the lips. 'I'm going to see if I can tempt her with a nightcap at the Light Bar,' she said, pointing over the road in the direction of the St Martin's Lane Hotel. 'And I will see you tomorrow,' she said, purring into Marcus's ear.

'Please come for a drink,' said Molly, as Marcus disappeared around a corner. 'I only had a couple of glasses at dinner. Marcus hates me drinking too much.'

'He knows what you're like, that's why,' said Summer cynically. 'No. I'm going home,' she said with finality, sticking her arm out to hail a taxi. Summer rarely stood up to her mother, but the last thing she needed just then was more cocktails and self-pity.

Molly just shrugged and they climbed into the back of a black cab, trundling round Trafalgar Square past the National Gallery, lit up and stately, and watched impassively as lovers walked round the fountains.

'You aren't filming next weekend, are you?' said Molly finally. She had seen the look of fear and confusion on her daughter's face at the mention of Adam, and her instincts for intrigue told her something was wrong. 'Why don't you want to go on the yacht?'

Summer stared out of the window. The yacht. Where Adam had promised to take her. Since they had first made love, anchored in the Solent, Adam and Summer had barely been apart, their passion swelling in ferocity with each meeting. Now they had arranged to meet on *The Pledge* at Porto Ercole on the Wednesday before Adam went on to Capri. Just the two of them, alone, together, entwined. How could Summer then reboard their love nest two days later, with his girlfriend playing hostess? How could she sleep on the boat, knowing that forty-eight hours earlier she had been lying next to Adam, kissing him, feeling him inside her?

She knew what she was doing was wrong. Selfish, immoral.

Many times, over the years, Summer had criticized her mother for willingly being 'the other woman', but now she was doing exactly the same. Even worse, she knew Karin; she owed her success to her. She hated herself for it, but the feelings she felt for Adam were too strong to deny – and, in truth, Summer felt she deserved this small ray of happiness.

She had never let anyone get this close before, and she didn't need a psychiatrist to tell her that her fear of intimacy and abandonment lay with Molly. What Summer had seen as a child. What she had heard at night. It was why, when all her friends in Toyko were out at clubs and going on dinner dates with rich businessmen, Summer had kept her distance and always gone home alone. It was why at twenty-four she had never had a proper relationship, regardless of her beauty. It was why she needed Adam so badly now.

'Come to Capri,' said Molly softly. 'Bring a friend if you want to. Marcus will ask Adam. Someone pretty. Pretty girls are always welcome on yachts,' she said, smiling slightly.

'I don't want to go,' said Summer, beginning to sob, the guilt, shame and sadness overcoming her unexpectedly.

Molly put her arm on her shoulder. 'You're being ridiculous,' she said softly.

Summer looked at her through misty eyes. She was going to tell her. She had to. The burden of what she was doing was too heavy to bear alone. And out of anybody she knew, Molly would know that feeling, of being the other woman and its sweet burden.

'I am seeing Adam,' said Summer simply, hoping for a second that her mother might not have heard her. 'I don't want to go because I'm already going. A few days beforehand. I'm meeting him in Porto Ercole.'

She held her breath and she looked at her mother, knowing that Molly wouldn't judge her for sleeping with somebody else's partner, but wondering for one moment if she would be angry for encroaching on her new wonderland, by bagging its prize.

Molly stared open-mouthed at her daughter, the glimmer of fury immediately softening as she realized with startling clarity the opportunity that had presented itself; wondering why she had not thought of it sooner. If Adam Gold was proving stubborn to her own advances, then having him as her son-in-law would be the perfect compromise. She smiled at Summer, one strap of her silk, crocus-yellow sundress falling off one shoulder, the curve of her rosy lips, slightly downturned with unease, and thought that she had never looked more beautiful.

She took her daughter's hand and squeezed it lightly. 'That's perfect. It really is perfect. You and Adam are perfect for each other.'

'Perfect. If it wasn't for Karin,' said Summer, a teardrop running down her cheek.

'Give it time, honey,' she said stroking her fingertips. 'Hang on in there and just give it time.'

Erin was hiding in a toilet cubicle at the Midas Corporation, her face buried in her hands, thick sobs welling in her throat. Her worst suspicions had been confirmed and the last few days all began to make sense as the pieces of the awful jigsaw fell together. It was part of Erin's daily routine to go through the trade papers for Adam: *Estates Gazette*, the property section of the *New York Times*, *Construction News*. In one building industry journal she had seen, to her horror, a news story about Julian. There, smiling at her, taunting her, was a head-shot of 'renowned architect Julian Sewell', accompanying a story that Julian had just been taken onto the board of Dreamscape Construction as vice president. She had known immediately how Dreamscape had got the information that had sabotaged the Midas pitch for the London Gallery. Every pitch, every development had its own file on her computer. Anybody accessing her computer would know exactly what Midas Corporation was doing – which developments they were pitching for, who they had been commissioned by and the intimate details of their costs and designs.

Erin tore off a piece of loo roll to blot her eyes and blow her nose. He'd used her, then discarded her. Had he ever really felt anything for her? When he whispered to her in bed, was it just his ambition talking? When his naked body pressed against hers was he simply going through the motions until he could get the information he wanted? Her mind flashed around every possibility – for all she knew, he might have manipulated that first meeting in the Piccadilly wine bar; hadn't he been waiting for a friend that never showed up? Their entire relationship was a sham. A knot of pain stabbed in her belly.

*

Erin took a deep breath and sat in the Eames chair in front of Adam. The sun was shining in through the window and making her squint. She felt nervous and pressured.

'What is it, Erin? I'm very busy today,' said Adam with impatience.

'I've got something, well, something bad to tell you.'

Adam glanced up. 'It can't be any worse than the news I've already had this week,' he said.

'Well, I think you should know that I've been dating Julian Sewell.'

'Oh yeah?' said Adam, looking up from a pile of contracts. 'I hope he's a better lover than he is an architect.'

He saw her crestfallen look and backtracked hastily. 'Sorry Erin, uncalled for. I've just been in a bad mood all week after the London Gallery fiasco.'

'Well, that's why I'm here,' said Erin, her voice wavering. She had his full attention now.

'Go on,' he said.

She put a copy of the magazine in front of him, the page of the story folded back.

'Fucking hell,' he said softly after he'd read it. 'It doesn't take a genius to work out what's happened, does it?' He looked up and gave Erin a cold stare. 'What did you tell him?'

Any trace of a smile had gone from his face and the tone of his voice made Erin shiver. It would have been safer to have kept quiet.

'Honestly Adam, absolutely nothing,' she said, 'I promise. I swear on my life, I haven't told him anything about any of the projects the company is involved in.'

'Well, he's fucking found out something, hasn't he?' said Adam, getting up from behind his desk and walking to the window, rolling the magazine up in his hands.

'I told him nothing,' begged Erin. 'He's never been in the office unattended. All I can think is that . . .' she paused, feeling her cheeks flush. 'He's stayed at my flat a few times. Maybe he's accessed my blackberry or my laptop.'

Adam turned and threw the magazine across the room, its pages fluttering. 'Do you have any idea how valuable this contract was to the company?' he yelled.

Erin nodded, unable to stop a tear sliding down her face.

'I should fucking fire you.'

That was it. All it took to make Erin crumble. She bent forward, sobs jerking from her mouth like machine-gun fire. She was going to lose everything. Julian, her job, Adam. Even Belvedere Road. Everything.

'Alright, alright, just stop it okay?' said Adam, his voice calmer. 'You, my dear, have been well and truly played.'

'He's a bloody shit,' said Erin, wiping her eyes with the corner of her sleeve.

'I won't argue with you there. That "bloody shit" has cost me a fortune in architect fees alone.'

'That's only the half of it.'

'If it's a broken heart, sugar, you'll get over it,' replied Adam curtly.

She took a deep breath and began to tell him about Belvedere Road and her dream of turning it into flats. How Julian had offered to do the drawings and put in the paperwork to secure planning permission. How he was now refusing to contact her and the clock was ticking for her to begin the conversion of the building while every month she was paying mortgage repayments through the nose.

'You're developing eight apartments?' said Adam, beginning to show the hint of a smile.

'With every penny I own,' she whispered.

'Initiative. I like that,' he mused, the smile growing on his face. 'That's the reason why I hired you.'

Erin wondered momentarily if Adam would be so encouraging if he knew she had exploited her position at Midas to buy Belvedere Road and tried to shake away the thought immediately. She was in enough trouble as it was.

'Will you at least give me a reference?' she said, biting her lip, trying to salvage something from the rubble. 'I'll find it hard to get another job otherwise and I have mortgage payments of over two thousand pounds a month. If I don't pay I'll lose the building. Lose my deposit. It was an inheritance from my dad.' At the thought of her family, Erin felt a little flutter of pride and resilience. She wouldn't let that bastard Julian Sewell ruin everything.

Adam was rubbing his mouth with his hand. Finally he puffed his cheeks and sighed. 'I'm not going to give you a reference,' he said slowly as Erin's heart plummeted. 'Because I want you to stay working for me.'

She stared at him, genuinely stunned. 'Thank you,' she whispered.

'Come on,' he said, taking her arm. 'Let's go talk to a few people in the residential department and see if we can find you an architect who can whip you up some drawings. I'm sure we must know somebody in the planning department too who can give us some advice. Where did you say it was?'

Suddenly, the departure of Julian Sewell from her life didn't seem quite so terrible. She looked at Adam Gold and laughed at his sudden enthusiasm for her project.

'Thanks Adam,' she sniffed.

'Okay. Enough of the pity already. Now, have you thought about how you're going to market the property . . . ?'

Erin was carried along by Adam's energy as he swept her out of the office, a wide grin on her face. She felt grateful, flabbergasted and more happy than she could have hoped only minutes ago. Turning to take a quick peep at Adam, she felt a warm, fuzzy feeling rear up in her tummy that she didn't want to go away.

Having spent three hours in a bar in Old Street, Julian Sewell was too drunk to notice he was being followed home. Even if he had been sober on the walk back to his flat in Hoxton, he would not have heard the purr of the prestige vehicle following two hundred feet behind him. Julian's mind was too full of other things. He was still celebrating his new position at Dreamscape Construction. He had the world at his feet and the phone numbers of two pretty girls in his pockets. He had no intention of calling either of them, even though he had accepted the offer of oral sex in the toilet. He had no intention of bringing her home. He didn't like women coming back to his flat. It was too intrusive, personal. He had allowed it once with Erin, but that was necessary. Ah, Erin. She had been a pretty good shag, he thought with a smirk. No, that little project hadn't been at all unpleasant. Almost a shame when she had to go.

The quickest journey back to his flat off Hoxton Square was to nip up the dark, deserted backstreets that ran north from Old Street itself. For one of the most fashionable areas of London, he thought, some of these alleyways wouldn't have looked out of place in a Jack the Ripper movie; you could almost smell the fog. There were a few spots of rain and Julian tutted as the droplets of water stained his tan leather jacket. He was still brushing at the drops when the footsteps caught up with him. Quickly, silently, an arm fastened itself around his neck, while a heavy boot kicked away his knees. Lying on the floor, the boot slammed into his face, again and again and again. The new vice president of Dreamscape Construction drifted out of consciousness, a trickle of blood oozing from his head onto the damp street. Quietly a Midas Corporation vehicle drove down the side street, turned into traffic and disappeared.

41

Karin loved her trips to Florence to visit the swimwear factories, especially in summer. Back in the office, she liked to pretend that her monthly trips to Italy were a chore that needed to be suffered but, as she drove through the lush green Italian countryside, how could she complain? Her routine was hardly backbreaking; she would check into her favourite room at the Lungarno Suites with its Tiffany blue walls and sun-dusted window, from which she could see the Duomo and taste the flower-fragranced air. She would then take the forty-five-minute drive out to the two factories, where she could cast over her perfectionist eyes over the manufacturing. After lunch with the factory manager, she would talk to the pattern cutters and the House models would try on her early prototypes, to which Karin would make the minor, crucial adjustments. Back in the city at night, she had a coterie of friends she loved seeing. The Italians had such a love of life, of food and, crucially, of gossip. They always had hilarious anecdotes about the back-stabbing world of fashion.

Karin was particularly excited about this visit, as she put her foot down on the autostrada heading out east of the city, her radio tuned into cheesy Euro-pop. Today, she was due to see samples of the Cruise collection, which were due to be shown at the Miami Swim Show trade fair later that month. Business was booming: after Cameron Diaz had been photographed in a black Karenza bikini on holiday in Hawaii, there had been another surge in orders from Fred Segal, Barneys and Neiman Marcus. But she couldn't rest on her laurels; she had to keep the brand moving forward.

Karin pulled into the car park of an anonymous-looking building in a small town in the Florentine countryside. It was usually packed full of Fiats, but today there was an eerie quiet about the place.

She walked to the main entrance and it appeared locked.

What the hell is going on? she thought, pulling out her mobile phone.

A small, thin-faced man in a pair of navy coveralls emerged from a side door.

'Where is everyone?' she asked in perfect Italian.

'Where eez everyone?' the man repeated back to her in English and threw his hands in the air. 'At home, *mia cara*, today it is, a, a . . . how you say stop work?' he asked.

'A strike!' She grimaced. She knew the Italians liked nothing better than a good strike, especially in summer or when there was an important football match on, but in five years of visiting Florence she had never been caught up in one.

'Where is Giovanni?' she asked.

'He not contact you?' asked the man. 'The strike is today and tomorrow. We see you Monday, perhaps?'

There was no point in arguing or demanding to see Giovanni, who'd probably headed to his villa on the coast. She got back in the car, but felt anxious, drumming her fingers on the wheel. Much as she loved the laid-back Italian attitude, she just couldn't adjust. Karin always wanted to be doing something. She ran through her schedule. She wasn't due in Capri until Saturday morning, so she could get an afternoon flight back to London but, what the hell, seeing as she was in Italy, she might as well enjoy its sunshine and its splendour. She knew that Adam's yacht was sailing down from Portofino where her boyfriend was buttering up some Italian investors on a corporate jolly. She could easily drive down to one of the ports along the way and join him. Or she could fly down to Naples and check into the Capri Palace Hotel for a couple of days; their famous leg treatments at the hotel spa were legendary all over Europe for keeping cellulite at bay. She picked up her phone.

'Adam. It's me.'

'Hi, honey. How's Florence? Another fabulous collection on your hands?'

'I'd only know that if I could see it,' she sighed. 'There's only a bloody strike. The factory is closed until Monday.'

Adam started to laugh. 'I can see the fumes coming out of your ears from here.'

'Where are you, anyway?' asked Karin, wedging the mobile under her chin as she rejoined the traffic on the autostrada.

'Still in Portofino. Just had some lunch at the Splendido. I can't wait to see you.'

Karin could almost see his sexy smile beaming down the receiver. 'Well, that's why I'm ringing,' said Karin. 'It seems a waste to fly back to London when you're here in Italy.'

'What are you suggesting, Kay?' She wasn't sure but he suddenly sounded distracted.

'That I join you on *The Pledge*.'

There was a pause and Karin felt a stab of annoyance.

'Honey, this is business. It's a bunch of dull investors, we'll be talking shop. You'll hate it.'

'Don't talk to me like some bloody bimbo,' she sighed, veering suddenly away from the hard shoulder. 'The boat's big enough that I can keep out of your way. '

'Kay. I'm not joking. Stay in Florence, go shopping, charge it to me. And I'll see you on Saturday as planned.'

'Fine.' She tossed the phone on the passenger seat and pressed her foot to the floor of the car so it shot off like a rocket back towards Florence. There was something about his tone which worried her. 'Charge it to me,' he'd said. *Well if he didn't want her in on* The Pledge, *it was going to cost him.*

Adam snapped the phone shut and turned over to face Summer, who was reclining on the top deck of *The Pledge* in a gold bikini that left very little to the imagination.

'Is everything okay?' she asked. She knew better than to pry but, hearing his lies on the telephone, she knew he must have been talking to Karin.

'Fine,' he replied, reaching over to rub his hand on her flat brown tummy.

Behind her shades, she squeezed her eyes shut to push any thoughts of Karin from her mind. It was Summer and Adam's first weekend away and she wanted it to be perfect – so far it had been. She had boarded *The Pledge* the night before at Porto Ercole. She and Adam had had supper at Il Pellicano, the de-luxe retreat hanging on the hillside just outside the port, laughing and kissing and enjoying the sunset like any other couple.

The next morning, the captain had sailed to Giglio, a small island off the coast, where he had dropped anchor in a quiet cove and they had dived naked into the cool water.

Now it was lunchtime. There was an ice box full of beer and white wine, cheese, olives, bread and cold langoustines the size of bananas. The walnut deck of *The Pledge* glinted in the sun, the water wrapped around it like jade shantung silk shot through with silver. The coast rose out of the sea, all granite cliffs, lapping caves and hillsides of scrub. Despite being the height of season, they were almost alone bobbing on the water – there was only the tiny white hull of one other yacht far away on the horizon.

Summer took a sip of Peroni, removed her bikini top and lay back on a towel in just a white thong, her sun-streaked honey-blonde hair that had been dyed back to its natural colour days earlier, fanning out around her head.

'Mmm . . . Are you deliberately trying to tempt me away from lunch?' asked Adam, crawling over on his hands and knees and rolling on top of Summer, taking one nipple between his lips.

'Adam Gold!' scolded Summer, widening her legs and then wrapping them around his body. 'Luigi is just over there,' she giggled.

'I pay him firstly to be a good skipper and secondly to be discreet,' smiled Adam lazily. 'Besides, it's nothing he hasn't seen before.'

As soon as the words were out of his mouth, Adam knew he'd made a blunder. Summer sat up and swung her legs away from him, pulling the towel over her breasts. She felt so stupid; *of course he did this all the time*. She had allowed herself to believe that the trip to Italy was a real step forward for their relationship. It was one thing meeting for afternoon sex in discreet boutique hotels around London; it was another spending two days together on Adam's yacht. She had taken it as a sign of growing commitment, even daring to hope he might end his relationship with Karin so that the two of them could be together properly. But 'nothing he hasn't seen before'? She accepted that Karin would probably have frolicked on the same deck she was sitting on now – but were there others?

The sea was calm, just the gentle flutter of a breeze.

'Are there others?' she asked finally. Adam propped himself up on one elbow and fiddled with his sunglasses.

'Summer, I thought we weren't going to talk about things like this,' he said, trying to touch her arm.

'Is that what we said?' she snapped, pulling her arm away.

He pulled a face and shrugged.

'I guess what you're telling me is that, if I ask you difficult questions, I'm likely to hear things I don't want to hear?' said Summer slowly. 'I'm not stupid.'

'No, you're not,' said Adam quietly.

There was a long pause as Summer stared up at the cliffs, watching the birds wheel round and round above them.

'So how about you move out of your mother's flat?' said Adam.

Summer sat up with a start, her pert, sun-bronzed breasts jiggling. 'What? What's brought this on?'

'Well, you can't think it's a good idea still to live downstairs from your mother.'

Summer frowned. 'Adam, what are you saying?'

He brushed his hand down her thigh. 'You don't want to become her, do you?'

Summer drew herself up on her knees so she was towering above him. 'I'm not sure I like the implication of this,' she said. 'Molly may have her faults, but she's my mother, Adam.'

'Summer, you're smart and beautiful and good. You don't name-drop endlessly. You don't do drugs. You don't want to spend my money . . .' He smiled wryly. He had taken her shopping the weekend before in Prada. As a VVIP he had half the shop closed off so they could shop in complete privacy. But if the store had been anticipating a big spender like Karin Cavendish who would spend £50,000 on his credit card without even blinking, they were disappointed by Adam Gold's new girlfriend. Summer had only been interested in a small leather tote.

'What are you saying about my mother?' repeated Summer. But she knew what Adam was saying. Molly was a party girl, a gold-digger, a single-minded bitch when the mood took her. And he was right, she didn't want to end up like her mother; not far off forty-five, unmarried, flogging gifts on eBay.

'Honey, I'm not saying anything,' replied Adam. 'She's with Marcus. So she's my friend.'

'Exactly. And she likes Marcus very much,' Summer added, not terribly convincingly. 'So please, whatever you're trying to suggest, don't.'

Adam pulled himself to his feet, facing her. 'Listen, there's a company flat we're having renovated. It's in one of the best squares in Notting Hill, a fantastic lateral conversation with solid oak floors and . . .'

Summer felt herself switch off. She enjoyed listening to Adam, learning from him, talking about books and movies and faraway places. But when it came to business she could feel herself cloud over.

'Well, what do you think?' asked Adam.

'Eh? Of what?' replied Summer.

'Of living there. It won't be for six weeks or so. But I think you need some independence and it'd be nice if we could have a little more privacy, wouldn't it?' he added, slipping his hand inside her bikini bottoms.

'Really? You're kidding?'

Adam shook his head. 'Now don't get too excited. I'll get a proper contract drawn up, naming you as my tenant.'

Summer could feel her pulse race with excitement. She would love to get out from under her mother's shadow and it would be heaven to have Adam coming around for long Sunday breakfasts, but still . . . There was a slight taste of something, well, *very Molly* about what he was saying. For all of Adam's philanthropic comments – did he really think she needed saving from her mother? – the setup had the distinct whiff of mistress. She didn't even know if it was possible to be elevated to mistress status when Adam wasn't even married. But when she looked into his dark brown eyes, all her misgivings melted away and she felt a stir in her groin. When she was with Adam she felt desired, protected. She also felt something she hadn't felt in a long, long time. She felt in love.

'Are you at least going to think about it?' asked Adam, putting his hands around her waist.

'I don't want to live there for free. I won't like how that feels.'

Adam nodded. 'I'll get a lease drawn up and we can fix a rent. Although I think you can rest assured it'll be very reasonable.'

He slipped the palms of his hands under the sides of her bikini bottoms and began to peel them down.

'And to answer your question,' his words became muffled as his mouth journeyed south. 'No, there aren't any others.'

42

Karin was sure she was being followed. At first she thought it was just paranoia brought on by stress and overwork, but it was happening too frequently to be just her imagination. At first it was nothing more than an eerie sense of being watched, the feeling of unseen eyes on her back or an involuntary shiver, even though it was seventy-five degrees outside. She had never been one to get easily spooked, but at the same time she had always possessed a sharp sense of knowing when something was wrong and it was making her jumpy. It made her close the curtains as soon as it went dark. It made her request the use of Adam's driver more frequently, although she did not tell him her suspicions – he would have laughed, especially as she often mocked his Manhattan security consciousness with his ex-SAS driver and his friends who had bodyguards and submarines that circled their yachts when they were on holiday.

She first saw him late on a hot, sunny afternoon in July. An apricot sun was sitting low in the hazy, pale blue sky and Karin had finished work early to enjoy the evening. Adam was in New York and she wanted some downtime to relax, perhaps sort out some paperwork. Swim Show Miami, the industry's most important trade fair, was only two weeks away and she needed to make sure they were prepared. Her house was just round the corner from a fabulous Italian deli and she strolled down there to get some beef tomatoes and buffalo mozzarella for an early supper on the roof terrace. Coming back, she cut through the South Kensington backstreets of tall white townhouses and hidden parks feeling relaxed and happy. Then she saw him. He was sitting on a wall at the end of her street reading a music magazine. His hair was lank and brown, pushed back over his ears, and his long face had a sullen expression. At first she thought he was just another teenager, but the way he had looked so directly, so intensely at her had made her feel deeply unsettled. As she passed, he began to follow her, the clop of his heavy trainers clearly audible behind her. She climbed up the stone steps of her house without looking back and slammed the door shut. Peering through the peephole she could see his distorted image standing outside and she quickly double-bolted the front door. *Don't be so silly, Karin,* she scolded herself. *He's only a kid.* She even managed a small laugh as she climbed the stairs to run a warm, oily bath. *He's only a silly little kid. What harm could he do?*

43

The only problem with living out in Buckinghamshire was the journey home, thought Molly, pressing her foot down on the accelerator. Marcus had given her his Maserati two weeks ago after he had bought a brand-new silver Jaguar XS. She loved the way it ate up the road. Even though she had not officially moved into The Standlings, she was fast beginning to think of 'the manor' as home. Her interior decorations were almost complete, most importantly the conversion of a bedroom into a climate-controlled 'his and hers' dressing room into which Molly had moved all of her extensive wardrobe. She was also delighted with the new Smallbone kitchen with its racks of shiny Global knives she would never touch and the brand-new panelled library designed to look 300 years old. The *pièce de résistance*, however, was the ten-man indoor hot tub, modelled on the grotto at the Playboy mansion. Molly had been itching to have one of those since she had been to a party there in the 1980s – now that was a great night out, she smiled. Marcus, however, had almost had a meltdown at the expenditure Molly was racking up, but even he had to admit the place looked amazing.

If she could have picked up The Standlings and dropped it in the middle of Kensington, it would have been perfect, but it wasn't. It was fifty miles outside of sodding London, which felt ten times longer after the two cocktails and the line of coke she had taken a couple of hours ago when she met some friends in Notting Hill for lunch.

She pushed her foot down even harder, wanting to get home for 4.30. She had discovered a wonderful woman in the village, a former beauty therapist at Dorchester spa who had down shifted

261

to Buckinghamshire and came round to Molly's once a week to do a very respectable manicure and pedicure. As she hit sixty mph on a B-road, her mobile rang and she reached across the passenger seat to grab it. She hadn't seen the slight bend in the road, and the car jerked as it mounted a roadside kerb. Molly dropped the mobile phone and tightened her grip on the steering wheel as she tried to control the vehicle. 'Fuck, fuck, fuck,' she muttered as the front left wheel bumped back on the tarmac. 'Shit, shit, *shit!*' she yelled, banging her palm against the dashboard as the sound of a police siren wailed behind her.

She'd been whisked through the court process. Molly had actually considered herself lucky to get away with a £2000 fine and a twelve month ban on her licence after she had seen the three po-faced country bumpkins on the magistrates' bench. No amount of Chanel or pearls was going to sway those inbreds, she thought. She was entirely correct. Molly was convicted of drink-driving when the bench completely rejected her mitigating plea that she had needed to drink vodka cranberry to sort out a nasty bout of cystitis. Still, at least she hadn't received a sentence of community service – imagine! Scraping chewing gum off railway bridges with her nails? – and hopefully her driving ban would mean that Marcus would finally sort them out with a Midas Corporation driver.

'Now we really have it to get this sorted,' said, Marcus seriously, sitting on one of the slate-grey sofas in The Standlings' drawing room with the cold, efficient manner of somebody who was dealing with a business problem. 'I have phoned Alcoholics Anonymous but apparently they don't take bookings. They say you need to initiate it yourself by going to a meeting. I think that would be a good first step, Molly.'

Molly sat back with the sulky, truculent expression of a grounded teenager. Marcus had spent too many years in America, she thought; he was beginning to sound like Oprah.

'I am not going to Alcoholics Anonymous because I am not an alcoholic,' she said, stubbornly refusing to meet his gaze. 'And before you ask, I'm not checking into the bloody Priory either.'

'Well, what about another rehabilitation programme then?' he continued soberly. 'I have a friend who has recommended a very discreet place in Wiltshire. It's tough, but apparently they have incredible results in three or four weeks.'

'Marcus!' Molly slapped her hand against the George Smith velvet sofa with a thud. 'You aren't listening! I am not an alcoholic or a coke-head. There is no problem to solve apart from finding the two-thousand-pound fine you're too stingy to pay for me.'

Molly got up and started pacing around the drawing room, while Marcus watched her closely, as if she was going to do something foolish at any time.

'Well, what are you going to do Molly? We cannot let the matter just rest here. You know I love you, but I do think you have a problem and we need to get it sorted.'

Molly knew that there was no wriggling out of this situation. Marcus had been like a dog with a bone since the offence; he'd got some crazy notion that this was all for her own good. *As if*, she thought. She had no intention of sitting on a plastic chair talking about her terrible childhood with a bunch of losers at AA, or disappearing off the circuit for four weeks to go cold turkey in the middle of nowhere. But it was clear from Marcus's belligerent expression that she had to do something. With an offer to move in to the Standlings full time surely just around the corner, she wasn't going to take any chances.

'I do have one idea,' said Molly, going to Marcus's chair and sitting on the floor, her chin on his knee. 'I know how much this means to you – to us – so I am going to stop drinking and I know of a fabulous way to start.'

'Molly, this is more serious than—'

Molly ignored Marcus' protests and pressed on regardless. 'My friend Donna runs a detox retreat at Delemere Manor. I know it's nothing official like rehab,' she said, trying to look as penitent as possible. 'But it's pretty much the same thing. Really rigorous, totally healthy. Organic menu, meditation and yoga, emphasis on spiritual and mental wellbeing . . .' She smiled up at him hopefully, creeping her fingers up to his crotch for good measure.

'It sounds more like a holiday,' said Marcus.

'It will be bloody hard work,' said Molly indignantly.

Marcus looked at her, seeming to weigh it up. 'OK,' he said finally. 'It's a start, at least.'

'Wonderful. I'll phone Donna and tell her to squeeze me in and then I think I'll pop into London to buy some new gym kit. And maybe get that pedicure. Can't have shiatsu with hangnails, can you?'

44

Couture. The very word made the hairs on the back of Karin's neck stand up. Couture reeked of class and exclusivity, excepting all but the very thinnest slice of society, and it was exactly where Karin wanted to be. She took her place on a dainty gilt chair on the front row of the catwalk and looked around. De Bouvier was one of the oldest ateliers in Paris, a small fusty, dusty brand heading for fashion obscurity until it had been bought by luxury goods conglomerate Raine-Laurent five years ago. Raine-Laurent promptly hired Coln Lindemann, one of the world's most exciting new designers, who had caused a sensation by breathing life into De Bouvier's ready-to-wear collection three seasons ago. Now Lindemann was poised to do the same for the couture division of the brand. The show was certainly playing up its old school heritage by showing in the Salle Imperiale at the Hotel Westin right by the Tuilieries rather than some marquee in the Bois de Bologne like some of the other big fashion houses. This was an old-fashioned gilded salon, with high painted ceilings, long crimson drapes and huge gold chandeliers with hundreds of bulbs, like teardrops, casting a flattering glow. Handsome assistants with fine bone structure and even finer sharp suits ushered the world's most powerful magazine editors, of American *Vogue, Harper's Bazaar*, *WWD*, celebrities and, most importantly, the atelier's clients to their seats.

'Isn't that Vivienne Delemere?' hissed Christina into Karin's ear. 'How does she manage to look so chic? She must be seventy if she's a day.'

Christina was dressed immaculately in a Balmain short skirt and silk ruffled shirt. She had told Karin she was in the mood to spend,

spend, spend, and who could blame her? Her divorce from Ariel was looking as if it was about to settle out of court. Fifty million pounds, said her lawyers, and that was before they started carving up the property.

Karin looked down at the show's running order on Christina's lap: her shopping list, she thought enviously. One sweep of the pen beside number twelve and that was £100,000 gone; £100K on one dress that would be worn once and then archived. Karin was beginning to wish she'd never agreed to come. But then how could she refuse when her boyfriend was encouraging her to spend, spend, spend too?

'Of course you should go,' Adam had said after she had told him of Christina's invitation. 'And I hope you will order something for yourself while you are there. Get them to invoice it directly to me. I know the directrice very well.' It was exactly the sort of gesture Karin was hoping for. Ever since the Capri trip on board *The Pledge*, she had been nursing a nagging suspicion about Adam's behaviour. Not that anyone else would have spotted anything; on the yacht Adam had been loving and attentive, in fact it had been quite the perfect weekend. Then, on the final evening, Karin had been tidying in their stateroom and found a matchbook from the Porto Ercole hotel Il Pellicano next to Adam's cigars. It looked new, unused. Hadn't Adam said he'd had lunch at the Splendido in Portofino? It was a tiny thing, but it had unnerved her.

The audience at the Salle was divided into three very distinct parts. The fashion editors who were lacking in millions but bristling with power, the celebrities who added a sprinkle of youth and glamour and then, finally, the actual customers. The haute-couture circuit had traditionally been a very small, very incestuous club of super-rich old-money women. The discovery of oil in Texas and the Middle East had added a dash of the exotic – the waste of those Arab women who bought couture to go *under* their burkas! thought Karin with a shudder; but it had been the post-*glasnost* explosion of Russian money which had almost single-handedly revived the art of couture. Still, it wasn't a young sport, thought Karin: most of the front row were over forty; couture dressing was as much an essential part of their look as a face-lift.

Loud classical music suddenly filled the Salle and a cone of light hit the runway as the first of the reed-thin models skated past them with the grace of a swan. Karin spotted a fabulous taupe dress made of the finest tulle with a train of ostrich feathers. It was beautiful, thought Karin, but . . .

Her critical eye was sizing it up, making mental adjustments. The beauty of couture, of course, was that the designer could adapt it whichever way the client desired. Karin would want the neck more scooped, the train of feathers less lavish. She knew her vision would be better than that of the designer himself.

'What do you like?' whispered Karin to Christina, who was busy scribbling notes on her running order. 'I want everything,' she purred. After the show Christina rushed off to an appointment at Chanel while Karin, never missing a business opportunity, remained behind to make small talk with the magazine editors.

'Karin, my darling. How on earth are you?'

Karin turned to face Lysette Parker, one of couture's highest-spending clients. Her husband Sidney was head of Jolie Cosmetics, which made him, with the likes of Leonard Lauder, one of the most powerful men in the cosmetics industry. Only Lysette's heavily lined hands gave away that she was nearer to fifty-five than forty. An ash-blonde bob bounced around her tight Portofino-tanned face, her sharp grey tailored trouser suit, a georgette blouse and a string of creamy pearls were the epitome of timeless style. Lysette was so elegant and refined and such a powerful player on the international social circuit that no one dared mention her roots, although everyone with an ear to the ground knew them. In the 1970s, Lysette had been working as a cocktail waitress in a Mayfair casino when she had met the young Sidney who, with family money, had taken over fading cosmetics company Jolie. Over the next thirty years, with Lysette as his hostess and trusted advisor, he had transformed Jolie into a vast empire.

'Karin, it's such a delight to see you in Paris.'

Lysette was far too elegant to mention that she had never before seen Karin at couture and that her presence was something of a surprise.

'It can get a little tedious, don't you find?'

Karin wondered if Lysette was being ironic or whether the allure of having the finest fashion artists create bespoke gowns had actually lost its charge.

'What are you doing now? How's the business?' gushed Lysette. 'I've so many questions; I insist you come to the house for tea.'

Accepting gladly, Karin followed Lysette into her Bentley waiting on the Rue de Rivoli, which sped them to an elegant townhouse on Ile St-Louis. Lysette led Karin into a drawing room with a huge window that overlooked the Seine, dazzling in the summer sun. A maid in a grey uniform served them tea and sugar-dusted madeleines.

'So how are you getting along?' asked Lysette. 'Do you have a man in your life?'

Straight to the point as usual, thought Karin with a wry smile. Lysette was not a close friend, but ever since they had met at Ascot almost ten years ago, the older woman had treated Karin like a favourite niece, always encouraging her to eat more and to get herself married off to a nice billionaire.

'I was so sorry to hear about Sebastian – you did get my card? – it must have been such a blow.'

Karin was momentarily thrown by the mention of her late husband and she stared out at the river. Lysette put her hand on Karin's knee. 'Sebastian was an angel, my dear, and we shall all miss him, but life goes on. A woman simply cannot stand still.'

Karin smiled at Lysette's legendary pragmatism. 'Well, I have been seeing someone . . .' she began.

'Oh good!' said Lysette, tucking a sheaf of pale blonde hair around her ear. 'And does he have good provenance?'

'Well, he's not a prince, if that's what you mean,' said Karin. 'But he is on the *Forbes* list. His name is Adam Gold, he's the CEO of the Midas Corporation.'

'Do you think you will marry him?'

Karin felt the porcelain teacup rattle in her hand. 'I . . . I don't know,' said Karin truthfully. 'He's reached his forties without ever having taken the plunge, and you do have to ask yourself if he is ever going to.'

'Now, now, Karin, all men are the marrying kind, it's just that you have to give some a little more encouragement than others. Are there any other obstacles? Religion? A disapproving mother?'

'I am sure he is seeing someone else, Lysette.'

She had finally said it. She hadn't told Diana or Christina, her closest friends. She had told Lysette Parker. She did not know the woman well enough to know whether she was discreet or a gossip, although there was something elegant and knowing about Lysette that made her want to unburden herself.

'Have you any idea who it is?'

Karin sighed. 'Possibly. There is a woman who he works with, although he always made it clear, even before we were together, that he would never involve himself with someone in the company.'

'Then how do you know it's her?'

'I don't,' said Karin flatly. 'But there have been a few incidents lately to make me suspect there is someone else.'

She told Lysette about their trip to Capri and finding the matchbook from Il Pellicano. As she unburdened her story, she could feel herself becoming more angry at the injustice, the betrayal. When Karin had finished, Lysette nodded and put down her cup and saucer.

'Now I'm going to tell you something that you may find shocking, my dear, but take it from someone who knows a thing or two about affairs of the heart. Adam Gold is very serious about you.'

Karin looked perplexed. 'How do you know?'

'Your relationship is such that it has created the desire for a mistress.'

'And that's a good thing?' said Karin, amazed.

'In my day, powerful, successful men did not want women who were successful in their own right. We had to stay at home, be the good wife, host dinner parties, perhaps produce children. That was it.'

'But everyone knows how important you were in building up the Jolie brand.'

'I have had the honour of being Sidney's muse, yes,' she said with a small smile. 'I have advised him about the desires of the woman on the street and the commercial triggers they respond to, but I have never been the alpha female. I have always known my position in our marriage. It's a supporting role,' she said, taking a sip of tea.

'Things have changed in business, that's true. There are women in the boardroom, running companies, they're even in the cabinet. But the nature of the alpha male has not changed a jot, my dear. He always wants a bigger car, a bigger boat, a bigger house, and he wants to win every game.'

Lysette paused to play with the pearls around her neck. 'Let me give you a piece of advice,' she said, dabbing her lips. 'If you think Adam is having an affair, accept it. If he *is* having an affair, accept it. Sidney and I love each other dearly and I consider our marriage successful, but don't you think I know that Sidney has slept with dozens of women over the years? Every time he gets another secretary, I get another diamond necklace. Sidney is getting the excitement he craves, which is bound to fade after thirty years of marriage; I get more beautiful things. And I get to keep all this,' she said, opening her palm to indicate their magnificent house. 'In return, Sidney loves me even more for being for so tolerant, so understanding. And, most importantly, he isn't going to leave me for any of those tarts.' There was a sudden hardness to her voice that hinted at her roots. Then she smiled knowingly. 'And, as you say, it doesn't hurt that I have helped him build up one of the world's most successful businesses.'

Karin was silent, mulling over Lysette's words. 'But I haven't helped Adam build up his business,' said Karin.

'Ah, but you are an asset, Karin. Never underestimate the alpha male, my dear. He might wine and dine you and give you diamonds, but he'll make his decisions strictly on a cold, hard business basis: he'll ask himself, "How much is she worth?" And you, Karin, are successful, beautiful and rich. As long as you don't try to play him at his own game, as long as you let him think he's in charge, you'll always be an asset. And men like Adam Gold want to hang onto their assets.'

45

Delemere Manor sat in the heart of the Delemere estate in the rolling countryside of Gloucestershire. Molly felt a frisson of excitement as her chauffeur-driven town car passed through the main iron gates and along the wide driveway lined with plush oaks. It was a picture-perfect scene of timeless aristocratic Britain. Herds of deer grazed on the greeny-yellow fields, parched with a hot early summer sun. There were proud copses dotted along the horizon, a lake bristling with long reeds, and then there was Delemere House itself, majestic in the distance, the top of its high Georgian windows peeking over a dense wood. Even to Molly, it seemed a little frivolous to turn the home of Donna and Daniel Delemere into an away-day foodie destination for ladies who lunch.

Molly wondered whether she would see Alex over the course of the weekend. Their passionate meetings at the Basil Street Hotel had become less frequent since her move to The Standlings and, besides, Alex could be so conservative. When Molly had suggested an assignation at the Delemeres' London townhouse, he had reacted badly, calling the idea 'disrespectful', so who knew how he would react to Molly appearing at his family seat.

The wheels of the car crunched on the gravel and came to a halt outside the honey-coloured pile, where Donna was standing on the step looking irritatingly beautiful and chaste in a knee-length Marni print sundress, her daughter Evie slung across one slender hip. Molly forced a smile as Donna waved; the fact that her friend came from one of the poorest areas of the northeast and could end up like this never ceased to irk Molly.

'I am so glad you could make it,' smiled Donna, popping her

head through Molly's open car window. 'I really didn't think this weekend was going to be your thing, but luckily I've been able to squeeze you into a room with my old friend Denise.'

Sharing a room? thought Molly with alarm. *What was this, the girl guides?* She waited a few moments to see if a valet would appear to carry her bags in, but when none was forthcoming she reluctantly took her case from the driver and followed Donna around the side of the manor house, the wheels of the suitcase dragging on the gravel. They came to a large courtyard full of blooming terracotta pots, on the far side of which was the barn that had been converted into the Delemere farm store. Molly paused to pop her head inside, drinking in the delicious smells of fruit, flowers and fresh bread. The shop was full of immaculately groomed women in white jeans and smock tops handling misshapen bundles of organic vegetables and loaves the size of Easter bonnets.

'I think the farm shop has expanded since the last time you were here,' said Donna, peering in behind Molly. 'We've had to build a private customer car park round the back. It's getting so busy, the noise was drifting too much towards the manor house.'

'What a shame,' said Molly insincerely. 'However, it must mean that business is booming.'

'It is,' agreed Donna, 'although that's less to do with our improvements than the growth of the luxury organic sector as a whole. We're just cashing in on what Prince Charlie's Duchy Originals and the Bamfords' Daylesford estate have done before us. But I'm just glad we've created something that people enjoy. Something that's good for them and good for the planet.'

What a crock of shit, thought Molly, following Donna towards another converted barn on the other side of the manor. Donna's eco-zeal was less to do with a commitment to the environment and more about her grubby desire to get her fingerprints all over Delemere Manor so that, when the time came, her 'invaluable commercial input' would translate into a fatter divorce settlement.

'So has anybody else arrived yet?' asked Molly as they walked into a big open-plan lobby painted in a palest sage green decorated with vases of lilies and cream squashy sofas.

'Well your roommate Denise is already here, and Karin and Christina are in room one. And do you know Diana Birtwell? She's here with her friend Rebecca. But that's it – as you know, this isn't a full course, just a dry run for the real thing when we get paying guests in, but Angela Appleby – she's the course leader – will give you the works, don't you worry!' she laughed. 'Now, why don't you go and unpack? The introductory session begins in forty-five minutes. You are really going to love it.'

Don't count on it, thought Molly as she dragged her case to her room.

Donna's old friend Denise Jeffries was sitting on a thin single bed in a small twin room that overlooked a field of grazing cows.

'Hi! I'm Denise,' she said, getting up.

'Molly Sinclair. I take it we're roommates.'

Denise was about forty with a head of red curls, a wide mouth and dry-looking skin that desperately needed a facial.

Molly dumped her case on the other bed and wandered into the hallway to find the other bedrooms. One door was open and she saw Karin and Christina changing into skintight leggings and crop-tops.

'Oh, hello. I didn't know you were coming,' said Karin, pulling on a ballet slipper.

'Can you believe we're not sleeping at the manor?' replied Molly absently, still looking around and surveying the property. 'I feel like I've arrived at scout camp.'

Karin pulled a face. It was the first time she had seen Molly since she had sent her on a wild-goose chase to the Villa La Vigie in Monte Carlo. Time, as well as Molly's dismissal from from the Midas Corporation, had softened the brunt of Karin's anger but she still found that she could be no more than civil to her.

'Oh, I think there's something fabulously Zen about Delemere,' said Christina, stretching her arms in the air to limber up. 'Don't you think it's such a wonderful escape from it all?'

Fine for you to be slumming it, thought Molly cynically, *when you've got a yacht and millions of dollars coming your way*. In fact, Molly had been delighted to hear that Christina Levy was attending the retreat. If the whispers were correct, Christina's divorce settlement was shaping up to be a very hefty one, and Molly couldn't wait to extract as many details from her as possible; she might even be able to sell them on to the newspaper diary pages.

Angela Appleby's introductory seminar was perhaps not quite the roaring success she had expected, but then she possibly under-estimated the effect of announcing that her charges would have to give up alcohol, all stimulants, red meat and men.

'During a detox, it is best to remove all distractions,' said Angela in a cheery voice. 'Your body needs time to heal itself and your mind to become clear. There is a reason Buddhist monks are celibate,' she added. Having absorbed this bombshell and having been promised that they would all be 'leaving Delemere on Sunday in a better place', the six women all adjourned to 'The Landing' – the open lobby where a fire had been lit and an organic buffet prepared on a long table covered in white voile.

'Apparently it's lights out at 9 p.m.,' said Christina, sipping at a ginger tea. Molly looked out of the window and saw the sky was bruising lilac as darkness was beginning to fall.

'I told you it was like school,' grumbled Molly still feeling hungry, despite the pumpkin seeds and carrot sticks.

'I didn't know you were a boarder, Molly?' said Karin, raising one eyebrow and watching with satisfaction as Molly's face reddened with anger.

'Anyway, goodnight everyone. I've had a hectic week so I could really do with an early one.'

One by one, the women retired, until Molly and Denise remained alone in The Landing. Molly had warmed to her roommate; she somehow detected a kindred spirit but she couldn't explain why. Certainly, Denise's life was the most removed from the other women on the retreat. She had travelled from Esher, where she lived with her husband Neville Jeffries, a scaffolding contractor, and two young sons. She wore no expensive jewellery, except for a large pair of diamond studs which Molly felt sure were just zircona, and her clothes looked like high street. But while Denise was probably the most advanced yoga student in the group, there was something about the lines around her mouth, the creases by her eyes, that suggested that Denise Jeffries had lived a life.

'Ahh, I love 'em to bits, but it's great to get away from the kids for the weekend,' said Denise, slumping back into one of the squashy leather chairs.

'My daughter Summer is twenty-four, but she still needs looking after,' smiled Molly, swivelling her legs up onto the sofa and stretching her toes.

'Wow. I didn't know you had a twenty-four-year-old,' said Denise, her eyes widening. 'Weren't you modelling back then, not playing mum?'

'You can do both, you know,' said Molly wryly. 'It was just a bit more difficult. I always think how far my career could have gone if I hadn't had Summer. It was tough seeing girls like Yasmin and Linda take off like a rocket.'

Denise nodded sympathetically. 'Yes, well, you've got a daughter though, haven't you? And anyway, you *were* successful. My brother used to love you!' Molly appreciated the compliment, but she could have done without that word again: 'used'. He *used* to love you. She sighed.

'I could so do with a drink right now,' she said. She had filched a couple of bottles of great claret from the Midas Corporation boardroom and they were lying like forbidden fruit at the bottom of her case.

'Should I see if I can find some tea or something?' said Denise, standing and walking around The Landing.

'No, a fine place like this calls for a good glass of wine,' said Molly, testing the water for a drinking companion.

Denise gave her the smile she was looking for. 'It's tempting, but we're not going find any on Donna's detox weekend, are we?'

'That's where you might be wrong,' said Molly, uncoiling her body and walking upstairs to the bedroom.

'Why did I agree to this?' slurred Denise. It was near midnight now and the two bottles of claret were lying guiltily on the floor between them, almost drained. 'I haven't drunk in ages and Donna will kill us if she finds out.'

The lights were off and the two women were sitting in front of the crackling amber fire. She was glad Donna had shacked her up with Denise, not uptight bloody Karin.

'How *do* you know Donna then?' asked Molly finally, who had waited all night for her moment. She had asked her before the introductory seminar, and her answers had been so vague that Molly had sensed there was much more to it than she was telling.

'We go a long way back, way before Donna lived like this,' said Denise, wiping a thin trail of red liquid from her lips. Molly noticed an inflection in her voice that she recognized as envy.

'Before she became the queen of detox,' smiled Molly, encouraging her. 'I mean, who'd have thought Donna the party girl would have ended up running a retreat?'

'Well, she did always know where there was money to be made,' said Denise.

'It didn't take a genius to work out that marrying a rich man was going to be a good thing, did it?' said Molly, probing gently.

'But Donna hit the jackpot, didn't she?' insisted Denise. 'Out of all the girls I knew back then, she was the one I thought least likely to do it. To, you know, get all this.'

'Which girls?' asked Molly, pouring the last of the claret into Denise's glass.

Denise paused before she spoke, fixing her slightly unfocused vision on Molly in what she obviously thought was a piercing stare.

'How long have you known Donna?' she asked.

'A long time too,' lied Molly.

'So you know?' said Denise cautiously.

Molly nodded convincingly, feeling a sense of welling euphoria that she was on the brink of discovering something potent.

'I was the one who sorted it all out for Donna,' began Denise. 'I had about a dozen girls, pretty party girls or failed models usually, girls that would always be up for anything.' She took a sip of wine and smiled almost boastfully. 'I wasn't always Denise Jeffries the bored housewife from Esher, you know. I was Denise Duncan, girl about town.'

Molly said nothing, like a shark that had sniffed blood but that was just waiting to move in for the kill.

'Do you know Adnan Hashemi?'

'Yes,' said Molly. She had of course heard of the now-dead Saudi arms dealer who had been a big player on the London social scene in the 1990s.

'I was his mistress for a little while,' said Denise. 'His wife still lived in Jeddah, and I had a little apartment overlooking Hyde Park. And for a small window of time, I had the most wonderful life', she said, staring at the fire. She turned back to Molly and took another sip. 'Adnan had friends. They liked British women and I knew a lot of pretty girls. Donna was young, maybe nineteen or twenty. She had come to London to train as a beauty therapist but was out on the circuit a lot. Legends, Tramp, all those, which is how I knew her. She was ambitious, she liked the high life, and Adnan's friends thought she was wonderful.'

Molly couldn't believe what she was hearing. 'Does Daniel know any of this?' she said softly, trying to disguise the surprise in her voice.

275

'What's there to know?' said Denise. 'That his wife did the international party scene for a little while? That some men gave her money and took her shopping? What's the big deal in today's day and age?' She shook her head, as if trying to clear the fog of alcohol. 'There's really very little to tell, and, even if there is, in whose interest is it to go delving too deeply?'

Molly raised her glass and smiled. 'I'll drink to that.'

46

Molly hadn't had so many compliments since she'd had that discreet Harley Street eye-lift two years ago. The turnout was spectacular. At least 200 people were milling around The Standlings' clipped gardens on a blistering hot summer's day and most of them were social A-list. There was a senior flight of executives from the Midas Corporation, and important bankers. She had also commandeered a handful of wealthy Europeans who were passing through London. Adam had been in touch with a raft of wealthy friends from New York, a software billionaire, a cosmetic mogul. And all for a little village fête.

Molly smiled with pride; she'd played this one perfectly.

As soon as the renovations on The Standlings were completed, Molly had been in a hurry to show them off to as many people as possible, but she knew a string of dinner parties would be both tedious and expensive, so had decided that the best way to show-case the house was to play to its strength as a quintessentially English manor. Her idea of throwing a Saturday afternoon garden fête came to her when she read an article about Liz Hurley's new life in Gloucestershire. As soon as she'd had the thought, she'd known it was genius. Genius. It would show a softer, philanthropic side, with key people from the village being invited for rustic colour and all profits from the tombola and coconut shy going to anti-seal-clubbing or whatever was hot that month.

The day of the fête, The Standlings looked like the Garden of Eden. The sun was shining, the flowerbeds were bursting with jasmine and sweet peas, the rose garden was in full bloom and the lawns had been mowed into two-tone stripes of soft and vivid emerald green. All along them, tents and stalls were doing a bustling trade. Molly's beauty therapist friend was offering Indian head massages by the potting shed, the Women's Institute were manning a jam stall and the raffle was bursting with all manner of pashminas, jewellery and perfume that had failed to meet their reserves on eBay. In the lower field, there was a bouncy castle in the shape of a pirate ship and the local scout pack were offering pony rides. Oiling the wheels was a jolly Victorian-themed bar run by Len Barry, landlord of the local pub, who had a stonking crush on Molly. Len was also overseeing the barbecue, which was grilling delicious meat and sausages provided by the Delemere farm shop. It was fun, it was elegant, it was respectable.

'I thought we were having a small barbecue,' laughed Marcus, hooking an arm around Molly's shoulder. They were standing on the terrace overlooking the lawns, the smell of candyfloss and sausages wafting around them.

'If you're going to do a job, you have to do it properly,' she smiled, resting her head on his shoulder.

'You're wonderful, you know that?' replied Marcus.

Molly moved even closer towards him, like a Siamese cat rubbing against its owner, knowing she had scored a bull's-eye.

The village fête idea appealed to Marcus's closeted country-gent side, the side that wanted to keep horses and play lord of the manor in his big house in the Chilterns. Ever since the drink-driving episode, she had felt her relationship with Marcus cool a little. He could be such a sanctimonious little prick sometimes, demanding she stop drinking, smoking, having fun. Well, if he wanted the dutiful little village wifey with no vices, he could have it, she thought slyly – the image of it, anyway. But today's triumph seemed to have warmed things right up and she knew her timing was perfect. When Marcus thought she was doing Pilates in the bedroom, she was listening, always listening. She had loitered outside his study late at night, eavesdropping, waiting for some nugget of information. And now, it seemed, it was here. Stock options. Cashing in. It was all music to Molly's ears. Something was brewing at the Midas Corporation and, one way or another, she was going to have part of it.

Karin was secretly seething. Either Marcus had instructed some top-flight events company, or she had underestimated Molly. The

Standlings village fête was fabulous; traditional without being stuffy, fun without being cheesy. She had even won a Hermès scarf on the tombola. And the turnout was remarkable; even the sprinkling of Great Horsham village locals gave it a certain homespun charm, although the presence of Diana and Christina – apparently they and Molly had all struck up some sort of bizarre friendship at the detox weekend – had made her bristle. But what had irked her the most was the presence of that glamorous blonde banker Claudia Falcon, whom she had spotted laughing with Marcus about ten minutes ago at the jam stall. The woman certainly looked good today. Her blonde bob had been pulled back into a chignon, she looked relaxed in a pair of wide linen palazzo pants, some Grecian sandals and a beautifully cut vest-top. *Stop being so paranoid and relax*, thought Karin. She took a deep breath and reminded herself what Lysette had said in Paris: *How do you know it's her?*

'You don't get this in Manhattan,' said Adam, coming up behind her, carrying a tankard of beer. 'It's a really good day, isn't it?'

'You fired Molly from the Midas Corporation, remember? Now is not the time to start eulogizing about her work. She'll have you for unfair dismissal before you know it.'

'I didn't fire her,' replied Adam, still smiling. 'Her contract was up. She was working on a case-by-case basis.'

Yeah, right, thought Karin, sipping her iced tea. *Nothing to do with her shagging around on your best friend.*

'Anyway, what are people like Claudia Falcon doing here?' she asked innocently. 'I didn't know Marcus wanted it to be a work thing.'

'It isn't. But why miss an opportunity like today to keep good people happy?'

'Kay, honey, there you are,' said Christina, trotting up with a large tumbler of Pimms and taking her arm. 'Come on, Molly is desperate for us to come look at the house. Diana and Donna are already in there.'

Karin rolled her eyes as Adam kissed her on the cheek and went to join Marcus and Claudia at the tombola.

'Can you believe this place?' said Karin to Christina, still trying to keep her eye on Adam. 'It's like a Jilly Cooper wet-dream.'

'I think it's rather fabulous. Highgrove chic,' said Christina as they climbed the stone steps away from the gardens into the house.

'She's hardly Camilla Parker Bowles is she?' said Karin.

'Not yet, darling, not yet.'

Inside, they found Molly was giving the guided tour to Diana and Donna in the master bedroom.

'Marcus didn't want anything structural done to the place so it's all cosmetic,' said Molly, pointing out the newly hung eau-de-nil silk damask walls and cream shot taffeta hanging at the windows. 'As you can see there's bags of room up here and lots more scope for improvement: a second study, nursery.'

'A nursery?' said Karin, lifting an eyebrow, 'and who would that be for?'

'You never know,' said Molly tartly, looking Karin up and down. 'Some of us are still of age.'

Molly took Karin and Diana downstairs for a look at the drawing room, then showed them through the French windows so they could sit out on the patio away from the crowds. They watched Molly and Christina walk arm in arm over to the bouncy castle, their high heels sinking into the grass.

'Can you believe she's thinking about a nursery?' laughed Karin. 'I bet her ovaries dried up about five years ago.'

When there was no response from Diana, Karin looked back at her friend. 'You're quiet.'

'Oh, I'm fine' said Diana. Karin frowned and searched her face for clues. Diana certainly looked impeccable, and things seemed to be going well for her family. Martin had just floated his online betting company, which had been valued at over £1 billion pounds, the offering heavily oversubscribed. Overnight, Martin and Diana were worth over £500 million, and they could have sold the shares five times over. But still, Karin thought she saw a sadness in Diana's face.

'Are you sure you're okay?' asked Karin. Under her wraparound sunglasses, Karin could see her friend's eyebrows crease into crooked lines.

'Not really,' she smiled weakly.

Karin touched Diana's knee sympathetically. 'Honey, what's wrong?'

A single tear rolled down from under Diana's shades. 'Last week I told Martin I had come off the pill and he almost had a seizure,' said Diana, pressing a fingertip on her cheek to blot the tear.

'Didn't you discuss it?'

Diana shook her head so a wispy tendril of hair escaped from her chignon. 'We've been married a year. I thought it was about time we started thinking about children.'

'But he doesn't?'

'Got it in one, girlfriend,' said Diana, dabbing under her shades with a table napkin. 'After I told him, it was as if he suddenly decided he didn't want to be married.'

'Come on, he loves being married to you,' laughed Karin gently. It was true. Every one of Diana's girlfriends had been envious of the energy with which Martin had pursued her. She'd moved in with him only three months after they had met at that day in Savile Row and within six months he had presented her with a twenty-carat diamond engagement ring that set a new yardstick for her circle's trophy jewellery.

'I thought so too,' said Diana, her voice cracking. 'But the issue of children . . . it's as if it's made him wake up and want to be young, free and single again.'

'But you did ask him if he wanted to have children with you before you got married . . . ?'

Diana's sob gave Karin her answer. It was so easily done; an unspoken issue was always an awkward one, and why bring up something that could break a deal? 'I didn't ask him then, no,' said Diana. 'But I asked him now. He said he didn't want any more kids. Said he just wanted it to be just me and him and no responsibilities, no decisions to be made other than where we should go on holiday, Miami or Mustique, Barbados or the Bahamas.'

'And I take it that's not your dream?'

'I love our life,' said Diana, her voice almost a whisper. 'But I've always wanted children. I never knew how much until Martin said he didn't want to have any more.'

Karin looked at her. Behind the grooming, the diamonds, the head-to-toe Gucci, was a traditional, blue-blooded Home Counties girl. Her family's star had fallen, their fortune dwindled to nothing, and in Martin she thought she could rekindle her family's glory by marrying well. But that's what she'd wanted all along; not the position, but the family.

'And is having children a deal-breaker?' asked Karin, trying to meet Diana's gaze.

She couldn't see her friend's eyes through the black lenses, but she could see the tiny sad nod of her head, the movement that said 'yes'.

Karin looked out at the Chiltern Hills, a smudge of muted colour in the sun, and shivered. It was funny how things changed. By the end of the summer, Diana could be falling out of the magic circle of millionaire wives. And Molly could be coming in.

Summer was standing by the hog-roast, helping the six-year-old son of the village butcher squeeze ketchup onto his hot dog. She was in a short white cotton dress so thin that the shadow of her body was visible in the sun, a stark contrast to the hazelnut brown of her long legs. It was the first weekend Summer had had off since Monaco and, while it had been enormous fun, she needed a break. Filming for 'On Heat', she had been to opera festivals, literary festivals, summer parties, Royal Ascot, the tennis, the Veuve Clicquot polo, Sardinia and St Tropez. Professionally, she had been on a steep learning curve, but she thought she was doing pretty well. Certainly, Simon Garrison kept saying that 'On Heat' was the best programme their production company had ever done. She took a swig of Pimms and the little boy ran off in the direction of the pony rides.

'Why don't you come and squeeze my hot dog?' whispered Adam into her ear, running his fingers lightly along her arm.

She turned round to see him looking relaxed in a pair of jeans and a navy polo shirt, while the sun had smeared a streak of colour across his nose.

'Adam. Don't,' giggled Summer behind her hand, looking round anxiously to see if anyone was watching. 'Where's Karin?'

'She's gone for a tour around the house with your mother. I think we're safe for a while. But, just to be sure, why don't you come and have your fortune read?' he asked, jerking his head towards a striped tent at the bottom of the garden. 'Meet you there in two minutes.'

Feeling a frisson of nerves and sexual excitement, she loitered for a count of 100, then followed Adam into the small tent. There was barely enough room for the two of them to move – and there was no sign of the fortune teller.

'Where's Madam Zorba then?' asked Summer as she felt Adam's hand slide up her thigh and under her panties. She groaned, every nerve end jangling with anticipation and the real prospect of getting caught.

'I crossed her palm with silver to make her go and take a coffee break,' mumbled Adam, biting gently on her earlobe.

Lifting her slightly into the air, he pushed her onto the tiny table behind her, slipping his hand up her thigh while his lips brushed her neck with kisses.

Summer arched her back and groaned softly. 'Adam, please. Don't. Someone is going to come.'

'Hopefully you,' smiled Adam, his fingertips dipping under her panties, finding her hot and wet. As he slid his finger over her clitoris, she gripped the edge of the table with desire, her nails clawing at the red baize of Madam Zorba's table. Gasping, struggling to regain control, she forced herself to think of Karin only 100 feet away. Suddenly Summer had a flashback to all the times she had lain in her bed at night, the sounds of her mother having sex filtering through the walls. Right then, Summer felt the same guilt and shame, the same uncomfortable mixture of desire and disgust.

'Stop it, stop it, Adam!' she hissed, pushing him away from her. As she sat up, the table flipped forward, sending Madam Zorba's tarot cards fluttering to the ground like butterflies.

'Hey! What the fuck has got in to you?' said Adam, pulling away from her sharply.

'This is *wrong*, Adam. It's all wrong.'

'Too right it's bloody wrong,' he complained. 'What are you stopping for?'

She pushed herself away from him and bent down to pick up the tarot cards. They were all face down on the grass and she quickly scooped them up and put them back on the table.

'Come on. We'd better go back outside,' she mumbled, smoothing down her dress. Adam tutted loudly and headed out into the fresh air, Summer following him. Neither of them saw the only two tarot cards upturned on the red baize. The first was the card of two lovers entwined. The second was the image of the hanged man.

From her vantage point on the terrace, Erin watched the activity of the fête panning out around her, feeling a uneasy sense of loneliness. She'd been grateful and excited when Marcus had invited her along earlier that week but, now she was here, she realized how socially unimportant she was. The people she knew best here – Molly, Karin and Adam – were too busy or uninterested to speak to her, and she found herself wishing that she was spending the afternoon with Chris, as she was increasingly spending her weekends.

283

Why didn't I invite him along? she cursed herself, taking a swig of lemonade. *I could have flirted with him in front of Adam.*

She stopped the thought in her tracks, knowing she was being ridiculous. Her crush on Adam was ridiculous. It was unprofessional, wrong and *unfair* that he was so sexy, unavailable and out of her league, she thought, catching sight of his sexy, handsome physique coming out of the fortune-teller's tent.

Something made her do a double take. As she looked more closely, she caught the thunderous expression on Adam's face and saw another figure coming out of Madame Zorba's tent: *Summer.*

Erin had been wondering where Molly's daughter had got to. Only twenty minutes ago they'd been having a giggle together on the terrace, catching up on all the gossip since the last time they'd met in Monte Carlo. Summer had proved to be the only friendly person at the fête, and Erin had welcomed her being around. But the sight of her now made Erin feel chilly, especially when she could now see Madam Zorba five hundred yards away at the Portaloos.

What were Adam and Summer doing alone together in the tent? Erin had felt a sickening, thumping realization of what she had just seen. For the past few weeks she had noticed Adam take phone calls with his office door shut. She had always assumed it was top secret business or just personal calls to Karin, but his uneasiness after such calls had recently made Erin wonder if there was another woman on the scene. Now she felt sure of it.

'There you are, Erin,' said Karin, striding out of the main house, fanning herself with a fête programme. 'I didn't know you were coming this afternoon. I don't suppose you've seen Adam, have you?'

Erin felt herself panic, glancing nervously down to Madam Zorba's tent. 'Karin. How great to see you,' she stuttered.

Karin stood at the edge of the terrace, surveying the grounds, her hand shielding her eyes from the sun.

Seeing Summer and Adam still shiftily standing together, Erin grabbed Karin by the arm and spun her around to face the house.

'Drink?' Erin smiled nervously, grabbing two glasses of punch from a passing waiter.

'Has this got red wine in it?' Karin asked the waiter, pointing at the tumbler.

The waiter nodded. 'Well, take it away. It'll give me a terrible headache. Get me an Evian, will you?'

The waiter mumbled apologetically and ran off in the direction of the house.

Erin was glad of the distraction, noticing over Karin's shoulder that Adam and Summer had now walked off in separate directions.

'So, Adam? You were looking for him.'

Karin nodded cautiously, examining Erin, whose cheeks appeared to have flushed slightly.

'We've got a dinner party tonight at the Rothschilds, and if we don't leave in an hour I'll never fit in a blow-dry.' The older woman narrowed her eyes, looking for a reaction from Erin. She had been on red alert all afternoon after seeing Claudia Falcon at the raffle, and Erin's behaviour was setting off more alarm bells.

'Erin, is anything the matter?'

'No, no, I'm just feeling a bit sick, that's all. Too much candyfloss and sitting in the sun, I expect.' She gave a wan smile.

Karin wasn't convinced, but she had little doubt that Adam's PA would be doggedly loyal to him even if she did know something, so she merely nodded.

'Ah, there's Adam,' Erin said, pointing in the direction of the raffle. 'Do you want me to run down and tell him you want to go?'

'That would be kind of you,' said Karin quickly. She put her hand on Erin's shoulder and smiled more warmly. 'It's so nice having you as Adam's assistant, you being my old PA and me basically getting you the job with Adam. I really feel as if I can trust you. *Rely* on you.'

Erin felt her cheeks flush again. 'Of course you can rely on me,' she replied in her most professional tone of voice.

Karin watched her run down the stone steps towards the main throng of the party. *I'll have to keep an eye on that one*, she thought. *She knows something.*

Summer had needed to take a walk around the entire grounds to cool off from her brush with Adam. She had just reached the stables when she noticed she was being followed by a very pretty blonde teenager.

'Hi, I'm Ellie Bradshaw,' said the girl breathlessly. 'I think you're beautiful. I've got your picture on my bedroom wall and everything.'

Summer had to laugh. It wasn't so long ago that she was feeling in awe of her mother's glamorous modelling friends, who would drop by the house. As she fell into step beside Summer, Ellie bombarded Summer with questions about London and Tokyo and modelling and all the famous people she had met. She was quite lovely, thought Summer, giving Ellie a sidelong glance. Sun-washed blonde hair, a small button nose. Her eyes were too small and close together to be truly beautiful, and the voluptuous figure busting out of her tight pink T-shirt ruled out catwalk, but she was certainly a very pretty girl.

'So what do you want to do when you leave college?' asked Summer.

'I've got a job in the pub this summer, but when I leave college next year I want to be famous.'

Summer laughed. 'Being famous isn't a career decision, Ellie. You have to do something to become famous.'

Ellie looked confused at this and Summer had to concede she had a point. There were plenty of people littering the magazines and tabloids who wouldn't be able to tell you what they did if their life depended on it.

'I was thinking about going on that pop programme on telly, but I can't sing,' said Ellie earnestly, 'And I'm not pretty enough to model.'

'You're really pretty,' said Summer frowning. She recognized that simmer of self-loathing from her own teenagehood. 'Anyway, not all pretty girls are models and not all models are pretty,' she added, suddenly feeling enormously protective of this sweet, vulnerable girl. She hadn't been much older than Ellie when she had gone to Japan. 'Don't worry, you'll find something you're good at and you'll have a great life, I promise.'

Ellie screwed up her face. 'Well, I wish it would hurry up and happen,' she said.

Molly's voice, announcing that the raffle was about to be drawn, suddenly crackled through a tannoy across the lawns.

Summer led Ellie towards the action of the fête. They were just passing the bouncy castle when Summer saw a face in the crowd and froze. Ricardo Lantis. He was dressed in a pair of white linen trousers and a shirt open to the waist, so you could see a thick black line of hair creeping up above the golden H of his Hermès belt.

'And which two lovely ladies do we have here?' smirked Ricardo as he saw them approach, turning to leer at Ellie.

'Who invited you?' snapped Summer, looking around.

'Your mother, of course,' smiled Ricardo.

'I'm Ellie, by the way,' said the girl, reaching out her hand politely. Ricardo lifted it to his lips and kissed it gently. '*Enchanté . . .*' he purred. 'Are you one of Summer's modelling friends?'

Ellie blushed furiously with colour. 'Oh no!' she giggled. 'I only work in the pub in the village.'

'Well, that's a pub I really must visit,' said Ricardo, still holding onto her hand.

'Ellie, can you go and check my raffle ticket to make sure I'm not missing out on winning,' said Summer, stepping between Ellie and Ricardo and pressing a yellow cloakroom ticket into her hand.

'Don't you dare, you old lech,' hissed Summer, as Ricardo's eyes followed Ellie trotting across the lawn.

'Ah, at last, the mouse roars,' smiled Ricardo, showing a mouthful of white teeth.

'I could have shopped you to the police that night, Ricardo. Don't start pushing your luck.'

'Shopped me to the police?' mocked Ricardo. 'Whatever for? Double parking the Bentley?'

'You put Rohypnol in my drink, you bastard. You wanted to have sex with me.'

Ricardo laughed, slowly, cruelly. 'I don't need drugs to score a fuck.'

'That's not the case though, is it?' said Summer, standing her ground, her hands on her hips. 'Men like you want to have sex with the woman they *can't* have sex with.'

Ricardo reached out a hand to stroke Summer's face and she jerked away. 'You're very spiky today, darling. It must be the sun.'

'Look who we have here!' said Molly, tottering across the lawns in her heels.

Summer shot her mother a sour glance. 'Ricardo was just leaving,' she said tartly.

'Oh Ricardo, you can't leave,' purred Molly, stroking the dark hairs on his arm. 'We're all going to the pub later. It's very quaint.'

Ricardo kissed her on the cheek before turning to watch Ellie again. 'I might see you there then,' he said, winking at Summer. 'Now, if you'll excuse me, I'll leave mother and daughter alone to congratulate themselves on a wonderful afternoon.'

'He's right, isn't he?' smiled Molly triumphantly after he'd gone. 'Marcus is practically wetting himself it's been so successful.'

'I can't believe you,' said Summer, shaking her head slowly.

Molly sighed theatrically. 'What have I done this time, darling?'

'You invited Ricardo Lantis,' replied Summer, her voice shaking. 'I told you what happened the night of our so-called date, and you still invite him to your home.'

Molly pursed her lips. 'Darling, I'm not exactly sure what happened that evening – you don't seem terribly clear yourself,' she laughed. The main thing she remembered about Summer's date with Ricardo was that it was the night her daughter had ended back at Adam Gold's house. 'But I can assure you that Ricardo is not the hazard to society you seem to think he is. You just got a bit drunk,' smiled Molly. 'We've all been there.'

'What bit don't you understand, mother?' snapped Summer. 'Ricardo gave me Rohypnol. He would have raped me. Look at him now, on the prowl for any young girl he can lay his hands on,' she said, instantly worrying about Ellie.

'Summer, Ricardo is an important businessman,' said Molly patiently. 'More than that, he's a good friend, a generous friend. He did not try to rape you and spreading lies like that could land you in a lot of trouble, young lady.'

'Well, now I know where your loyalties lie,' said Summer, unable to look at her mother. Just then there was a roar from the crowd.

'Speak up, darling. I can't hear over the noise. Ooh, listen. I think they've just called out the number of my raffle ticket. I'll see you later.' As she watched her mother totter off towards Marcus, Summer couldn't stop a tear escaping down her cheek. There was a garden bench a few feet away from her and she sat down on it, hugging herself protectively as she watched everyone laughing and drinking punch in the distance.

'I take it you didn't win the raffle,' said a voice behind her.

Summer rubbed her cheek quickly when she saw Erin. 'I never win,' she said, forcing a smile.

'What's wrong?' asked Erin, taking a seat beside her.

'Nothing,' said Summer quickly as another tear trickled down her face.

Erin felt caught between compassion and curiosity. What *had* happened between Adam and Summer in Madam Zorba's tent?

'You can tell me, Summer.'

Summer exhaled deeply and looked in the direction of Ricardo

288

Lantis, whom she could now see handing Ellie a glass of punch. 'That man over there is a beast,' she said motioning over at Ricardo. 'If Adam sees him here he will go ballistic.'

Summer realized she had said too much already and looked away. She liked Erin and trusted her, but it was enough that her mother knew about her affair with Adam. Anybody else knowing would be too dangerous. 'I'm sorry, Erin. It's nothing.'

'Do you want me to tell Adam anything?' she said gently. Part of Erin was desperate to know more, the other part did not want her earlier suspicions about Adam and Summer to be confirmed.

'No. Just forget it,' replied Summer. 'Don't mention anything to Adam.' She turned to look at Erin, her eyes pleading, wondering if she had any idea of her relationship with Adam. 'Please Erin, don't say anything at all.'

47

Karin was determined to look particularly sexy tonight. As she walked into her bedroom, she thought of Adam across town, having dinner with Claudia Falcon, and frowned. Despite her pep talk with Lysette Parker in Paris, Karin was still convinced that Claudia was a threat. She was attractive, powerful and Adam needed her; it was a potent combination. *Well, we'll see who's got what it takes tonight,* thought Karin, letting her white bathrobe slip off her shoulders onto the floor.

Karin was due to join Adam and Claudia for drinks at Boujis in Chelsea and she was going to look dynamite. She picked up the deep-lilac silk dress lying on the bed and smiled to herself as she pulled it on, feeling the thin fabric skim over her naked body. She had decided against wearing underwear. Her breasts were round and firm enough not to need a bra and she loved letting Adam find out halfway through the evening that she was *sans* panties.

She glanced at her gold Cartier watch on the dresser; it was almost 9 p.m. Damn, she was late. Outside it was darkening quickly, the sky the darkest lavender streaked with spaghetti-thin lines of gold. Slipping on her shoes and grabbing a jacket from her wardrobe, she turned off the light. Remembering she hadn't closed the curtains, she turned back towards the window – and suddenly saw movement. She snapped back away from the window and peered round the curtain, making sure she stayed out of view. She gasped: there was a man sitting on the low wall at the end of her courtyard garden. She recognized him instantly – it was the boy she had seen hanging around her house, the one who had unnerved her with his intense stare. And now he was here, staring up at her window, his face pale, eerie and ghoulish in the dusk.

Karin found herself squeezing her hands into tight fists. She told herself sharply it was not fear, but she was overwhelmed by a sudden sense of vulnerability. How long had he been there? Minutes? Hours? Was he there every day? Nausea swept up her throat as she realized her curtains had been open, lights blazing as she had undressed. She stepped away from the window and pulled her mobile out of her bag, quickly dialling 999.

'Operator, there's an intruder on the premises,' she hissed.

'Is he in your house, madam?' asked the voice at the other end of the line.

'What? No, he's in the garden,' snapped Karin.

'Are you in immediate danger, madam?'

'Of course I am!' said Karin, her voice rising. 'There's a pervert rapist stalking me and he's sitting on the wall looking at me naked.'

'The man is naked?'

'NO!' cried Karin. 'I mean he was looking at me when I was changing.'

'We'll see if there's a patrol car in the area. In the meantime, we would advise you do not leave the house.'

'But I'm meeting my boyfriend at Boujis, I have to go!'

'We really would advise you wait until the officers arrive.'

Karin sighed. 'Oh, very well, but I shall expect a lift to the club afterwards.'

Adam put an arm protectively round Karin's shoulder. 'You'll be okay, honey,' he said, burying his nose in her hair.

She shrugged defiantly. 'It's fine, I'm just a bit shaken up, that's all.'

She had telephoned him straight after ringing the police and she had been delighted that he had left his dinner with Claudia Falcon at once.

Adam turned to face her and she could see both admiration and concern. She felt a little flutter of excitement in her stomach. There was nothing like a little bit of jeopardy to test a person's feelings. 'We'll get the security on your place tightened up,' said Adam seriously, putting his strong hands on her shoulders. 'I can get CCTV installed tomorrow. Fingerprint entry pads on every door. Everything.'

She took his hands and gripped them. She hated to show any weakness and she was not going to start now. 'It's okay, honey, really. I don't want to become some paranoid freak. What do you always say about those rich guys that travel around in bulletproof cars? You become more of a target, don't you? No, it's sweet, but really I'm okay. He's just a kid.'

A middle-aged policeman came across to speak to them, introducing himself as Sergeant Danners. 'Do you want to go through what you saw, Miss Cavendish?'

'I caught a pervert spying at me from the garden. He was probably there ages.'

She gave Sergeant Danners a description of the youth and accepted the cup of tea that Adam had made for her.

'Is this the first time it's happened?'

She shook her head. 'I've noticed him several times before, just hanging around.'

'Hanging around?' said Danners.

Karin shuddered. 'He doesn't actually do anything, but I think he's following me.'

'Did you report any of these previous incidents?'

'No. But I wish I had. I think I know who he is as well. I was driving by a house on Pelham Grove, just around the corner from here, about a week ago, and I saw him coming out of the big white house at the end of the street. I think he lives there.'

Adam stood to face the man. 'So what's going to happen now? You caught him red-handed, didn't you – surely it's an open-and-shut case? We know where he lives . . .' 'Stalking, voyeurism, lewd conduct in an open space,' said Karin, shivering. 'I give you full authority to press charges on any count you want.'

Danners smiled politely. Working in this part of London where wealth and self-importance went hand in hand, he was used to dealing with victims who felt they knew more about police procedure and criminal law than he did.

'Well, this is possibly an offence under the Protection from Harassment Act,' he said gently. 'Obviously we need to identify who this man is. For us to start any sort of procedure against him, he needs to have done it at least twice.'

'Of course he has! Haven't you been listening to what I've just told you?'

'Once identified, we can get a harassment order against him.

However, there does seem to be a lack of tangible evidence that constitutes "harassment". Letters, emails, CCTV footage.'

Karin rolled her eyes dramatically. 'So he's going to get off scot-free is what you're telling me?' cried Karin, her voice full of disbelief.

Danners shook his head patiently. 'No, Mrs Cavendish, that's not what I'm saying. We could start off with a police warning. That sometimes deters people, although not always. If the harassment then continues, it heightens our chances of a successful prosecution.'

Adam put a hand on Karin's knee and turned to the policeman. 'Officer, if both the police and the Crown Prosecution Service fail to have this man properly and fully prosecuted, I am prepared to go to the highest level to make it happen.'

Sergeant Danners allowed himself a small smile. He had little doubt this imposing businessman would actually be able to do what he said, but he stood his ground nevertheless.

'I assure you, there will be a full investigation,' he said evenly. 'First of all we'll go and check out this house on Pelham Grove, and in the meantime I can give you the number of a local support group aimed at people who have had similar experiences.'

Karin snorted. 'Whatever.'

Sergeant Danners moved away and Karin curled her body into Adam's. 'I've heard about people like this. Erotomaniacs; they become fixated with someone, fantasize that they are in a relationship with them. They can spend *years* stalking them.'

Adam squeezed her arm and kissed the top of her head. 'I don't think that's going to happen, honey.'

'Will you stay?' she asked softly, looking up into his eyes. 'Or are you going back to your dinner with Claudia?'

'I'm staying right here,' he whispered.

She squeezed his fingers and smiled, but deep down she was frightened.

48

Sharif Kahlid was a man whose glory days were long behind him. At sixty-seven, his once handsome face was lined and the dark eyes which had sparkled in his youth had dulled and seemed to have shrunk back into his thin face. His small apartment, in a purpose-built block at the back of London's Edgware Road was full of mementos from three decades of glamorous travel around the world: African carvings, a gold Buddha on the mantelpiece, a silk wall-hanging from the Forbidden City in Beijing. Now merely gathering dust, they were the only physical reminder of a glittering jet-setting lifestyle that had come to an abrupt end the second his employer had died. Sharif's employer had been Adnan Hashemi, the well-known arms dealer. As Adnan's private secretary for almost thirty years, Sharif had led a life of vicarious luxury; taking private jets from Gstaad to Palm Beach, Beirut to Antibes at the beck and call of his wealthy, powerful boss. But that life had ended four years ago with Hashemi's heart attack and Sharif was still finding it hard to adjust to a humbler existence. His only luxury now was cooking for himself; buying a small amount of halal meat from the many Lebanese shops around Edgware Road, adding okra and star fruit and serving the curries to himself on vast white platters, pretending he was at a banquet in Marrakech, or a yacht party in St Tropez.

Sometimes, when he'd had just enough arak, he could almost believe it was true. But, in the cold light of day, Sharif knew he was a has been, a spent force, the last sparkle of glamour tarnished away years ago. Until the day Molly Sinclair knocked on his door.

'Forgive me for not being able to entertain properly,' said Sharif, pouring a mint tea in a small amber glass and handing it to Molly. 'Your visit has taken me a little by surprise.'

Molly took the glass from the little man and smiled. Yes, she was sure he was going to be just the man for the job.

Ever since the detox weekend, when Denise had drunkenly confessed that she had been Adnan Hashemi's mistress, Molly had become obsessed with knowing the rest of the story. Yes, Denise had told Molly that she had introduced Donna Delemere to several of Adnan's friends, but Molly had spent long enough on the international party circuit to know what *friendship* meant between young, pretty blondes and ageing arms dealers. The question was whether that friendship involved the exchange of money. Determined to find out, she had tracked down Hashemi's private secretary, Sharif, having heard he was down on his luck and knowing that he might be willing to talk, if the price was right.

'It's been a long time, Sharif,' smiled Molly. She hardly knew Sharif – their paths had crossed briefly at various nightclubs in the 1980s – but she knew a man like Sharif Kahlid would respond to flirtation and familiarity.

'Indeed,' he replied. His accent was clipped and precise; the product of an English public school education. 'Although I am interested to know how you found me. I suspect our social diaries are rather different now. There is little need for me to travel in the circles I once did.'

'Oh come, come,' laughed Molly, 'don't be so modest. You were a player, Sharif. An important man. People like you don't disappear without somebody knowing where you are.' She touched his arm and his lip curled upwards.

He sat back in his worn leather chair, crossed his legs and folded his hands in his lap. 'So, how can I help you, Molly?' said Sharif. 'I assume there is a purpose to this social call?'

Molly was glad to cut to the chase, feeling uncomfortable in this small flat stuffed full of weird ethnic trinkets. 'Did you know a woman called Donna Jones about ten years ago?'

'Perhaps. I was in the line of work where I met many, many beautiful women,' he responded, raking his eyes appreciatively over Molly.

Molly reached into her handbag and produced a photograph of Donna and Evie from the christening. 'The hair would have been blonde when you knew her,' she said, handing him the picture.

He pursed his lips and cocked his head. 'Possibly I recognize her,' he said slowly, handing back the photograph. 'What do you want to know?'

There was a defensive edge to his voice and his face was set in a challenging, defiant expression. Sharif had clearly done much more for his employer than booking hotel rooms. Wanting to make this as easy as possible, Molly picked up a leather folder from her feet and unzipped it slowly, opening enough for Kahlid to see it was full of twenty-pound notes.

'A donation to the cause of your choice,' she said, watching Kahlid's eyes widen.

'You didn't answer my question,' he said finally.

'I'm acting for a friend,' said Molly flatly. 'A friend who needs to know about Donna's past.'

'Yes, I heard Donna married very well.'

'She did. And that is why my friend wants no surprises about her.'

Sharif got up silently and went into the small kitchen to fill the kettle and put it on to boil, which he did with the elegance of a colonial butler.

'Adnan was a very rich, powerful man who loved the company of women,' said Sharif, returning to his seat. 'When he was staying in London, where he would often entertain other important, rich men, they would want fun after they had concluded business. Donna Jones was one of a dozen girls who provided entertainment, not only to Adnan's friends but to Adnan himself.'

'Entertainment? You mean sex,' said Molly matter of factly.

'Indeed,' replied Kahlid with a cautious smile. 'Mostly with just one girl, sometimes two or three girls at one time. Donna was one of the more shy girls, but she was very popular, very charming and very adventurous.'

'And was there payment involved?'

Kahlid let out a low, gravelly laugh. 'You are clearly uninitiated in the ways of this world.'

'Was there payment involved?' repeated Molly.

He nodded. 'Payment kept things simple.'

If knowledge is power, then Molly felt its electric charge rush around her body. For years she had been made to feel inadequate by Donna's marriage and her charmed new life. But that choking knot of envy was now easing, melting away as Molly realized that Donna's destiny was now in her hands.

'How did you meet Donna?' asked Molly, trying not to show her excitement. 'Through Denise Duncan?'

Sharif nodded. 'Denise was the sometime lover of Adnan, yes, and she introduced Donna to our circle. The first time I met Donna was at a party we threw in Mayfair. There were many, many important men there and Donna was picked out by one of the highest spenders. That first time, I don't think Donna expected to be paid for her, ahem, companionship,' he smiled. 'But I think she was pleasantly surprised when she was.'

'The first time? So Donna entertained more than once?' ventured Molly.

'Of course,' replied Sharif. 'She became one of Mr Hashemi's favourite girls. Sometimes she was his travel companion. You know, she would stay with him as he spent a week in St Tropez or Hong Kong perhaps. That would be a fifty-thousand-dollar date,' he laughed. 'I assume my employer found it value for money. Anyway, over the course of around two years Donna would have received –' he steepled his fingers in front of his lips as he did the mental calculation '– in the region of two hundred thousand pounds, and that was just from Mr Hashemi – there were many others. Mr Hashemi also helped pay her bills and bought her gifts like handbags. I remember she liked Chanel.'

'How do you know?'

Sharif laughed again. 'I know, Miss Sinclair, because I arranged for the handbags to be bought. And I gave her money.'

Molly could hardly believe her ears. She had expected a few indiscretions, but nothing on this scale.

'There were other men apart from Adnan, you say?'

Sharif nodded. 'Yes, there were other clients I was aware of. Men of similar status and wealth as Adnan. Girls were always introduced by word of mouth, a very discreet process. Donna had a very good reputation.'

Molly put her hands together on her lap and leant forward. 'Would you be prepared to sign an affidavit swearing to this?'

'Is that really necessary?' Kahlid asked, surprised. 'Adnan had nothing to hide – his lifestyle was well documented. But some of the girls we used to use . . . Some are high profile now, respectable. They would prefer to keep this quiet.'

Molly wondered who else was paid by Adnan Hashemi for sex?

She'd heard many rumours that certain actresses, models and society wives had been escorts in their past.

'I assumed, of course, that a man of your standing would continue to be loyal to Adnan,' she smiled, reaching into her handbag and bringing out another handful of twenty-pound notes. 'But would I also be correct in saying that, now he has passed away, your loyalties may have shifted slightly – to yourself, perhaps?'

'Very true,' shrugged Sharif, his eyes glistening once more.

'Well, I suppose we should talk further about the level of my donation to your chosen charity,' said Molly, beginning to count the notes out slowly.

'Oh, I think you'll find me a reasonable man,' said Sharif. 'Very reasonable indeed.'

'So? What have you discovered?' asked Alex Delemere briskly. Molly and Alex were sitting in a corner booth in a fish restaurant in Pimlico. Usually he would put his hand over hers as they dined, but today Alex had a steely look reserved for the boardroom not the bedroom. This was business not pleasure.

'Everything I suspected is true,' said Molly, taking a sip of mineral water. 'Donna was a high-class call-girl, commanding five thousand pounds a night. Her clients were mainly Arabs, including the Saudi arms dealer Adnan Hashemi.'

Lord Delemere looked at Molly for a long moment, absorbing this information with an impassive face. 'No wonder it's not come out before,' he said finally. 'I doubt she runs into any arms dealers among Daniel's group of friends.'

'She's been smart,' said Molly matter of factly. She idly wondered what Donna had done right. After all, her friend Denise, the one-time madam and longtime lover of Hashemi, was now relegated to being the wife of a Surrey businessman. Donna, the younger, more naïve friend meanwhile makes a fortune, then marries into aristocracy. She must have had a few tricks up her sleeve, thought Molly.

'It's disgusting,' said Alex, 'I must tell Daniel immediately.'

'Now don't be so hasty,' said Molly, touching his sleeve. 'I have been giving this some thought and we both know Daniel is no fool. He knows you don't like Donna, so telling him she was a call girl would just look vindictive. He won't believe you and you run the risk of him siding with his wife instead of you. No, the information has to come from a third party.'

'Who were you thinking? You?'

Molly laughed. She had no intention of looking like a trouble-maker either. That certainly wouldn't suit her long-term plan.

'No, darling. Of course not. I was thinking of a newspaper.'

'You want a grubby tabloid to expose it?' said Alex incredulously. A waiter approached him with the wine list and he waved him away. 'This is my family's reputation you're talking about,' he hissed.

'Precisely,' said Molly coolly. 'Your son's wife used to be a prostitute and it will come out sooner or later. The wise thing to do is to expose her now, while you can control the situation. You know every newspaper proprietor in the country. The story can be spun to vilify Donna as a money-grabbing fortune-hunter with Daniel as the victim. His reputation might take a blow in the short term, but he will recover quickly with good PR.'

She folded her hands. 'The priority is to get Donna out of Daniel's life, Alex. Remember, the longer you leave it, the lengthier the marriage, the bigger the divorce settlement.'

At the mention of the money involved, Alex looked anxious, rubbing his forehead.

'Yes, I think you're right, we must act,' he said, looking at Molly shrewdly. 'You've clearly given this a lot of thought, haven't you?'

'Of course I have,' she smiled, waving the sommelier back over. 'Now you just leave everything to me.'

49

It was the hottest day of the year and the Guards Polo Club was buzzing. Anyone who mattered was sipping champagne in the Cartier tent in the Smith's Lawn enclosure.

There was always gossip to dissect when high society, Hollywood and big City money collided, but today there was only one topic of conversation on anyone's lips: Donna Delemere, society wife, daughter-in-law of one of the richest men in England, had been a hooker! Karin had nearly choked on her wheat-free pancakes when she had opened her paper that morning.

High Infidelity! read the headlines. *Delemere wife – Call Girl: Society wife plays high-class escort to arms dealer.*

It was a genuine shock and, even now, hours later, as she mingled with the beautiful and the rich in the Cartier enclosure, she still found it hard to take in. After all, there were plenty of women in Karin's social circle that she would have put money on having been high-class hookers sometime during their ascent to the top flight of society – but quiet, mousy Donna? Karin had read every word of the shocking story, praying that she hadn't been name-checked as a 'friend', and when she was satisfied that her brand name hadn't been sullied with the scandal, she had called Donna to extend her support. Not surprisingly, she had not been able to reach her. Her mobile was turned off and the Delemere home phone went straight to a terse message on the answerphone.

'Isn't it incredible?' said Celia Chase, *Class* magazine's editor-in-chief, sidling up to Karin as she was examining the table plan just inside the Cartier marquee. 'I don't think I can remember such a scandalous summer.'

Karin's first thought was to jump to her friend's defence and give this stick-thin blonde a piece of her mind, but she needed the press on side at all times, so she smiled politely. 'I can assure you it's a pack of lies,' she said, taking a sip of mineral water to moisten her lips. 'I haven't spoken to her yet, but I'm sure she'll be instructing her solicitors as we speak.'

'Someone else asking about Donna?' said Molly, walking over to Karin, her arm protectively around Marcus's waist.

'Poor thing,' said Karin, playing with the little Cartier lunch pass that was pinned onto her cream chiffon dress. 'The knives are out for her. At least she can count on us, anyway.'

Adam came over and gave Karin a kiss on her bare shoulder. He looked handsome in a cream two-button suit and a pale blue shirt with a high collar. 'We've just been invited into the Chinawhite tent after the match. What's that?' he asked, taking a flute of champagne from the outdoor bar.

'Big club in London. Good DJs,' said Molly. 'Kind of a Moroccan vibe. They have a tent here every year.'

'Moroccan vibe, eh?' said Marcus, sipping his Pimms. 'So there'll be belly dancers and hookahs?'

'No, Donna's not here today,' sniggered Adam.

'Honey!' cried Karin, slapping him on his arm, 'this isn't funny. Donna is my friend. People will be talking about us.'

'I thought that's what you loved,' he smiled.

'Not like this,' she said seriously.

What a wonderful afternoon, thought Molly, sitting down for lunch in the marquee. She loved the Cartier International Day: an amazing social scene plus sexy Argentinian polo players cantering up the pitch in those fabulously tight jodhpurs – what more could you want? Adding to her pleasure was the reaction to the Donna Delemere revelations; it was playing out exactly as she had hoped. People who had never met Donna revelled in the delicious gossip and delighted in speculating on which other well-known names had been high-class escorts to Adnan's circle. The Sunday newspaper that Alex had chosen had done a brilliant job: in an eight-page special, they had boasted how they had smashed an international vice ring involving top models and personalities who would service the world's most wealthy men for £10,000 a time. The whole thing, they had claimed, was masterminded by London madam 'Bettina

B', who they were now calling Europe's Heidi Fleiss. Molly smiled to herself. In another life she could have been a tabloid reporter.

As for the people who did know Donna, Molly could tell by their embarrassed disquiet that the story had suddenly stirred up all sorts of unwelcome concerns. They all had something to hide somewhere down the line; seeing one of their number sliding back down to the bottom of the heap made them very nervous indeed.

Serves you all right for being such judgmental bastards, she thought, fixing a stare on Karin. Molly knew what women like that said about her. That she was a washed-up nobody. A slut, a whore. Well, look who really is the whore, Molly thought triumphantly. One of their butter-wouldn't-melt inner circle.

The rest of the day passed in a whirl of socializing. Molly kept bumping into people she hadn't seen in ages, people to whom she could boast about going out with Marcus Blackwell, about how happy she was, about her fabulous renovations at The Standlings. It was wonderful. Finally, Molly and Marcus left the grounds in Marcus's convertible, taking a quick exit out of the park to avoid the traffic jams. With the sweet summer evening breeze ruffling through her hair, and Marcus's hand reassuringly on her knee, Molly was filled with a glorious molten happiness. It had been a perfect day. They were only ten minutes from home when her mobile phone rang. She sighed; there was always something.

She snapped open the phone, but didn't recognize the voice at the other end. 'Who is this?' she said, frowning.

'It's Patsy Jones, Donna's sister,' said the voice. 'Forgive me calling, but I needed to speak to you.'

'What's wrong?' asked Molly, noting the crack in the woman's voice.

'It's Donna. Daniel's left her and, well, Donna's taken an overdose.'

50

The following evening, Molly drew up to Delemere Manor in Marcus's chauffeur-driven car. There was the inevitable pack of paparazzi by the gates, of course, but as the house was buried in a thousand acres of parkland, there was an eerie quiet around the house itself. What Molly found even more disquieting was that she had heard no word from Alex. She had met him on the previous Friday evening in the arrivals lounge at Heathrow to arrange full payment to Sharif Kahlid. Alex was due to fly out to Spain that evening, wisely putting himself beyond the reach of reporters when the story broke, but he hadn't been in touch since; he clearly hadn't heard about Donna's overdose. She had thought about trying to contact him but decided it was better to visit Donna and find what had really happened first.

Donna's sister Patsy answered the door of Delemere Manor; Molly instantly remembered her from Evie's christening. In her late thirties, she had dark blonde hair that straggled to her shoulders, and a once-pretty face that looked permanently tired. She looked completely out of place in the hallway of the manor with its marble busts and Old Masters on the walls. Molly idly imagined them in some nineteenth-century period drama, with Patsy cast as the galley cook and Molly the lady of the manor, ruling everyone with her iron fist.

'I'm so glad you've come,' said Patsy in a small voice, as she led Molly into a small drawing room. 'It's been awful. Photographers trying to scale the walls, reporters phoning all morning. I can't get in touch with Daniel at all and Alex and Vivienne are in Spain. Donna doesn't want to tell him until she has spoken to Daniel, but when we couldn't track him down . . .' Patsy tailed off, her voice wobbling. '. . . Well, anyway, Donna said you would be the best person to call.'

Molly took off her jacket and threw it over a Hepplewhite chair and nodded sympathetically. 'I take it she's back from hospital?' she asked.

'Yes,' said Patsy. 'It was only an overnight stay. She took paracetamol but not enough to do any real damage. The Delemeres' family doctor has been wonderful; sorted out for Donna to see a psychiatrist. One of the best, apparently.'

Molly smiled, her face a mask of concern, secretly wondering why she over all of Donna's other friends had been requested. The least of all evils, she thought; Karin and Christina would scare the bejesus out of the likes of Patsy.

'Well, let's go and see her,' said Molly decisively. 'I can't imagine how awful this whole episode has been for her.'

Molly followed Patsy up the sweeping mahogany staircase, down a corridor and into the master bedroom, where Donna was lying like a thin child in a heavily swagged four-poster bed. She was propped up on a thick wedge of white pillows, trying to read a magazine in the early evening light pouring in from the long Georgian windows. *Lucky bitch*, thought Molly.

'Thanks for coming,' she said with a weak smile as Molly sat on the bed beside her. 'Sorry for dragging you all the way out here.'

'I'm a country girl myself now, remember,' said Molly, squeezing her hand. 'It didn't take long and, anyway, I would have come at whatever time of day or night, you know that.' She looked around the bedroom. 'Where's Evie?' she asked.

'With the nanny. She's fine.'

There was an awkward pause before Molly asked the obvious question. 'Oh Donna, why? I know you're in a bad place, but you've got a little daughter to think of now.'

Donna turned away and gazed blankly out of the window. There was a long silence before she spoke, her voice even and measured, as if she was resigned to the great

'It doesn't feel great when everyone you know – and everyone you *don't* know – is judging you and talking about you. When you know they are calling you a slut and a slag and a whore.'

She turned back to look at Molly. 'And yes, when you know that it's going to haunt your child in the playground for the next fifteen years. And you know that it's your fault for once being foolish and short-sighted when you should have been old enough to know better.'

Donna shifted uncomfortably on her pillow and reached for a glass of water.

'Your friends aren't saying anything of the sort,' said Molly, not sounding entirely convinced. 'And people you don't know will have something better to gossip about tomorrow.'

Donna shrugged. 'The doctors said I might have had some un-diagnosed postnatal depression.'

'And what do you think?' asked Molly.

'I think I should have gone to see a doctor a while ago.'

'So why didn't you?'

'Because postnatal depression is not the sort of thing you are supposed to have in the Delemere family,' said Donna.

Molly looked at her, pale and fragile between the sheets and silently agreed. Donna was weak. Burying her problems like her precious bloody organic vegetables beneath the soil, only to have them rot and fester. She didn't belong in a family like the Delemeres', which had prospered over the generations through strength of char-acter and resilience. It made Molly angry. She was glad Donna hadn't actually topped herself, of course, but, hearing her sad, pathetic story had only convinced Molly that she was doing the right thing; she was helping the Delemeres.

'What can I do, Donna?' she said. 'Just tell me.'

'Find Daniel,' said Donna, her eyes pleading. 'I don't even know if he's heard what has happened because he left his mobile phone here and he's not answering at the London house.'

'So when did you last see him?'

'We were tipped off about the story on Saturday night. Daniel left soon afterwards.'

Molly nodded gravely, but inside she was skipping with glee. She couldn't have scripted it better if she had been a Hollywood screenwriter.

'And what do I tell him?'

Finally the tears began to roll down Donna's pale face. 'Tell him the truth,' she gulped. 'Tell him I love him and that I'm sorry.'

'I will,' said Molly. 'You can trust me.'

51

The cottage in the grounds of Cliveden, one of England's grandest estates, was everything Chris had said and more. From the main house, that splendid honey-coloured Palladian pile, a driveway snaked away through lush parkland down to the River Thames. A short walk along a private towpath and there it was; a cute little Victorian cottage perched right on the edge of the silent water. It was a remote, peaceful spot, where the only sounds were ducks, insects and the occasional miniature deer scrabbling through the undergrowth on the hillside above the cottage. Erin loved it, and was smitten by the romantic history of the place.

When she had arrived from London two days earlier, Chris had taken her on a stroll along the river, passing another quaint cottage which, he told her, was where Christine Keeler had stayed in the early 1960s. Erin had vaguely known the story, but Chris had vividly filled in the lurid details: the beautiful high-class call girl who partied with the rich, glamorous aristocratic Astor set and had almost brought down the government when she had become entangled with cabinet minister John Profumo at a party held by Cliveden's swimming pool. It only added to the glamour of the place for Erin. She found that Chris had already moved a desk for her by the window in the living room, where she could sit and write and watch the sun setting over the river. It was spectacular, thought Erin now, lifting her head from her laptop, a blood-red sky reflecting in the water and staining it pink and gold. She had settled down to do some work after supper but she was restless. It was her first-ever Monday off work since she had started at the Midas Corporation and she just couldn't relax.

'What's the matter?' said Chris, looking up from a notebook. He was sitting in an armchair wearing gold-rimmed glasses, which Erin thought made him look more vulnerable, *cute*. She closed her eyes and stubbed the thought out like a cigarette.

'Nothing,' she said, still staring out of the window.

'Erin . . .' scolded Chris.

'I can't think of anything to write about,' she said, doodling some circles on a notepad in front of her.

'Erin, there's a billion things to write about.'

'Yes, well, everything I want to write about has been done already,' she said hopelessly, getting up and flopping onto the sofa.

Chris moved across to sit next to her. 'Listen, there're only seven basic plots in the world, so your work is always going to have some similarity to something already written.'

'Seven storylines?' she repeated. 'Don't be ridiculous.'

'It's true, and Shakespeare used most of them.'

'So now you're going to tell me that *When Harry Met Sally* is just a rewrite of *Hamlet*?'

'No. But take horror for example. It's always the old "overcoming the monster" plot-line. You know, *Moby Dick*, *Alien*, all those.'

Erin laughed. 'Overcoming the monster. That's my memoir of my brush with Julian Sewell.'

Chris took his glasses off, smiling. 'I see you've finally come to your senses. I tried to tell you he was a wrong 'un.'

'No you didn't,' she laughed.

'Well, I would have if you'd given me the opportunity. I never saw you for dust when he was on the scene.'

'And to think I thought I meant nothing to you,' Erin teased.

They both looked at each awkwardly and Erin began scribbling on her pad again. 'Will you let me read what you've written then?'

'No,' said Chris.

'Why not?'

'Because it's not finished.'

Erin groaned. 'Well, tell me a bit more about this overcoming the monster thing. I like the sound of it.'

Chris put a cushion at the back of his head and stretched his legs out.

'Overcoming the monster is one of the most basic plots in storytelling,' he said. '"Little Red Riding Hood" is a good example, or

"Hansel and Gretel". Even James Bond – it's good versus evil, where good has to conquer the bad to get the precious treasure, the princess, to save the world, whatever.'

Erin thought about it for a moment. 'It sounds like Karin and Adam,' she said.

'I heard Karin was a bit of a monster,' smiled Chris.

'No, Adam's the prize, the treasure,' said Erin thoughtfully. 'Karin guards him like a Minotaur or something. Every woman that comes into contact with Adam seems to be after him – to her at least. Except they're not all good,' she said, frowning. 'Certainly not women like Molly Sinclair.'

'They sound like a right bunch of gold-diggers.'

'Well, yes and no.'

'No?' said Chris, laughing, 'but the man's a billionaire!'

'I mean, they are not doing anything that women of their age weren't doing a hundred years ago – and it was entirely respectable to do it. Marrying for money, position in society.'

'Bloody hell. Listen to you,' said Chris, a note of surprise in his voice. 'It's like the feminist movement never happened.'

'But that's the point. It has,' said Erin. 'The women who chase Adam Gold have choices. Chase the career or chase the man. Gold-diggers chose the man. And I guess women like Karin want both.'

'Well, that's what you should write about!' said Chris suddenly, slapping the arm of the sofa. 'Adam's wonderful world of women!'

'I can't do that,' said Erin uncertainly, 'I'd get fired.'

'But you wouldn't be writing about him or Karin or Molly or anyone, not specifically,' said Chris, sitting up, 'You can create a world. A literary beau monde. It's what Fitzgerald made a career out of. *The Beautiful and the Damned, Tender Is the Night.*'

'Oh, I love that book,' smiled Erin, relaxing into the sofa. She hadn't felt like this in ages. Clever and creative and capable.

Chris had moved nearer to her on the sofa. Part of her felt hot and uncomfortable, another part of her was buzzing at the banter between them and the possibility of something happening. She glanced up quickly at Chris and suddenly noticed how long his eyelashes were. Even though it was a warm night, he had lit a fire, and the logs spat and crackled.

Suddenly Chris stood up, as if he had sensed the change in atmosphere between them. He walked into the kitchen to open a bottle of red wine: a medal winner, he told Erin. That meant nothing to her, but it tasted sublime, like blackcurrants and spices on her tongue.

'Umm, I like your job,' she laughed softly.

'I like it too, but I could think of a better way to make a living.'

'Oh yeah? Doing what?'

'Being able to make a career out of writing,' he said, sitting down next to Erin again. 'It would be brilliant. Me and my girl being able to live away from London, somewhere like this.'

His fingers touched hers on the cushion and Erin felt a spark jump between them. She waited for a moment to see if it was mistake, to see if Chris would remove them, but he kept his hand on hers and looked at her with a nervous expression completely out of character with the confident, womanizing Irish man-about-town.

'Chris, I . . . Dammit!'

Erin's mobile buzzed loudly on the desk. She had promised him she would switch it off, but she had left it on vibrate, just in case. They both looked at the phone humming insistently.

'Are you going to answer it?' said Chris, raising an eyebrow. Erin thought he looked annoyed, but she ignored it.

'It might be work,' she said weakly, feeling the electricity between them vanish as she said it.

'Fuck work,' said Chris angrily.

Erin looked unsure. The phone was still vibrating. It might be important.

Chris followed her glance and jumped up, grabbing the phone. 'Erin. You have a few days off,' he said, holding the phone in his fist. 'You're entitled to a break and you have a book to write, or should I say a book to start, otherwise you are going to get fired by your agent.'

'But you don't understand,' said Erin, raising her voice. She snatched the mobile from his hand and ran through to the kitchen. Through the closed door, Chris could hear a muffled conversation. When she returned he fixed her with a sour expression.

'You're going back to London, aren't you?'

'I have to,' said Erin. 'There's been a fire in the Midas Corporation mine in Kazakhstan. Adam is freaking out. He has to fly out there.'

'So why do you have to go back to work? He has other people that can sort things out, doesn't he? I mean, they managed okay before you came along.'

Erin flung her mobile on the sofa angrily. 'Chris. The Midas Corporation is a multi-billion-dollar business. I can't just turn my loyalties on or off as it suits me. I am Adam's assistant, I have to be there whenever he needs me. And he needs me now.'

Chris started shaking his head slowly. 'You're desperate to be part of that world, aren't you? No wonder you can't bring yourself to write about the women who hang around Adam, because you appreciate what they're after.'

'Oh, don't be such a shit,' she snapped. 'Forgive me if I enjoy my job, and forgive me if I want to help my boss. Adam saved me from a mundane life in Cornwall, and I'll never forget it.'

A small smile of resignation pulled at Chris's lips. 'You're in love with him, aren't you?'

'I am not,' said Erin, blushing furiously, feeling as if she'd been caught out. Chris saw her expression and shook his head sadly.

'Well, I guess I can't blame you. He's super-rich and good looking, and so are his friends. I just thought you were different,' he said softly.

'I'm leaving,' she said, moving towards the door.

'Oh, don't be stupid,' said Chris, moving across to stop her. 'It's late and it's dark.'

'I thought you were my friend,' shouted Erin, pushing him away.

'I am,' replied Chris, touching her on her shoulder. 'That's why I'm saying this.'

Erin looked at him intently and shook her head. He'd touched a raw nerve and she hated him for it. 'I'm going back to London,' she whispered, and ran upstairs to pack.

52

Imogen Sanders, one of the UK's top casting directors, worked out of an office in a little row of pastel-coloured mews houses in Notting Hill. After spending ten years in LA working with some of the biggest names in the film industry, she had returned to her home town to set up on her own. Right now, Imogen was the hottest casting agent in the capital; she was the woman who producers and directors turned to when they were looking for hot British talent.

'So, tell me about yourself, Summer. Your likes, dislikes. What you want to do with your life,' said Imogen, smiling kindly at Summer Sinclair. In her twenty or so years in the business, Imogen had seen hundreds, if not thousands of models, desperate to move into acting. While most of them had a face that the camera loved – big mouths, button noses, perfect ivory teeth – only a handful of them had the x-factor to make them into stars. Imogen had already seen Summer's showreel before she had got here – just a few rushes from some cable TV show which was endearing in its raw naïvety, but Summer's beauty was unmistakable and she certainly had on-screen charisma. The question was: could she act? If she could, thought Imogen, Summer Sinclair could make the hottest entrance to the movie scene since Cameron Diaz blasted onto the screen in *The Mask*.

'Tell you about myself?' smiled Summer trying to relax into her brown leather armchair. 'Well, as I'm twenty-four, I guess I'm a geriatric model. I came back from Japan to ease myself into retirement, but my TV career has kind of taken off. I got my break into TV when the "On Heat" presenter literally jumped ship; she's cruising the Med with her multimillionaire lover as we speak,' she smiled wryly.

Imogen nodded, urging her to say more.

'Likes and dislikes? I like being in love, chocolate biscuits and sailing. I don't like sitting in front of you with no acting experience to my name. But I've spent a lifetime on photo-shoots and I feel like I've spent my whole life playing a part as Molly Sinclair's daughter, even though I don't really like parties and the London social circuit.'

Summer looked at Imogen anxiously, having no idea whether she was making a good impression or embarrassing herself totally.

'My dear, most of us spend half our lives acting, even if we don't realize it,' she said, taking a sip of water. 'As for your lack of acting experience, we're not looking for someone with a CV as long as Julia Roberts'. This is going to be a blockbuster movie, but the producers and the director are looking for an unknown or a relative unknown for the female lead.'

'How come, if it's a big-budget picture?' asked Summer, confused.

'Unknowns are getting more of a shot in bigger roles in Hollywood these days,' Imogen explained. 'Traditionally the studios wouldn't take a chance on an actor with no track record: big names equalled big box office. But when half the budget is going on special effects these days – and *Krakatoa* is going to have *incredible* special effects – the studio might not want to pay a big A-list female lead twenty-five million dollars.'

'I suppose not, when she's going to get upstaged by a volcanic eruption,' smiled Summer.

They both laughed. Imogen liked her and she knew Luc, the director, would like her too. Summer's was a fragile, refined beauty, but there was a toughness behind her eyes that suggested she had been through a lot. And she was going to have to be tough if she wanted to survive in the Hollywood jungle.

Imogen passed Summer a copy of the script; she could almost feel the pages crackle with excitement and promise.

'Don't worry,' said Imogen, 'this is just a read-through, we're not doing it to camera or anything. So take your time and start whenever you're ready.'

Summer looked down at the pages intently, although she did not need to read the words. She had received the script a few days before and had repeated them over and over until they had become part of her. The scene was powerful, packed with emotion. In it, Marien, the character she was auditioning for, had just survived the initial blast of the volcano, but she had just found her sister dead and was screaming her anger and frustration at the sky. Summer took a small breath and closed her eyes just for a moment, thinking about her experience at Ricardo Lantis's mansion and that night in the pink bedroom, and suddenly the rage welled into her throat. She opened her mouth and the words poured out. It was like music to Imogen Sanders's ears.

Wow! thought Imogen, unable to take her eyes from Summer's face. *This girl is fantastic!*

53

As Adam's Learjet banked into Moscow's Domodedovo Airport, Karin leant over to peer out of the window. The city was one of her favourite places in the world with its romantic wedding-cake buildings and tsarist glamour, today lit up by bright sunshine. She had grown up in the dying days of the Cold War, when Russia was seen as a sinister state, a vast nation that had presidents with their finger on the nuclear trigger, bread queues, cold winters, wolves and snow. But a very different Russia now lay a thousand feet beneath her. A country of division. Poverty still gripped the nation, but there were pockets of immense wealth and luxury. Moscow was now a city where armour-plated Hummers and Bentleys drove the freeways, where beautiful girls dressed in Prada and Gucci and where the chic restaurants rivalled those in Manhattan. The price of a Karenza swimsuit, however, sold in the grand GUM department store, was still a good deal more than the average annual wage.

'Thanks for coming, honey,' said Adam, smiling over from the cream leather seat opposite her. 'You know I'm grateful.'

'My pleasure,' smiled Karin. She wanted to reassure him but, looking at his drawn face, she could tell he was anxious. Only six weeks earlier, the Midas Corporation had put forward a bid to build a huge skyscraper in the centre of Moscow. It would have been a vital foothold in Russia's burgeoning luxury real-estate market for Midas – much desired by the company. But Adam's tender had been turned down; Moscow still fiercely guarded its own territory, and contracts were routinely handed out to the richest, best-connected Russian developers. Adam had been bitterly disappointed until Mikhail Lebokov, an oligarch with interests in everything from oil to construction, had called about the possibility of subcontracting the development to the Midas Corporation. Mikhail had requested a meeting at his dacha – his second home just outside Moscow – to discuss it further.

Adam had been excited by the call and was confident of reaching a deal; Mikhail had purchased three Midas penthouses in Miami and New York, and was known to be a big fan of the company's work. But the fire in the Kazakhstan mine had changed everything. The Russian newspapers had jumped on the story and Adam had spent the last week on a damage-limitation exercise, trying to demonstrate that there was no breach of safety regulations. But he had no idea whether it would affect Mikhail's desire to work with the Midas Corporation.

'Do they live nearby?' asked Karin. She was already hot, despite the air-con in the back of the car. Summers in Moscow could be sweltering, and today was sticky and warm, with no breeze. She had changed into her most glamorous Russian wives outfit: tight Dolce at Gabbana black trousers and a Chloe vest with a smattering of diamonds around her neck and wrists.

'They have an apartment in Moscow,' said Adam, watching the city fly by. 'But no Muscovites of their wealth stay in the city in the summer. They all have dachas just outside in the countryside.'

They travelled for thirty minutes west of the city down the Rublovka highway. Here the buildings thinned and made way for heavy woods of birch and pine, the strong sunshine making patterns through the branches on the road in front of them. After half an hour, they turned off the highway and wound through a series of smaller roads dotted with clusters of expensive-looking dwellings. Karin peered over the top of her sunglasses. She had never been this far out of Moscow before. She had always imagined Russian country homes to be like Hansel and Gretel cottages, but these were like small but showy mansions, albeit surrounded by redcurrant bushes and a clear, cloudless blue sky. She pressed her nose against the black glass as they drove past, taking in the high walls, security cameras and iron gates.

'Is it one of these?' asked Karin.

'These are probably worth ten million dollars a throw, so I doubt it,' smiled Adam. 'I think Mikhail will have gone for something a little more impressive.' The car took a right-hand turn up a gentle slope into a more thickly wooded area and they stopped outside a huge pair of cherry-wood gates. As these swung open, Karin had to gasp.

'You're right, it is impressive,' she said. 'I think I'm going to like it here.'

Mikhail Lebokov was around forty. He had dark hair flecked with silver and, although he was not a handsome man, his muscular physique and alert blue eyes gave him a striking look. His wife Daria was even more impressive. In her mid- to late twenties, her dark blonde hair fell straight and glossy down her bare back. Her face was heart-shaped, her lips were full and smiling. She was beautiful.

'Welcome Adam and Karin,' said Mikhail, leading them into the house. There was a Japanese theme throughout. The floors were made of cherry-wood and bamboo. In the heart of the dacha was a courtyard walled with glass, at the centre of which was a steel pond of koi carp and water lilies. On the way out to the terrace, Daria told Karin there was a whole wing for staff at the back of the house, which included a French chef, Thai masseur and an English butler, who had once served in the household of a minor royal.

'You must be hungry after the long journey, *da*?' said Mikhail, motioning into the vast grounds. A sumptuous lunch had been spread out on a long cherry-wood table, covered with an ivory parasol the size of a parachute.

As Karin sat down she took a moment to assess Mikhail. He was polite and gracious, she thought, watching him direct the butler to bring them cold drinks, but there was a distance to his manner that suggested Adam might have an uphill battle securing the skyscraper contract. She was glad she was prepared.

'Karin. I saw you looking at the art on the way through the house,' said Mikhail. 'You like the Bacon and Warhols?'

'Of course,' she said. She had heard that Mikhail was an important collector of art; he was the rumoured buyer of a $50-million Picasso at auction, and she had been genuinely impressed by what she had seen on the walls. 'However I like the Russian art even more.'

Mikhail looked confused. 'The Kandinskys and Chagalls are in the bedroom and library. I don't think you have been there yet.'

'I actually meant the two works by Nesterov in the corridor behind us and the Grigoriev over there. That one was painted during the artist's time in France, I believe.'

'It is my turn to be impressed,' said Mikhail with the hint of a smile. 'Few Western friends recognize important Russian artists.'

Karin nodded thoughtfully. 'Most people seem to think Russian art is all about Malevich, Chagall and Kandinsky, but I am a big fan of the artists less well known to the West.' She shrugged modestly. 'I have to thank my late husband. He was an art historian and owned a gallery.'

As lunch was served – Sevruga caviar, cold meat and exotic salads – Mikhail leant across the table and began to talk with passion about his collection. As he listened, Adam threw Karin a grateful glance and she smiled back. The truth was, Sebastian had never had any real interest in Russian art at all. But Mikhail was not to know that.

Finally Mikhail turned to Adam. 'And how are you enjoying London?' he asked, draining some mineral water from a crystal tumbler. 'It is easier for Americans to fit into the London establishment than us Russians, yes?'

'I haven't had any problems so far,' he replied cautiously, detecting an edge to Mikhail's voice.

'What about the gentlemen's clubs? Do you belong to those?'

Adam shrugged. 'Clubs like White's, you mean?' He shook his head. 'That English old-boys' club scene isn't really my thing, to be honest.'

'I have tried to join Hamilton's. Are you aware of it? It is the most exclusive club. But they, how do you say, blackballed my application. It is ridiculous. Do they think Russians are thugs? Criminals? Not worthy of drinking with them?' Karin noticed that Mikhail's hand had curled into a fist. 'I have a good mind to buy their little club and close it down.'

Karin cleared her throat. 'I don't think that will be necessary, Mikhail. My late husband was on the membership committee of that club. A lot of his friends are still members. I'm not making any promises, but how about I introduce you to some of them socially and see how you all get along?'

Mikhail's fingers began to uncurl. 'Really? That would be most kind of you,' he said, smiling. 'Very kind indeed.'

*

After lunch, Adam and Mikhail went into the library to talk business, leaving Daria and Karin alone.

'Would you like the grand tour?' asked Daria, seeing Karin's eyes darting around. 'We only finish the property six months ago, so some of it is still new to me.'

'Oh, yes please.'

Karin was about to get a lesson in how vast wealth and good taste could make a home into a palace. 'I am a big fan of your swimwear,' said Daria, as she led Karin upstairs towards the bedrooms. 'When Miki said he was due to meet Adam, I insisted you come along too. I read a lot of English magazines, you see.'

Karin immediately liked Daria, who seemed much more approachable than many of the Russian wives she had met in London. In fact, she seemed a little lonely. The dacha was surrounded by high walls, and there had been a platoon of security on the gate when they had entered. Karin suspected it would be like living in a gilded cage.

Still, as they moved through the house, Karin marvelled at every room. Daria's dressing room was the most spectacular, filled with exquisite clothes of every kind. There was a climate-controlled closet for Daria's collection of sable minks, and shelves of cashmere sweaters, colour-coded like the rainbow. The walls were lined with rails upon rails of designer clothes, many of them, judging by the cut and exquisite embroidered fabric, clearly couture. On another rack, Karin was pleased to note, were about thirty Karenza swimsuits and bikinis. Catherine the Great was rumoured to have over 5000 dresses, but Daria couldn't have been far off that number, thought Karin, spying another glass closet devoted entirely to long gowns.

'Wow,' said Karin, unable to disguise her envy.

'I got a taste for clothes when I was modelling in New York,' she said frankly. 'You see, I'm from a very small village near Kiev. My parents were poor. I used to help them on their fruit stall and I wore rags until I was spotted by a model agent. I guess now I am making up for all the dresses I never had when I was a little girl.'

What a transformation, thought Karin, looking at elegant Daria. It was hard to picture her in rags.

'Do your parents still sell fruit?' she asked, fascinated.

Daria laughed. 'Mikhail has moved my parents into the next

village. Now they do very little, but I'm not sure they prefer it that way.'

They walked out of the house and into the grounds, slowly sipping iced mineral water from Baccarat tumblers, the smells of the summer countryside – grass, pine and berries – filling the air. After ten minutes of walking they came to a lake filled with tiger lilies. Next to it stood a cherry-wood lodge with a black pointed roof and low eaves. It looked like a painting of imperial Japan.

'It's a Japanese teahouse,' said Daria, beaming. 'I come in here for calm.'

Her childlike pride in the little house made Karin smile. She was still reeling at the sheer scale and luxury of the dacha, but for Daria, this was clearly the jewel in the crown.

They stepped inside. It had the same cherry-wood floors as the main house. Karin followed Daria's lead as she took off her heels and changed into a pair of white slippers. They sat down on a teak lounger with cream cushions and Daria poured some tea.

'Excuse me for asking,' said Karin, breathing in the cherry blossom from a tree standing just outside the shuttered window of the house, 'but why exactly do you need calm? Everything seems rather good in your world.'

Daria's expression instantly changed from the excited little girl playing house to the more knowing expression of a woman who had seen more in her life than most twenty-somethings. She fixed Karin with a searching look.

'You are a woman dating a very wealthy man, Karin,' she said frankly. 'I'm sure I don't need to tell you what I mean.'

'I'm not sure I understand,' replied Karin, taking a small sip of green tea.

'My husband has a mistress,' said Daria simply. 'It has always been this way since very soon after we married, and until recently I have accepted it. In our circle, a mistress is on the list of things for men to have, like a yacht and a 737.'

Karin saw the sadness in her eyes, and for a moment she thought about her own recent paranoia. 'I'm not quite sure having a mistress is acceptable,' said Karin cautiously. 'But rich men will always take what is thrown in front of them, that's true. Men are weak, whether they come from Moscow or Manhattan.'

Daria nodded, staring at the branches of the cherry blossom tree waving slowly in the breeze.

'I have never been worried before,' she said quietly, 'but his latest is troubling me. She lives in London, she is very beautiful. Her father is rich, important and connected.' Her eyes had half closed, making them look feline, like a cat sizing up its prey. 'I know she calls him all the time. I hear them talking on the telephone when he thinks I am asleep. I think it is getting serious.'

'But Daria, you're beautiful. Why would he look at another woman?' she asked, genuinely curious and surprised at Daria's candidness.

'I am his wife,' shrugged Daria, 'a mother. This immediately makes me less sexy than a beautiful eighteen-year-old he sees twice a month.'

Karin nodded. 'And is there anything else that makes you think it's serious?'

'We have a couple of apartments in your city, and I think she now lives in one of them.'

'That's outrageous,' cried Karin, feeling a sudden sense of solidarity with Daria. 'You must tell Mikhail that you know and that you won't tolerate it.'

Daria laughed softly. 'And when he calls my bluff, then what do I do?'

'Well, I will tell you what we would do in England. We would go and see a divorce lawyer.'

'In Russia we now have London's boutiques, your restaurants, your bars; but we do not yet have your divorce laws. If I divorce Mikhail I will be lucky to end up with an apartment as big as this teahouse.'

Karin looked at Daria and her sad big blue eyes, eyes that knew she could be back selling fruit as quickly as she had escaped it.

A fire suddenly burned inside Karin as she found herself becoming protective of this woman. 'Well, you have to fight back,' she said quickly.

'How?' said Daria.

'Why do you think Mikhail likes this woman so much? Surely she is no more beautiful than you?'

'Mikhail loves glamour. He loves status. This mistress – she runs around with a very glamorous crowd in London.'

'Then so shall you.'

She laughed. 'I live in Moscow.'

'Do you want to save your marriage?' asked Karin sharply.

320

Daria nodded.

'If Mikhail is as impressed with the London scene as I think he is, then he might sit up and take notice if his wife is a major player. A woman other women want to be, and other men want to sleep with. Men can be simple creatures. A rich man likes the woman that every other man likes; he wants other men to look at him and envy him not just for the money in his bank but for the woman in his bed.'

Karin put her hand on Daria's knee. 'You have to put the excitement, passion and glamour back into your marriage.'

Daria looked at Karin with those little-girl eyes. 'Can you help me?'

Karin laughed. 'You will have to help yourself, but I can help you make a start. Next time you are in London, give me a call. I can introduce you to everyone who is worth knowing. Even the committee members of the Hamilton Club,' she smiled playfully.

'And then let me help you,' said Daria, looking at Karin shrewdly. 'I am still Mikhail's wife, the mother of his child, and he wants to keep me happy. I think that, in twenty-four hours, Adam may just have his contract to build the skyscraper.'

The two women looked at each other, each recognizing how they could help each other, and smiled.

'I'll drink to that,' said Karin.

'Thanks for coming, honey,' said Adam, pulling Karin close. 'Mikhail loved you.'

It was 2 a.m. and they were back at the Moscow Park Hyatt hotel, lying between crisp white sheets; but Adam was clearly wide awake. It was always the same way when he was trying to land a deal, when an almost feral energy inside him made him jumpy and on edge.

'I aim to please,' smiled Karin. 'So when do you think you'll hear about whether he's giving you the contract?' she asked, running her finger up and down his arm.

Adam shrugged and popped another goosedown pillow under his head. 'Don't get too excited just because we managed to charm him at dinner. I'm sure that was just one of many hoops I'll have to jump through before Mikhail even thinks of giving the job to Midas,' he said, frowning.

'Oh, I wouldn't be so sure,' said Karin, stroking his hair.

She'd been wrestling all evening with the dilemma of whether to tell Adam about her conversation with Daria. To tell Adam ran the risk of denting his ego. He was a Master of the Universe, he could close any deal, talk anybody into anything; did he really want his girlfriend interfering; single-handedly *influencing* a billion-dollar development? But then again, if Daria had the power she said she had, then there was no way Karin was going to keep quiet about swinging the deal.

'What do you mean?' asked Adam, prossing himself up on one elbow.

Slowly, cautiously, Karin recalled her conversation with Daria, and waited in silence to hear Adam's reaction.

'Fuck me, Dr Ruth,' he said, smiling. 'It really has been worth you coming.'

Karin's heart was pounding. 'So you're pleased?'

He flipped up the duvet and rolled on top of her. 'I've got a feeling that you are going to be really, really good for me,' he whispered into her ear as his lips began a trail of moist kisses down her neck.

The next day, Mikhail rang Adam as they were on the way to Domodedovo Airport. He would be delighted to subcontract the building of the Moscow Supertower to the Midas Corporation. Sitting on the black leather seat of the Mercedes beside Adam, Karin had to turn her head to look out of the window to stop Adam seeing her Cheshire Cat grin. She took his hand and squeezed his fingers, silently predicting that, by this time next year, she would be Mrs Adam Gold.

54

There was no answer at Eton Square. Molly had tried the front doorbell of Donna and Daniel's house and peered in through the windows, but there was no sign of life. Luckily, she knew exactly where to go. Daniel's father Alexander owned a small apartment in Holland Park, where Molly and Alex had occasionally met for sex. It was like a tiny literary bolthole, crammed with books and journals, and Alex had told Molly nostalgically that Daniel had used it to revise for his finals twenty years earlier. *It was the perfect place to lock himself away*, Alex had told her.

'Well done. You found me,' said Daniel flatly as he buzzed Molly into the small top-floor space. He was standing by a window that overlooked the park, arms folded across his chest. It was a bright day, but the sun was shining on the opposite side of the street, which gave the room a sombre cast that perfectly matched Daniel's expression.

Molly sat down on an antique leather sofa without being asked. 'Donna's sister has been trying to reach you.'

'Well, I haven't wanted to be found,' said Daniel tartly. He looked up and glared at her.

Molly frowned and avoided his gaze, a little unnerved by his hostility. Okay, so he was angry and upset, but he didn't have to take it out on *her*, did he?

Daniel shook a cigarette out of a packet and lit it, giving a small shake of the head.

'Starting smoking again wasn't part of the plan, but when you've got every bloody hack in London chasing you for a comment . . .'

'Well, I think you might need that cigarette,' said Molly.

'What do you mean?'

Molly paused before speaking.'It's Donna. She's okay now, but she took an overdose.'

Molly saw his jaw slacken and more colour drain out of his face. '*What?*' he said, his voice small and cracked. He walked over to the sofa and sat down, burying his head in his hands. 'Jesus,' he said, muttering to himself. 'I am so stupid. I've been so bloody selfish.'

'I think you left your mobile at Delemere so nobody could reach you,' said Molly. 'But don't worry, Patsy is with her. Evie is okay. And Donna's okay too, really she is.'

All of a sudden he looked up; Molly could see his fingers were curled into a tight fist. Daniel was not usually an aggressive man – he was certainly the most placid of the husbands in Molly's circle of friends – but the atmosphere was now prickling with enmity. He jumped to his feet and took a step toward Molly. 'Donna is clearly not okay, you stupid fucking bitch,' he said through clenched teeth.

Molly stood up, holding her hands out in front of her in a placating gesture. 'Now calm down, Daniel. What I meant was that it could have been so much worse, but the doctors have all said she is going to be fine.'

Daniel stood there, clenching and unclenching his hands, his shoulders shaking with suppressed violence.

'You've not cottoned on that I know, have you?' he sneered, shaking his head slowly. 'That I know what a vicious, conniving little cow you really are.'

'I honestly don't know what you are talking about,' said Molly, her voice shaking, tripping over her heels as she tried to back away from him.

'Oh, I always knew you were self-seeking,' spat Daniel, 'but I really didn't think you would have the gall to do what you have done and then come here posing as a friend of my wife. '

'But I am a friend, Daniel,' said Molly, backing right up to the door. 'I don't know what you think has happened, but I haven't done anything except come to find you, to tell you about Donna and to say she is sorry. She is so sorry.'

'*Sorry?*' yelled Daniel, lunging across at Molly and gripping her arms, pinning her against the doorframe.

'Sorry? You're the one who should be sorry, you sad little whore!'

Daniel's face was only inches from hers, his eyes blazing with fury. She could feel his arms shaking and his fingers pressing into her flesh. Molly was terrified, unable to utter a single word, barely breathing.

Suddenly, Daniel released her and turned away, walking back to the window. He stared out at the street and shook his head slowly. 'Donna thinks we were both tipped off about the story on Saturday night, but a friend at the newspaper had told me a couple of days earlier. I had tried to get an injunction to stop it being published, but was unsuccessful,' he said flatly. 'So, I hired a private investigator.' He barked a hollow laugh. 'When a reporter tells you that your wife was a high-class hooker, you want to find if it's true or not.'

The look on his face was one of anger and confusion as he ran his hand through his blond hair. Molly was unable to do anything except stand frozen by the door.

'It didn't take a Sherlock Holmes to track down Sharif Kahlid.' He looked up at Molly with probing, accusatory eyes. 'At first he wouldn't talk. But it's amazing what a suitcase full of cash will do. Apparently you found the same thing out yourself.'

Molly opened her mouth to defend herself, but she knew it was pointless.

'The investigator, terribly good at his job, I might add, followed you.' He wagged a finger in the air while walking over to a walnut bureau. He opened it and removed a large brown envelope, flinging it onto the coffee table.

'I have pictures. Go on, open it. Meeting my father at the Hilton at Heathrow Airport on Friday afternoon. I assume you met to have sex as well as to conspire. I have to admit, I really didn't think you were my father's type.'

'But that's bloody illegal!' blustered Molly, regaining a little of her composure. 'You can't just have me followed!'

Daniel seemed unnaturally calm now. His voice had regained its cool elegance and was beginning to sound more icy with every word. 'I could strangle you right now if I didn't pity you so much,' he said. 'Really, I'm serious. What would drive you to destroy my wife's life? Are you so stupid that you believe my father will somehow want you more? That he will be so grateful for this information, that he will somehow divorce my mother so he can marry *you*?' He gave a cruel laugh that made Molly shudder. She couldn't believe that little, mousy Daniel Delemere could be so icy, so devastatingly brutal.

'Or is it just plain envy, Molly? Are you that twisted, that bitter?'

Molly puffed her chest out. How dare he suggest she was bitter?

'I care about your father and he cares about his family,' said Molly defiantly. 'You could have a brilliant career Daniel, in politics, in the Lords. But not when you have *a whore* by your side.'

'A whore?' he spat. 'I only know one of those, and she's standing in front of me.'

Molly flinched at the look in his eyes. She held up her hands again. 'Daniel, see sense. You don't need someone like Donna in your life.'

'And who do I need?' asked Daniel coolly. 'Someone like you?'

Molly looked away, cursing herself. She couldn't understand what had gone wrong. She'd been looking forward to Daniel being single and back on the market once more, but he was being so *irrational*.

He looked at her once again, and his face actually softened.

'Donna has done things that she undoubtedly regrets, Molly, things that *I* regret,' he said. 'But I love her, and you don't marry someone's past, Molly. You marry the person.'

He walked to the door and picked up a leather holdall that was sitting packed and ready. 'Now, if you'll excuse me, I was about to return home to my wife.'

Molly watched Daniel climb into his Audi and drive away, then picked up her mobile to phone Alex. 'Are you back in the country?' she asked urgently.

'I've heard about Donna. Patsy phoned Vivienne,' he said slowly. 'We're coming back to England immediately.'

'It's nothing serious, she's fine,' said Molly. 'But I think I need you to talk some sense into Daniel. He knows what we did.'

There was a long pause before Alex spoke again. 'I didn't want it to turn out like this. I don't think we should see each other again.'

Molly felt her heart in her mouth. 'Alex, wait!' she said, pleading. 'Don't be ridiculous, Daniel is just angry and confused. He'll forgive you and he'll do the right thing and get rid of Donna. We just need to let the dust settle for a while.'

'Molly, I have to go. We're leaving for the airport. Goodbye.'

The line went dead and Molly threw her phone back in her bag.

55

Something was in the air. Erin could feel it. Most of the time she was privy to all of Adam's business affairs, but over the last few days she was feeling increasingly excluded from what was going on. Adam's door was closed most of the time: people were in and out and she could hear a lot of raised voices coming from his office. There had been several long meetings and lunch dates with someone called Claudia Falcon; Erin had googled her and found out she was a prominent securities banker.

Erin had assumed she knew everything about Adam's business, but she was obviously mistaken. She only knew what Adam *allowed* her to know. Feeling frustrated and highly curious, she carried on with her emails, straining her ears for any more snippets of conversation. She knew that whatever was going on behind those closed doors was clearly either very good or very bad, and she was desperate to know which.

Sebastian Cavendish hadn't wanted to be buried. He had told his wife, many months before his death, that he hated the idea of his expensively maintained body rotting away beneath the surface of the soil. Against the staunch wishes of his family, who wanted him to be buried in the village church where the Cavendish's still owned a Grade I listed manor house and were treated like local royalty, Karin had carried out Sebastian's wishes. He had been cremated, his ashes strewn in the grounds of his parents' house, and a David Linley-designed bench had been placed in a quiet corner of Holland Park where Sebastian used to go to read his papers.

It was hard to believe that was only a year ago, thought Karin, resting her elbow on the open window of her car as she drove towards Holland Park. Today was the first anniversary of Sebastian's death and yet, honestly, she struggled to remember what life was like with him in it. Her new life with Adam was so true and sure and established, it had snuffed out all memories of a time before he existed.

Perhaps today would feel different, she thought. It was 11 a.m., and the morning skies were soft and hazy, promising another warm day. She parked the car in a metered bay on Addison Road and walked towards the park. She saw a old man, a neighbour who she recognized, and they nodded. His eyes looked apologetic. He clearly knew who she was. The tragic, beautiful widow who had lost her husband in a boating accident and had moved out of the area within months of it happening.

As Karin walked into the park towards Sebastian's bench, she recognised another familiar figure moving towards it from another direction. Karin's first instinct was retreat, but she could see she had been spotted.

Dammit, that's all I need today, thought Karin, as she drew level with a cool, smartly dressed blonde. She was about forty, but looked good on it, thanks to her elegant, regal bone structure. Helen Cavendish, Sebastian's sister. It had been her husband Matthew's business partner who took out the charter of the *Zeus* every August, and thus Helen had been a guest aboard the yacht the night of Sebastian's death.

For a second the air was filled with awkwardness, and then Karin gave a small smile. She had not seen Helen for many months. There was little love lost between them. Helen had been the ringleader of the argument over the burial and Karin also felt sure that Helen felt bitter about not receiving a penny from Sebastian's estate. It was hardly Karin's fault that there was nothing left to give after Seb's debts; she had been lucky that the house was in her name.

'Karin. It's been a long time,' said Helen quietly, holding her handbag in front of her like a shield.

'I'm surprised to see you here,' replied Karin, taking a seat on the bench. 'After all, you did disagree with the idea of this.'

'Well. There's not much else to remember him by now, is there?'

Karin shrugged. 'We can still remember though.'

Helen sat down next to Karin, perching on the edge of the wood as if she feared her coat becoming dirty from it.

'Yes, we can.' Her words were clipped, her expression sour.

'Is there a problem, Helen?' asked Karin.

Helen looked at Karin and paused before replying. 'Matthew and I are divorcing.'

'Oh, I'm sorry,' replied Karin.

Helen gave a small snort. 'Are you, Karin? He told me what happened in Turkey the night Sebastian died.'

Helen's remarks were like a bomb blast from nowhere. Karin had a flashback to a memory she had long tried to forget. For a second she thought about denying everything, but from the cold look on Helen's face, it was clear that she knew the truth.

'Helen, I don't know what Matthew's told you—'

'He told me that after Seb took the tender back to the yacht, you tried to seduce my husband.' Her tone was flat and without accusation.

'Matthew seduced *me*,' Karin replied softly, 'but I don't suppose it really matters, does it?'

'No, it doesn't. He doesn't matter. You don't matter. But what does matter is what happened to my brother that night,' said Helen, looking far off into the distance.

Karin knew what she was implying; exactly the same thing all those society gossips had said.

'Helen, it was an awful accident,' said Karin. 'No one knows how or why, but we just have to accept that.'

Helen glared at her, her eyes full of accusation. 'You and Matthew slipped back to the boat. Why didn't you tell the police?'

Karin sighed. 'Because I was with your husband. There was enough hurt without bringing all that up.'

'Matthew gave you your alibi, didn't he?' continued Helen. 'He said he saw you dancing on the dance floor all evening,' she snorted. 'Bloody liar. Truth was you were both having sex together back in the cabin.'

'Helen, please.'

Helen swivelled round, her lips in a tight line, her eyes pooled with anger. 'Matthew came back to the club before we had noticed he was missing. You, on the other hand, remained on the yacht. What happened, Karin? What happened to Sebastian?'

Karin could feel frustration and anger rising. 'Okay, look. It's true,' she said, her voice rising. 'But when I got back to our cabin it was empty!' She took a breath to compose herself. 'I didn't know where he was.'

A small white dog had trotted up to them and was sniffing around their feet. A warm breeze had picked up and rustled through the trees.

'Things have turned right around for you this year, haven't they, Karin?' said Helen coolly.

Karin looked at her hands. 'In the last six months, yes, I suppose they have.'

'Your new boyfriend is very rich. I suspect he has a yacht of his own.' Karin sat up.

'What are you suggesting, Helen?'

Helen rose slowly and slung her handbag over her shoulder. 'You know exactly what I'm suggesting, Karin. I'm watching you.'

Helen put two fingers to her lips, kissed them, and then put them down on the arm of the bench. 'Goodbye, Seb. I miss you,' she whispered, and walked off into the park.

Karin folded her arms in front of her, her eyes watching Helen go, but her mind completely lost in thought.

56

Whoever said modelling was glamorous, thought Summer groggily, leaning her head against the window of the people carrier as she watched the north Norfolk coast slip by, a blur of fields, cottages and grey sky. It was 6.30 a.m. and she was on her way to her next modelling assignment. Well, modelling-stroke-acting, she corrected herself. She actually knew very little about the job ahead of her, except it was a video-shoot for DHP Records' bright new hope. The record executive who had booked her, a middle-aged cockney man called Phil Harrison, had been unusually vague about the details of the shoot, which had sent Summer's imagination into overdrive – what if it was someone really big like Justin Timberlake? Knowing her luck, it would Cliff Richard.

The people carrier dropped her off on the edge of a wide, dark, sandy stretch of beach and she walked over to a small herd of trailers on the edge of the sands.

'Ah, here she is, looking gorgeous,' smiled Phil Harrison. Phil had clearly dressed for the season not the weather and looked faintly ridiculous in a long shearling coat and a pair of flip-flops.

'Fucking freezing, isn't it?' he said, glancing at a giant watch around his chubby wrist. 'You'd never believe it was August, wouldja?'

Summer smiled sympathetically. 'Is there anywhere I can grab a coffee?' she asked.

'Go ahead, darlin',' he said, jerking a thumb towards a trailer. 'Talent's not here yet, but that'll give you time to meet the director and go through my vision for the video.'

Phil put an overfamiliar hand on Summer's shoulder. 'To give you a heads-up, I'm thinking Helen Christensen in Chris Isaak's "Wicked Game" video, know what I mean? I'm thinking you, running along the sand, gagging for it. I'm thinking bleak, moody, sexy. I need to see sex, Summer. Show me sex.'

'I think you mean *Helena* Christensen, Mr Harrison,' said Summer icily and moved towards the trailer, knowing it was going to be a long day ahead of them.

In the six months since Charlie McDonald had last seen Summer Sinclair, he had become the next big thing in the record industry and he was miserable. While on the surface it was every schoolboy's dream to be groomed as the next platinum-selling rock artist, he couldn't help but feel as if his identity had been hijacked, and that he was being taken places he didn't really want to go to. Sure, he loved the attention and the limos and the interviews, but was it really him?

Everything about him had changed, he thought mournfully, catching a glimpse of himself in the rear-view mirror of the black Mercedes that was transporting him to the video-shoot. That DHP Records had insisted he get rid of his band was painful enough, but when they had cut his hair, brought in a stylist and a personal trainer to revamp his image, and had even changed his name to CJ, he was beginning to wonder why they signed him in the first place.

The car slowed as it reached the edge of Brancaster Beach and Charlie felt a little jolt of nerves in the pit of his stomach. When his manager Rob had started talking about a video featuring a sexy girl for his debut single 'Smile', Charlie only had one girl in mind for the job. Summer Sinclair. After their night at the Monarch, it had taken him months to get over her. The process was helped along by the stream of groupies, music PRs and female rock journalists who suddenly seemed to find him irresistible. And, while Charlie had not been a monk, when he had seen the Karenza advert plastered all over London, he had realized that he had to see her again.

There was a slight salty breeze, a weak early morning sun beginning to crack through the folds of steel-grey clouds as Charlie walked across the sand to the trailer where Summer was sitting reading a book.

'Ah, Summer, meet CJ,' said Sean Clarkson, the video director gruffly, impatient to start filming. 'CJ, meet Summer. You two are in love, now can we all get to our places?'

Summer looked up, squinting in the early morning sun at the incredibly good-looking man in front of her. For a split second she did not recognize him: his hair was shorter, darker; stubble sat around his jaw; his blue jeans and loose white shirt screamed sexy Texan cowboy, not clean-cut groom.

'Charlie? Charlie! What the hell are you doing here?' laughed Summer as Sean rolled his eyes and vanished into the trailer.

Charlie smiled bashfully. 'I'm the talent, allegedly.'

'I had no idea it was you,' she said, shaking her head. 'You've done brilliantly. I didn't even know you'd got a record deal. I feel an idiot.'

'You weren't to know. My debut single hasn't even been released yet and can you believe my management want to call me CJ,' he winced.

'The record company seem so excited about you. Gosh. This is great. And what a coincidence.'

Charlie looked embarrassed. 'Well, I could lie and say this is an incredible coincidence, but when the record company said they wanted a gorgeous model for the video, I said I knew just the girl.'

She slapped his arm playfully. 'You just wanted to see me in a meringue again.'

'Maybe I just wanted to see you,' he said softly.

Summer felt her heart flip and felt instantly guilty. She was in a relationship with Adam. She shouldn't be looking at other men. 'You never phoned,' she said softly. 'And things are a bit different now.'

Charlie looked puzzled. 'Well no, I didn't phone because I lost your number, but I did come round to see you.'

Summer looked at Charlie, confused. 'Sorry? When did you . . . ? Where?'

'I came to see you at your flat. But your mum said you weren't there. Didn't she tell you what happened?'

Summer frowned. 'No, she didn't. Perhaps you better had.'

'Darling, everything I do is in your best interests,' said Molly, sitting back on the sofa and examining her teeth in a silver compact mirror. Summer had only just arrived home from the Norfolk shoot when Molly had breezed in to show her the results of a Wimpole Street teeth-whitening session. Summer hated confrontation at the best of times – especially with her mother – but she was so angry at Molly's meddling that, for once, she couldn't keep it in.

On the journey back from Norfolk, Summer had tried to rationalize why Molly had lied to Charlie McDonald, but there was no obvious, acceptable explanation, and it incensed Summer even more that her mother was showing no signs of remorse.

'You lied to me and you lied to Charlie McDonald,' said Summer with irritation. 'How could lying be in my best interests? You had no right to send him away and tell him I had a boyfriend. He's a great guy.' The force of Summer's feelings surprised her.

'Oh, I had every right,' said Molly, coolly snapping her compact shut and looking at Summer with disdain.

'When a third-rate male model turns up at your house and starts sniffing around, a mother has to act. I mean, honestly Summer, he was so unkempt that at first I thought he was homeless.'

'You weren't to know he was about to get a million-pound record deal,' replied Summer sarcastically.

'Hmm, that was unfortunate, yes. But things have worked out for the best, haven't they?' said Molly. 'If you'd have started a relationship with this Charlie, Adam Gold would have slipped through the net. This boy's record deal might sound like a lot of money, but, believe me, once he's paid his record company back for tours and videos, there's not that much left over.'

Summer laughed incredulously. 'It's always about money with you, isn't it? But you're missing the point as usual, mother. It's not about who's better off, or even who I prefer.'

'Then what the hell is it about?' snapped Molly.

'It's about the fact that you lied to me, mother. It's about you interfering in my life and trying to manipulate my choices and decisions.'

The night with Ricardo Lantis suddenly slipped into Summer's head, and she tried to blot it out immediately. There was no point making this conversation any more complicated than it needed to be, but it gave her added resolve to be strong.

'Oh, for God's sake, Summer, I'm only trying to do the best for you, it's all I ever do. What do you want from me?'

'I want my life back, mother. I don't want you interfering in it again.'

Molly stood up suddenly, her eyes flashing and angry. 'Don't talk to me about interfering,' she yelled.

Summer recoiled in surprise and fear.

'You are the one who has interfered in my life since the day you were born. I could have had everything without you. The brilliant career, the rich husband; but how could I, with *you* hanging around?'

At first Summer was too shocked to speak. The unspoken resentment that Summer had felt underpinning their life together had finally surfaced, was finally out in the open.

'Don't, mother, please,' cried Summer.

'Even when I found someone, you had to poke your nose in and spoil it for me, didn't you?' said Molly, looking at her daughter sourly. 'You and Graham bloody Daniels deceived me perfectly, didn't you, with your filthy little goings-on. I devote my life to you and that's how you repaid me? Think about that before you start accusing me of meddling in your life.'

'Stop it, stop it!' screamed Summer, sinking to the floor sobbing. 'Stop it, stop it!' she repeated over and over again, her hands over her ears, her eyes tightly shut. Without another word Molly left the flat.

57

The beautiful Ibizan finca La Toreador had been taken out on a three-week August rental by Diana and Martin which, as far as Karin was concerned, was perfect timing. August was a flat month in the fashion industry, and it neatly coincided with her thirty-second birthday. Arriving at the finca on the eastern coast of the island late on Friday morning, she knew that Adam was going to love it. He wasn't due to arrive until later that evening, but as Diana had arranged for Karin to get a lift on a private jet owned by one of Martin's friends, Karin figured she was better off getting to La Toreador sooner rather than later. Besides, she smiled to herself, shielding her eyes as she gazed up into the cornflower-blue sky, the extra hours at the villa meant that she could have a beautiful tan in time for that evening's soirée.

Having been shown to her room by the housekeeper, Karin took a few minutes to wander around the villa, before joining the other guests who were out by the pool. It was a huge whitewashed finca on the side of a hill overlooking the eastern coastline. It had recently been featured in Russian *Vogue* and it was easy to see why they had called it the last word in rustic chic. Expensively pared down, it had white voile curtains wafting in a soft breeze, the colour scheme was cream and chocolate brown, while the furniture was a mixture of rattan and heavier, more expensive pieces of oak. There were ceiling fans and big squashy beds covered with Portuguese linens, while at the window were pots of lavender and bougainvillea and orange, peach and lemon trees growing in the garden. In the 1960s, La Toreador's bacchanalian parties had been legendary, and it hadn't slowed down much since – only the week before it had hosted a supermodel and her rock-star boyfriend with a legendary drug habit.

Karin had a shower and changed into a skimpy snakeskin Karenza bikini, with a dramatic décolletage with low hipster pants. She smothered herself in a factor four suntan oil that smelt of coconut and lime, then fastened a sheer brown sarong around her slim waist. She then made her way to the back of the finca, where a huge kidney-shaped pool shimmered in the hot Balearic sun. Although it was almost lunchtime, a couple of people were having a very late breakfast under a vanilla-coloured parasol, while the rest of Diana's house guests were lounging around the pool on a mixture of sun-loungers and big white day beds. At the sound of Karin's bejewelled flip-flops clattering across the terrace, Diana swung off her sun-lounger, her voluminous fuchsia kaftan billowing in the breeze.

'The birthday girl!' she smiled, spreading her arms in extravagant declaration, 'Now the party can really start!'

Karin embraced her friend and narrowly avoided knocking her oversized Gucci sunglasses with her own huge Prada shades as they air-kissed a greeting.

Diana tapped one of the white-coated Hispanic-looking waiters on the arm. 'A cocktail for the new arrival please!' she said, before showing Karin to a sun-lounger next to hers. 'How incredible is the finca? I told you, didn't I? Turns out that the owner used to be a stylist before she met her husband. Now all she does is shop for herself, never other people. Isn't that fabulous?'

'Who's here then?' asked Karin, sipping her drink. Diana wafted a manicured hand across the swimming pool.

'Not everyone's up yet,' she whispered with a wink. 'We were all at Pacha last night, which was a bit crazy. You should know most people here.'

'Where's Christina, still sleeping?'

'Surprisingly not,' said Diana. 'A friend is in town with a yacht and they've sailed over to Formentera for the day. She said she wanted to shag a beach bum.'

Karin tried to examine faces that were obscured by wide-brimmed hats and newspapers. She could just make out Sabrina Love, a thirty-something society jeweller, adjusting her Pucci bikini alongside her German hedge-fund banker husband Frederick. A well-known model was passing what looked suspiciously like a spliff to a notorious music producer. Notting Hill socialite Melissa Craig and her property developer husband were here; apparently the baby had been left in London with a 'smashing' Australian nanny. It was a real mixed-bag, thought Karin, from hip Holland Park to monied Belgravia – the only thing they all seemed to have in common was their love of a good time, which Ibiza in August could always provide in spades.

As she looked around the pool, satisfied that her body in the skimpy Karenza bikini looked better than everyone else's, Karin decided that she was glad to be back.

'I don't recognize her,' said Karin, looking over the top of her sunglasses towards the other side of the pool, where a small, slim blonde lay, in a leopard-print bikini and matching headscarf worn warrior-princess style.

'That's Tracey,' said Diana.

Karin sat up. 'Martin's ex wife is here?' she hissed.

'And the kids,' said Diana slowly. Karin gaped at her friend, appalled. 'For goodness' sake, honey, you've got to put your foot down!' she whispered. 'What sort of holiday is it going to be for you with her running around . . .'

Diana lowered her voice and looked embarrassed. 'You know we've been arguing about having a baby?'

Karin nodded cautiously, knowing she was going to disapprove of what she was about to hear. 'Well, Martin said I should make more of an effort with his kids and with Tracey. I figured if I can show him how good I am with children, maybe he'll reconsider about us having children together.'

'You actually believe that?' said Karin tersely.

'I have to hope,' she replied, looking sad. 'Anyway, they are my step-children. It's probably a good thing if we all get to know one another a little better, don't you think?'

Karin took a sip of apple juice and looked away from her friend, knowing there was nothing she could say to make Diana change her mind. When they had married, Martin had known he was lucky to catch Diana with her breeding and grace, but now the tables had completely turned. Karin did not like to see her friend in this frightened state of submission, desperate to please her husband but secretly knowing that it was ultimately futile.

Karin settled into her sun-bed and picked up her Sidney Sheldon novel, but the sun quickly became too hot for her to read without feeling exhausted.

'Karin. I see you've arrived, looking lovely as ever. Missed a great night out yesterday.'

She looked up to see Martin sitting on the end of her sun-lounger, wrapped in a white waffle robe. His eyes were bleary and he was squinting in the sun.

He leant over to Diana on the adjacent bed and tapped her thigh. 'I'm starving. Can you go and hurry the help up with lunch? They seem a bit slack.' He pulled off the robe to reveal a garish pair of swimming trunks and stretched his arms to the sky. 'Think I'll take a quick dip while I'm waiting.'

As he jumped in the pool, two little girls, around six and eight, ran towards him, shrieking and firing huge fluorescent water pistols.

'Look how far we can spray people,' they screamed, squirting their guns over at Tracey, who shot up like a bullet.

'Gerr'over here!' she screamed, as the other guests were beginning to look up and tut.

'I'm, um, I'm going to check everything's okay with lunch,' said Diana, pulling on her kaftan. 'A couple of Italian chefs have come over from Ibiza Town. One used to work in the River Café, you know.'

'I'll come with you,' said Karin. 'It's getting a bit boisterous around here.'

'That's Chloe and Emma, Martin's girls. They are very lively.'

Karin and Diana walked down to a huge wooden gazebo at one end of the pool. Beneath the shade of the wooden slats lay a long table that could comfortably seat twenty. Two waiters in white uniforms were beginning to set it with white crockery and big glass dishes of food; bowls of pasta, mountains of mozzarella, tomato and avocado, large rustic-looking tarts. Diana began to direct the waiters, while Karin sat in the shade watching Emma and Chloe running around the pool causing havoc, shaking her head at how badly behaved they were.

'Come in the pool, sweethearts,' shouted Martin, 'you can do that later.'

Encouraged by their father's refusal to tell them off, and their mother's failure to move from her sun-lounger, Chloe and Emma were now hysterical with power, running at full speed towards the gazebo, their guns aloft.

'This is outrageous; you've got to stop them,' said Karin. Diana stepped out in front of them and put up a hand like a traffic policeman. The two girls had no intention of stopping, however, as Emma splayed out her arms like an aeroplane, clearly aiming to fly kamikaze-like into the table while Chloe charged at Diana, holding her long water pistol like a lance.

'Stop it!' screamed Diana, trying to grab Emma. Seeing an opening, Chloe swerved sideways and swung her water pistol along the top of the table, sending plates, glasses and bowls of food smashing to the floor.

'You little minx!' shouted Diana, grabbing Chloe's arm sharply. 'Look what you've done.'

Chloe started howling, clutching her arm as Martin jumped out of the pool and Tracey came running over, tottering in a pair of four-inch rope wedge heels.

'My arm! Diana's hurt my arm!' screamed Chloe, going pink in the face.

'Don't move darling, you might have dislocated it!' said Martin flashing Diana a filthy expression.

'You stupid cow!' screamed Tracey at Diana, curling a protective arm around Chloe. 'What have you done to my baby?'

'I'm so sorry, honey,' said Diana kneeling down, trying to soothe Chloe, who flinched away from her, screaming.

'Good with kids, are you?' snarled Martin to Diana, moving Chloe and Tracey away from the gazebo. He put his arm across Tracey's shoulders; she was now beginning to cry hysterically. All the guests had crowded round them and someone was already making a call to the local doctor. Karin touched Diana lightly on the arm.

'Don't worry, she'll be okay,' she whispered, but Diana's eyes were filling with tears.

Martin announced that he was going to take Chloe to the hospital in Ibiza Town, while the waiters desperately tried to remove what remained of lunch off the floor. Diana meekly followed them to Martin's four-by-four, where Chloe was helped into the back seat by her fussing mother and driven away. Diana stood there help-lessly, watching them leave. As the car swung off the drive, Chloe turned and gave her a smug little smile.

Summer was on such a high, she thought she was about to burst with happiness. She was in love with a billionaire and now she was going to be a movie star! When she had received a phone call from Luc Balzac the day before, offering her the part of Marien in *Krakatoa*, she had assumed someone was playing a practical joke. Luc assured her he could not be more serious. She was one of the last principal parts to be cast, and rehearsals were due to start in six weeks; then there were four weeks of filming at Pinewood studios, followed by another eight weeks on location in Mexico.

'Don't let me down,' he had purred in a sultry voice as rich and soft as warm brandy.

'I won't,' breathed Summer, 'I promise I won't.'

'Well, I hope you're still going to talk to me after you've won your Oscar, Miss Movie-star,' smiled Adam, rolling over in the emperor-sized hotel bed to look at Summer, her hair splayed out on the pillow, her naked body covered in just the slightest sheen of sweat.

Summer beamed, but shrugged modestly. 'It's only one role,' she said, 'let's not get too excited just yet. But I can't believe filming starts so soon. Two months in Mexico as well. Think of the tan.'

'Mexico?' said Adam, surprised.

Summer smiled. 'I know, I know. Krakatoa is in Indonesia. But apparently Mexico always gets used as a location when the studios want somewhere hot and steamy.'

'I didn't mean that,' said Adam, stroking his finger across her forehead. 'I don't want you to leave me for two months.'

Summer's heart leapt; the man she loved wanted to be with her all the time. But her happiness disintegrated moments later as Adam glanced at his watch. Then again, what did she expect? When she had called Adam to tell him the news about *Krakatoa*, he had suggested meeting the following afternoon in a discreet boutique hotel in Knightsbridge: that was their relationship. Illicit, forbidden. She would spend days waiting for him to call, and would drop everything to go and be with him when he did. That was the price, she told herself, of being in a relationship with a busy billionaire – a busy billionaire who was in a relationship with someone else. But Summer couldn't stop herself. Two hours in his company, being on the receiving end of his full attention and charm, was like a delicious drug that made her feel more beautiful and sexy than she would have ever dared thought possible.

'Have you got to go?' she said softly, reaching out to stroke his face.

He nodded. 'I've got to be at the airport at three p.m. or we'll miss the slot for Ibiza.'

'So you're away this weekend?' she asked. He never told her his plans and she rarely asked.

'I have to,' he said, 'it's her birthday.'

Her. Karin.

'You stay at the hotel as long as you want,' he said, climbing out of bed and reaching for his clothes. 'All weekend if you'd like. There's a little spa. Get them to send me the bill. '

She nodded slowly and he saw the look of hurt on her face. 'Look. I've got you something,' he said, reaching into his overnight case and pulling out a delicate chain. He reached over and fastened it around her neck. It was an antique diamond pendant in the shape of a teardrop. 'To say congratulations.'

Summer felt emotion choke her throat as she ran to the mirror to admire the chain. 'I love it,' she said. But she would have swapped it gladly for one more night together.

The sound of Adam's bag thumping onto the limestone floor woke Karin up from an early evening siesta. She had been wearing just a tiny pair of bikini bottoms while she snoozed on the cool white linens, and she wrapped a towel around her body as she climbed off the bed; she didn't want the housekeeper blundering in. Karin peeked around the bedroom door and grinned.

'Adam!' she cried, 'you made it.'

Adam walked towards her and pulled the towel away, dropping it to the floor. 'Of course I made it, birthday girl,' he murmured, planting a warm kiss on the side of her neck. 'Just look what I'm missing.'

She squealed as he picked her up and carried her back into the bedroom; they fell together back onto the bed, Karin wrapping her long legs around his body like snakes.

'Has the party started?' she giggled, as his lips trailed down her neck to her erect nipple.

'It has now,' he said, and pulled his polo shirt over his head.

After they had made love, Karin and Adam took a shower together. The bathroom window was slightly open to let out the clouds of steam, and already Karin could hear the sounds of laughter and clinking glasses coming from outside. They didn't hurry.

By the time Adam and Karin finally stepped outside, there were at least fifty people on the terrace. Word had got around about Diana's soiree at La Toreador, and everybody who was anybody wanted to come: the beautiful people, the club hags, the Euro-trash. Some planned to stay all night, eating, drinking and dancing; others would use it as a warm-up for the nightclubs, which didn't really get going until 2 a.m.

Karin and Adam picked up cocktails from the bar by the swimming pool. On the other side of the water, Karin could see Christina dressed in white palazzo pants and a matching bandeau bikini top. She looked fabulous. She was openly flirting with a small, rotund man with a moustache. Wearing a crumpled linen jacket, shorts and flip-flops, the object of Christina's breathless attention looked rather shabby and dull.

'Is that who I think it is?' asked Adam with a half-smile.

'Let's go and find out,' she said, taking his hand to walk around the pool to where her friend was standing. Christina spotted Karin and squealed with delight, greeting her with an embrace as if she hadn't seen Karin for years.

'Darling, I must introduce you to my new friend, Reggie Bryce. Reggie, these are my *bestest* friends in the whole world, Karin and Adam.'

Adam extended a cautious hand towards the man.

'We've met, right?' asked Reggie in his Texan drawl as they shook.

Adam nodded. The billionaire community was a small one. Reggie Bryce was a Midwestern supermarket magnate who was fast catching up to the hugely wealthy Walton family, the owners of Wal-Mart. The name wasn't lost on Karin either. Recently divorced, Reggie's wife had won one of the biggest-ever settlements the world had seen. But Reggie could afford to lose a billion dollars here and there. He had plenty. And Christina clearly had designs on a few of them.

'We met on Es Calo Beach this afternoon,' gushed Christina, 'and I insisted he come and join us tonight. Reggie was five berths down from the *Big Blue* at St Barts at New Year. Isn't it crazy how small a world it is?'

'Es Calo? Isn't that the nudist beach?' said Karin, looking at Reggie's bowling-ball physique and suppressing a smile.

'It's very liberating, Karin,' scolded Christina. 'Reggie agrees, don't you, honey?'

Reggie wasn't listening. Instead he was looking at Christina as if she was a mouthwatering delicacy.

'My yacht the *Crusader* is in Ibiza Town,' he said to Karin and Adam, not taking his eyes off Christina. 'I'd love you to come for lunch if you're not busy.'

Karin nodded. 'Well, it's my birthday tomorrow, so I hope you have cake.'

As the night wore on, the music was edged up louder and louder. As the moon sprayed glitter onto the swimming pool, a lithe tanned man with Vilebrequin trunks around his ankles was standing by the deep end spurting Cristal into the water like a Formula One driver while, in the shallow end, two Swedish models were kissing. All around them the scent of sex and drugs drifted like clouds.

'Shall we go and circulate?' asked Christina, linking her arm through Karin's. Reggie patted Christina's bottom as they left and he returned to discussing economic sanctions in the Sudan with Adam.

'What do you think?' she giggled to Karin as they walked away.

'I think he likes you,' smiled Karin.

'I made a vow to myself after the Ariel tragedy that, next time, I would date up. I owe it to myself after everything that happened,' she said with a slight waver to her voice. 'Between you and me, Reggie's asked me to stay on with him after the weekend. He's spending the next two weeks touring the Med. Do you think it's too soon?'

'But you hardly know him,' said Karin, slightly shocked.

'We've got so many friends in common it's not funny.'

'I think you've made up your mind,' smiled Karin playfully.

'Mmm . . . maybe,' said Christina with a smirk. 'Anyway, I'm simply exhausted after all that small talk. Do you fancy a naughty pick-me-up?'

Karin tried to not look disapproving. When it came to drugs, her circle of friends split between the dos and the do nots. If you did them, it was with a vengeance; it was not unknown for entire City bonuses to be blown in one summer on coke and opiates. If you abstained, it was usually because you were a member of Narcotics Anonymous. For Karin, taking drugs had no moral overtones, it was simply an issue of control. She'd smoked the odd joint at boarding school but had hated the way it made her feel – woozy and nauseous and not quite tuned-in – so she had mostly avoided the various drugs that had come in and out of fashion on the social scene over the years.

Christina tapped her on the waist. 'Stop being such a puritan, Kay. We need to celebrate the start of my beautiful new relationship.' They made their way to Christina's bedroom and Karin sat back on the bed while her friend rifled through a cream vanity case. She looked up. 'Shit. I'm all out. Will Adam have any?'

Karin shrugged. He was a very light user and sometimes kept a wrap in his wallet. She wasn't sure he'd take kindly to her going through his belongings but, ever since she'd found the mysterious matchbook in Capri, she was always looking for a reason to have a snoop.

Their bedroom was just next door and she went through. She could see Adam's Brioni linen jacket slung across the back of a high-backed leather chair and, picking it up, she slid her hand into the inside pocket, her fingers brushing against a bunch of keys, and a money clip holding together a sheaf of notes. She pulled out a butter-soft leather wallet and opened it. Ignoring the platinum and black credit cards, she slipped a finger into the silk lining and pulled out a piece of neatly folded paper.

'Tina. I've got . . .' her words trailed off as she realized it wasn't a wrap of cocaine but a folded receipt. Her heart leapt as she saw it was from a jeweller on Bond Street: a 'gold and diamond teardrop pendant' costing £1500. *Fifteen hundred.* Her elation was immediately replaced by a twinge of disappointment.

'So. Has he got any?' asked Christina, appearing in the doorframe.

'No,' replied Karin quickly. 'I'm going to find Adam.'

Karin was standing by the swimming pool, a glistening electric blue against the black of the night, staring into the darkness.

She was sipping a mojito slowly, alone with her thoughts, when Adam crept up behind her and pulled her close.

'Unless I'm very much mistaken,' he said, showing her his watch, 'it's gone midnight and that means one thing . . .'

'It means I'm twenty-nine again,' smiled Karin, resting her head on his shoulder.

Adam nodded and took her hand, leading her inside, the laughter of the crowd growing faint behind them. 'I might have been late today,' smiled Adam, 'but at least I come bearing gifts. I take it you can't wait another minute for your present?'

Karin tried to look enthusiastic. 'Patience has never been one of my virtues.'

'Well then, step this way for the show and tell . . .'

He pulled her into their bedroom and Karin slipped off her sandals and arranged herself elegantly on the bed, letting the ceiling fan woosh a stream of cool air across her body.

Adam rummaged in his black suitcase, then walked back to Karin with his hands behind his back. 'Close your eyes and hold out your hands,' he teased.

Karin sat up and did as she was told. 'Happy birthday, honey,' whispered Adam, placing a warm kiss on her lips and a package in her upturned palms.

Karin opened her eyes to see a long claret box tied up with a gold ribbon. She tore off the ribbon and flipped up the lid, which opened with a satisfying click.

Lying on a bed of black velvet was a string of clear and prim-rose-coloured tear-shaped stones, sparkling in the lamplight. She gasped, her hand flying to her mouth. It was exquisite. Adam took the bracelet and fumbled to fasten it around Karin's wrist.

'Diamonds and canary diamonds,' he said, grinning. 'Do you like?'

Karin was staring at the delicate string around her wrist with a bemused expression. 'I like a lot . . .'

'But . . . ?' asked Adam noticing the quaver in her voice.

'But this didn't cost fifteen hundred pounds . . .' There was a trace of laughter in her voice.

'I don't follow.' Adam sank on the bed and looked up at her.

Karin cursed herself for the slip, realizing she'd have to confess for looking in his wallet.

'It's nothing.'

'No, tell me,' pressed Adam.

'Well, I found a receipt in your wallet and I thought . . .'

Karin saw it immediately – just a flicker of something in Adam's expression that sent a cold shiver down her spine. When she had first found the receipt, her reaction had been one of disappoint-ment, anger even. Their relationship seemed to be going well – very well in fact – and Adam had a lot of money. Had she misjudged the situation so terribly. Did he really think so little of her? But now the penny dropped. The necklace wasn't for her. It was for somebody else.

'Who is it for?' she said softly, unconsciously fingering the bracelet.

'Who is what for?'

'The necklace, the receipt in your wallet.'

Adam stood up, suddenly angry. 'What were you doing in my fucking wallet?' he snapped.

Karin was not to be deflected. 'Answer the question, Adam,' she said calmly. 'Who is it for?'

'It's for Erin,' he said coolly. 'It's her birthday, so I thought I'd get her a little trinket.'

'Erin's birthday? Really,' said Karin sarcastically. 'You forget she used to be my assistant. Her birthday isn't in August at all.'

Karin didn't have a clue when Erin's birthday was, but she knew she had to bluff him.

They locked stares and she saw him take a small, sharp intake of breath. She knew Adam Gold, the businessman, the ruthless negotiator, had been caught out.

'Adam, tell me the truth.'

Her voice was high pitched and shrill and she could feel her heart beating faster. She caught herself feeling fearful and inse-cure and hated herself for it. The last six months with Adam had gnawed away at her confidence so much that she was beginning not to recognize herself. She glared at him, baiting him to lie further.

'It's Claudia Falcon, isn't it?' she said calmly.

Adam had walked away from her and stood at the window, staring out into the blackness. In the distance they could hear the low hum of laughter from the party.

'It's not Claudia,' he said softly.

'Then why have you been spending so much time with her?'

'Business!' shouted Adam.

'Yeah, right,' said Karin sarcastically.

'Look. We are putting together a financial deal – a takeover bid for the Astley Retail chain. We have to do it by stealth.'

'Oh yes, stealth being the right word, when you're fucking the banker.'

'I'm not fucking Claudia,' he said, twisting round to face her.

'Adam, I'm not stupid. I've seen the way you are together, I can see—'

'Claudia is gay,' he said with finality.

Karin stopped in her tracks, stunned. Gay? That was a turn-up for the books. She felt her anger reboil as she realized he'd distracted her from the big issue. The necklace and who it was for. She knew she had let herself slip, her anger betraying her vulnerability and insecurity. But she'd come too far now to pretend it didn't matter.

'Adam,' she said softly, walking up behind him, 'the best birthday present you can give me is the truth.'

She could see their faces reflected in the glass, both sad and uncertain.

'Karin . . .' he began, then he stopped and took a deep breath.

'There is someone,' he said finally. 'The necklace was for someone else.'

'Can I ask who?' Karin's voice was little more than a cracked whisper.

He turned to face her and for a moment Karin expected the worst, but he gently picked up her hand and placed it in his. She wanted to snap it away but she felt drained of strength.

'The necklace was for someone who doesn't matter half as much as you matter to me,' he said, stroking her fingers with the curve of his thumb. 'Someone who doesn't even come close.'

She snatched her hand away from his and stepped back. 'How dare you?' she spat. 'How dare you treat me with so little respect. You're lucky to have me. You know that, don't you?' she said defiantly.

Adam reached forward and touched her arm. 'Kay. I'm sorry. I'm so sorry. It was a mistake. I was weak. I was foolish. Give me the chance to make it up to you.'

She took hold of his arm and threw it away from her. 'There's no second chances, Adam. I'm not like all the other women you've taken advantage of.'

He picked up her hand again and began unfastening the bracelet from around her wrist. She felt a rush of warm tears sting at the back of her eyes, wondering if she had pushed him too far. He was taking it all away from her. *Everything*.

'So this is it?' she said softly, biting her lip to stop her voice from cracking.

'Sssh,' he said softly, lifting her fingers to his mouth and kissing their tips.

Karin just stared at him, the tears flowing down her face now. 'What . . . what are you doing?' she croaked.

'I want to make it up to you,' he said quietly.

He held her left hand in his and began to wrap the bracelet around her third finger. Karin felt her heart skip a beat as the cold diamonds pressed against her skin.

'I'm afraid I'm going to have to improvise,' he whispered as he held the glittering bracelet in place and sank to one knee.

'Karin, will you marry me?'

Karin looked down at him, his eyes so blue in the lamplight, her third finger obscured by diamonds, and began to laugh softly. Then she nodded. Adam pulled her down to him and pressed her hand against his face.

'Baby, I want you. I love you. I need you,' he said, kissing each finger in turn.

Karin laid her head against his. 'The feeling's mutual,' she murmured, before words were lost in the swell of a passionate kiss.

58

'What do you mean, they're *engaged*?' Molly spluttered to Marcus, trying very hard to conceal her emotions after he had told her the news. 'They've only been going out two minutes! I have bottles of shampoo on the go longer than their relationship.'

'Well, she's done something right, because I never thought I'd see the day when Adam headed down the aisle,' smiled Marcus. 'They're having a party to celebrate as soon as Karin can organize something suitably grand. Probably at Adam's palazzo on Lake Como.'

That final detail made it even more painful for Molly. She didn't even know he owned a villa in the Italian Lakes. She had been to the Versaces' villa on Como and had often pictured herself in the role of a beautiful contessa. It was really all too terrible, especially when he had seemed to be getting along with Summer so well. She took a long drag of her Sobranie cigarette and began to think.

Engaged. Summer had almost choked on the word when she repeated it back to Adam. Moments earlier she had been feeling so happy. Adam had driven her out to the Fat Duck restaurant in the tiny Berkshire village of Bray, one of the few three-Michelin-starred restaurants in the country. She had been thrilled that Adam had wanted to see her the moment he'd arrived back from Ibiza, and was looking forward to a perfect night together. Instead, just as the starter had arrived, he'd said those three little words: *'I'm getting married'*.

'Why did you bring me somewhere so special to tell me you were engaged?' said Summer, aware of a large tear trembling on her eye-lid.

Adam folded his napkin on his lap and looked around in case anybody was eavesdropping. 'Honey, it's only just happened,' he whispered. 'I wanted to tell you as soon as possible and I was going to bring you here anyway.'

'Don't make it sound like you're doing me a favour, you insensitive bastard,' hissed Summer.

He leant over the table to stroke her cheek and she jerked away from him as if she'd been stung.

'You've always known about Karin,' said Adam. 'This doesn't have to change anything.'

'Of course it changes things. You're getting married.'

'Don't get all fucking sanctimonious, Summer,' said Adam sharply. 'I've been in a serious relationship the entire time we've been seeing each other. You're not exactly in the best place to be taking the moral high-ground.'

'But you've just made a commitment to her. That's what changes things.'

Aware that a waiter was looking at them, Adam leant forward. 'What hasn't changed is the way I feel about you. I care about you.'

'So much so that you're marrying Karin,' said Summer, taking a glug of Chablis.

'Summer. Karin knows I've been seeing someone.'

Summer thumped her glass down on the table. 'Oh I see,' she said sarcastically, 'so you proposed as a way of saying sorry?'

They looked at each other, neither one knowing what to say.

Summer looked down as a tear landed on the white tablecloth. 'I want to go home,' she whispered.

'Don't be silly,' said Adam. 'We've only just got here.'

'I feel sick.'

'Summer, stop being dramatic.'

Shaking her head, she pushed her chair back with a screech, ran to the toilets and threw up violently.

59

Early September was Erin's favourite time in Port Merryn. Although it was still warm and sunny, the tourists had begun to clear so the streets and harbour had reclaimed their still charm. Knowing her Audi wouldn't fit through the tiny village streets, she parked it at the top of town and walked down the winding lanes, taking it all in. Seagulls squawked, the air smelt clean and salty and there was space to breathe. Only a year ago it had been this very quietness that had driven Erin half mad, but now it was a welcome relief to stroll in the sun and relax. Things had been getting a little too stressful in London in recent weeks, and the fresh air seemed to unjumble all the knotted thoughts in her head.

She'd greeted the news of Adam's engagement with mixed emotions. She tried to tell herself that, if he was genuinely happy with Karin, then she was happy for him, but the little stab of disappointment she'd felt when Adam had told her still refused to go away. She was also saddened at the deterioration of her relationship with Chris. After their argument at Cliveden, the only contact she had had with him had been a few awkward hellos in the corridor of Peony House. The last two times she had seen him with a pretty redhead, but he hadn't even bothered to introduce Erin to her, which had irritated Erin inordinately.

She shook her head, trying to forget about London, and walked down the steep cobbled path into the village. She had to admit she felt a little nervous being home and she couldn't quite place why. After all, this was Jilly's seventieth birthday – that was supposed to be great fun, wasn't it? Everyone was coming, Jilly had assured her over the telephone: friends from the village; even Erin's only

352

other living relatives – her aunt Louisa, who now lived in Australia, was making the trip over specially.

Erin realized that a lot of her uneasiness was down to guilt. She wished she had thought of throwing her grandmother a party herself, but she had been so busy with Adam's summer schedule and now the wedding plans. It was no excuse, of course, and she was determined to make it up to her. She had gone to Gray's Antique Market and bought her a beautiful gold brooch encrusted with topaz and pearls. It had cost her a week's salary, but she hoped her grandmother would love it as much as she did.

The back door of the house was open, so the background noise of the party, Sinatra and the low hum of happy conversation was pierced by the loud caw of seagulls.

Erin stood in the doorway and looked on at the scene: Jilly surrounded by a throng of well-wishers, a large glass of red wine in one hand and a plump iced cupcake in another. She had dressed up in a red and cream floral dress, open-toed sandals over tan tights, her grey hair fastened on top of her head with a big tortoise-shell clip.

It was good to see her grandmother so happy. To think Erin had nearly not moved to London because she thought that Jilly couldn't cope without her. Well, she was glad to be proved wrong. The other thing that Erin noticed was that the house seemed tidier. No piles of glossy magazines on the kitchen table, no trainers strewn across the floor, no laptop on her desk. No sign of her having lived here at all, thought Erin, feeling a little cross.

'It's Erin,' shouted Jilly in a merry voice over the music and hubbub.

A dozen smiling faces turned to look at her. She could see Janet with her swollen pregnant belly, Eric MacIntosh, the landlord from the local pub; almost every one of the party guests knew her and shared a history, in some cases a whole life. She felt welcome. She felt at home. She took a sip of white wine from her glass and helped herself to a sausage roll, grinning. She'd been so used to being served Krug and exotic canapés at parties, something as plain as a sausage roll was a treat.

'What are you doing hiding all the way back here?' said a strange voice. Erin turned to see her aunt Louisa, her arms open wide. 'I'm the one who doesn't know anyone,' said Louisa after giving her a squeeze. 'Come and mingle with me.'

Erin smiled warmly. Louisa was a dead-ringer for Jilly, only about twenty-five years younger. It had been three years since her last visit from Perth and she had aged a little. Her strawberry-blonde hair had streaks of grey at the temples, and her skin was more lined and bronzed from the West Australian sun where she had lived for the last twenty years. But Erin noticed that their eyes were the same: deep green and framed with long lashes. The same eyes that Erin had looked into as a child; her mother's eyes. She looked at her aunt and wondered if this is how her mother would look if she was still alive.

'So, what have you been doing?' asked Louisa, looping her arm through Erin's. 'It's been ages, tell me everything.'

'Just taking some time out,' smiled Erin. 'I drove up this morning so I'm pretty knackered. Still, I didn't have as far to come as you, did I?' Louisa laughed and grabbed a bottle of Chianti from the dining-room table.

'I suppose. The jet lag hasn't hit me yet, so expect to see me in a pile on the floor a little later.'

She grabbed Erin's glass and filled it to the brim. 'Speaking of motoring down from London, Jilly tells me you have a fancy new car and some high-flying job. I want to hear all about it.'

Erin felt a little embarrassed thinking of her blue Audi. She had also been careful to tone down her appearance today. Gone were her standard office attire of Jimmy Choo heels and the Gucci suits; instead she wore a pair of jeans, a pretty pale blue Gap top and some gold ballet flats. The last thing she wanted was for people to think she had 'gone all London'.

'It's really nothing fancy,' shrugged Erin, 'I'm only a personal assistant. It pays quite well but I have to work every hour God sends.'

'"Only a personal assistant"?' mimicked Louisa. 'Only to some billionaire. Apparently you've been swanning off around the world in private jets and helicopters.'

Erin laughed at the suggestion. 'It's not as glamorous as you may think. I'm the one cleaning up the champagne bottles at the end of those jet-set parties, not enjoying myself.'

'So, what happened to your book?' asked Louisa, remembering the pages of chatty letters she used to get from her niece talking of her dream to write the great British novel.

Erin shrugged uncomfortably and tried not to meet her aunt's gaze. 'I have an agent,' she replied, trying to sound breezy.

'That's brilliant. So you must have written something?'

'Well . . . I did,' said Erin slowly. 'But I've had to start again. I'm much more excited about what I've written this time.'

At least that much was true. After Cliveden, Erin had begun work on her novella on a fictitious London beau monde, exactly as Chris had suggested. She wasn't sure if she was writing out of enthusiasm for her subject matter, or to show Chris that she didn't need his help but, whatever the reason, she had managed to craft over 15,000 words in three weeks – and it was pretty good, she thought. All she needed was to polish it a little and she felt ready to give it to Ed Davies.

Her aunt smiled. 'Well I shall be the first one in the queue to buy a copy. But, in the meantime, I think it's time we found the birthday girl and have a family toast.'

She waved at Jilly, who was opening another present in the middle of the room. She turned to an elderly ruddy-faced man in a yellow jumper and kissed him on the cheek before she came over to join Louisa and Erin.

'I need some fresh air,' said Jilly, taking Erin by the hand and leading the two women outside to stand in the sun. The village sparkled in front of them, the sun bouncing off the whitewashed walls of the cottages, the grape-green sea rippling in the harbour.

'So who was that man?' asked Erin, raising an eyebrow.

'Which one?' asked Jilly playfully.

'The man you just kissed on the cheek,' said Erin.

'I was just saying thank you for my present. Just being polite.'

Louisa and Erin didn't miss a slight blush on Jilly's cheeks.

'It's Jim Latimer. Erin, you don't know him,' said Jilly quickly, pre-empting her granddaughter's next question.

'He moved into Port Gaverne about six months ago. Retired, widower. I met him at the choral society . . .'

There was an excited hesitancy in her grandmother's voice that made her wonder if Jilly and Jim did more than sing together. Maybe her grandmother had moved on more than she thought.

'Oh, I've been meaning to ask you,' said Jilly. 'Jim's taking a trip to London next Saturday. He has a grandson in London too. I thought perhaps . . .'

'Oh, I'm away next weekend,' said Erin, feeling a wash of guilt. 'What about the weekend after? I'd love to make a fuss of you.'

'Not to worry, lovie,' said Jilly, trying not to look disappointed. 'Where are you off to this time?'

'Lake Como.' She tried to say it casually but didn't miss Louisa's raised eyebrows.

'My boss, Adam, is getting married to my former boss Karin. They're having some glamorous engagement party in Adam's villa in Italy.'

'Is that the boss you like and the former boss that's a bit of an old cow?' said Jilly, her intelligent eyes twinkling. Jilly might be seventy, but she didn't miss a trick.

'Something like that,' said Erin. 'Actually, I can't wait. I will no doubt be made to work like a dog – they've been trying to arrange this huge bash for a hundred and fifty people in less than three weeks – but the palazzo is supposed to be gorgeous.'

'Gosh,' said Louisa, loving all the jet-set tittle-tattle. 'If the engagement party is being held in an Italian villa, where will the wedding be?'

'I've no idea,' said Erin. 'I heard Adam talking about having it in Nassau or a private island in Greece which could be lovely. It will be super-glamorous, wherever it's held, although one thing is making me laugh already.'

'What?' asked Louisa, seeing a mischievous grin on her niece's face.

'The thought of their vows. I found out the other day that Karin's real name isn't "Karin Cavendish", it's plain old "Karen Wenkle" – at least that's what it says in her passport. All her flights are booked under the name of "Wenkle". That's not going to sound quite as glamorous when the priest reads out the vows, is it?'

Jilly's face went pale, her eyes suddenly clouding over with displeasure. 'Karin Cavendish is Karen Wenkle?' she repeated.

'Well, yes,' said Erin, her smile fading. 'What's wrong?'

Jilly and Louisa shot each other a look.

'How old is Karin?' asked Louisa, taking a nervous gulp of wine.

'Thirty-two. It was her birthday the day after they got engaged.'

Jilly was nodding, as if calculating dates. Again Erin caught a glance between the two older women, a look loaded with apprehension.

'Gran, what's wrong? Louisa?' She looked at her aunt who was staring at the ground. 'Louisa, tell me!'

Jim Latimer walked out into the garden. He had a purposeful stride and smiling eyes. He was holding a glass of champagne. 'You'd better start drinking this, Jilly, or it'll lose its fizz.'

He glanced first at Jilly and then at Erin, as if hoping for an introduction. Jilly looked at Jim and shook her head in a tiny movement. Jim took the cue. 'It'll keep,' he said, and moved back indoors.

'Gran, tell me,' urged Erin.

Jilly drew a breath, as if she was about to speak, and then held it for a moment, letting her glance drift up the hillside behind the house. She fixed her gaze on the line where the hill met the sky and the silhouetted shape of a herd of cows. Then she sighed deeply.

'What's this all about?' said Erin, exasperated. She had a thumping sense of foreboding, but couldn't possibly fathom how Karin had been the catalyst for this conversation.

'Your father's death, his suicide . . .' said Jilly quietly. 'As you know, it was because of financial problems.'

Erin nodded. She had been told about how and why he died when she was fourteen. Back then she had been angry, frustrated, cheated; unable to compute how something as trivial as money could drive someone to abandon his family, to end his life.

'Your father did a lot of business with a London jeans wholesaler,' continued Jilly. 'Your dad's firm made jeans for lots of different companies, but as orders increased from this one particular company, the MD of that the company – WD Fashion – insisted that your father stop supplying to other clients or lose his business.'

'So what happened?' asked Erin.

'Your dad did what was asked but, after twelve months, WD Fashion transferred all their business to somewhere in the Far East; basically left your dad's business high and dry. Didn't pay your father anything they owed him, either: you know the trick – they filed for bankruptcy and then started trading under another name two minutes later.'

'But what's this got to do with Karin?' asked Erin, frowning.

Jilly paused. 'WD Fashion was owned by Terence Wenkle. A real East End shark, possible criminal connections. When your dad tried to get his money back, he was threatened and intimidated. Your father's business was ruined, but Wenkle's went through the roof. Within the year he was living in some fancy house in Surrey, his daughter sent to boarding school – your typical nouveau-riche lifestyle. Your father couldn't stand it. That was the life *he* wanted for his family. While Terence Wenkle was living the good life, the bank foreclosed on your home. You were only four at the time, so you all came to live with me. Erin, it was awful. Your dad was such a strong, confident man, but the whole business had sapped every ounce of self-worth from him.'

Erin looked out beyond the village where the sun was fading, smudging apricot behind the high hills.

'And Karin is Terence's daughter?' asked Erin.

'It appears that way,' said Jilly grimly. 'Karen was about seven years older than you. I've seen pictures of Karen – sorry, *Karin* – in the *Daily Mail* but I hadn't made the connection without the surname.'

'It seems an awful coincidence that you ended up working for her,' added Louisa.

'Coincidence?' asked Erin, feeling a knot of dread in her stomach. 'I know Karin Cavendish, and nothing is ever a coincidence with that woman.'

60

For the one hundred and fifty guests going to Adam and Karin's engagement party, it was a long and weary journey. The early start to get to Heathrow, the two-hour flight to Milan's Linate Airport on the specially chartered 737, the ninety-minute drive to the shores of Lake Como in a fleet of Mercedes and then, finally, the short trip by motor cruiser to the palazzo itself. But there was not one person who did not agree that it was worth the wait as the launch finally docked at the jetty. Adam Gold's palazzo was magnificent: a sumptuous wedding cake of a building transported to a magical timeless setting by the glistening waters. It had Doric pillars, painted ceilings and long windows that looked out onto gardens bursting with flowers of saffron, scarlet and blue, tumbling down towards the cyan-blue waters of the lake. Adam had bought the property lock, stock and barrel from an impoverished comte, and with it came a catalogue of superb art and marble statues, some by Canova and Bellini. No one could fail to be impressed.

Karin threw her vanity case on the canopied bed in the master bedroom and flopped down next to it. It had just gone noon and a glorious September afternoon stretched out in front of her. The sun was streaming in through the windows and dappling the marble floor with spots of light. It couldn't be more perfect. Their engagement party was the hottest, most exclusive ticket anywhere on the social circuit from Miami to Monaco. Any social triumph or professional success she had had up to this point was just a starter for the main course. Today, Karin Cavendish had arrived. She was now up there with the Lynn Wyatts, the Lily Safras, the queen of a new generation of super-wealthy society wives: glamorous, powerful women who enhanced their husband's success and ruled with charm, style and mega-wealth.

Adam came over and sat on the bed, stroking her hair. 'I don't know about you but I'm tired already,' he said with a slow smile. 'I could do with me and you crawling into this bed right now, and not being disturbed until Monday.'

'Well, sorry to break it to you but we have a hundred and fifty people about to descend on the pool for cocktails and we have got to be charming and chatty to every single one of them.'

Adam sighed. 'Whose idea was it to have a party anyway?'

'Don't look at me,' said Karin. 'The whole world has been waiting for Adam Gold to get married. You know you didn't want to go quietly.'

Karin had a shower and changed into a bikini and a long sheer black kaftan shot through with gold thread. She had skin that tanned within minutes, so there was no need for make-up, except a little liquid blush and a slick of gloss across her lips. Throwing open the French windows that led into the grounds she could see that waiters in white tails were already putting out champagne flutes onto long tables covered in starched ivory tablecloths. Around thirty-five guests were staying at the palazzo; the rest were staying at the big five-star hotels around the lake: the Villa d'Este and Villa Serbelloni. A fleet of motor cruisers were due to bring them over any time now: it was 1 p.m. She held up a hand to shield her eyes and squinted at the lake, a slab of shimmering silver in front of her. She frowned. Nobody was allowed to be late to her engagement party. No one.

Erin had never seen anything like it. Not in the movies, magazines or coffee-table books. She didn't know that she was in the smallest room at Palazzo Verdi, an attic garret once used for the servants, but she wouldn't have cared. To have any room in this hotel was, to Erin, like having her own little pocket of heaven. Feeling like a Greek goddess, she stopped unpacking her suitcase and pushed open a small window to let a gust of warm, sweet-smelling air rush onto her face.

She was determined to enjoy herself this weekend, she thought, gazing at the lake with its steep cliffs and cream and terracotta villages. How could she not? She was in a picture-postcard movie set, she was off-duty – Adam had insisted this weekend would be all play and no work for his hard-working executive assistant: it should have been the most perfect weekend of her life. Perfect except for two words: Karin Cavendish. Despite her own feelings for Adam, she had accepted his engagement with a detached resignation. After all, who was she kidding? Adam was never going to want anybody like her and, while Erin knew from experience that Karin could be hard, demanding and sometimes insufferable, she was still cut from the same cloth as Adam: successful and glamorous.

But now Erin felt cheated. Karin was a fraud. She wasn't that much different to Erin – she had just spun her own story better, bluffed her way into a world far beyond her beginnings. She thought back to Jilly's revelations at the party and grimaced. One event had elevated Karin's life into the vaulted glittering theatre it had become, and sent Erin's tumbling to the ground. Surely it wasn't a coincidence that she had ended up working for Karin – it was a plan. A plan to suck Erin into a more glamorous world, to give her a taste of what should rightly be hers, but because her role was servant and not master, she could only taste it and fully enjoy it. Karin might have taken Adam, but she had taken something much worse from her. She had taken her life, and now she was dangling it back in front of her like forbidden fruit. A jumble of questions rushed through Erin's mind. How could she? Why would she? And how was she going to get even?

Well, this is more like it, thought Molly, stepping out onto her own private terrace in a tiny scarlet bikini. She scooped her hair up into a ponytail and surveyed the villa, deciding that, with the exception of the room that had the huge balcony next to them – presumably Adam's – she was definitely in the best bedroom in the house.

'Why does Adam not come out to this place more?' asked Molly, as Marcus walked out to join her in a pair of cream linen shorts and a plum polo shirt. 'We could have spent all summer here if he hadn't been hiding it away.'

'He's only had it about twelve months,' said Marcus, handing her a chilled cocktail. 'Maybe next year.'

'Why can't we have a place like this?' she pouted. 'Everyone I know has a summer place. I think it's time we started seriously keeping up. I don't mind starting to look; I can visit some estate agents when I go to Milan for the shows.'

Marcus shifted uncomfortably and moved over to the rail. 'Oh look, I think the boat has come from the Villa d'Este. Shall we have a wander downstairs and meet them?'

Molly walked over and put a hand on his shoulder. 'You know how you hate being the first at a party,' she murmured in his ear. 'Let's go back into the bedroom and think of some way to waste a bit of time.'

Marcus smiled and took her hand. She hoped he wasn't going to be tiresome over the issue of overseas property. A woman like her needed a villa or two. *But then again,* she thought, *I can be very persuasive.*

The grounds of the palazzo were so enormous that it had been easy for Summer to find a secluded spot away from the braying guests where she could think. Staying at the villa also brought with it the very real possibility of being confronted by the happy couple, Karin and Adam. *So why have you come?* Summer asked herself for the thousandth time. She felt physically sick just being here, but when Karin had phoned her personally to invite her, insisting she would not take no for answer, Summer could not think of a believable excuse. Molly had also been insistent, convinced that her daughter could still convert her relationship with Adam into something more substantial. 'Look, darling, fucking Adam is one thing,' she had said, 'but this could be your last real chance to stand side by side with Karin and show him that he is with the wrong woman.'

Worst of all, Adam had insisted she come, particularly when he'd found out that she had a modelling job in Milan on the Monday after the party.

'It will look odd if you're not there,' Adam had told her in bed a week before the Como party, when Summer was once again feeling hesitant and guilty about attending. 'You're the face of Karenza swimwear. Don't make her suspicious. You know what she's like.'

Summer had desperately wanted to finish their affair after he'd told her about his engagement, but when he had appeared at her flat, several days after their dinner at the Fat Duck, Summer had found it impossible to resist him. Life without Adam had felt so wretched, empty and pointless that she came to the swift conclusion that she was prepared to accept their relationship on whatever terms it now came.

But it didn't make her feel good. Summer sat down on a bench she had found between two long cypress trees and pulled her feet up so her knees tucked under her chin. She picked a fuchsia-coloured flower and began to tear the petals off slowly, letting them twirl to the ground one by one. Molly was right. This was probably the last real chance of reclaiming Adam from his fiancée before the wedding plans went so far it would get too messy and embarrassing to stop them. And what her mum didn't know was that she had a much bigger reason to make it happen. Her period was two weeks late. A home pregnancy test had confirmed that she was pregnant.

By eight o'clock the sun was setting, spilling russet-gold light across the lake, the cypress trees surrounding the grounds silhouetted black like sentry guards. Erin had gone out to wander through the gardens, cool and sweet-smelling in the dimming light. As she had walked across the terrace, Erin had spotted Karin sitting alone on a wall by the swimming pool, smoking a cigarette. She knew this was her opportunity. She took a deep breath to compose herself and went down to sit beside her, the stone cold under the thin fabric of her dress.

'I didn't know you smoked,' said Erin, wondering if she was coming across as strange, forced. She certainly felt it.

Karin shrugged and threw the cigarette stub on the floor. There was a gentle hiss as it fell in a splash of water from the swimming pool.

'Haven't smoked in ten years, but sometimes needs must,' she smiled. 'It's been a big day.'

Erin glanced up at her ex-boss, her face illuminated by the light shining from the palazzo. There was a slight lift to her brow, a subtle flare of her nostril; it was the arrogant yet slightly surprised look of someone who knew they could get whatever they wanted but still couldn't believe their luck that it had finally arrived. It made Erin press on.

'You know, I went home to Cornwall last week to see my grand-mother and I was telling her where I was going. She asked me how you were going to top this for your wedding. You're going to have to go some.'

Karin smiled slightly, but Erin thought she looked flustered to hear her talk of home. 'Yes, I heard you'd gone back to see your family. Adam does get terribly panicked when you're not around, but I tried to tell him that you have your own life and you're not at his beck and call twenty-four hours a day. After all, you're not Julia Roberts in *Pretty Woman*.' Karin laughed a little harshly. 'At least, I hope not.'

As Karin rose to leave, Erin touched her arm. 'What, darling?' she said, irritated. 'I really have to get back to the party.'

'My grandmother told me something about you while I was back in Cornwall.'

Karin's brow furrowed. As she turned towards Erin, her foot kicked over a glass of red wine that Erin had left on the floor.

'What? Something she read in the gossip section of the *Daily Mail*?'

Erin felt a flutter of sickness in her stomach. Karin had a formidable presence: not just with her imperious manner, but in her four inch Manolo heels she stood over six feet tall.

'I know your real name is Karen Wenkle.'

'Oh, darling that's no big surprise. You've worked for me before. You've probably seen my passport.'

'And I know your father was Terence Wenkle. The man who destroyed my father's business. My grandmother told me everything.'

Karin snorted and turned away from Erin, opening her tiny clutch bag to take out another cigarette, which she promptly lit. 'Well, I'm surprised you didn't know that either,' said Karin, blowing smoke back over her shoulder at Erin, 'Do you walk around with your eyes and ears closed?'

Erin looked up at her ex-boss who was holding her cigarette aloft and staring out into the darkness. Erin felt more bold having come this far. 'Did you know who I was when you gave me the job?'

Karin nodded. A gust of wind blew a sheaf of raven hair across her face.

'So why do it?' snapped Erin angrily. 'Did you want to rub my nose in everything you've got and I haven't? Or was it pity?'

She had felt so angry for so many years about her father's death, and now she had someone to project all that raw, violent emotion onto.

Karin pushed the hair out of her face and took a step towards Erin, her eyes cold. 'I gave you the job as a favour,' she said, her mouth curling, 'because I thought you could do with the break, you ungrateful cow.'

Karin turned away from Erin, looking momentarily embarrassed that someone had seen a chink in her armour.

'So it was a coincidence? Me working for you?'

'Yes,' said Karin. 'Well, in so far as, when I was recruiting for the PA job, I asked for some girls to be sent over from an agency. You were one of them. I recognized your name. Erin Devereux – it's fairly distinctive. I was old enough to know what happened with that business with your father. I was sorry for what happened. I still am.'

'So you gave me the job because you thought it would make up for things?' said Erin sarcastically.

It was dark now and the temperature had dropped. The pool was like a sheet of black ice surrounded by the greyness of the lawns. Karin wrapped her arms around her body to protect herself from the cold. 'Do you want the truth, Erin? The truth is that giving you the job *did* make me feel a little better about what my father had done. '

Erin laughed bitterly. 'Does Adam know he's marrying Mother Teresa?'

'I saved you from some shitty little life in Cornwall.'

'My life wasn't shitty,' said Erin, suddenly full of protective pride.

Karin rolled her eyes and began to walk away, but Erin stood in front of her. 'You *used* me to make you feel better about having a ruthless crooked shark for a father,' she said. 'You are only where you are today because he shafted and murdered people, to make money and give you opportunities.'

Karin's expression instantly hardened. 'Erin, darling, I would be up here, and you would be down there, regardless of what our fathers might have done twenty-five years ago. It has nothing to do with where we came from, but who we are.'

'Well I'd certainly hate to be you,' said Erin as calmly as she could, her cheeks blazing with humiliation.

'Really,' smiled Karin, lifting one perfectly shaped eyebrow. 'I've seen the way you look at Adam. You expect me to believe you wouldn't rather be the successful businesswoman about to marry Adam Gold? That you'd rather be the failed writer who answers his phones? I don't think so, darling. Now, if you'll excuse me I have to get back to the party.'

She turned back to look at Erin. 'Oh, and Erin? I suggest you stop having little tantrums like this; otherwise you might find it's the last party you ever go to.'

The pink champagne was flowing, the ice sculpture was melting, the atmosphere fizzed with the chatter and laughter of everyone having a fabulous time at somebody else's enormous expense. There was dancing in the ballroom, cigar chomping on the terrace and, in the conservatory, transformed into a casino for the evening, Molly and Summer were standing over the blackjack table, wondering when their luck was going to turn.

'Well? Have you spoken to him yet?' asked Molly, eyeing her daughter up and down. Even in such glamorous company, surrounded by New York and London's most gorgeous creatures, Summer Sinclair stood out with her natural beauty. Her face did not need Botox or eye-lifts or any of the other cosmetic procedures on display in the palazzo. Her long thin silk Versace gown, in the palest apricot, made her skin seem to glow; her hair, dyed back to its natural honey blonde, made her look like a pearly goddess who had just stepped out of an oyster.

Summer placed a pile of blue chips in front of her and watched as the croupier dealt the cards. A queen and a seven.

'Seventeen, signorina?'

Summer bit her lip. 'Stick,' she said.

The dealer flipped over his cards. An ace and a jack. Twenty one.

'I don't seem to be having much luck tonight,' said Summer, pretending to concentrate on the croupier raking up all the losing chips. She didn't want to talk about Adam. She didn't want the pressure from her mother. She felt sick enough at the prospect of seeing him tonight, let alone speaking to him.

'We make our own luck, darling,' replied Molly, taking Summer by the arm and leading her away from the table. She led her into a corner behind a pillar and fixed Summer with her best 'displeased' glare.

'What are you playing at, Summer?' she snapped. 'I've counted at least half a dozen opportunities when you could have caught him on his own, but you don't seem to have taken any of them.'

Summer looked at her mother, who had the confident self-important air of somebody on coke.

'I want you to go and find him now,' said Molly, pushing her face up close to Summer's. 'Because if you don't, I will.'

The enormous sweeping marble steps that led from the French windows of the ballroom down to the edge of the lake were like a set from an Audrey Hepburn movie, the perfect place for a heroine to finally kiss her hero to a swelling string quartet and tears from the popcorn-munching audience. *Well, there was going to be nothing like that tonight*, thought Erin, walking to the final step and sitting down so that her feet almost dangled in the water. *Not for me, anyway.* She rested her elbows on her knees and listened to the gentle lapping of the lake. If she half closed her eyes it was as if she was back in Cornwall, walking back home from the Golden Lion pub in the village, always taking a minute to pause on the harbour wall and listen to the waves. She looked up at the palazzo behind her, its windows glowing yolky light, illuminating men in tuxedos like tiny penguins. She pulled a face. She wasn't in Cornwall any more and she had never felt more lonely.

She heard a gentle tapping behind her and Erin looked up. High heels coming down the terrace, then the shape of a woman coming down the stairs towards her. For a second Erin thought it was Jilly. There was the same volume of grey hair piled on top of her head, the same slender figure showing the slight gnarl of age. As she came closer, Erin could see that the woman was a lot more polished than Jilly. The silver hair was brushed and coiffed, her long dress was made of blue silk that screamed Oscar de la Renta and shimmered in the low light. She had a strong face, but the same intelligent, questioning eyes as Erin's grand-mother.

As she got closer, Erin saw that it was Adam's mother. Erin had only spoken to her briefly at the airport, but Erin knew quite a lot about her. She knew that she lived in Greenwich, Connecticut, that she had been sixty-seven last birthday and had received a walnut Steinway piano from her only son. She knew all this because she had bought it and arranged for it to be delivered at Adam's request. She also knew that Julia was going to receive a Hockney painting for Christmas, which Adam had just bought from a recent Sotheby's sale and which he was keeping for her until 20 December, when he would spend two days in Connecticut before flying off to spend

Christmas in St Barts with Karin. It was the most important job skill for a PA: you had to know.

'What are you doing out here all alone?' asked Julia Gold. 'Didn't you know one of Europe's most glittering social occasions is occurring right behind you as we speak?' She smiled kindly. '. . . Or so I read on *Page Six* anyway.'

'I don't think I'm here to enjoy myself,' smiled Erin, immediately warming to her.

'Just because you work for Adam, doesn't mean he doesn't want you to have fun. He's not that bad, is he? Or have I raised a monster?'

'He's not bad,' smiled Erin, 'for a global tycoon.'

'Funny, most people expect him to be like that.'

'Me too. I come from Cornwall, where there aren't too many billionaire industrialists. I'd watched *Wall Street* and that's how I expected everyone to be. Hideous and ruthless.'

'So I take it you've survived? Not been chewed up and spat out?'

Not by Adam, maybe, thought Erin. *But try his fiancée.*

Julia Gold was too graceful to crouch on the floor like Erin, who had got the hem of her long midnight-blue dress dirty and dusty. Instead, Julia rested elegantly against a pillar and looked thoughtfully out at the lake, which had now turned black and was framed by the looming shadows of the cliffs surrounding it.

'It's funny,' said Sarah after a pause, 'I never thought Adam would end up doing what he does. I don't know how much you know about our family?'

Erin shrugged. She knew a little colour from a *Forbes* magazine feature she had read on Adam, but her boss gave out very little personal information on himself.

'Adam's grandfather Aaron was a very rich man, but Adam's father didn't inherit a cent because Aaron didn't approve of our marriage. Adam's father and I were happy and comfortable enough and we did our best for Adam, but we couldn't really afford the fancy prep schools or those exclusive summer camps.'

She paused and looked back at the magnificent palazzo in the background. 'Adam was very driven from an early age. He was good at everything, he made sure of it. He always used to say, "We'll show grandfather, we don't need him." I don't know if you know, but Adam is a wonderful artist. He had a place at Parsons to study graphics. But he didn't think a career in art could make him money. Not the serious money he wanted, anyway. So he studied economics at Yale and dropped out when Wall Street came calling.'

'I really didn't have Adam down as the creative type,' said Erin, genuinely shocked.

Julia shrugged and smiled. 'Well, now he buys art instead of painting it. I still have some of his old drawings hung up in the house. They mean more to me than any Hockney.'

Erin thought of Julia's very expensive Christmas present and winced.

'And what do you want to do with your life, Erin?' asked Julia suddenly.

'Why do you ask?'

The old woman smiled kindly; even in the dark Erin could see the lines around her eyes crinkling with amusement. 'I consider myself to be a fairly good judge of character, and I wouldn't have put you in the ruthless world of business.'

'Oh dear,' said Erin. 'Don't tell your son that.'

Julia looked embarrassed. 'Oh, I didn't mean it like that. It was meant to be a compliment. And anyway, Adam thinks you're marvellous.'

Erin felt her heart flutter. 'Anyway, I wouldn't say I'm "in the world of business", as you put it,' said Erin. 'I'm only his executive assistant – his PA really. It started off as a way to make money while I was writing a book, but now Adam says I have a future with the company and that maybe I could eventually move into marketing or something . . .'

'I knew it!' Julia looked remarkably gratified. 'I knew you were a creative soul.'

Once again, Erin didn't know whether it was an insult or a compliment.

'Well, don't hold your breath, Mrs Gold,' said Erin. 'I think I've been sidetracked.'

'Really?' said Julia thoughtfully. 'Well, let me ask you a question, then. Would you rather have a library lined with beautiful first editions or a bookshelf stacked with your own novels?'

'Oh, the second one, definitely,' said Erin immediately. 'That's what I've always wanted. Just to see a novel I've written in a bookshop.'

'So why are you wasting your time with Adam?' asked Julia.

The words 'For the money' were on the tip of her tongue, but she kept her mouth closed. But she could see that Julia was right. Who was she to look at Molly Sinclair, even Karin, and criticize them for money-grabbing and social climbing, when she was prepared to shelve her own ambition for a fat pay cheque?

'I've written something I'm pretty pleased with. I gave it to my agent last week and he loves it too.'

'Can I read it?' asked Julia.

Erin hesitated before recognizing the enthusiasm in Julia's eyes. 'I have my laptop with me, but I'm sure you don't want to read it at the party.'

'I'm nearly seventy,' smiled Julia, 'it's too boisterous for me back there. I want to be tucked up with a good book.'

'Are you sure?'

'I'm sure, Erin. Now come on and impress me.'

Karin stood on the terrace of the palazzo's master bedroom feeling a discomfort she couldn't quite place. She had come upstairs for an aspirin, but she knew that her headache wasn't the source of her disquiet. She leant against the balcony and looked out at the pool shimmering beneath her in the streaky silver moonlight. She shuddered, thinking back to the earlier scene with Erin Devereux, wondering if she been a little hard on her. There had been no reason to imply she was bitter and jealous; Erin was just a lonely, angry kid who had just discovered the grim truth about her father. *Well I can empathize with that*, she thought, kicking off her heels and sitting down on one of the balcony chairs. Karin knew full well that her father Terence Wenkle was the ruthless bully that Erin had described. Yes, she worshipped him, because he had treated her like a princess and told her she could be whatever she wanted to be in life. But she also knew he was a crook, a liar, a greedy con man who didn't care who he walked over to get what he wanted. She remembered the first time she had heard the Devereuxs' name. She had been ten. The Wenkles had moved from their Essex detached house to a mansion in Surrey with a stables and a swimming pool, because 'Daddy was doing so well.' One evening, after she had been sent to bed, she was creeping downstairs for her new Sony Walkman cassette-player when she had heard the raised drunken voices of her parents. Not daring to go any further, she had waited on the top step, listening to her mother shouting at her father.

'*Terry, you shouldn't have done it. You shouldn't have made him drop all his clients if you knew you were going to drop him.*'

'*Business is business. It's not my fault if he trusted me.*'

'*Think of his wife, Terry. Think of his little girl Erin. He killed himself because of you and now that little girl hasn't got a dad.*'

'*It's not my fucking problem.*'

Then Karin had heard the unmistakable sound of a backhanded slap followed by her mother's scream. Karin had covered her ears with her palms to stop herself hearing any more and had run back to her room, hiding under the duvet, praying for it to stop. People had said that Karin's steely ambition stemmed from the confidence Terence Wenkle had instilled in his daughter, but deep down Karin knew it was something else. Her desire to succeed was a desire for re-invention; to wipe clean all traces of Terence Wenkle from her life and forget that she was really just a gangster's daughter from Essex.

She took a glug of water to wash down her aspirin and thought about heading back downstairs. It was gone midnight and out along the driveway she could see guests stepping into cars to take them back to the Villa d'Este, but the party was still in full swing. The sound of the jazz band floated up to the balcony, along with a rumble of merry conversation. Karin slipped her heels back on and turned to go back into the bedroom. Her fingers were on the brass door handle when she saw two shadows behind the thin voile curtain. Still suspicious of Adam's womanizing, she froze, immediately wondering if he would have the audacity to bring anyone into their bedroom. It was Adam alright, but the other voice was male and it was raised, angry. Curiosity made her wait outside in the dark to listen.

'Listen, don't worry,' said Adam, 'the team are in place for the Astley Stores takeover. Marcus says the shares should bottom out any day now, then we can move. We just have to wait.'

The other voice seemed doubtful, anxious. 'Retail really isn't your bag, is it Adam? So why should I trust you? Everyone else says that Astley's is a busted flush. String of profit warnings and no doubt more to come.'

Karin heard Adam laughing. 'I told you not to worry, didn't I? The Astley CFO has been on our payroll for the last eighteen months; he's been helping to run the company down. That "busted flush", as you put it, is now open to a sale. With a strong management team, we can easily turn the company around.'

The other voice sounded impressed.

'You SOB, you have Astley's CFO in your pocket? That's genius!'

'That's only the half of it,' continued Adam. 'The real money is in the real estate. The Astley retail group owns a small logistics company that have derelict warehouses right in the middle of a riverside brownfield site in Wandsworth. Fifty-one per cent of the company is owned by the Astley family, but they won't authorize a sale of the warehouses because they've been land-banking it for years.'

'Who owns the rest of the site?'

Adam laughed again. 'Me. Through various companies, of course. We got it cheap because the Astley land was blocking any sort of development. Who else would want it?'

Karin could hear the other voice laughing now. Curiosity got the better of her and she quickly snatched a look at the man Adam was talking to. She recognized him as Jonathan Parsons, the chairman of Murray and Spink, a major investment bank whom Adam had introduced to her earlier in the evening.

'Once we get control of Astley Retail and transfer the Wandsworth land to Midas, it becomes a fifty-acre riverside side worth two hundred and fifty million. I've already got a raft of investors lined up to build the biggest shopping mall in South London.'

'And your share prices go up even further . . .'

Adam laughed again. 'Call your broker. Buy Astley. Buy Midas Property, my friend. You can't lose. Now, what do you have for me?'

'How does Ginsui, the electronics company, take your fancy? Computech are about to make a move on it. An announcement is being made this week.'

Karin stood outside, goosebumps on her skin. She had a plan and she knew it was a beauty. What Adam was talking about was share manipulation and insider dealing. Not just the grey-area, skirting-round-the-edges-of-the-law sort of stuff she knew many big businesses indulged in. No, this sort of dirty play could get you two years inside. She could now hear Adam laughing. 'I'll put a call into my broker immediately so he can move on it as soon as trading opens on Monday.'

She heard the door click, as if Jonathan was leaving the room, and then heard Adam make a call to his broker; she waited outside on the terrace until she was sure Adam had left the room. For a second she thought of her father and shivered in the cool night air. But then she looked around her – the magical setting of Palazzo Verdi, the twelve-carat diamond sitting on her finger, the party filled with the most important people in society. And she pushed Terence Wenkle out of her mind. She'd come too far to get distracted by principles now.

Summer was sitting by the fountain in the palazzo's courtyard, letting her hand trail in the cool water, when she saw Adam descending the sweeping flight of stairs from the bedrooms. He was lighting up a cigar and heading in her direction. She felt a rush of butterflies as he came nearer, then a flood of disappointment as she realized he hadn't yet seen her.

'Oh, hello. I haven't seen you all evening.' Adam gave a weak smile, but he looked her up and down approvingly.

'Can we go somewhere to talk?' Summer's voice faltered as she said the words. Adam's eyes darted around and he looked distracted, unwilling. He took a puff of his cigar.

'Listen, I haven't seen Karin in about half an hour,' he said. 'I'd better go and find her because some guests are beginning to leave already.'

She could tell he was in no mood for a quickie in the flower-beds. Though that was not what she had in mind anyway.

'Please Adam, I just need a few minutes in private.'

'It's hardly private at my engagement party,' he said with a small smile. 'Okay, there's a rose garden behind that line of trees. I'll come in a few minutes.'

It was almost pitch-black at their rendezvous point; just a little amber light trickled into the circle of tall, spindly rose bushes at the back of the house. Summer sat on a wooden bench feeling isolated and uneasy, until she heard the sound of footsteps on the grass, and then Adam was standing there holding a glass of champagne. One glass. Not two. He sat down next to her and said, 'You look beautiful.' He said it almost apologetically.

Summer shrugged. She knew she looked good. She'd had her hair freshly highlighted at Aveda, plus four hours of treatments at the Bliss spa, telling herself it was in preparation for the job in Milan, but knowing in her heart of hearts it was to look her very best for this evening.

She'd been rehearsing what to say to Adam ever since she realized what might be happening to her body but, sitting here in the semi-dark with his knee pressing lightly against hers, she knew that she just had to spit it out.

'Adam. I'm pregnant.'

There was silence. She looked at his profile in the dark and saw his Adam's apple bob slowly up and down. His gaze remained fixed in front of him. 'Are you sure?' he said finally.

Summer almost laughed out loud. 'My period has gone AWOL. I'm never late.'

'That doesn't mean much, does it? I mean you hardly eat anything. That plays havoc with your system.'

She'd told him a few weeks earlier that she'd been bulimic in her late teens, but she was surprised he would throw it back at her now.

'And I've taken a test.'

He stood up and anxiously rubbed his mouth with his hand. 'Jesus, Summer. Nice thing to drop into conversation at my fucking engagement party.'

'When did you want me to tell you? In nine months' time?'

He paced back and forth and took a deep slug of champagne. Finally he sat back down and touched her knee gently.

'Look. When you get back to London, see a doctor. Get it confirmed. Home tests aren't always accurate. Anyway. What about your movie role? That doesn't fit in with having a baby.'

Summer didn't need a doctor to tell her that her body felt different, the swell of her breasts just a little more round. 'Adam, we're going to have a baby. That means more to me than any role in a bloody film.'

His jaw tightened and he met her gaze. 'Summer, I'm getting married,' he said slowly.

She knew what he was trying to say. That a baby with her was not part of the equation. Summer bit her lip to stop a hot rush of tears welling up. 'Adam, it's not too late,' she said, her voice pleading. 'You're not married yet.'

He was looking more and more angry now. 'Don't even think about it, Summer.' His voice was low, controlled and steely.

'Think what?'

He carried on looking at her, his lips curling aggressively. Summer tried to catch a breath but it wouldn't come.

'Why can't we be together?' she asked, her voice quavering.

'Because I'm getting married. How many times do I have to say it?' He rubbed his forehead. 'You're a stunning girl, Summer, but I love Karin. This is the first time in my life I've been willing to make this sort of commitment, and there can't be any complications.'

Summer couldn't stop the tears from flowing now and Adam found himself putting an awkward arm around her shoulders.

'What's wrong with me?' she sobbed into his jacket.

'Shit, Summer.' He exhaled and stroked her hair. 'There's nothing wrong with you. We've been having a great time, haven't we? If I hadn't met Karin, then who knows, but I did and I love her and I'm sorry if you've got the wrong impression. I would be lying to you if I said anything different.'

Summer jumped up and glared at him, wiping her tears away vehemently with her fingers. 'You selfish shit!' she sobbed.

Adam stood and drank the last of his champagne, tossing the flute into the bushes. 'Look. We'll talk tomorrow.'

'I'm going to bloody Milan tomorrow,' she cried.

'Well, we'll talk when you get back.' He paused awkwardly. 'We'll sort something out.'

'Thanks,' she spat under her breath as she watched him leave the rose garden. 'Thanks for nothing at all.'

In the master bedroom, Karin unzipped her sheer red Valentino gown and let it shimmer to the ground until she was standing there in just her La Perla bra and thong and her four-inch, crystal-encrusted heels. Adam slipped off his dinner jacket, threw it over a chair and walked over to her, smiling as he undid the buttons of his white shirt.

'A successful evening I'd say, Miss Cavendish,' he said, taking her hand and leading her to the bed. Karin lay back on the cool linen and shut her eyes, feeling Adam kiss her ankles and then work up her long, bronzed legs with feathery brushes of his lips.

'Mmmm,' she murmured contentedly. 'That's good. You did seem a little distracted this evening, though. Is everything alright?'

Adam took off his shirt while Karin sat up and unbuttoned his trousers. He shrugged. 'No, everything's fine. More than fine, in fact.'

He pulled Karin towards him to kiss him and she lowered her lips down over his firm stomach, her fingers peeling down his cotton boxers until her face brushed his hardening cock. She pushed him on his back and kneeled to straddle him. Lowering her head so her long hair brushed over his thighs she took the tip of him into her mouth and moved her tongue in delicate circles, lower and lower until the lips were moving up and down the whole of his cock, fast, slow, hard, soft. She knew how to pleasure a man while being totally in control; she'd made it her life's work. He was groaning and grabbing her head to push himself deeper and deeper into her mouth. She lowered her mouth so far down him that the tip of his cock hit the back of her throat and his springy pubic hair brushed her lips. Then, suddenly, she pulled away, uncoiling her body back up to look at him.

'Fuck, Karin what are you doing? I was almost done.'

Still straddling him, her high heels pushed down on the bed, she put her hands on her hips, knowing she looked like a wanton Amazon towering above him.

'I know why you were distracted tonight,' she smiled.

'What are you talking about?'

'I heard your conversation with Jonathan Parsons earlier. In the bedroom,' she said. 'I was on the terrace.'

She got off the bed purposefully and picked up a white Frette gown and slipped it on.

Adam lay there for a second, naked, his cock still rigid, before a look of exposed vulnerability clouded his expression and he pulled the sheet over him.

There was a padded gilt Louis XV chair in the corner of the room and Karin sank into it, crossing her legs so that the robe opened and flashed a long expanse of thigh.

'I'm not sure what you heard, Karin, but it was business,' he said tersely. 'My business. Business you don't know anything about.'

She stared at him, knowing she had to play it carefully. This was her roll of the dice. She could win big, or her whole house of cards could come tumbling down.

'Adam, I know enough about business to know that what you were talking about is illegal.'

'Honey, please. Stay out of this.'

'I'm going to be your wife, Adam,' she cooed. 'I think I deserve to know if my husband might be looking at a jail sentence this time next year.'

'Quit it, Karin.'

'No, I won't quit it. I am here to support you. We're a team. I want to know your business. I'm big enough to handle the truth.' She smiled a smug little smile.

Adam took a sip of water from a crystal tumbler by the bedside table and looked at her for a long moment.

'Obviously you discuss this with no one.'

'Obviously.'

Adam smiled. There was a hint of arrogance about it that Karin didn't like. 'So, come back to bed,' he said, patting the bed beside him. 'I was enjoying myself.'

'I just want it to be worth my while,' said Karin, fixing him with her gaze.

'And by that you mean . . . ?'

'If I am going to support you, I don't want to feel vulnerable.'

'Why the fuck would you feel vulnerable?'

'Because you want to get married in the States.'

'Well, yes,' he said. 'I thought the house in Miami would be perfect. It's private. Nobu can do the catering, but I thought I would leave all the planning to you.'

'I'm not a bloody fool, Adam,' snapped Karin, standing up. 'You want to get married in the States because you want a pre-nup.'

There. She had said it. The p-word. The elephant at the table. Everyone knew that a pre-nup was not worth the paper it was written on in Britain but, if a couple married abroad, and one of the partnership was American, it was another story.

Adam shifted uncomfortably and pulled the sheet a little tighter around his body. 'Come on, honey. Let's not talk about this at our engagement party.'

'We need to talk about it, Adam. When better?'

'Look,' he said finally. 'And this has nothing to do with my respect for you or the hopes I have for our marriage, but I have got to safeguard my position. I've seen too many men screwed over, companies ruined.'

'Don't talk about companies ruined, Adam, bearing in mind your little conversation earlier with Jonathan. If someone blew the whistle to the FSA about what you've been up to, I think you'd be in serious trouble.'

Adam shrugged. He had faced far more ruthless negotiators than Karin and come off the victor. 'You have no proof whatsoever,' he said.

'Oh, the FSA can be very thorough in their investigations. Haven't you just put a call in to your broker to buy twenty-seven thousand shares in Ginsui. That will leave a trail.'

Adam raised his eyebrows and nodded. 'Look, when we get back home I will call my lawyer in New York. I will talk to Marcus and we can work something out, Karin. I want a pre-nup. I need a pre-nup, but that doesn't mean I want to shaft you over either. They can work two ways, and I will be more than accommodating.'

'I don't want a pre-nup.'

'So what do you want?' he said, lifting an eyebrow.

'I want a share in the company.'

'I don't own all the shares in the company.'

'So? Adam, transfer some of your shares over to me. You have enough of them, for heaven's sake. I need to safeguard my position. Particularly as what I know puts me in a very uncomfortable position.'

'Are you trying to blackmail me?'

Karin put her hands on her hips, her robe falling open. 'Adam. This is not blackmail, it's self-preservation. You would do the same. But don't forget . . .' She slipped her robe off completely and stood at the end of the bed, unhooking her bra and peeling off her panties slowly.

'Don't forget what?' said Adam, unable to tear his eyes away from her body.

'That so long as we're together and happy, we are on the same side,' she whispered, crawling onto the bed, naked except for her heels, ready to finish what she'd started earlier.

61

At eight in the morning, when all of the guests were still asleep in their Baroque fantasy bedrooms, Summer was up, dressed, packed, and ready to go, dressed in a pair of jeans, a white T-shirt and some Tod's loafers she always wore for travelling. The kitchen had sent blueberry pancakes up to her bedroom and, twenty minutes later, Federico, Adam's kindly Italian butler, tapped on her door to tell her that her car had arrived to take her to Milan.

She had a room booked for that night at the 3 Rooms, the tiny boutique hotel favoured by the fashion crowd, and had already called ahead to see if she could have an early check-in. She wasn't due in Milan until that evening, but Summer couldn't have left the palazzo soon enough. She hadn't been able to sleep all night. Every time she had closed her eyes she had seen a vision of Adam in the Rose Garden, dismissing her pregnancy as if he was talking about yesterday's news. After writing a note to Molly, she stuffed it quickly under her bedroom door and waited impatiently on the front steps of the palazzo while the driver put her case into the boot of the car. She was just about to climb into the back seat of the Mercedes when she heard the sound of footsteps in the entrance hall. With a sinking feeling in her stomach, she turned round. She could see Karin standing behind her, her arms folded across her chest, cream silk dressing gown tightly wrapped around her.

'What are you doing, sneaking away at the crack of dawn?' she smiled, a little crease of suspicion between her eyebrows.

Summer could feel herself blush and cursed inwardly. 'I have a job in Milan. Thought I'd better set off before the party gets going again and I don't want to leave.'

Karin didn't reply; she seemed to be staring straight past Summer. Summer reached up and fingered the delicate chain of the necklace that Adam had given her nervously. Suddenly she had the strange thought that the pendant was what Karin was staring at. But that was just paranoid, wasn't it? There was no way she could know the little teardrop was from Adam, was there?

Karin flashed her a big smile, but Summer could see that her eyes looked dead. As she moved to embrace her goodbye, Summer could feel Karin's thin fingers press hard into her shoulders.

'It was such a pleasure to see you,' said Karin. 'I really appreciate you making the effort to come, especially when you hardly know Adam.'

They locked eyes and Summer had to look away, such was the intensity of Karin's stare. Summer clambered into the Mercedes and stared straight ahead as she ordered the driver south to Milan.

'I can't believe Summer has left already,' grumbled Molly, sitting on her balcony and reading the message her daughter had pushed under her door. Marcus looked up from his newspaper and took the glass of fresh, sweet orange juice off his breakfast tray.

'I thought she had a job in Milan?'

'Not until tomorrow. I can't imagine why she wouldn't want to hang around the house'.

Marcus lifted an eyebrow at the casual way Molly had said 'house,' as if she was talking about a three-bedroom semi in London, not a magnificent, twenty-bedroom palazzo.

'She's a big girl,' smiled Marcus, wondering why his girlfriend seemed so agitated. 'Anyway, there's not much happening today. I think there's a boat going over to Bellagio, if you fancy it.'

Molly pulled her sunglasses down over her eyes dramatically. 'It was a big night yesterday, baby, I'm not sure I can face bobbing on any water today. I might just hang about the pool.'

The truth was, Molly wanted time alone to fume. How dare Summer just swan off and leave the party? Hadn't she warned her that this was her last opportunity to close the deal with Adam? After this weekend, Karin's claws would be well and truly into him. She had already heard her boasting about how she was moving into Adam's home as soon as they got back to London. Molly refused to believe that Adam was off the market until he was walking down the aisle but, with Karin Cavendish shacked up in his Knightsbridge duplex, any manoeuvres were going to be far more difficult. She knew she should have gone after Adam herself rather than hand him to Summer on a plate. Summer lacked the killer instinct required to land a man like Adam Gold. *She, on the other hand . . .*

Karin lay back on the sun-lounger by the pool and accepted a copy of Italian *Vogue* from Christina, who had grown weary of looking at the pictures and instead was now peering through a pair of opera glasses at the villa's Riva boat putting across the lake.

'Diana is so antisocial sometimes,' said Christina, squinting at the bright sun glinting off the water. 'Why on earth did she want to go on that Bellagio trip instead of making wedding plans with us?'

She rolled over to look at Karin. 'I mean, there's so much to discuss. Who's going to do your wedding dress? And I insist you have a trousseau. I suggest maybe ten or twelve couture pieces by Lacroix.'

'I don't think Diana's in the mood to talk about weddings,' said Karin, flicking through the magazine to see if she could see any Karenza credits. 'I asked why Martin wasn't here this weekend and she burst into tears and said she hadn't invited him.'

'Well, at least she finally showed some backbone,' said Karin. 'Although that has to mean the marriage is in trouble.'

Christina shrugged. 'Maybe so, but she can't go leaving him now. Twelve months of marriage? She'll get next to nothing in a settlement. She has to hang in there at least three years, or have a baby.'

'But that's the problem,' said Karin, sipping her peach iced tea.

'Anyway, back to the happy day,' said Christina, tiring of Diana's problems. 'May I ask if you've discussed a pre-nup? If he's insisting on one, I have a great lawyer that can make it work for you.'

Karin smiled. 'We discussed it briefly, yesterday. And it's sent him into a sulk.'

She and Adam had hardly spoken all day. They had had incredible sex the night before – one of Karin's heels had gone though a Lalique bedside lamp when things were getting particularly frisky, but in the cold light of day, she could tell that he was brooding about her demands for a share in the company. She felt he was being ridiculous. They only had to look at Diana and Christina to know how precarious the institution of marriage could be. Surely he could understand her wanting to safeguard her position, especially given his cavalier attitude to fidelity.

Karin squeezed her nails into her palm. *Summer Sinclair*. Ever since she'd discovered that *she* was the one Adam had been messing around with, Karin had taken it on the chin, vowing to deal with it as soon as the celebrations were over and she was back in London. But what had unsettled her the most was not that Adam was obvious enough to pick someone as flagrantly beautiful as Summer, but that he was arrogant enough to think he would not be found out.

She pulled her sunglasses over her face and shut her eyes, wanting to think. There was a right way to handle this situation, to manipulate Adam into getting exactly what she wanted; she just had to think about what it was. And when she did, Adam would regret the moment he had laid eyes on Summer Sinclair.

Molly was drunk. And high. Coke in the afternoon never agreed with her, but, she needed a little pick-me-up to get through the day.

Marcus had gone into Bellagio with about ten others. There were masseurs on call by the pool who were pummelling guests and, as the sun sank in the sky, sunbathing became a bit redundant. Molly was a little bored and restless. She'd flicked through a Jackie Collins novel and painted her nails hot pink, lost in thought. She decided to take a walk in the grounds, and pulled a short, sheer kaftan over her bikini top before she set off to explore, wondering how she could get Marcus to invest in a property of this size.

The grounds were vast, and it took Molly over half an hour to walk round the perimeter. In a far corner of the grounds, looking down over the palazzo, was a small marble temple almost obscured by a line of cypress trees. She was alone out here; somehow the birds seemed louder, the air more sweetly fragrant with the scent of frangipani and lilies. She was about to turn to leave when she saw a solitary figure sitting on the little marble bench reading a book. It was Adam, dressed in a pair of shorts, a thin cashmere sweater and some deck shoes. There was a bottle of red wine beside him that Molly noticed was almost empty. She almost shuddered at the perfect serendipity of the moment.

'So you've found my little hiding place.' He put down his book and poured what was left of the bottle into a goblet that was sitting on the floor.

'I didn't think I'd find anyone out here.'

'Well, if you don't mind sharing a glass, this is an excellent wine.' Molly read the label. Petrus.

'Ooh, my favourite,' she smiled, taking the glass from him and sitting down on the bench opposite him, the cold pinching the back of her thighs.

'Feeling antisocial?' she asked, raising the glass to her lips. He shrugged.

'I know how you feel,' added Molly.

'I thought you never felt antisocial,' said Adam, knocking back the contents of his goblet.

'You'd be surprised,' said Molly coquettishly.

Molly noted with excitement that Adam was drunk, and his mouth had a little downward turn as if he was anxious.

'Weekend parties always seem like a good idea at the time . . .' he said slowly.

'But by Sunday afternoon you just want to tell everyone to bugger off?' laughed Molly.

The temple was small and confined. They were only three feet apart, but the enclosed space made it seem even closer. When they didn't speak, she could hear the sound of their breathing.

Adam shrugged, not sharing the smile, and drowned the last of his wine.

'Shouldn't you be with Marcus?'

'We're not joined at the hip,' she said.

For the first time she saw him approach something resembling a smile. He held up his glass as if he was examining it. 'Do you know what I like about you, Molly? You think like a man.'

'Is that supposed to be a compliment?'

Adam nodded. 'What you see is what you get. Me and you are similar creatures. We're straightforward. Maybe even selfish, but at least we're honest. What I can't stand is women who pretend to be one thing and then try to fuck you over.' His mouth was in a tight line, his voice aggressive, eyes staring forward, cold and hard.

Molly felt a smile pulling at her lips. *He has obviously had a fight with Karin.* She felt dizzy with glee. She knew now was her moment to strike.

'Maybe you're just choosing the wrong women.'

He lowered his voice so she could hardly hear him. 'Maybe.'

She moved across the marble bench so she was sitting right next to him. She pulled the empty glass from his hand, finger by finger, and ever so slightly ran the tip of her tongue over her lips.

'Come on. Let's get back to the party,' she whispered. She could tell by the way he was looking at her that he had no intention of going. 'Not unless you want to stay here,' she added softly, resting her fingers on the line of his shorts. She ran her other hand down the stubble of his cheek and he caught it and pulled her fingertips into his mouth.

'Adam, don't,' she whispered, willing him with every bone in her body to continue.

He pulled her towards him and her foot knocked the bottle to the floor with a hollow clatter. They stood up together and began pulling at each other's clothes, urgently. Molly's kaftan came over her head in one swift movement, and he unclasped her bikini top with one hand, so her small, brown nipples jumped out in his face. He pinned her against the temple walls, her arms over her head, her skin smarting as it hit the ice-cold marble, while the fingers on his other hand pushed her bikini briefs to one side. She moved her feet apart to widen her legs, moaning as his fingers slid into her. Adam's lips slid down her neck to take a hard nipple in his mouth. They didn't speak, just grunts and gasps. He fumbled to pull down his boxer shorts and pulled at the strings of Molly's bikini briefs so they fell to the floor.

His cock was hard. His fingers pushed roughly back into her, feeling her wetness, while his hand guided his cock inside her. His body pressed against her, pushing her harder against the marble wall. It didn't feel so cold now. Molly clasped behind him, digging her nails into his buttocks until he cried out.

He thrust into her with such force that her head banged on the marble. She glanced at his face and saw his eyes closed, his teeth biting into his lip. It was raw, urgent and, for Molly, disappointingly quick. He withdrew his cock just before he came, his hot juice spilling onto her thigh.

'Fuck,' he grimaced through clenched teeth. No emotion. It wasn't sex with a new lover; the start of something, a promise. It was hard and cruel, a fuck against women. It was a beginning and an end.

He raked his hand through his hair and looked up at her, his eyes glassy, and reached for his sweater. 'We probably should both keep that quiet,' he mumbled.

Molly nodded, her stomach churning with disappointment.

They gathered up their clothes and got dressed in silence, but outside, Karin Cavendish had heard everything.

Karin sped away from the temple in a hot fury. An affair with Summer Sinclair was one thing; if Adam was going to be unfaithful, then at least silly impressionable models were never going to be a long-term threat. But to have sex with Molly *at their engagement party*? It beggared belief. Putting aside the complete lack of respect on Adam's part – it was Molly! *Molly Sinclair!* And Molly was a far more dangerous prospect because she knew how to play the game. Molly was not a pretty lovesick puppy like Summer, who would dote on Adam's every word, gaining his affection but not his respect. Molly was an operator. Karin had witnessed first hand over the last six months how Molly was able to manipulate men. But could Adam see that? Men were notoriously blind to the obvious flaws that a woman could see. Did Adam see a tramp who'd be up for a quick shag in the bushes in the desperate hope that he would fall in love? Or did he see a former top model, about his own age, with a steely, independent core that Karin knew he found attractive? Well, she wasn't going to take any chances. It was time to fight back.

That evening's party was quieter than the previous night's main event. There was a hog-roast in the garden, low tables and cushions by the pool, tea-lights everywhere, and guests were dressed more casually – long sparkly kaftans and jewelled flip-flops rather than the couture gowns of the day before, giving the whole evening a sultry Moroccan vibe. Karin found Marcus sitting alone on a leather pouf by the pool, picking at some baklava and watching the guests mill around. Seeing that Adam was within eyeshot on the other side of the pool, she positioned herself next to Marcus and turned on the charm. She knew she was looking hot. Her long chocolate-brown chiffon dress was almost sheer, revealing a tiny bronze bikini and an incredible suntanned body underneath. She had accessorized with a pair of metallic Grecian sandals, a copper bangle pushed up her arm, and a slim gold lariat hung around her neck, making her look every inch a modern day Talitha Getty. Rather appropriate, she thought, smiling. Except without the drug habit of course.

'Where's Molly?'

'Around, around,' laughed Marcus, trying not to notice the curve of Karin's breast peeping through the low neckline of her dress. 'Phoning Summer, I think. She took off early this morning to Milan, so I think Molly just wants to check everything is okay.'

'She just adores Summer, doesn't she?' smiled Karin, knowing the irony was lost on Marcus. 'I know she'd do anything for her. I'm quite envious of their relationship. In fact, I'm quite envious of Molly full stop. Wonderful daughter, fabulous boyfriend.'

Adam stared at Karin from the other side of the pool with undisguised fury. What was she doing? He excused himself from Claudia Falcon and stalked over.

Marcus looked up. 'Just going to get a drink,' he said. 'Fancy one?'

Adam grunted and sat down on his vacant pouf.

'What are you doing?' he asked Karin immediately Marcus was out of earshot.

'What do you mean?' asked Karin innocently, playing with her lariat.

'Hanging off fucking Marcus with your tits out, that's what I mean.'

'Hardly,' sniffed Karin, delighted that she had provoked such an immediate reaction. 'Anyway, I didn't have you down as the jealous sort.'

'I'm not,' said Adam coldly, snuffing out a dying tea-light with his finger-tip.

'Well, don't behave like it, then. It's only Marcus, what's your problem?'

'My problem,' growled Adam, watching Marcus coming back towards them balancing three cocktails, 'is that you are flirting with him and Molly is just over there making a phone call.'

'Of course,' replied Karin. 'It's all about Molly.'

Her eyes locked with Adam, and for a second she thought she saw a fleeting moment of panic in his expression. *That would do for now*, she thought.

'I think there's more mint than rum in these things,' said Marcus putting the glasses on the low table. 'Probably just as well with the amount I've drunk this weekend.'

'A bad workman blames his mojitos,' laughed Karin, standing to leave the table.

'Going somewhere?' asked Adam tartly.

'Looks like Molly is off the phone,' she smiled sweetly, pointing

386

over to the gazebo, where Molly was snapping shut a mobile phone and putting it in her clutch bag.

'I'm going to leave you gentlemen and go and have a girly gossip.'

She looked at Adam, who was nervously running a finger around the sugary rim of the glass, and smiled broadly at Marcus. 'I'll see you later.'

The gazebo was away from the main throng of the party and much quieter. Karin could just hear the strains of a clarinet floating on the air, and the low murmur of background chatter. Molly was walking back to the pool and having trouble with her kitten heels in the grass. 'You should have used the phone in the house,' said Karin, looking her up and down. She did look good, she thought begrudgingly. Molly's blousy leopard-print dress was so short it barely covered her thighs; her tawny hair hung loose on her shoulders, and even her low heels gave her a statuesque appearance.

'It's fine,' smiled Molly. 'I can get reception out here.'

'So, how's Summer? I'm surprised she took off so early this morning.'

'She's okay,' said Molly, trying to dodge around Karin to continue back to the pool.

'What did she have to say?'

'How did you know that was Summer?'

Karin shrugged and took a sip of drink. She made the silence hang in the air to unnerve Molly. For a second they could hear the crickets in the trees and the quiet splash of waves lapping on the shore.

'She really did miss all the action this afternoon, didn't she?' said Karin casually. 'I think she'd have found it quite interesting if she'd hung around.'

Molly flicked her hair behind her shoulder and pushed her clutch bag under her arm, gripping it with white fingertips. 'Well, we've both been to Bellagio before, and you can only do so much lounging around a swimming pool,' smiled Molly lightly, even though the expression looked troubled.

'That's right, isn't it?' Karin pressed on. 'I saw you getting a bit bored of sunbathing earlier, although frankly I didn't think that was in your nature.'

They were only thirty or so feet away from the main action. Marcus lifted a hand in the air to wave. Molly's face looked frozen, as if she'd had a Botox overload.

'Look, Karin, I've got to get back. Do you want anything from the bar?'

Karin shook her head politely and adopted a butter-wouldn't-melt expression.

'No, I just wanted to know what you thought of the grounds when you went exploring. Did you know they were designed by Luigi Belmondo, Italy's answer to Capability Brown?'

'They were gorgeous,' smiled Molly thinly. 'Although I didn't really have much of a look.'

'What did you think of the temple?'

Despite the darkness, Karin could see Molly's face redden and her long fingers grip her clutch bag even harder.

'I don't think I saw that,' she said.

'That's odd, because I could have sworn I heard you in there. Either that or it was a wounded pig squealing.'

'Oh fuck,' mumbled Molly.

'Exactly,' said Karin coolly. She paused for a long moment, her head cocked to one side, examining Molly's face carefully.

'So what was it like having sex with my fiancé? Or should I say, your daughter's lover?'

Molly was now so red in the face she looked sunburnt. Karin took a breather, surprised after everything that had happened that she was enjoying it.

'I think that maybe the hostess was drunk this afternoon,' said Molly, finally lifting up her chin arrogantly.

Karin snapped. 'The final insult!' she laughed harshly.

'Well, what do they say about it taking two to tango?' said Molly, realizing that there was no point pretending. 'I can't even begin to think how bad your sex life is when your fiancé has to come looking to me. No, to *us*.'

'Well, you should know all about a bad sex life, isn't that right, Molly? It must be hard trying to orgasm when you're too busy thinking about bank balances.'

'Fine, have your fun. I'm not going to listen to this,' said Molly, trying to push her way past Karin.

'Oh yes you will,' said Karin, grabbing a handful of leopard-print chiffon. 'What do you think is going to happen, Molly? That Adam will break off his engagement with me and propose to your little daughter? To you?' she mocked. 'Don't you understand? Nobody marries a nobody.'

Molly tried to pull herself free. 'I'm really not listening to this.'

'Not only will you listen to me, I'm going to make sure Summer does too,' hissed Karin. 'I wonder what she'll make of all this. She's a terribly sensitive young girl.'

Molly went white. She knew she was cornered and desperately tried to think of a way out. 'Karin, don't,' she said gently, trying appeal to a better nature that Molly wasn't even sure Karin had.

Karin pulled back, for one moment surprised by the pleading expression on Molly face. She had never before seen even a hint of her vulnerability. She let her speak.

'Slag me off all you like,' said Molly. 'Hate me for what I did this afternoon, but please don't tell Summer. Please.'

'If you're so desperate for me not to tell Summer, why *did* you screw Adam?' she asked coldly. 'You weren't being quite the caring mother then, were you?'

Molly looked down at the ground, examining every blade of grass, hoping that, when she looked up, Karin would be gone and the whole conversation would have been just like a nasty acid trip. After all, she could hardly tell Karin the truth, that she wanted Summer to be engaged to Adam. For the money, for the status, for the reflected glory. But that, as the weeks of Adam and Summer's illicit afternoon sex had yielded nothing except Adam's engagement to Karin, Molly had decided to wade in and have a go herself. No, she could hardly tell her that.

'It was just a fuck,' whispered Molly. 'He was drunk, so was I. It was over in five minutes, it meant *nothing*,' she said, her voice getting louder, stronger, more desperate. 'Summer doesn't need to know. Please. She loves Adam. It will crush her.'

Karin fell silent, her face expressionless. They could hear the crickets again and the tension that moments earlier had swelled between them like a giant wave just ebbed away. For just one second, Molly thought that Karin was going to let the matter rest. But then she opened her mouth and her top lip twisted into a snarl.

'I'm going to tell Summer as soon as she gets back to London,' she said. 'And I'm going to tell her *everything*.'

62

The plane ride home on Monday morning had been quiet, the atmosphere on the 737 subdued and bloated. Champagne and croissants were available, but most people chose to sleep. Erin, however, had spent the entire flight staring out of the cabin window, her eyes searching the swirls of clouds beneath her, wondering whether she should listen to Julia Gold, whether she should say goodbye to her life with Adam. Much as she loved the excitement, importance and – on occasion – sheer luxury of her job, a life with Adam Gold meant a life with Karin. And, at that moment, Karin's very existence seemed too painful a reminder of what had happened to her father. She thought about her pep talk with Julia, wondering if the old lady was right, that she should try and make a career writing books. But if only she knew it was going to work out – after all, having an agent was one thing, actually selling her book was quite another – it might make a decision to leave the Midas Corporation easier. A Mercedes was waiting at Heathrow for Erin to take her back to the office; she was hoping that it was going to be a relaxed day ahead. Adam hadn't joined the rest of the guests on board the party plane; his Learjet had been waiting for him at Milano Linate to take him on to Paris for a meeting, and he hadn't needed Erin to accompany him.

She was back at her desk by noon, when her mobile rang. She hesitated before picking it up. Even though she had officially been 'off-duty' at the weekend, she had still been pestered with a hundred and one requests from party guests, who expected Erin to fix the plumbing, press their clothes or order them a helicopter. She looked at her phone, hoping it wasn't some disgruntled party guest complaining that their Louis Vuitton boîte flacon had been left at the palazzo, or that they had lost a pair of holistic flight slippers on the plane. She took a deep breath and pressed 'connect'.

'Ah Erin! Finally. I've left you a message on your home phone, but I suspect you've been out gallivanting?'

Ed Davies, her agent. Erin hadn't spoken to him since she'd sent the first fifteen thousand words of her new novella over to him and had been discouraged by his silence.

'Sort of,' said Erin warily, 'I've been in Italy for the weekend.'

Ed chuckled indulgently. 'Well, I should have told you this news before you went away so you could celebrate.'

Erin pulled a face. She doubted anything could have lifted her spirits from the mood she'd been in Como.

'So what's happened?' She hoped he wasn't going to ask for a rewrite. Any more setbacks from Ed Davies would knock her confidence even further.

'Well, I got those fifteen thousand words from you. Sorry I haven't been in touch, but I've been in Tuscany for the last couple of weeks. You know how the publishing industry gets very quiet over summer? Anyway. It starts picking up now. Editors want to snap things up before the Frankfurt Book Fair.'

Get on with it, thought Erin with irritation.

'So I sent your manuscript to an editor over at Millennium Publishing who I thought might like it.'

'You sent it out?' said Erin, her heart pounding. 'But I, I didn't think, I mean I . . .'

'Yes, yes, I know you didn't mean for me to show it anyone,' said Ed. 'But I rather liked what you'd delivered. Not a great deal of it, but what was there was super.'

Erin's mouth had gone dry with anticipation. 'So . . . what did they think?'

Ed paused for dramatic effect. 'They loved it! Charles, the editorial director over there, said it reminded him of *Bonjour Tristesse*.'

A smile spread across Erin's face. Françoise Sagan, the sixties French novelist, was one of her favourites, and *Bonjour Tristesse*, the story of a troubled little rich girl, was her masterpiece.

'Anyway, the best news is that he's made a pre-emptive offer of forty thousand pounds for a one-book deal, which I think is super considering it's only a part manuscript.'

'Oh gosh,' said Erin, her heart flip-flopping at this totally unexpected development. 'What do we do?'

Ed chuckled again. 'Ball's in your court, my dear. But what I would say is that Charles won't hang around with something like this. He definitely wants to get it out by summer next year. So that means he wants the book delivered by Christmas.'

'Christmas?' said Erin, panicking. She'd written just a few chapters and, while it was only ever going to be a short novel, Erin knew that it would mean leaving work immediately to get it done.

'Yes, well, I wouldn't normally encourage an author to stop work,' said Ed, 'not until they were very established anyway, but there does seem to be an issue of time here.'

'I . . . well, I need to think about it,' said Erin.

'Okay, but Charles has given us 48 hours to accept his offer.'

Erin's heart felt as if it had been turned up to maximum volume. 'Then what?'

'Then the offer lapses. Of course there may be other publishing companies interested but, to be honest, it's a gamble. Why don't you sleep on it and get back to me in the morning?'

By 8 p.m., Karin was exhausted. After the flight home she had popped into the office, answered some emails, called her PR, who had been inundated with calls from journalists wanting details about the party, and then had returned home for a long soak with Jo Malone bath oils. As she wallowed in the silky water, she let her mind drift back to the party. She couldn't remember a more eventful forty-eight hours, and it had filled her with a rush of different emotions. Guilt and discomfort at Erin's outburst, rage and heartache at the revelation that Summer was Adam's secret lover. And, as for Adam and Molly . . . In the quiet of her bathroom she could still hear the raw, frantic moans of them having sex in that marble temple. She felt sick.

Karin picked up a sponge and squeezed it over her face. She had to get some perspective, she thought: focus on the positive. Because if she played this right, the positive could be very good indeed. Her knowledge about Summer and Molly gave her leverage, and the conversation she'd overheard between Adam and Jonathan Parsons trading company secrets – well! Everything had changed with that one twist of fate. Yes, she thought, on balance this weekend had strengthened her position. And that could only be a good thing in the long run.

Smiling to herself, she got out of the bath, rubbed herself down with a fluffy white towel and slipped on a thin Sabbia Rose dressing gown.

She padded downstairs and noticed that the big vases of Verbena roses in the hallway were dying. She tutted; her housekeeper Reya had the week off to go and see relatives in Estonia, so she supposed she would have to deal with it herself. Not in the mood for supper, she opened a packet of organic rice cakes and began to nibble at one as the phone rang. She perched on a kitchen bar stool to answer it and smiled as she heard the voice. 'Ah, Molly. What a surprise to hear from you.'

He couldn't help himself. The papers were full of pictures of her because of the party. He couldn't believe she was getting engaged. The pain at the thought of her being lost for ever was searing. He just had to come, to see her. To look at her. Pretend she was his. One last time.

It was a balmy evening. Warm for September. The sky had darkened to a deep purple, but in Karin Cavendish's back garden it was almost pitch-black. There were a few lights on in the house. Two upstairs, three downstairs. It looked like a face laughing at him.

One of the kitchen windows was slightly open, the blind only half down. From a distance he could only see her torso, a hint of breast hidden behind coffee-coloured silk. He had to get closer so he could see her face and a tumble of hair. She was on the phone. He heard her voice floating on the breeze like the smell of honey-suckle, sweet and heady. He closed his eyes, feeling drunk, taking in every sensation for one final time. He loved her. He wanted to be with her. He knew she could never be his.

63

Erin was going to resign. She had chosen to wear her chicest power-dressing outfit: a black crêpe Donna Karan dress with three-quarter sleeves, and some Gucci heels she had bought herself with her first pay-packet. Looking into the mirror, pulling back her strawberry-blonde locks into a severe ponytail, she wondered if she didn't look too much as if she was on her way to a funeral, before deciding such a formal, sombre look was probably appropriate. It was the end of something – the end of her new life. In eight months, her life had been transformed from unemployed misery, living in her grandmother's cottage in Port Merryn and dreaming of one day becoming an author, to a jet-setting PA with a fast car, faster lifestyle and a chic apartment. She was going to miss them all, but the phone call from Ed Davies had changed everything. Eight months ago, she had zero options; now she had too many. Now, she had the power to make positive decisions about her life, but she wasn't entirely sure if she preferred it to the narrow options of her life in Cornwall.

Erin had spent the entire night tossing and turning, knowing that the decision she was about to make would change her life forever. It was an embarrassment of riches, really. To stay as executive assistant to Adam Gold, sexy billionaire, or finally to have the chance to make her dream come true and become a novelist. This time last year, she knew the decision would have been instantaneous, obvious: write that book, get it published and see it on the shelves. That would have been a lifetime's ambition fulfilled. But, somewhere along the road her dream, once so clear in her mind, had become murky and opaque. An author's life was a lonely life and forty thou-

394

sand pounds wasn't going to buy the trips on the private jets and the blue Audi parked outside her fantastic flat. Then there was Belvedere Road, which she hardly dared think about. Planning permission still hadn't come through and, if she didn't get it developed and let within the next couple of months, she was going to have to sell the building: she could only go on haemorrhaging mortgage payments for so long. In so many ways, staying with Adam would be the easy, safe option. But she had to make a decision and the decision she had chosen was the decision she knew her mum, her dad and Jilly would have chosen for her. She would choose her *own life*. Not somebody else's. She picked up her clutch bag and made for the door. It was time to stand on her own two feet.

Eight hours later, she still hadn't told Adam. It had been a busy day; he had been tied up in meetings all morning, there had been an investors lunch, followed by his session down at the Bath & Racquet Club and, before she knew it, 5 p.m. had rushed around. And the truth was, Erin was terrified about resigning. Erin had only 'left' one job before, a waitressing job when she'd been a student at Exeter; she'd been so scared of the slimy manager, Keith, she had decided that the simplest solution was to stop going in to work. She'd spent the entire duration of her time left in Exeter avoiding the restaurant, and Keith had left two messages on her answer machine accusing her of stealing her uniform. She had briefly considered using the same tactics at Midas, but had quickly decided that the grown-up thing to do was to resign face to face. The prospect, however, was making her sick.

'Erin can you just step through one minute, please?' called Adam from his office. 'And can you get me a drink?'

Right. This was it. She was determined she was going to do it. It was tempting to wait until the end of the week, of course – surely Friday afternoon with its natural finality was the best time to hand your notice in? – but Ed Davies had called her three times demanding to know what to say to Millennium Publishing. As she was on a month's notice at Midas, it meant she had to move immediately. She grabbed a cup of black coffee and walked through. The sky outside his office window was a lacklustre gunmetal grey.

'Sit down, Erin,' said Adam. 'Why don't you get yourself a coffee?'

Erin looked puzzled. It was the first time ever he had asked her to sit and share a drink.

'I'm fine, thanks. I've just had one.'

Adam rested his elbows on the desk. The sleeves of his white shirt were rolled up to show his firm, tanned forearms as he sipped the coffee.

'So, did you enjoy the party?'

It was the first opportunity they'd had to discuss it all day. Erin couldn't exactly tell him the truth about Karin and her father and how miserable it had made her, so she chose to be vague. 'It was a wonderful party,' she smiled.

'Well, I think you did a brilliant job helping us to pull it all together like that in such a short space of time.'

'That's what I'm here for,' replied Erin, wondering if maybe she should leave *the deed* until first thing tomorrow morning.

'And, actually, that's what I wanted to talk to you about,' said Adam. Erin's attention snapped back to the man sitting in front of her.

'I stopped off at the Lanesborough to see my mother on the way back from the airport today.'

She quickly averted her eyes away from him. Damn, damn, damn, she thought, suddenly realizing how stupid she had been to divulge her dreams, the details of her novel and, worst of all, how she had an agent to Julia Gold. No matter how kind and supportive Julia had seemed, there was no getting away from the fact that her loyalties were obviously going to be to her son. It was true Erin wanted to leave the Midas Corporation, but the last thing she wanted to do was to get fired.

'Actually, Adam, there's been something I wanted to talk to you about as well.'

He held up an imperious finger. 'Hear me out, Erin. My mother mentioned she'd been speaking to you – she seems quite a fan actually – and she told me you'd begun your writing again. Apparently she's read your manuscript. Says it's fantastic.'

'Adam, don't take that the wrong way. I haven't been doing it in work time, but it's been going well and—'

The finger went up again. 'You don't have to make excuses for challenging yourself. How do you think I've made so much money? I get bored with one thing and it's onwards and upwards to the next. You sitting down and writing your novel just makes me remember what I thought when I first met you.'

'Adam, I—'

'That you're made for bigger and brighter things than being my assistant.'

Erin was desperate to make him stop, but by now she was too intrigued by what he had to say.

'I'll cut to the chase; there is a fabulous opportunity for you in Moscow. We're talking a lot more responsibility, I want to capitalize on all this entrepreneurial spirit you have and, obviously, we're also talking a lot more money, your own flat, choice of car and so on. Alternatively, if you want to stay in London because of your little development in Crystal Palace, I think we can rustle up something for you in marketing. But either way, I think it's time we stepped up a gear.' Adam Gold had a way of talking to people as if everything he said made the most perfect sense in the world.

'But Adam, I came in here to tell you—'

'Erin,' he interrupted, 'I don't expect you to answer me immediately. I hope you've enjoyed being my assistant and, if you're enjoying it too much and you think I've jumped the gun, then just tell me. But at least think about it overnight and tell me tomorrow.'

Erin just sat there, open-mouthed. She couldn't say a word. Adam Gold was too insistent, too persuasive to turn down, at least at that moment.

'Now then,' he said, continuing with his air of authority. 'I need you to do something for me.'

'Umm, okay, what is it?' asked Erin, busy thinking how she was going to stall Ed Davies and Millennium Publishing.

'I need you to check on Karin.'

Erin groaned inwardly. If she could just give in her notice right at this second, she need never see that bitch again.

Adam went on. 'I haven't spoken to her since Monday morning when we were all at the villa.' He looked up, the hint of a wry smile on his lips. 'I know it might not seem like a long time, but she usually rings. I've tried her a few times and there isn't any reply on her mobile or at home.'

'You want me to go round?' asked Erin. Adam nodded and fished in his pocket, pulling out a tan crocodile-skin key-holder and unclipping a small gold key.

'I'm sure everything is fine,' he said, passing it over. 'We had a bit of a . . .' he stopped, not knowing how much information to offer. 'We had a little disagreement over the weekend, so she's probably just in a mood. But can you just go round and check she's okay and get her to ring me? Thanks, Erin. I really couldn't manage without you.'

Erin stood up and nodded. *If only that were true*, she thought.

Tap, tap, tap, tap. Summer rolled over, not sure if she was dreaming or awake. She opened her eyes and glanced at her alarm clock. Midday. Tap, tap, tap. She could hear it again. She pushed back the duvet and sat up on her elbows. It was coming from the front door – a sharp insistent rapping of the letter box. Molly. It had to be.

'Where on earth have you been?' said Molly, charging through the door. Summer had to rub her bleary eyes and do a double take. Molly was wearing no make-up, her skin looked tired and lined, and she was in a pair of skin-tight navy yoga pants and white T-shirt, her hair tied up in a messy ponytail. She couldn't remember the last time she'd seen her mother looking anything but immaculate.

'Summer, did you hear me?' she snapped, 'I've been frantic about you.'

'I've been in Milan,' said Summer. 'You knew very well where I was.'

'But I thought your plane got back last night. I've been sick with worry'.

Summer raised an eyebrow. 'I did get back last night, but it was late. You don't usually send out the search party.'

Molly tried to look hurt. 'I thought your plane got in at seven o'clock. I knocked for you a couple of times but there was no reply. I didn't know what to think,' she said. There was a pause. 'There's nothing wrong, is there?' Sun was blasting in through the flat's French windows, bouncing off the pale cream walls, lighting the room up with a seaside brightness. It didn't do Molly any favours, thought Summer. She looked as if she hadn't slept a wink. Perhaps she really was worried.

'No, no. Nothing wrong. My plane was delayed, that's all,' said Summer yawning.

'It was a good party though, wasn't it?' said Molly eagerly. 'I must phone to thank Karin. You haven't spoken to her yet, have you?'

Her speech was quick and somehow forced and for a minute

Summer thought her mum was high. 'No. I've not spoken to Karin since.'

Molly began picking at a bowl of grapes on the coffee table. 'Well, I thought you might have met up with Adam in Milan. Isn't that where he went after the party?'

'He's been in Paris,' said Summer, lowering her eyes.

'So you did speak to him at the party?'

There was a silence. A charged quiet like the lull before a thunderstorm. Summer walked out of the room into the kitchen, where she got a bottle of mineral water out of the fridge. Molly had got up to follow her, but Summer returned to the lounge and flung open the French windows, feeling the warm morning sun on her face.

'What is this? Twenty questions? Yes, I spoke to him.' She still had her back to Molly and was staring intently at a little apple tree in the garden, its branches dotted with small, stunted fruit.

'Well, what happened? You looked gorgeous on Saturday. I couldn't believe it when you just left the party on Sunday when you could have taken the boat out with him that afternoon and spent some time together and—'

'Mother, I'm pregnant.'

Summer shut the French doors again and turned back inside. Molly's eyes widened towards an expression that hovered between horror and joy.

'Adam's?' she asked.

Summer nodded and the tears began to roll down her face.

'Well, have you told him?' Molly walked over and put an arm around her shoulders. 'You've got to tell him, honey. This makes all the difference. A baby makes a difference.'

'It makes no difference to him,' said Summer flatly. 'He said he loves Karin. He said he wouldn't leave her.'

'Karin doesn't matter now, honey,' Molly said, stroking her hair. 'Things change. This has changed things. You're beautiful. He'll want you. And now you're having a baby.'

'Yes. It's a baby. It's something growing inside me, a little person. Not a meal ticket.'

Molly looked at her daughter and saw that her eyes were hollow, her mouth set in a fixed, defeated expression.

'I didn't mean it like that,' Molly blustered. 'But be practical, darling. You two belong together. If this baby can make that happen then that's wonderful, and if it can't, then we can get a lawyer and make it worth your while.'

Summer pushed away from Molly angrily. 'Why is it all about the bloody money for you?' she shouted. 'Is that all really you care about? Do you give a shit that I might love Adam? Do you care that I want him to be with me because he loves me, not because I missed a pill and got pregnant and won't get rid of it?'

'I just want what's best for you, Summer,' said Molly, her voice cracked and wobbly.

'You want what's best for *you*,' said Summer with uncharacteristic force. 'You chase money; you crave it. You think that money will be the answer to all your problems, but it's not and look where it's got us.'

'What do you mean, "Look where it's got us"?'

Summer laughed a hollow laugh. 'I'm pregnant to a man who doesn't love me. You're forty-three and alone, with a fucking reputation, when you could be married and happy and not sponging off rich men and spending your money on drugs and parties!'

Summer sat down on the edge of the sofa, too exhausted to continue. She thought back to the vicious spat she and Molly had had after the shoot in Norfolk and considered what good it had done. It certainly hadn't changed Molly's attitudes or behaviour – so what was the point of raking it all over?

Outside a blackbird was twittering. The sun had disappeared behind a cloud and, for a second, the air cooled. She looked at her mother, who had a small, pinched look on her face, her jaw tight, her eyes bitter and distant.

'I don't think we should talk about it any more,' whispered Molly, lowering her head. At first there was a sniffle, which became louder and louder. When she looked up her eyes were rimmed with pink and her cheeks damp with tears. 'I had you for love and look where it got me,' she said, wiping her cheeks.

Summer didn't know which surprised her more; the fact that Molly was crying – Molly *never* cried – or what her mother had just said. Summer knew the story of her father, Jeff Bryant. Molly had met him on the New York club circuit in the early 1980s before the shadow of Aids had stopped the rampant bed-hopping and life was just one long party between modelling assignments. Bryant was old New York money, dabbling in the flourishing world of advertising. When Molly had told him of her pregnancy, she'd been dropped like a hot potato, and he'd refused to see her or take her calls. Molly moved back to London and she had never heard from Jeff again. Summer had never for one moment thought that Molly cared so much about him.

'You never said you loved Jeff,' said Summer softly. 'You always told me that he was just a party boy you met on the circuit.'

Molly took a deep breath and looked up at Summer sadly. 'Jeff Bryant wasn't your father.'

'What?' Summer placed her glass of water on the coffee table, stunned.

It was several seconds before Molly spoke.

'The summer before I met Jeff, I met an English artist called James Bailey at a gallery party. An *artist*. I was terribly impressed. Assumed he was a new Basquiat, a Keith Haring, one of those hot new names that were making waves on the New York society circuit at the time. He wasn't.' She laughed harshly.

'Lived in a walk-up in Hell's Kitchen, not backed by any hot dealer, just a struggling artist trying to make his way, doing what he loved best in a city that was the centre of art.'

'He's my father?' Summer struggled to say the words.

'He was so handsome,' said Molly, smiling at the memory. 'Women would turn and look at him on the street. And he was a good man too. A very good man.'

'You loved him . . . ?'

Molly gave the smallest of nods.

'So you got pregnant, and you loved him. What the hell happened?'

'We'd been dating maybe three months when I found out I was having you. I remember the night I went round to tell James. It was a baking hot New York night. There was no air-con in his tiny, dirty flat. I'd been on a job for *Mademoiselle* magazine that afternoon and the other model at the shoot showed me the engagement ring she'd just got from some Wall Street banker.' Molly looked at her daughter and her eyes were sparkling. 'Oh, it was beautiful, Summer. I can see it now. A diamond the size of a fingernail, glinting in the studio lights.'

Summer started shaking her head but Molly pushed on with her story. 'I looked around his tiny apartment, littered with fucking paint and brushes, and just thought, what the hell am I doing? For about two minutes it had seemed so romantic. A long, hot summer dating this sweet, lovely artist but—'

'But what?' Summer said sourly.

'But when you're given this body. This face,' she said, pointing to herself, 'I knew I could get more for myself. I knew I could get more for *you*.'

'So you ended it with James?'

Molly nodded, her face a mask of defiance. 'I met Jeff Bryant the following week at The Limelight. He was rich, Summer, really rich. Father owned half of Boston. He was the rebel son but he was still the heir. I told him I was pregnant with his baby a few weeks later.'

Summer snorted. 'You thought you could trap him but it back-fired. He blew you out and you came back to London?' said Summer, filling in the gaps. 'And did you ever tell James about me?'

'No,' said Molly, 'it was the only way, honey. James was decent. He would have wanted us to have stayed together and be a family. Well, I wasn't going to hang around on the bloody breadline as a mother and artist's muse.'

'But you were making your own money!' said Summer.

Molly laughed. 'Not much. I was modelling just before the money exploded in the fashion industry; when Linda and Christie and Naomi came along you could stick another zero onto your rates. I was successful, sure, but the money wasn't fantastic. Back then you needed a rich man, darling, to give you a life.'

'And my father still doesn't know about me?' asked Summer.

'No. It was for the best,' said Molly, a note of pleading in her voice. 'I wanted a better life for you. If I've ever pushed you with Adam, it's because you don't want to end up like me.'

'But James is my father. I have a right to meet him, to know him.'

'It's not possible. Not now.'

'Why?' snapped Summer.

'Because it's been too bloody long!' shouted Molly.

'Maybe for you, but not for me,' said Summer. 'Do you know where he is?'

'Summer, please. Let it go.'

Summer looked at her mother, dishevelled in her casual clothes, her hair messy, with lines on her face and puffy eyes from crying. She looked more like a stranger than ever before.

'Get out,' said Summer.

'Summer, please. We need to talk about Adam, about the baby.'

'Please, Molly, just get out. I need to be on my own.'

And, as Molly shut the door quietly behind her, Summer sank to the floor and began to sob, wondering how everything could have unravelled in her life so quickly.

64

There were a few lights on in Karin's house, glowing blush-pink behind the curtains as the dusk began to fall. For a few moments Erin sat outside in her car, the engine switched off, listening to the background noises: distant cars on a busier road, a breeze blowing leaves along the pavement. She didn't get out of the car until she felt calm, knowing another scene with Karin would get her nowhere.

The house was grand, thought Erin as she walked up the steps, although too prim and pretty to be intimidating. Set a little back from the road, it was a tall, slim, white building with a shiny black door and Georgian windows with flower-filled window boxes. She rapped on the door with the big brass door knocker. Nothing. As much as she wanted to avoid Karin, the last thing she wanted was to let herself in with Adam's keys. It seemed so intrusive and presumptuous. She could be doing anything in there – *with anyone*, she thought cynically. She walked round to the side of the house. A side window that looked onto the kitchen was slightly open. She peered through and called Karin's name. The house remained silent.

After trying her mobile and land line one more time, Erin resigned herself to letting herself in. The door creaked open. The only sound was the tapping of Erin's heels on the wooden floorboards. In front of her was a wide staircase lined with thick cream carpet; to the left of the entrance was a formal lounge. It was completely quiet. No hum of a television or bubbling of a pan on the stove, just the quiet of an empty house. She walked through the kitchen, a stunning space with white lacquered units and granite work surfaces. It was a show kitchen, a kitchen to be looked at, not cooked in thought Erin, Erin walked around the central Island; a lone bottle of wine stood on the side.

'Karin. Are you home?'

Feeling more confident she was alone, Erin walked though into a big open dining space that ran along the back of the house. Erin put her car keys on the glass table; the jangle as they hit the surface unnerved her. Yesterday's newspaper was on the table, along with some Italian magazines and a packet of chewing gum. She could see that the dining area ran into the lounge. Walking towards it she felt a sudden sense of unease. And then she saw her. Erin held her mouth and felt bile come up her throat. Karin was lying on the floor, dark hair splayed out round her, rivulets of blood spreading from her head like Medusa's snakes. Oh, the blood. There was so much blood.

She edged closer, forcing herself to look, to see if there was any sign of life. Erin retched again and her knees gave way. She scrabbled around on the floor, reaching for her mobile in her bag, her hands quivering as she tried to punch in Adam's number.

'Erin,' said Adam, his voice sounding irritated. 'I'm at dinner, can I call you or Karin in half an hour?'

'Please come quickly,' whispered Erin, barely able to say the words. 'I'm at the house. Karin's here. I think she's dead.'

The police got there quicker than Adam. Before Erin had time to process what was happening, the house had been cordoned off, red and blue lights swirled on the street, while officers were milling around with notepads and radios, barking orders and being deliberately vague about what they were doing.

Detective Chief Inspector Michael Wright from Scotland Yard's murder squad did not look as if he belonged in Karin Cavendish's drawing room. In fact, he didn't look as it he belonged in any drawing room. Michael Wright was a cop cliché, at home in the pub and the bookies, lived and breathed the job for twenty years which had cost him his marriage and his health. He smoked forty Lambert & Butler a day and his drinking problem had escalated after his wife Lynn had kicked him out of the house three years earlier.

Sitting in the exquisitely decorated room, staring absently at the Colefax & Fowler wallpaper, DCI Wright wondered how he had failed to raise himself to this level. What choices had he made. He glanced over at Adam Gold, mentally comparing their take-home pay, and suppressed a snort. He had failed in the rat race and he had also failed in his calling, he thought grimly, watching Karin's body wheeled out of the house. He had failed to clean up the streets and keep this woman safe. But, by God, he would catch the culprit, he thought. The monster who took a life. He ran his hands through his hair and took stock of the scene. Some facts had already been established. The pathologist had estimated the time of death between 8 and 10 p.m. the previous evening. Cause of death was a severing of the carotid artery. She had been smashed over the head with a glass object that lay shattered on the carpet.

'Can we go over what you know one more time, Mr Gold?' said Detective Chief Inspector Michael Wright, looking at the smartly dressed man sitting opposite him.

Adam nodded, his head bowed. Michael didn't like the CEO of the Midas Corporation; there was something dirty about him. Experience and police statistics also gave him more solid reasons to be suspicious of a victim's partner; and nobody made as much money as Adam Gold without being a ruthless bastard. But he wasn't about to mention that right now. Men like Gold were connected and could stir up a whole lot of trouble with his superiors if he put a foot wrong.

'We'd just come back from our engagement party in Italy,' said Adam flatly. His eyes looked blank. 'I flew to Paris on business and came back on Monday evening when I went out with my vice president for dinner. Karin and I did not spend every evening together – we're both extremely busy business people – although we do usually speak. When I hadn't heard from her by this morning I was a little worried, so I sent my assistant round to her house. And she found her.'

On the face of it, it looked as if Adam's young assistant had disturbed an intruder. Both the back and side kitchen windows were slightly ajar, although there was no sign of a struggle.

'So, who were you with between eight and midnight yesterday evening, sir? I just have to establish who was where,' said Chief Inspector Wright, pen poised over his notebook.

'My colleague Marcus Blackwell. My assistant can give you his number to confirm it.' Adam took a business card out of his pocket and gave it to Michael. 'This is my private number. The number for Erin, my assistant, is on there too.' He rubbed his eyes with the palm of his hands and exhaled.

'I realize this is very difficult, Mr Gold,' said Wright with practised sympathy. 'If we can just establish a few more things about last night, I can leave you alone. I'm sure that's what you want.'

'Haven't I given you enough yet?' snapped Adam.

'I'm afraid the investigation will be quite intrusive,' continued Wright. 'We need to build up as big a picture as we can about Karin's life. Friends. Enemies. And are you sure Ms Cavendish had no enemies?'

'Enemies, no,' said Adam, shaking his head. 'But I assume you will be checking out that wacko who was harassing her over the summer?'

Michael Wright looked up quickly. 'A wacko? Who was this?'

'Some kid named Evan Harris. Parents live in a house that overlooks the back of Karin's. He was caught peeping and following her over the summer. We got out a harassment order eventually.'

'And has he given her any trouble since?'

Adam shrugged. 'No, but he's a little weirdo. If you don't investigate him thoroughly then I will arrange for some other people to do so.'

Wright closed his notebook. 'Don't throw your money around, Mr Gold. I can assure you we'll do our job properly.'

He glanced in the hallway. He could see the girl Erin Devereux, who had found the body, still waiting. As he was looking, his sergeant Jim Beswick pushed past her, clearly in a hurry.

'Anything, Beswick?' asked Wright.

'Evan Harris, sir. Some kid that lives close by.'

Adam and Wright flashed a look at each other.

'He harassed Miss Cavendish over the summer,' continued Beswick in a lower voice, wary of being overheard by suspects.

'His fingerprints are already on file and they match prints on the window ledge by the kitchen window.'

'What are you waiting for?' growled Michael Wright. 'Let's bring him in.'

Erin arrived home just as it was getting dark, never more thankful to see her apartment. She had been questioned by the gruff Chief Inspector for forty minutes and had felt guilty for every one of them. She was sure she must have looked it, too.

Just as she was putting her key in the lock, she heard the noise of a door opening. She turned round.

'Hey Erin,' said Chris with a look of concern.

'Hi,' she said quietly, silently willing him to be nice. The thing she needed right now was a friend, not a reminder of how things had soured between them.

'I was about to come and see if you're okay. I heard about Karin from the newsroom at work.'

She nodded, feeling a tear slide down her cheek, the events of the past month suddenly becoming too much to bear.

He moved towards her and folded his arms around her. She stayed very still, inhaling the smell of the jumper, feeling momentarily protected.

'Let's go inside,' he said, pushing her front door open and leading her to the sofa.

Erin curled up on the sofa, hugging herself, while Chris went straight over to the kettle.

'Did you know I found her?' said Erin quietly after Chris had returned and sat down opposite her.

Chris shook his head and handed her a cup of coffee. 'Do you want to tell me about it?'

She wanted to trust Chris. *Had* to trust him. She was too scared, lonely and anxious to carry the burden alone. Chris moved across to the sofa and she swung her legs around, tucking her feet under him.

'I'm scared the police are going to think I did it,' she whispered.

'Don't be daft. Just because you found the body, it doesn't mean the police will be suspicious,' he said, his voice upbeat and reassuring.

Erin looked at him, hesitating. 'If I tell you something, do you promise you're not going to think I killed her?'

'Of course not,' he said evenly, his curiosity prickling.

'I had a fight with Karin in Como,' she said, and began to tell Chris the story Jilly had told her days earlier and Karin's response when she had confronted her. As she did so, she began to see just how bad, just how guilty she looked, and she became scared.

'Chris, if the police find out about our families, I'm screwed, aren't I?' she said, a feeling of dread growing in her stomach. 'If they find out that my dad committed suicide because Karin's father ruined his business – well, it doesn't look good does it? It could look like a motive for murder, look as if I want revenge.'

Chris remained silent and Erin felt a chill. 'I didn't do it,' she whispered.

'I know that,' said Chris, moving closer and stroking her hair. He looked awkward and then stopped. She surprised herself by wishing he would do it again.

'But you're right, it doesn't look good. If you're interviewed again you should tell the police what you've just told me. Better you tell them than they find out on their own.'

'Well, let's hope they find who did it quickly. Do you have any friends at the newspaper who might know if they have any suspects?'

'I could give my mate Mark on the crime desk a ring. He's bound to be involved in the story.'

Erin felt a glimmer of hope. 'Oh can you do it? Please?'

Chris nodded and reached for the phone.

65

If Summer Sinclair had watched the six o'clock news she would have seen that Karin Cavendish's death was the dominant story. Instead she had run a hot bubble bath and switched off her mobile, lowering herself into the hot water, oblivious to everything happening outside her bathroom door. In fact, at that moment, oblivion seemed like a desirable option to Summer; a little voice in her head kept telling her to slip under the suds and not resurface. But, as she lay there letting the water cool around her body, she forced herself to consider her situation in a more optimistic light. *There has to be an upside to all this*, she thought, popping bubbles between her fingertips. It was such early days with her pregnancy she could possibly still take the role in *Krakatoa*. More importantly, the situation concerning Adam could be a lot worse. Although he seemed to be in a state of denial about Summer's pregnancy, Adam had not mentioned the dreaded word 'abortion' – there was a little sparkle of hope there at least. A baby meant that Summer would always have him in her life, even if eventually their child became just a reminder of their time together. And there was still the chance that, as Summer's pregnancy progressed, Adam might have a change of heart and want to raise their child together. It was a slim hope, but a hope nevertheless.

She felt a sudden surge of anger that James Bailey, *her father*, had been denied that opportunity. While Summer wanted to get some distance between herself and Molly after their latest row, she was desperate to find out more about James – who he was, where he lived. The funny thing was that, throughout all those years that Summer had believed Jeff Bryant was her natural father, she had never had any real desire to meet him; stubbornly rejecting him for turning his back on Molly and herself. But James Bailey had had no idea that Summer even existed. He'd been duped, and they both deserved the chance to get to know one another. If he wanted to, of course. If he was even still alive.

She climbed out of the bath feeling more positive but slightly headachy, which she put down to the humidity in the bathroom. An hour later, however, the dull thud in her head had spread down her body, with sharp cramps in her stomach. She rubbed her palm lightly against her tummy, hoping that it would pass, but as the minutes ticked by and the pains began to get more frequent, she began to become frightened. Any pregnant woman in her first trimester was always haunted by the idea of miscarriage, and Summer was no exception. Heart in her throat, she crawled into bed and curled tight in the fetal position, finally managing to drift into a light sleep. But when she woke, just as the light was creeping through her curtains, she was sweating and nauseous and, with a rising sense of panic, she realized the pains had become stronger. She staggered to the kitchen to make herself breakfast, but she couldn't face it; besides, the cramps were coming every few minutes now. Adam had insisted she see a top Harley Street obstetrician and an appointment had been pencilled in for the following Monday, but Summer knew it wouldn't wait that long. She looked upwards. Despite the row, she needed Molly's help now more than ever. She climbed the stairs, her head swirling, and knocked on the door. Her heart sank as she realized there was no one home. The ache was really gaining pace now, like a boulder that was beginning to roll down a steep slope, picking up dust and sharp shards of rock as it went. There was also a nagging sensation around her shoulder, as if she had pulled a muscle. She knew her local GP often saw patients without an appointment if they turned up at the surgery, so Summer pulled on some jogging bottoms and a sweater to leave the house. She had only just set foot on the pavement when a pain seared through her abdomen, so sharp and severe it was as if she was being sawn in two. She wondered if she could make into back into the flat, but her legs felt too weak. She clutched onto the front garden wall and vomited onto the pavement. She tried to breathe but could feel no oxygen reaching her lungs; her head was so dizzy it was as if a ball bearing was whirling maniacally around her brain. The pain was almost unbearable now and her sight was blurring, until the houses and trees on the street were just a series of muted colours and shapes in front of her eyes. She tried to reach for her mobile phone but all strength had abandoned her body. The last thing she felt was a soft thud against the side of her head.

'Can you tell us what happened?' asked a soft female voice as Summer opened her eyes a fraction. She was disorientated and frightened, but she could tell she was in an ambulance. Two paramedics were staring at her, one male, one female, their faces fixed in concerned expressions. The sounds around her were distant and distorted, as if she was listening to them through water.

'A neighbour found you on the street but couldn't really tell us anything. Are you suffering from any known condition?' asked the female paramedic as the siren screamed in the background. A tear trickled down her cheek. 'I'm pregnant,' whispered Summer as she began to lose consciousness once more. 'I'm pregnant.'

Summer opened her eyes, squinting in the bright fluorescent light. She could see the dirty, peeling paint of a ceiling and faces staring down at her, at least five or six. Doctors in white coats, and nurses.

'Where am I? What's happening?' she croaked.

A female doctor spoke. 'I'm Doctor Shaw, Summer. Your pregnancy is ectopic, which means that the fetus is growing outside of your womb.'

'My baby. Is it okay?' whispered Summer.

'Your Fallopian tube has ruptured. You've had morphine to ease the pain, but we're going to have to take you into surgery immediately.'

Summer was conscious enough to know that this was not good news. And the pain was still there, consuming her whole body like fire. A nurse had picked up her hand and was checking her pulse. Summer did not miss the urgent, concerned glance she gave to the doctor.

'The pulse is very low,' said the nurse.

Doctor Shaw pointed towards the door, ordering everybody into action. 'We need to get her to theatre now,' she said urgently. 'Has anyone been called, is anybody with you?' asked the doctor as Summer could feel her bed being pushed along. She was scared, so scared, she could feel the life beginning to drain out of her body,

412

'Am I going to die?' whispered Summer, trying to lift her hand off the bed.

Dr Shaw put her hand over Summer's. It felt warm and strong. 'Who should we call?' she said kindly. Summer could read the older woman's face. A flash of pity, concern and sadness that the doctor could not disguise.

'My phone,' whispered Summer, 'my phone is in my bag. Molly Sinclair.' Their disagreements were suddenly irrelevant. She wanted her mother to be there.

Her bed was being wheeled faster now, through some swinging doors, the bright lights of the hospital almost blinding her. Summer's hands were trembling. If she was going to die, she didn't want to die alone. It was becoming too difficult, too draining to speak. She lifted her hand off the bed to motion to the doctor, but drifted into unconsciousness once more.

Detective Chief Inspector Michael Wright sat in the semi-darkness of his two-bedroom flat in Putney. It was a cramped space, sold to him as 'a bijou apartment in the best part of London'. He snorted to himself as he took a cold beer from the fridge, thinking about Karin Cavendish's palatial home. Not that all her money did her a great deal of good, he thought, lifting the beer to his lips. He rubbed his temples and groaned. What a day. He'd spent three hours interviewing Evan Harris, but had still not been able to charge him. His solicitor had been particularly sharp and aggressive; it appeared that the boy's parents had money and had instructed some expensive hotshot to help their son. Michael knew he should be at the station, but he was so tired he couldn't even think straight any more, and the cold beer sliding down his dry throat was the only pleasurable experience he'd had in days.

He sat in a frayed armchair, not bothering to turn on the light. The glow from the street cast a dim light that suited his mood. It was moments like this when Michael Wright found he could think most clearly, when his mind was relaxed by alcohol and he sat alone with no distractions, slotting the pieces of his case together, like a jigsaw, until it all made sense and the picture became clear. As he turned the pieces over in his mind, Wright felt a sense of unease; something in the investigation didn't seem right. All the signs pointed to Harris: the boy's bedroom had been full of newspaper cuttings about Cavendish, he had a harassment order against him and, mostly importantly of all, when the prints of Karin's windowsill had matched those in the file, Harris had finally admitted to being in Karin's garden the night of her death. He was an obsessive, an eighteen-year-old loner who clearly had abandonment issues. Whilst he still lived with his parents, it was obvious Evan saw little of them; from what Michael could sense he was desperate to love and be loved by somebody. But that didn't make him a murderer.

What troubled Wright the most was the lack of forensic evidence. Michael doubted Karin had struggled. He had worked on countless assault and murder cases where the victim had put up a fight. There was always something: telltale blood spots, fibres from the murderer's clothes, skin or hair under the victim's fingernails. But in Karin's case, the initial pathologist's report suggested that there was nothing. She hadn't struggled. She had been caught unaware. And that meant she probably *knew* her attacker.

The previous day's evening news had gone heavy on the death of Karin Cavendish; since then information from the public had begun to filter through. Two of Karin's neighbours had both spotted a grey sports car parked outside her townhouse between around eight and half past. Michael wasn't sure how significant the detail was. A sports car parked in a Kensington street was hardly unusual, but he filed it in his mental database anyway.

Michael stretched out his legs and held the beer bottle to his forehead. What had Evan said about a phone call? The kid had claimed that, when he'd been standing by her window, Karin had received a phone call from someone called Maggie. Of course, he had asked the telephone company for a list of calls to and from Karin, but the process was slow. Suddenly, he jumped up and walked over to a sparse bookshelf. Michael wasn't a big reader: he didn't have time. There were a few golf magazines, a DIY manual, some picture books on World War Two and a handful of thrillers. He pulled out the book at the end of the shelf: *The Big Book of Baby Names*. He had always wondered why this book was on his shelf. When he had left the marital home three years ago, it must have been slipped into his hurriedly packed box of belongings. He smiled at the memory of him poring through the pages with his ex-wife Lynn, with her bloated pregnant belly and their giddy excitement about parenthood: he'd been unable to throw the book away; it was a connection to happier times. Before the drink problem kicked in, before work consumed his life. Before Lynn began to hate him for never being there.

He flipped through the yellowing pages before he came to the section on girls' names – M. He put on his glasses and began to read the names, saying them out loud: 'Maggie . . . Mandy . . . Molly.'

He grabbed a piece of paper and scribbled them all down.

66

At 8.30am DCI Michael Wright walked into the Midas Corporation building for his appointment with Adam Gold, suffering only slightly from a hangover. Many people would have thought it was strange that a grieving man should be in work, but years in the force had taught the detective that people responded to grief in different ways; for some the best method of coping was for business to carry on as normal. After being shown into Gold's office, Wright settled into a chair opposite Adam's desk and fixed him with a searching look. *God, he looks worse than me*, thought Michael. There were bags under Adam's eyes and a permanent crease between his brows.

'Can you tell me if the name Maggie means anything to you, Mr Gold?' he began.

Adam simply shrugged and shook his head.

Michael pressed on. 'What about Mandy, or Molly?'

'Molly? Yes,' said Adam, looking up alarmed. 'Molly Sinclair is in our circle of friends.'

'Molly Sinclair the model?' asked Michael. 'She was a friend of Ms Cavendish's?'

Adam nodded. 'Although I have to say that Molly and Karin have never particularly seen eye to eye.'

Wright made a note and looked up curiously. 'What do you mean by that? Did they have a falling out?'

'No, no specific reason that I am aware of.' He paused. 'I guess it was just social competitiveness.'

'Competition enough to be a motive for murder?' asked Wright quickly.

Adam scoffed. 'Molly Sinclair is many things, but a murderer is not one of them.'

So what is she exactly? thought Michael, thinking back twenty years to police college when a picture of Molly Sinclair had been sellotaped to the inside of his locker. Legs as long as Africa. That famous tumbling tawny mane of hair. She had more sex appeal than those skinny page three girls, was more natural and earthy than any *Playboy* centrefold. She must be roughly his age now. Mid-forties. Was she married? Wealthy? What if she wasn't? Perhaps Gold was right, thought Michael, perhaps there was an element of jealousy. It couldn't be easy to sit back and watch younger women like Karin Cavendish snagging the handsome, rich men she would once have attracted.

'So, what about Harris?' asked Adam. 'I thought you had arrested him. Is there any reason why you're extending the investigation?'

Michael Wright smiled to himself. How many times did coppers make that mistake? Spending all their time trying to nail the prime suspect when the real killer was roaming free, reading the papers and laughing at the police. Michael Wright wasn't one of those men. Until he was absolutely sure that Harris was his man he was going to keep an open mind, and that if that meant digging deep, then so be it.

'One last thing,' said Michael, putting his notepad in his jacket pocket. 'Do you know who Ginsui might be?'

'I'm sorry I don't. Why do you ask?'

'No reason, Mr Gold,' said Wright, standing. 'Thank you for your time. I'll be in touch again soon.'

Summer had been lucky, very lucky. After her Fallopian tube had ruptured, she had suffered massive internal bleeding, a plummeting pulse rate, and had needed an emergency blood transfusion. The surgeons had just got to her in time, however, and Summer woke to hear just how close she had come to death. She also heard that she had lost the baby; growing inside her left Fallopian tube, it had never had a chance, which sent her spiralling into a state of despair.

Molly meanwhile had telephoned Adam, who had insisted she be transferred to a private room in the hospital. Disappointed that he did not seem to have immediate plans to come and see Summer, Molly accepted his offer anyway, hoping the hospital bill would be enormous.

Molly sat at her daughter's bedside, holding her hand, for three days. Summer was as pale as the inside of an eggshell. Her honey-coloured hair, spread out on the hospital pillow, seemed to have lost all its shine and lustre. Her eyes were shut, just two subtle dark crescents on her perfectly oval face. She looked tiny and broken, her thin frail body under the sheet. Molly's eyes misted as she thought of her daughter alone and in pain. She had been in the flat when Summer had tried to wake her. After her argument with Summer, she'd gone to meet a friend for cocktails and, as she hadn't been able to drive back to Marcus's place, she had crashed at home, too far gone to hear Summer's frantic knocking.

For the first time in a long time, Molly felt disgusted with herself; Summer's condition – God she almost died – had been a slap in the face, a wake-up call that made Molly realize just what kind of mother she had been these past years. Sitting at her bedside, Molly had wondered how she could make it up to her daughter, and only one idea had seemed appropriate.

She heard the sound of the door creak open and soft footsteps on the floor. Thinking it was another nurse doing their regular check on Summer, Molly glanced up. It wasn't a nurse, it was a man in his late forties, tall and stockily dressed in a navy-blue suit and tie. He looked as if he had been handsome once, but his jaw now was jowly and his dark brown eyes were serious.

'Molly Sinclair?'

'Yes', said Molly, surprised.

'You've been a difficult woman to track down,' he said gruffly.

'And you are . . . ?' she asked, feeling a slight sense of unease. Molly put a protective hand on Summer's arm.

He slipped his hand in his pocket and brought out a wallet. 'Sorry, Chief Inspector Michael Wright,' he said, flipping the wallet open to reveal his ID. 'I'm looking after the Karin Cavendish investigation.'

His eyes wandered over to Summer and his shoulders seemed to stiffen. 'Is she okay?'

'She will be,' said Molly, squeezing Summer's fingers. 'She will be.'

'Miscarriage?'

'Ectopic pregnancy,' she said quietly.

A ghostly quiet settled on the room as Molly tried to work out what the inspector knew.

'I know this is a bad time, but I need to talk to you about the death of Karin Cavendish,' said Wright.

'I know, I heard about that. It's dreadful.'

'So you won't mind me asking a few questions? It won't take long. If you'd just like to come through to somewhere a little more private.'

'According to my mate Mark, the police aren't entirely sure that they've got their man,' said Chris, leafing through a pile of the day's papers in Erin's living room, looking for more news on the case.

'So the police don't think it's that stalker?' asked Erin, looking up from a news magazine.

Chris shrugged. 'Mark says they're not confident enough to charge him. Your mate Adam Gold has apparently been put under the microscope, too, but he has an alibi. However, Molly Sinclair has been taken in for questioning.'

'Molly?' said Erin. She had suspected months earlier that Molly was after Adam herself but, after the summer fête at The Standlings, Erin had become convinced that Summer was Adam's bit on the side. *Which of them was it, and would either murder Adam? Surely not Summer?*

Erin felt a stab of guilt. Even if it was for selfish reasons, she still wanted Karin's murderer found, and she knew the fact that Adam had a mistress would undoubtedly be of interest to the police. But Erin was struggling with the idea of putting Summer into the frame. She was so sweet. A good person. They had had such fun in Monaco and at The Standlings. *There was no way that she would have murdered Karin . . . Was there?*

'Fancy a drink?' asked Chris, peering down at Erin's wine rack.

'Umm, I think I'm becoming an alcoholic.'

'Well, we're under stress,' smiled Chris, pulling out a bottle of red and opening it with a practised flourish. As Erin watched Chris pouring the wine, she had a sudden flash of *déjà vu*. Something that had been nagging at her suddenly became clear, and she cursed herself for not acknowledging it sooner.

'Listen, something has been bothering me,' said Erin, leaning forward, 'and I've only just realized what it is.'

'What?' asked Chris.

'Karin is a neat freak. A total perfectionist who doesn't like a hair out of place.'

'So?'

'So, when I first went into the house that night, I remember seeing a bottle of wine on the kitchen side.'

Chris had a doubtful expression. 'Erin, plenty of people have booze lying around the kitchen.'

'Not Karin,' said Erin. 'She's very particular like that – everything in its place. She drummed that into me when I was working for her. She'd certainly have put her wine away in the cellar. And there was nothing else on the kitchen surfaces that night, nothing at all. I remember thinking it was like a show home.'

'Couldn't she just have bought it that afternoon, or fetched it from the cellar? Who doesn't like a glass of wine when they come home from work?'

Erin frowned. 'The bottle in her kitchen was a bottle of red. Karin hates red wine. I heard her say once it gives her such a headache she thinks she's allergic to it.'

Chris was looking at her with confusion. 'So what does all this mean?'

'I think Karin had a social call the night she died. Someone was at the house with her.'

Chris was starting to warm to the theory. 'Well, it can't have been a casual caller. Your mum or your best friend wouldn't bring a bottle, would they?'

'And think about it – who would bring a bottle of *red* wine round?' said Erin. 'Not a friend like Diana or Christina – they'd know she'd prefer a cup of green tea.'

They looked at each other, both feeling they were on to something.

'A lover?'

'Possible,' said Erin, thinking out loud. 'Anyway. Won't the bottle have been checked for fingerprints?'

'They could easily have been rubbed off by the murderer on his or her way out, if he or she had brought the wine round.'

Erin nodded thoughtfully.

'Anyway. What was the wine?' asked Chris.

Erin laughed. 'I've only just remembered it was there, let alone what vineyard it came from. Anyway, what does it matter?'

'Ooh, a great deal,' replied Chris, walking back over to Erin's wine rack. 'You're saying that whoever brought the bottle round is Karin's killer. Well, the choice of wine a person brings round to somebody's house says a great deal about them. For instance, if you go to a girlfriend's for a gossip –' Chris pulled out a bottle and held it up – 'I bet you take a five-quid bottle of Pinot like this: cheap, cheerful. You don't care about the wine. It's just a prop.'

'So you're saying I'm cheap, Mr Scanlan!' laughed Erin, throwing the cork at him.

He ducked and grinned, but continued with his line of thinking. 'But say I was coming round to your house to seduce you . . .'

'Promises, promises,' laughed Erin before she could help herself.

'Well, say I was rich and knew a lot about wine and wanted to impress you – which of course I would,' he added with a grin, 'I'd choose a very, very expensive bottle of vintage claret. A night-time wine. A romantic wine, a wine that said something about my status and taste, like a Petrus or a Château Margaux. A wine that deserved to be shared with somebody special.' Chris was nodding thoughtfully. 'You need to find out about the wine, Erin.'

'Won't the house be all cordoned off?'

'Probably. But it was Karin's home. I bet Adam could get in and I bet you could too. You just need an excuse.'

67

The interview room was cold and windowless and smelt of cigarette smoke. To Molly it felt like a trap. She shivered, wondering if it was some sort of sick retribution for not attending her father's funeral. For having sex with Adam Gold. For exposing Donna Delemere as a call girl. She stopped herself. This was no time for superstition. She had her reasons for everything she did in life. She didn't deserve punishing.

'What am I supposed to think, Molly?' said Michael Wright evenly. 'You don't have any alibi for that evening. Evan Harris was at Karin's window and heard her on the phone to a Molly. He heard her say "See you later." Given those facts, anyone would suppose that it was you arranging to pop over.'

'I admit I called Karin that evening,' said Molly defensively. 'But if she said "see you later", I can assure you it was just a figure of speech.'

'What did you call Karin about?' asked Michael, swirling some tepid tea around in the bottom of his paper cup.

'Simply to thank her for a wonderful party,' she replied inscrutably.

Wright blinked at her. 'What about the grey car that matches the description of the one you drive? It was seen outside Karin's house one hour after the phone conversation, at around eight thirty. I repeat, what am I supposed to think? You went round to see her that night, didn't you?'

'I did not!' snapped Molly, feeling so flushed she had to undo another button on her shirt. She felt it was definitely time to instruct a solicitor.

'Can I ask you who the father was of Summer's child?'

Ever since he'd left the hospital he'd been curious. He'd asked around the girls in the station, who all seemed to be devoted to the gossip magazines, if they knew who Summer Sinclair was involved with. Michael was aware that Summer Sinclair was a celebrity, and if she had some glamorous boyfriend, he knew it would be common knowledge. However, when the general consensus was that Summer was single, Michael's curiosity had turned into suspicion. Unless it was the immaculate conception, he reasoned, *somebody* had made her pregnant. Was it too much a stretch of the imagination to think it was Adam Gold? Summer was certainly beautiful enough to attract a lover like that. And if Adam was the father of Summer's child, then Molly had the strongest motive in the world: motherly love. With Karin out of the way, Summer and Adam could live happily ever after.

Molly had folded her hands on top of the table and was now sitting tight-lipped. 'To ask about the paternity of Summer's child seems both irrelevant and, at this time, in very poor taste. If you're going to continue with this line of questioning, I must demand to have my lawyer present.'

Michael switched off the tape recorder and drank the last of his tea. It was going to be another long day.

Erin had found her mission to get back into Karin's house surprisingly easy. There were two constables on guard at the top of the steps to keep the press and prying neighbours away, but she had spotted Chief Inspector Wright in his car outside. Erin had explained that she had left her keys to the office inside. She wasn't sure whether Wright had believed her: he had seemed wary, but had still accompanied her inside to look. The keys were never found, of course, but there was enough time to quickly inspect the bottle of wine still sitting on Karin's black granite worktop.

'You're kidding me,' said Chris, reading the name Erin had copied down from the label. They had met for lunch in an American-themed diner off Kensington High Street.

'Nineteen forty-seven Château Henri Jacques, are you sure?'

'That's what it said. What's wrong?' asked Erin, taking a sip of her Diet Coke.

'It's a red wine alright,' said Chris with an incredulous expression. 'It's also one of the finest wines in the world. Extremely rare and will probably have been sold through an auction house like Christie's or a very high-end wine merchant.'

'If it's so rare, do you think we'll be able to find out who owned it?'

Chris smiled and shovelled a handful of French fries into his mouth. 'I like your thinking and, actually, I think I know just the man who can help us. I warn you he's very eccentric, but what he doesn't know about wine you can write on a postage stamp.'

Montague Cruickshank, known to his friends as Monty, was managing director of the most prestigious wine merchants in Mayfair. His family had owned the company since 1765, and his forefathers had advised and supplied every wine lover from Churchill to Mountbatten on the very best wines to buy both as investments and for sheer sybaritic pleasure. Chris had given Erin a crash course on the world of wine on the way over to Cruickshank's shop just south of Piccadilly. It was a world that was notoriously stuffy and exclusive, but Monty was one of the most exuberant and good-natured characters on its scene. He was also privy to more gossip than most newspaper editors, having access to the cellars of some of the most exclusive and expensive homes in the world. Heads of state, kings and billionaires sought his advice on their private wine cellars, serious collectors asked him about the very best wine investments; Hollywood stars bought from him to impress their friends.

Cruickshank and Sons was located in a quiet mews in St James's. With its elegant maroon frontage, blacked-out windows and lanterns outside the front door, it felt quite Dickensian. The shop door opened with a tinkle.

'How do you know about this place?' said Erin, feeling compelled to whisper.

He laughed. 'That's like asking an art lover how they know about the Louvre. It's world famous. I come in at least once a month to pick Monty's brains for a feature I'm writing. There are literally millions of pounds' worth of wine on the premises, and Monty brokers hundred-thousand pound sales between private clients every week.'

The shop was lined from floor to ceiling with shelves stacked with bottles of wine and an old-fashioned polished wood counter. Behind it stood a middle-aged gentleman in a red waistcoat.

'Is Monty around?' asked Chris.

No sooner had Chris opened his mouth than a booming voice could be heard from a back room. 'Christopher, is that you?'

A giant of a man in a navy three-piece suit loomed in the doorway. At six feet four and seventeen stone, Monty Cruickshank had a round, florid face, intelligent green eyes and a sweep of grey hair over a high forehead.

'I thought it was about time I paid you a visit,' smiled Chris, shaking his huge hand.

'He obviously wants something,' smiled Monty to Erin in a theatrical stage whisper. 'But before we settle down to good conversation, I have to ask you, young lady, do you enjoy wine?'

'I'm no expert, but I'm an enthusiastic drinker,' grinned Erin, instantly warming to the man.

'The best kind, dear lady, the best kind,' said Monty, clapping her on the arm. 'Well, shall we go directly to the cellars, my dears?' he boomed, leading them through the shop. 'We had a wine tasting a couple of hours ago for some hacks. You probably know them, Christopher. Frightful bores, but I have half a bottle of an excellent Latour 'eighty-two left over. You simply must try it' – he kissed his fingers – 'just heavenly.'

Erin felt like Alice in Wonderland as she stepped through a heavy wooden door and descended into Cruickshank's cellars. The stone stairwell was cramped but, once they were in it, wasn't as cold or dirty as she'd imagined. The brick walls had been pointed, the high arched roof, supported by wooden mahogany beams, looked like a beautiful church. At intervals, between the dark racks containing thousands of bottles of wine, were gold-framed paintings of old distinguished vintners. To their left was a door with a glass porthole, and from inside came the sound of laughing and the tinkling of glasses. Erin peeped inside. It was as if she was looking back in time. A twenty-foot-long table was piled high with food and wine, like a banquet worthy of Henry VIII. She was even more surprised to see the glamorous famous faces sitting around the table. Two supermodels, a pop star, a handful of big society names.

'Serena Balcon, the movie star, is having her birthday meal here,' explained Monty. 'We do get a lot of high-profile names to the private cellar.' He smiled, looking at Erin's bewildered face. 'There's no better place to eat, drink and be very, very merry. And, of course, none of those dreadful paparazzi.'

Monty handed Erin a glass, poured a ruby-coloured liquid into it and motioned to her to drink it. It felt warm and fragrant, like a ribbon of ripe summer fruit, as it slipped down her throat.

'What can you taste?' asked Monty, pouring himself a measure and tipping his head back to drink it.

'It's kind of fruity and floral.'

Monty had his eyes closed, his nostrils flaring slightly. 'Let yourself go, my dear. Concentrate on each sensation, every flavour on your tongue.'

Erin shut her own eyes and let the flavours swill around her mouth. 'It's very full and fruity. Maybe blackcurrants and cherry. And it has a woody, leathery taste afterwards. It kind of tastes like autumn. I like it!'

'Ah, within the bottle's depths, the wine's soul sang, as our friend Baudelaire would have it. Very well done, my dear,' said Monty warmly, 'I'm glad you appreciated such a good wine.'

Erin beamed across at Chris and he smiled back. 'Actually, that's what we wanted to talk to you about, Monty,' said Chris. 'A very good wine.'

'Oh, do tell,' smiled Monty, leading them back up the stone stairwell. 'Let's adjourn to the office, shall we?'

They made their way back upstairs and then up to a spacious wood-panelled office above the shop. It was a like a gentleman's study, full of leather-jacketed books and pictures of men drinking wine. Monty took his seat behind a bottle-green leather-topped desk and Erin and Chris sat in front of him.

'I wanted to pick your brains on the Château Henri Jacques forty-seven,' said Chris, leaning forward.

Monty's eyebrows rose almost comically. 'My word, now there's a beauty. Is it for a feature you're writing?'

Erin noticed that his eyes were shining with passion and interest.

'Sort of an investigative piece,' Chris said in a low voice. 'Tell me what you know.'

Monty took a cigar from out of his top drawer and clipped its end.

'One of the rarest wines in the world,' said Monty, raising the cigar to Erin as if asking her permission to smoke it. 'Hardly ever seen commercially. There were very few bottles of it in the first place, in fact. The vineyard was exceptional but very small, and the owners liked to keep most of it for their own consumption, which I can fully understand. I've never tried it,' he continued, looking almost apologetic. 'But my father had. Apparently it was quite the most perfectly balanced wine he had ever tasted.'

'How many bottles are in existence? Do you know?' asked Chris, feeling a surge of professional interest.

Monty shrugged. 'Impossible to quantify. There will be several in private cellars. However, a bottle of it did surface almost a year ago at a Christie's auction in New York. It was part of a collection belonging to a recently deceased Swiss count that had apparently been in his cellars for thirty years. The family wanted to get rid of the whole collection,' he sighed. 'It nearly made me weep.'

Chris sensed that Monty knew something vital. 'Was the collection broken down into individual lots at auction?'

The older man nodded. 'The entire cellar was worth millions, but it would still have found a buyer. However, yes, it was broken down. I probably still have the catalogue somewhere, as I attended the auction myself.'

'And did you bid for the Henri Jacques, by any chance?'

'Of course,' laughed Monty. 'However, bidding went through the roof. There was serious money in the room that day. As you know, my friend, wine is the new art.'

'So who bought the Henri Jacques, can you remember?' asked Erin. She could almost hear her heart hammering out of her chest.

'It was done on the phone,' said Monty, finally lighting the cigar and letting the nutty smell spiral around the room. 'But I always like to find out, keep a note of major or interesting acquisitions, as I often broker sales between private clients. Anyway, an American wine merchant friend of mine identified the buyer – a New York property tycoon called Adam Gold. You'll probably know the name, he's been all over the news the last few days. His fiancée has been murdered.'

All night, Erin tossed and turned under her duvet. She was exhausted, but her mind was far too active for sleep, plagued with doubt and anxiety. She knew should have phoned Inspector Wright with the information they had learnt at Cruickshanks, and Chris was threatening to do it for her, but something was holding her back. Was it fear? She felt a creeping uneasiness and wished that Chris was with her. Armed with information that incriminated a rich and powerful man made her feel inexplicably vulnerable. She looked at her clock. One a.m. Too late to phone him?

She reached for her mobile, which was glowing a dull green in the darkness, and dialled Chris's number.

'I don't know why, but I'm scared,' she whispered.

'I'll be right there.'

Chris stayed with her till morning, sleeping on the sofa under a duvet he had transported across the hallway. When her alarm trilled at 6.30 and she staggered into the lounge, she saw Chris was already awake and frying bacon. He moved a pile of papers and magazines from the kitchen table to make a space for her, spilling a few onto the floor. Picking them up, he found a large sheet of waxy paper.

'What's this?' he asked, unfolding it to see a large architect's drawing.

Erin snatched it back from him and folded it up, hiding it away under the coffee table. 'It's nothing, just something from work,' she said briskly.

Chris looked at her curiously, but let it drop and turned back to the stove. 'Listen, I don't want to sound like a broken record,' he said, putting a bacon sandwich on the table in front of her. 'But I really think you should call that detective. And I'm not sure you should be going in to work today, given what we know about your boss.'

'I *am* going to work, Chris,' she said defiantly. 'I'll call Michael on my lunchbreak, I promise.'

Her voice sounded confident but she didn't feel it. She was apprehensive about seeing Adam, but she felt drawn to the office. Besides, Michael Wright was possibly not going to take her seriously with a far-fetched notion about rare bottles of wine stashed on Karin's kitchen counter. She needed more evidence, and she knew that the office was the only place she had any chance of finding it.

'Erin. I'm serious,' said Chris, touching her arm and seeking to meet her gaze with his. 'This is getting dangerous. We shouldn't be meddling. I don't want anything to happen to you,' he added softly.

'It won't,' whispered Erin. 'I'm just going to do my job.'

'Well, if you haven't called Wright by this evening, I'm going to call him myself.'

'But what if Adam's innocent?' said Erin. 'What if the wine

theory is just bogus? We're playing with people's lives here. If he's suddenly a suspect, that will get out in the media; his reputation won't ever really recover from something like that.'

'And what if he's guilty, Erin? What then?'

68

The Midas Corporation offices had been understandably sombre and quiet following Karin's death. Adam seemed to have retreated into himself and spent the whole time in his office with his door closed.

Colleagues scurried around, but there was no chitchat in the kitchen or hallways; everyone just put their heads down and worked.

Erin had barely sat down at her desk when her phone rang.

'Can you step inside a moment, please?' said Adam, his voice low and flat. She'd had little interaction with him over the past few days and a flutter of nervousness appeared in her stomach. But why? Did she really think Adam was a murderer? As she walked to his office, she began to wonder. The police said that Adam had been with Marcus on the night of the murder, but where? And for how long? But surely Adam's alibi must have been convincing, or wouldn't DCI Wright have arrested him by now? The questions tumbled around her head as she sat down in front of Adam.

'Are you okay?' asked Adam, registering Erin's mood.

She nodded.

'Well, I appreciate you being here,' said Adam. Erin looked away. His once-sexy chocolate eyes suddenly felt penetrating, cold and unnerving.

'I'm sorry you had to find Karin,' he continued. 'I feel terrible about sending you around.'

'You weren't to know,' she said, feeling herself flush. It was the first time they had talked about what had happened. Adam pushed his lips together in a tight line.

'Well, the police tell me that the body may be released in the

430

next few days,' he said sombrely. 'And I know Karin would have wanted an appropriate send-off. Could you find a hotel room for a reception after the burial? Something chic. She loved flowers. Let's have lots of flowers.'

'Lilies? Roses? She liked Verbena roses. Or did you have anything in mind?'

'My ex-assistant Eleanor used a fantastic florist for an event at the beginning of the year. Phone them up, tell them what we want. I want it to look beautiful.'

Their eyes locked and Erin felt a wash of fear up her spine. She blinked hard to stop her eyes betraying her.

'Are you sure you're okay?' asked Adam. 'I can cancel my lunch and we can go to talk if you like.'

Erin shook her head a little too vigorously. 'I have plans. I'm sorry.'

'Well, how about later tonight? I'm on a site visit this afternoon and then going to Mikhail's party tonight, but I don't have to stay long. People won't expect me to, anyway.'

She felt her heart beginning to beat faster and the adrenaline pump around her veins. He had never showed this much concern for her feelings or emotions before. She was only there to serve and make his life easier. Now he wanted to get her alone.

She stood up quickly and smoothed her skirt down nervously. 'It's fine, Adam. It really is,' she stuttered. 'Now I had better go and find the number of the florist. As soon as you know a date for the funeral, can you let me have it? Thanks.'

She returned to her desk in silence and sat motionless in her chair, her head bowed, her fingers locked together on her lap, willing her heart to slow down. She had to stay normal, she didn't want him to suspect anything. Keep working, don't show him you're flustered, she told herself. Taking a deep breath, she clicked on her computer to look for Eleanor's wonder-florist. Luckily, Eleanor had been a very organized woman and had left a folder on Erin's desk of her contacts, diary entries, addresses and notes. It was the inside track into Adam's life: where he went, what he did, his likes and dislikes.

Erin clicked on a folder labelled 'entertaining' and found the details of several florists. One name, however, was highlighted in bold, and Erin scribbled down the name and number. She was just about to close the folder when her eye was drawn to a file called

'Christmas Gifts'. Intrigued, she clicked it opened and started reading a long list of presents that Adam had given to his family and friends the previous Christmas, all carefully documented by his former PA. *Well, it wouldn't do to send Mummy a Hockney two years on the run, would it?* she thought. But it was an impressive line-up. Art, designer clothes, handbags, spa weekends; they had all gone to his family, assistants, godchildren and friends. Not to mention the cigars, wine and hampers that had gone to clients and contacts. It was only halfway down the page that she saw something that made her heart leap into her mouth. She looked around her anxiously and quickly closed the file.

Last Christmas, Marcus Blackwell had received a bottle of 1947 Château Henri Jacques.

Chris was having a very late lunch at his desk, a quiet booth located behind the newsroom. His cubicle was an untidy space, spilling over with papers, magazines, press releases and a mountain of chocolates, sauces, exotic spirits and brand-new soft drinks, all received from manufacturers and vintners vying for Chris's attention and column inches. He had finished his stories for the week and was using the free time at his disposal to catch up on the last few days' press, his mind wandering between the world's events and thoughts of his own involvement in one particular news story. The Karin Cavendish story had cooled in the press at least, he noted, flicking through all the tabloids and broadsheets. Just a small piece in the *Mail*, nothing new. He was just scanning the *Financial Times* when a headline on page nine caught his attention: *Computer Giant Ginsui In Takeover Bid.*

His eyes widened as he tried to remember his conversation with Erin days earlier. When Michael Wright had interviewed Erin on the day she had found Karin's body, he'd asked her if she knew who Ginsui was. Apparently Karin had written the name as a diary entry for the day she died. Wright had clearly assumed Ginsui was the name of a *person*, thought Chris, chewing the tip of his biro. But it was the name of a company, a large Japanese computer manufacturer. His mind began to ponder its significance but his thought process felt blocked.

Ginsui, Ginsui. Ginsui. Why would Karin have an appointment at Ginsui?

Over the top of his booth he could see some of his colleagues

432

walking around the newsroom, fetching coffee, walking between departments; the usual semi-frenetic activity as deadlines loomed for the first editions of tomorrow's paper. Out of the corner of his eye he could see City Editor Alistair Crompton heading to his office in the corner of the room.

'Are you busy?' asked Chris, popping his head round the door.

Alistair smiled up at him. 'I've got a phone interview in about five minutes, but grab a chair.'

Chris grabbed a plastic cup and filled it with water from the cooler before sitting opposite Alistair, a balding man in his fifties with red cheeks and a jovial manner.

Chris paused a moment before he spoke. He knew he had to tell Alistair the facts as he knew them. 'What would you say about a friend of mine who had the word Ginsui written in her diary four days before the takeover was announced?'

'Does this friend invest in stocks and shares?'

'Let's say they do,' said Chris, taking a sip of water.

'And is this friend connected? Do they have friends, contacts, advisers in the City?' continued Alistair, pouring himself a cup of tea from a pot in front of him.

'This friend is very rich and very connected. Her boyfriend owns a number of investment companies.'

'Then I'd say it sounded a little suspicious,' smiled Alistair.

'Why?' asked Chris, his heart thumping.

'It could of course be entirely innocent. Maybe your friend was reminding herself to go and buy a Ginsui computer,' he said, smiling cynically. 'On the other hand your friend could have been tipped off to buy shares that were certain to rise in value. Maybe she'd written it in her diary to remind her to buy them.'

'Insider dealing?' asked Chris.

'It's rampant,' said Alistair, sipping the tea. 'Far more so than the FSA would care to admit.'

'Where would somebody completely unconnected with the electronics industry get a tip-off about Ginsui?'

'There can be hundreds of people who know market-sensitive information prior to a takeover. A banker, a broker, a lawyer, a financial PR. Any connected friend could have tipped her off. It could even have come via the boyfriend if he's a big City player and he'd heard something.'

Chris suddenly felt a cold chill. Had Adam been feeding Karin share tips? Could that have had anything to do with her getting murdered? Money was always a strong motive.

He thanked Alistair and headed quickly back to his desk. He had to get in contact with Erin. If she hadn't contacted Inspector Wright already he was going to do it himself. This was getting serious.

Driving his navy-blue Ford down Knightsbridge, Michael Wright slapped the palm of his hand against the steering wheel with frustration. They had been forced to release Evan Harris twelve hours earlier and he just did not have enough evidence to arrest Molly. The forensic team working in Karin's house hadn't thrown up any strong leads, except that the murder weapon was a glass candlestick that had smashed on contact with Karin's neck. Only half of the candlestick was on Karin's floor in pieces around her body. The other half the murderer must have taken with him or her.

He was banging his head against a brick wall with this case. It was a high-profile murder; a rich, beautiful socialite beaten to death in her own home. It had dominated the newspapers for days. The powers that be would want a successful conviction, and Michael knew they did not have a strong enough case against either of the primary suspects. He was due to speak to Summer Sinclair at the hospital in a couple of hours; he was determined to find out who the father of her child was and where *she* was on Monday evening, because that could put a different complexion on everything. In the meantime, he was going to return to Karin's house and look again. Long experience told him that there was always something else, always something that had been overlooked. He had to find it. His mouth set in a thin, determined line and he stepped on the accelerator.

Erin had spent the last two hours staring at her computer screen wondering what to do. She had tried the phone number Michael Wright had given her, but she had only reached the incident room at Scotland Yard, where an unfamiliar voice had told her that Chief Inspector Wright would not be back until later. When Erin had been asked if any of the other officers could assist her, she had quickly declined. She knew that her wine-bottle information was just a theory, and she had a feeling that only someone like DCI Wright would take it seriously.

Adam had gone out immediately after their meeting, being unusu-ally vague about where he was heading. She knew he had been invited to Mikhail Lebokov's drinks party that evening, but that didn't start for another two hours. She had a sudden thought and walked down the corridor to Marcus's office. As she had suspected, the room was empty, but his PA Candy was sitting outside, making full use of her boss's absence by applying a layer of topcoat to her freshly painted scarlet fingernails.

'Hi honey,' smiled Candy, 'listen, I'm dying for a cigarette. Do you mind watching the phones for ten minutes.'

'No problem. Where's Marcus?' asked Erin nonchalantly.

'Gone for the afternoon,' she smiled. 'Place is like a bloody ghost town.'

Erin waited until the lift doors hissed shut, then stepped into Marcus's office and pulled the door behind her. Her palms instantly felt clammy the moment she entered, but she forced herself onwards, not really knowing what to look for, but feeling certain that the answer was in here. Marcus's office was like Adam's, only smaller. There was a row of expensive walnut shelving containing box files and property law books, back issues of *Fortune* magazine, big glossy coffee-table tomes on the great architects like Gehry, Rogers and Foster and, sitting on its own, in a silver frame, a picture of Marcus and Adam somewhere hot and sunny. They looked much younger and Adam had his arm around his friend's shoulders. She picked it up and ran a finger over the glass, thinking. Marcus had given Adam his alibi, and in the process had given himself one; what if neither of them were where they said? Feeling more bold, she moved over to the desk, looking but not touching. It was a very ordered desk. Documents in neat piles. A black fountain pen sat at right angles next to a crystal paperweight. She glanced towards the door again, her ears straining to hear. Nothing. She opened the slim drawer at the top of the desk. More papers. Letters, bills and taxi receipts. And then she saw something. A wink of colour between leaves of white. She pulled it out between her thumb and forefinger and gasped. It was a picture of Marcus and Karin together. Karin was sitting next to Marcus by the swimming pool in Como, her head thrown back, laughing, her hand on Marcus's knee, his expres-sion one of pride and pleasure. Erin remembered thinking at the time how inappropriate it was for Karin to be flirting with Marcus.

What if he'd taken it the wrong way?

At that moment, the sun came out, sending a glare against the gloss of the photographic paper. Erin could see that it was smudged with fingerprints, as if it had been handled a hundred times. What if it was Marcus who had gone round to Karin's house with his impressive, expensive bottle of red wine? Hadn't witnesses reported seeing a grey sports car outside Karin's around the time she was murdered? The police had assumed it was Molly, but Erin remembered the two vehicles sitting on the gravel of The Standlings at the summer party. Molly's dolphin-grey Maserati and Marcus's silver Jaguar. To a casual observer they could be the same car. She shut the door and hurried out of the room with the photograph.

69

When Mikhail Lebokov came to London he always threw a party, and when one of the richest men in the world throws a party, everyone makes sure they drop whatever they're doing and attends.

Erin got out of the black cab and stood looking up at Chelsea's exclusive new waterside development soaring into the sky. Although most super-rich Russians lived in townhouses in Belgravia, Kensington and Mayfair, Mikhail had bucked the trend by buying the most luxurious penthouse flat on London's stretch of the Thames. Word was that it cost £50 million, also making it London's most expensive apartment. She glanced at her watch, wondering whether there was time to try Michael Wright's number again. She had called again only twenty minutes ago, and the officer answering the phone had assured her he was due back soon and would call her immediately. In the meantime she knew that she had to speak to Adam.

The lobby of Mikhail's apartment block was the size of a tennis court, lined with walnut and beginning to fill with beautiful young women and immaculately dressed older men.

Two well-built men wearing charcoal suits and headsets stood by the chrome lift doors with clipboards, looking less like greeters and more like KGB bodyguards. Perhaps they were, thought Erin nervously.

Luckily Adam and Karin had been sent individual invitations, which had both been delivered to the Midas Corporation in a black lacquered box, so Erin had been able to pick up Karin's invitation from the office. She fluttered it at the security guard,

437

trying to stop her hand trembling. Clearly the man had never heard of Karin Cavendish and nodded her through. She watched in wonder as the glass lift sped up the outside of the building, London disappearing below her as they reached the penthouse on the fifteenth floor.

The apartment was incredible. A huge bronze sculpture that Erin recognized as Henry Moore dominated the large hallway. Inside, it was a masculine flat, decorated in taupe and tobacco brown, with a few bursts of colour from some of the most famous artists of the modern era. Erin was no expert, but even she was impressed to see a Francis Bacon and a row of Andy Warhol's 'car crash' silk-screens.

She walked through into an enormous lounge, sparsely furnished with a big black lacquered table, a bus-sized grey sofa and a six-foot-tall plasma screen. Tonight, however, the spaces were filled by the beautiful and powerful of London, laughing, drinking and chatting. Her eyes scanned the room for Adam, but all she saw were unfamiliar faces. This was not some show-off celebrity shindig, this was an exclusive gathering for Mikhail's closet friends and business colleagues.

A waiter handed her a cocktail and she walked up a chrome and glass stairway clutching the ebony handrail. The crowds thinned out as she reached a mezzanine floor that led out onto a rooftop garden that echoed the Japanese theme of Mikhail's dacha outside Moscow. Sculpted trees obscured the London skyline, koi carp swam in a black marble pool, while cherry-wood and cream linen day beds provided a place to sit. But it was too cold to linger this evening, and Erin quickly saw that she was alone up there. Cursing, she perched on a day bed, opened her mobile and dialled Adam's number. It rang twice before he answered.

'It's Erin,' she said sharply, 'I need to speak to you urgently. I'm at Mikhail's party – I thought you were going to be here.'

'I'm on my way,' said Adam, sounding bemused. 'What's the problem? What are you doing there?'

She paused a moment and then decided it was too late for keeping theories to herself. 'I think I know who killed Karin, but I need to ask you a question and you have to answer honestly.'

'Go on,' said Adam cautiously.

'Where were you really on Monday night?'

It was a few moments before he spoke. 'I went to see Summer. But when I got there, there was no reply at her apartment, so I went home alone. I had no alibi so I asked Marcus to cover for me, to stop things getting complicated with the police.'

'So you didn't see Marcus all evening?'

'Summer, what are you suggesting? That Marcus did it?' he replied, sounding incredulous. 'What on earth would make you think such a thing?'

'I'll explain later but I think Marcus did it. And try and get in touch with Chief Inspector Wright. I'm having no luck.'

She snapped her mobile shut, stood up and took a big swig of cocktail to calm herself.

'I thought we were friends, Erin. That's no way to go talking about friends, is it?' said a voice behind her.

Erin whirled around to find Marcus was standing only feet away, a thin half-smile on his face.

'Marcus, what a surprise, I didn't think you'd be here . . .' she stammered.

'Clearly,' he leered. 'I'm a guest of Mikhail's architect. And it's a good job I came, isn't it? Now you and I can have a private chat about the little lies you've been spreading about me.'

'It's nothing, Marcus, honestly,' she said, wondering if he had heard the whole conversation. He grabbed her arm and ushered her further into the garden, into a long seating area, shielded from the house by clipped hedges.

Marcus pushed Erin roughly against a low wall on the edge of the roof and brought his face close to hers. 'Now, why on earth would you think I'd do such a thing as to kill Karin?'

Erin stood frozen, her heart hammering with fear. 'Tell me!' hissed Marcus, his fingers digging into her arm.

'You brought the expensive wine round, didn't you?' whispered Erin, not knowing what to say except the truth. 'And it was your car outside Karin's that night,' said Erin, so softly it was barely audible.

'She was a tease. Like all women,' growled Marcus, his face twisting as he moved closer towards her.

'But what about Molly?' said Erin, trying to think of anything that might distract him. 'You're in love with Molly.'

Marcus snorted. 'Ah, yes Molly. Sweet, greedy Molly. I thought I could fall in love with that one, until I discovered she's exactly the same as all the other gold-digging tramps I've ever been out with. So she uses me and I use her. She's a very good fuck,' he whispered, his eyes narrow and cruel as he reached up with his other hand to stroke Erin's face.

'Let go of me!' she cried, trying to wriggle out of his grasp, but he was too strong. She was helpless as he jerked her away from the wall and marched her towards a set of wrought-iron stairs that led up to an elevated extension of the building.

'Where are you taking me?' shrieked Erin, terrified now.

'We're going for a chat,' he said flatly, pushing her up the steps.

'Marcus, please,' begged Erin. 'If it was an accident, just tell the police. We can work this out.'

'Don't think I'm going to rot away in jail when it should be Adam doing the time. You do know about that, of course,' he snarled, pushing her on to the flat roof. 'The insider dealing, the illegal trading? Yes, of course you do, you're his assistant. You're up to your neck in it.'

Erin shook her head. 'No! I don't know anything, Marcus. Let me go and I won't say anything.'

Marcus shook her arm violently, then pulled her in close. 'You don't know anything? Well let me educate you, young lady,' he sneered. 'Adam Gold is running on empty. He's borrowed so heavily against his own stock that one day soon – and it will be soon because the property market can't stay buoyant forever – it's all going to come crashing down around his ears. Karin wouldn't have stayed with him. She wouldn't have wanted to stay with a pauper, with a bum.'

The very top of the building was flat and empty except for an air-conditioning unit, a large satellite dish and a low brick perimeter wall, the only barrier from a hundred-metre drop. Erin's hair whipped around her face in the wind and hot tears run down her cheeks.

'Marcus, please. It's dangerous up here.'

'No one is going to believe you, Erin. No one is going to listen to the rantings of Adam's lovesick little PA. Because you were in love with him, Erin, weren't you? The whole floor used to laugh about the way you hung on his every word. And when they find you, they'll say you couldn't stand the way he loved Karin – and you jumped.'

'Marcus! NO!'

The cry came from behind them on the iron stairs. Marcus spun round to see Adam coming towards them. Erin jerked away and Marcus stumbled over a cable, going down on one knee. It gave

Erin just enough time to push past him and run to Adam. He pushed her behind him.

'Erin, go and tell Mikhail what is going on up here. Get him to send his men,' Adam whispered quickly.

'Don't you go anywhere, Erin,' said Marcus, taking slow, considered steps towards the perimeter wall, 'or I'll jump,' he shouted, his voice carried in the wind as climbed onto the wall.

'Get down, Marcus. Please,' said Adam as calmly as he could, extending a hand towards him. For a moment, all they could hear was the whistle of the wind a hundred metres above the Thames, then Marcus began to make a choking sound, and Erin could see his face crumble.

'I didn't mean it!' he screamed. 'I didn't mean it because I loved her! And she loved me!'

'It was an accident Marcus, I know,' said Adam coolly, inching towards his friend.

'She toyed with me, Adam, likes she toys with everyone. She flirted with me in Como, but when I went round to see her she treated me like a stranger. She said I'd got the wrong idea,' he shouted, his baritone voice wobbling. 'How could she say that after all the looks, after all the signals she was giving me? But she said she loved you. *You.* There was a glass candlestick on the table. I picked it up . . .'

He was sobbing now, a deep choking coming from his throat like a car refusing to start.

'I didn't mean to kill her. The candlestick smashed. The end of it cut into her neck. There was so much blood,' he said between sobs. Marcus's feet shuffled closer to the edge.

Erin clenched her fists. 'No!' she screamed.

Adam lunged forward and grabbed Marcus's wrist, just as his feet slipped off the wall. Adam was pulled forward, jamming his feet against the wall, holding onto Marcus who was hanging over the edge of the building. Erin ran forward to help him, watching Marcus's watery eyes full of hate and fear.

'You always had everything I wanted,' he said softly, looking directly at Adam.

'I'm not letting you go,' snarled Adam through gritted teeth, reaching another arm over the edge to grab Marcus's body more firmly and, with Erin's help, slowly began to hoist him back onto the roof.

The two men stumbled back onto the concrete floor as Erin turned to see Chief Inspector Wright and Chris running up the iron stairs to the roof.

'Chris!' shouted Erin, running into his arms.

'It's okay,' he whispered, pulling her tight. 'It's over now.'

70

News of Marcus's arrest was all over the media by the next morning. Summer sat up in her hospital bed, watching a lunchtime bulletin on the small television screen beside her bed, still trying to make sense of it all. Molly had phoned her the night before, sobbing hysterically, still refusing to believe that Marcus had killed Karin. And while Summer had to take her mother's grief at face value – who wouldn't be distraught to find out their partner had been in love with somebody else and then murdered them? – she knew Molly was also mourning the end of life at The Standlings. It looked like her old rival Karin had finally got one over on Molly, even from beyond the grave.

'I think you can go home this afternoon,' smiled a nurse, putting a tray of food on Summer's table. 'We've just got to wait for the consultant to do his rounds.' She hovered at the door, eyes flickering to the TV screen, hoping that Summer would volunteer some information about the case. Summer's connection to Karin Cavendish's murder was no secret around the ward: they had been forced to field phone calls and visits from insistent reporters, all wanting a quote from Summer. But she was a nice kid, thought the nurse, shutting the door and letting her watch the news in peace. On top of the life-threatening ordeal she had just gone through, she didn't deserve to be hassled.

When she was alone, Summer lifted up her pyjama top and stroked the scar along her abdomen. It was over with Adam, she knew that now. He knew about the baby, he knew about her emergency – he had paid for the room – but he hadn't visited her in hospital. She could try and justify it a million ways – after all, his

443

fiancée had just died – but if he had *really* cared, he would have come. Summer knew she was lucky to be alive. She'd pull through. She wasn't going to be a victim any longer. It was time for a fresh start. Rehearsals for the film started in six weeks; filming would begin in the New Year. A whole new chapter of her life was beginning and she was going to enjoy it.

Hearing the door open, she looked up expecting to see the doctor. It was Molly. Her eyes were red, she looked drawn and haggard, but was trying to smile.

'Am I allowed to say you've looked better?' smiled Summer as Molly came to sit on the bed.

'I could say the same about you,' she retorted, and they both started laughing. Summer lay back and expected Molly to start jabbering on about being hassled by reporters, but she surprised Summer by being quiet and looking nervous.

'Mum? What's up? Is anything wrong?'

Molly walked over to the bed and sat on the edge of the mattress. There were so many things she wanted to tell her daughter. Some, like her own tryst with Adam, she could never reveal no matter how much she wanted to share the truth. Other things, like the recent death of Kenneth Sinclair – a grandfather Summer had never known – she would tell her in time. But there had been something Molly had wanted to do right now. Something she had to share.

'Listen, honey, I wanted to try and do something right for once in my life,' she said, her voice cracking.

'What do you mean?' asked Summer, perplexed.

'I've found him. I've found your father,' she said quietly.

She opened her bag and removed a piece of paper which had James Bailey's address and telephone number written on it.

Tears were now streaming down Molly's face, and the regret she had been suppressing for so long suddenly overwhelmed her as she handed the piece of paper to Summer.

'I hope you'll forgive me one day. I hope you'll both forgive me.'

Summer moved her fragile body forward and held her arms out towards her mother. Molly pulled her daughter's head towards her shoulder and just held her.

'Of course I forgive you,' whispered Summer.

It had been a long night. More police statements. Erin was exhausted but strangely energized. It was over. It had been a strange sight

444

seeing Marcus in handcuffs, weeping, his cool, intelligent façade broken.

Adam, Chris and Erin walked out onto the street outside Scotland Yard where Adam's jet-black Maybach car was waiting for them. It had been raining, the night sky was charcoal black and a sour breeze blew in from the Thames. Adam's driver jumped out of the front seat and opened the door nearest the kerb.

Adam stood in front of it waiting for Erin to jump in. 'I take it you want to go straight home?' smiled Adam. His face looked tired and drawn. For the first time since she had met him, he looked old. She paused to look at Chris who was hanging back from the car. Adam nodded at him. 'You too.'

He shot a look at Adam and shrugged. 'I've got my bike. I'd better not leave it in town all night.'

He turned to Erin. 'I'll see you back home in about half an hour. Are you sure you'll be okay?'

'Chauffeured all the way the home in a Maybach? Of course I'll be okay,' she grinned. 'Seriously, I'm fine. Just a little shaken, but glad it's over.'

She went up to him and hugged him. 'We would never have got him without you,' she whispered in his ear.

The door of the car shut with a heavy thud as Erin sank back in the leather seat, watching Chris unlock his bicycle from a railing opposite the station. The car pulled off onto Whitehall and she craned her neck to watch Big Ben's face shining like a moon. London's architecture was spectacular if only you bothered to look up, she thought.

'I don't suppose this is a great time to hand in my notice,' she said, turning to Adam, who was reaching for a decanter of brandy in front of him. For a moment he had a look of complete surprise, then he shrugged and gave a soft laugh.

'I always knew this day would come sooner rather than later,' he said. 'My mother said your book was too good to waste.'

Erin laughed to herself. 'It's not just the book, though,' she said. 'That building in South London. The one I bought? I found out this morning that I've got planning permission and I need to get started on work right away.'

'Spoken like a tycoon in the making,' he smiled, taking a sip of the deep orange liquid.

A *tycoon*, thought Erin. Suddenly she felt scared and exposed.

She had no job, an empty building, and three-quarters of a book to write before Christmas. Only a few weeks before, the future had seemed full of promise; now it was so uncertain.

'Oh God, Adam, what do I do now?' she said.

Adam laughed. 'You'll be fine,' he said, lifting his glass in toast. 'Believe me, you'll be more than fine. But if you will allow me to make one request, as your outgoing boss,' he said, looking out of the window as the car stopped at the junction with Trafalgar Square. 'There's a very nice guy about to pull up next to us on a bicycle, and I think he could do with some company home.'

Erin turned to see Chris was drawing level with the Maybach on the inside lane.

'You know me better than I know myself,' she grinned as the car window purred down.

'Pull over!' she shouted to Chris above the noise of the traffic. 'I'm taking you for dinner!'

Erin got out of the car as Chris pulled his bicycle onto the pavement. The Maybach tooted its horn as it drove off around Trafalgar Square.

'Dinner? You can't afford me,' he smiled as they stood together under the flashing lights of a theatre. *Has Chris always been this good looking?* she asked herself as she suddenly felt her heart flutter. She felt contented and comfortable next to him, and realized that, over the past six months, it was moments like this, when it was just the two of them together, that she had felt most happy.

'That car suited you,' he said softly.

'Nah. It's not my style,' she smiled, touching her fingertips ever so gently against his.

'What is your style?' he said, moving closer so their faces were only inches apart.

'Someone like you,' she said. He moved in to kiss her but she put a hand against his chest.

'Not so fast,' she said. 'What about the redhead?'

'What redhead?' asked Chris, pulling away.

'The pretty redhead I saw coming out of your flat.'

'Oh, you mean Jenny,' he replied, a little embarrassed. 'Poor girl hasn't heard from me for a couple of weeks now.'

'Oh yes, lover boy?' teased Erin. 'And why not?'

He shrugged. 'It wasn't fair to date someone when I'm in love with you.'

His lips touched hers in a featherweight kiss that felt as sweet and delicate as a flower petal. When they finally uncoiled from each other, Chris picked up his bike and started pushing it with one hand, his other laced between Erin's fingers. Trafalgar Square was lit up like a fairground, thought Erin, the illuminated frontage of the National Gallery spilling a soft buttery light onto the puddles. She didn't want to go home; she wanted to savour the moment forever.

'I've given my notice in to Adam.'

Chris gave an incredulous laugh. 'Well, it really has been a strange day.'

'And I have another confession, too. Remember those architect's drawings you saw in the flat the other day? They weren't from work, they're mine. I bought a bit of a building wreck a few months ago to convert into apartments. The mortgage payments have been killing me, but planning permission has come through and I'm starting immediately. I hope I can get a bank loan now I haven't got a job; otherwise I'll have to sell it.'

'You're developing apartments?' said Chris, nearly dropping his bicycle. 'What about the book?'

'I want to do both,' she said firmly. 'I know I can do both.'

'I don't doubt you for a minute,' said Chris honestly. 'But why didn't you tell me about your building?'

'I guess I didn't want to admit to you, to myself, how crazy I was being. I mean, what do I know about developing property? I guess I was seduced by the life at Midas; thought I could do it too.'

He stopped and reached over to stroke back a lock of hair that had fallen in her face. 'You're not crazy. Just brave and clever. That's what I love about you.'

Erin felt herself blush. 'Well, it's a scary prospect. I have a builder on standby ready to start, and I guess I'm going to have to project-manage it myself.'

'If you want any help, just shout,' he said .

'Oh, I'll come knocking alright. Make sure you have a big stock of brandy at the ready at the end of every day.'

'I didn't mean that. I've got a bit of experience in property development. I sort of dabble in property myself.'

It was Erin's turn to look surprised. 'You dabble in property? In what way do you "dabble"?' she asked cheekily. 'Define "dabble".' Their heads were only inches apart and she could feel his warm breath on her lips.

'I own Peony House,' Chris said quietly.

Erin jumped back. 'You own my flat! My tenancy agreement says the landlord is JuniorCon Ltd or something.'

He nodded. 'Well, I'm embarrassed to say it's me. Peony House was bought and developed by my father's property company. He transferred it over to me a few years ago when I told him I wanted to be a journalist and wasn't going to join the family firm. I formed a limited company just to manage the building. It's my nest egg.'

'I thought you said your dad was a builder?'

'He is. He's got a building company. The Scanlan Group.'

Erin was shaking her head in disbelief. Scanlan were one of the biggest home-builders in Ireland. George Scanlan – Chris's father, presumably – was an aristocratic industrialist of the old school, building schools and hospitals with his spare cash. Erin backed away from Chris, shaking her head.

'Erin. What's wrong?' asked Chris, leaning his bike against a lamppost.

'I thought I was through with rich men,' she whispered through a half-smile.

'Don't hate me because I'm loaded,' laughed Chris, taking her in his arms and kissing her as Big Ben struck midnight. It was a new day. A new start. A new life together.

EPILOGUE

Once *Krakatoa* had finished filming, and word spread about what an exciting new acting talent Summer Sinclair was, she was inundated with offers of roles. With money in the bank and a lot more promised, she moved to a bright, airy apartment in Chelsea that overlooked the Albert Bridge, which twinkled gloriously and made every night feel like Christmas. She also began getting to know James Bailey. An art teacher who lived in Dorset, he had a warm and friendly wife who had welcomed Summer with a generosity she had never encountered before, while James's two teenager daughters Katie and Alice couldn't believe their luck at having *the* Summer Sinclair as a half-sister. It was going to take a long time to catch up on all the wasted years but she had the rest of her life to do it. She had spent years, looking for a father figure but, now that she had one, she wondered how she could ever have found the forty-something men on the Cipriani and Chinawhite circuit attractive.

At the *Krakatoa* premiere in London, with the paparazzi screaming her name and glowing reviews in the trade papers, she couldn't believe how far she'd come in the last twelve months. After her ectopic pregnancy and the end of her relationship with Adam, she had felt that she could never feel happy again. She smiled to herself and turned behind her, where Charlie McDonald was signing autographs for screaming girls behind the crash barrier. In a midnight-blue suit, his blondy-brown hair flopping onto his face, he looked gorgeous.

Charlie looked up and grinned. And, as their eyes met, the noise and people seemed to bleed away until it was just the two of them.

Lovers. Friends.

He walked over to Summer and whispered in her ear. 'Come on, honey. I think it's time to go in.'

He squeezed her hand and she felt safe. Life got better all the time.

Adam Gold was investigated by the FSA. He vigorously denied receiving any tips about share purchases of Ginsui and, since there was little or no evidence to the contrary, he was cleared of insider dealing. His appearance at the FSA's Canary Wharf offices did not however, go unnoticed, and Midas Corporation's share price wobbled. For six months it looked as if the company might even go under. But when Midas suddenly announced it was to build a thirty-acre residential, shopping and leisure complex by the Thames the company's fortunes recovered. Adam climbed twenty-five places on the *Sunday Times* Rich List. He moved more heavily into philanthropy. A Karin Cavendish scholarship fund for gifted students at St Martin's College of Art was one of several donations. Adam Gold is still single. Huge sums of money are exchanged at charity functions to sit next to him.

Christina Levy is about to move into Reggie Bryce's twenty-bedroom mansion in Bel-Air which has a bowling alley, a soccer pitch and en-suite everything. She considers herself to be going home. Reggie's place is only fifteen miles away from Christina's childhood home, a trailer in the Valley.

Diana Birtwell finally left Martin, who went running back to Tracey and their children. His Internet business promptly stalled. Diana is pregnant with an Icelandic sportswear millionaire, four hundred places above Martin on the *Sunday Times* Rich List.

Donna Delemere's organic food empire goes from strength to strength. In time, Donna and Daniel forgave Alexander. Alex in turn grew to respect Donna for her sassy business skills and forgiveness.

Molly would have stood by Marcus during his time in prison; she had grown terribly fond of The Standlings. Marcus, however, had other ideas and insisted she moved out after his arrest. 'It was all a sham,' he'd told her after the trial. 'I don't love you. I love Karin.'

Molly posed nude for an American men's magazine and is currently living off the proceeds. After bemoaning the lack of decent men in London – it was quite pathetic, she would tell anyone who would listen, how men were only interested in twenty-two-year-olds in skinny jeans – she decided that she could do worse than reunite with Harry Levin. He refuses to take her calls.

Marcus is serving ten years for manslaughter in HMP Risley. With good behaviour he is expected to get out in six.

Adam begged Erin to do two months' notice in return for a large bonus. 'This is the last thing you do for me. You've got a book to finish and a building to develop,' he told her, promising to give her a large bonus for the duration of her stay at Midas. Erin's last job in his employment was to go and box up everything in Karin's home.

'I'm kind of going to miss him,' she told Chris while they were taking silver photoframes from the expensive looking cabinets and covering them in bubble wrap.

Chris looked bruised. 'You don't feel anything for him still, do you?' he asked, taking her hands and pulling her towards him.

She shook her head softly. She didn't hate herself for falling for Adam. Every girl was allowed an unsuitable crush, an unrequited love. But true love was a different beast, she thought, looking at Chris. Love crept up quietly on you. She didn't need the fancy restaurants or the private jet to have fun with Chris. She just needed him there. And, standing in Karin's hallway, he had never looked more handsome; her feelings towards him had never been more certain.

'There's only one person I'm in love with, and he's standing in front of me.'

'In that case, I think we're wasting money,' he said with a smile.

'How do you mean?'

'Two apartments. How about, after this, we go home and move all your stuff into mine? I've got a feeling the landlord might let you off a month's notice.'

He grinned, and Erin rested her head on his shoulder. 'Stuff that,' she laughed. 'How about you move into mine?'

Suddenly it felt strange, laughing and kissing in Karin's house, and they moved away from each other, speeding up the packing.

The underfloor heating was turned off. It was the middle of November and the air had the sharp pinch of winter. It was quiet, still and haunting.

'Who is going to get the house?' asked Chris to fill the silence.

Erin shrugged. 'Karin's got no family, but there was a will. Adam gets the house and most of her shares in the business. Can you believe she wanted Diana to have twenty per cent of her shares?'

'Maybe she wasn't all bad.'

Erin didn't want to speak ill of the dead and said nothing. 'Adam wants all the personal belongings boxed up so he can collect them later.'

'Let's split up. It'll will be quicker. And I can't wait to get you home,' he grinned.

While Chris stayed downstairs to pack away Karin's books into boxes, Erin went upstairs to her bedroom. What a beautiful room, she thought, standing gingerly at the doorway. Cold, bright sunlight flooded in through the long windows hung with heavy cream shot-silk drapes. The en-suite bathroom was still piled high with expensive beauty products and creams that would never be used. A white fluffy towel had a smudge of black mascara on it. She shuddered and walked to the wardrobe and opened it. A row of beautiful clothes, acres of silk and chiffon and tulle in all the colours of the rainbow.

She folded them carefully in layers of plastic and tissue and loaded tea chests until the closets were empty.

The last thing she had to clear was Karin's dressing table, which was in front of the long windows that looked out onto the sleepy Kensington street. It was a beautiful piece of furniture. Venetian glass with carved black-wood legs and a tall concertina of mirrors in the shape of Doge windows, beautifully etched with flowers. Erin traced her fingers over it and smiled. If there was one thing she did not regret about this year, it was how she could recognize and appreciate beautiful things. That was a gift for life now. She sat on the stool, putting the bottles of perfume into a shoe box, her jewellery into a leather pouch she had found in the dressing room. Hundreds of thousands pounds' worth of things, folded and stored away in boxes. What would be the fate of all these beautiful things, she wondered? Finally she opened the drawer. It was empty except for a couple of bottles of nail polish, a silk scarf and a wooden box.

Erin heard footsteps at the door and turned round to see Chris.

'Are you nearly ready? I bet the traffic is bad, so it will take us ages to get home.'

'Nearly done,' she said distractedly, holding the box in the palm of her hand and removing the lid. Sitting on the red velvet lining of the box was a small shiny silver object.

'Wow, that's nice,' said Chris, picking it up and feeling the satisfying heaviness between his fingertips.

'What is it?' asked Erin.

He held it up between his thumb and forefinger to show her. 'A cigar cutter. It's a beauty,' he whistled. 'Solid silver. Asprey,' he continued, looking at the hallmark.

Erin took it from him. Her fingerprint left a greasy smudge on the metal.

'Look, there's a message on it. "Dear Seb. All my love. K." I wonder why she's kept this locked away in a box?'

'I dunno. Who's Seb, anyway?'

'Karin's husband who died last year. He fell off a yacht in Turkey and drowned. It was all pretty murky. For a while they didn't know if he fell or was pushed. I heard that for a time they thought Karin might have done it, but the police decided it was an accident.'

'She had a pretty tragic life really, didn't she?' said Chris, pulling on his coat and waiting for Erin to finish.

She closed her fingers around the cigar cutter. 'Yes. I suppose she did.'